BONNIE DUNDEE CLAIMS HIS BRIDE.

# BONNIE DUNDEE


BY

GEORGE EMMETT.

Author of "Tomahawk & Rifle," "Red Hugh the Backwoodsman," &c.


---

PROFUSELY ILLUSTRATED

BY

HARRY MAGUIRE.

---


Publishing Office:

HOGARTH HOUSE, ST. BRIDE'S AVENUE,

LONDON, E.C.

# CONTENTS.

George Emmett

# BONNIE DUNDEE!

## OR, THE CAVALIERS OF KING JAMES.

GALLANTLY HE FOUGHT HIS WAY THROUGH THE DUTCH TROOPERS.

### CHAPTER I.

#### THE THREE CAVALIERS AND THE FAIRY BARK.

Flash all your swords like Tartarian hordes,
And scare the prim ladies of Puritan lords;
Our steel caps shall blaze through the long summer days,
As we galloping sing our mad cavalier lays.
Then, banners, advance! by the lilies of France,
We are the gallants to lead them a dance.

It was in the turbulent reign of the brave sailor king, James II., the period when England was the arena of a strange and unnatural rebellion, when Dutch guile abroad and black treason at home were on the point of obtaining a signal victory over blunt honesty, though allied, alas! with foolish indiscretion and that evil genius which has been an attendant upon every member of the princely house of Stuart.

For many years the people of England, like those of Scotland, had been prepossessed against all the measures of King James, and to his brave army alone did this unhappy monarch look for support in the coming struggle; but, notwithstanding that for years he had been a father, rather than a captain, to his soldiers, and had watched over their interests with the most kingly and paternal solicitude, quarrels and disgusts broke out between them, and he was yet to find that he leant on a broken reed. The strict amity subsisting between him and Louis of France excited the jealousy of the nation, who dreaded an invasion of French and Irish Catholics to enfore the entire submission of the Protestants.

Supported by the Puritan party, William of Orange and the "reformed" nobles at home began busily to undermine the very foundations of his throne. Burnet, the historian of the Reformation, negotiated between the parties, and paid agents intrigued, giving circulation to William's pamphlets, until a formidable body stood organised to co-operate with the Dutch troops directly they should land.

James had endeavoured, previously to this, to initiate William into his plans of toleration, and had deputed to him the celebrated Quaker, William Penn, to advocate religious freedom of worship, for though a Catholic, the dearest wish of King James's heart was that all his subjects should have the widest civil and religious liberty. The caustic William, however, listened with far higher relish to Burnet's reasonings, whence he hoped to derive solid personal advantages.

In this posture of affairs, an event occurred which seemed likely to blight the hopes of the perjured son-in-law and incipient usurper. The Queen Maria d'Este gave birth to a son, but as no extremes approximate more closely than those of meanness and selfish ambition, the adherents of the House of Orange pronounced the infant a foundling, and under pretext of a French campaign, William, by augmenting his forces, prepared to carry his measures with a high hand.

Up to this time, James obstinately closed his eyes to the danger of his position. The proffered aid of France he haughtily rejected, and when urged imperatively to defensive arrangements, he found on all sides but feeble co-operation.

The memorial of William the Stadtholder, penned in Holland by Burnet, but published as the embodied sentiments of the British Puritans, obtained rapid circulation, and sowed the seeds of disaffection broadcast through the land.

Still when William landed at Torbay the apathy of the people so discouraged him that he thought of returning to Holland, and would doubtless have done so had not numerous desertions from the Royalists re-animated his hopes.

Amongst these the most notable were Prince George of Denmark, the Duke of Grafton, Churchill, afterwards the celebrated Marlborough, and the file of traitors closed with the Princess Anne, the King's favourite child, who, on hearing the bitter tidings, is said to have exclaimed, "May God help me, for even my own children abandon me!"

Meanwhile, however, the cavaliers of Scotland remained true to the dynasty, and Grahame of Claverhouse, now Lord Viscount Dundee, at the head of ten thousand leal hearts and true, had marched into England, closely invested Carlisle, whose citizens were distinguished for the zeal and patriotism with which they had hailed the advent of William, the new Regenerator of the Faith; but the formidable force which Dundee commanded, and his own terrible *prestige*, had struck terror into their hearts, and they at length showed some signs of a wish to surrender to the King's troops.

One bright moonlight evening in the October of 1688, three figures muffled in cloaks were reclining on the bank which sloped downwards to the clear glassy waters of the Eden, some two miles below the grey walls of Carlisle, whose embattled towers shone in the mellow light.

About half a mile to the left glittered the white tents of the royal army, the heavy folds of England's standard and those of the blue Scottish banner that surmounted the scarlet and white pavilion of Dundee slowly unfolding to the light westerly breeze that stirred the waters of the river, and rustled the thick autumn foliage of the many trees that adorned the verdant banks.

A few light flaky clouds were slowly drifting below the higher ether, which glittered with stars, casting a passing shadow upon the murmuring stream and green fields, as with ever-changing form they passed away to the eastward.

Few sounds were audible, save the gentle murmurs of the breeze, the lower rippling of tiny waves against the banks, and now and then the flourish of a trumpet, the neigh of a horse, or the faint echo of laughter and revelry from the distant camp.

The latter indications of life were, however, but occasional, for the royal army, as a body, was sunk in profound repose, and equidistantly along the sloping hill-side of Tupsley gorse gleamed the lurid watchfires of the outlying pickets; while the flash of steel often revealed the dark forms of the sentries, as the moonlight shone upon their morions, corselets, and shouldered pikes.

"Our last night of camp-life, I presume, Dundee?" said the chivalrous Dumbarton. "Tomorrow, I trust, we shall sleep in Carlisle."

"Nay, why in such haste, Dumbarton?" returned the Viscount; "I intend not to assault the city until the midnight after. My plans must not be hurried; nevertheless, I invite you to sup with me on Thursday at the castle; and, as an inducement to come, I will pledge myself to lay before you some of old Greysteel's choicest wine. They say that he is a good judge of grape-juice."

"I will back his crop-eared, lantern-jawed, nasal-twanged chaplain, the Reverend Zerubbabel Makepeace, to be a better," replied Dumbarton, with a sarcastic laugh, as he impatiently cast a pebble into the stream; "but wine or no wine, I will be with you. They say that the good town is but badly stocked with edibles; but if there be no other dish at hand, we will cut off the head of the traitor Governor, and serve it up as a first course."

"There will be many a red hand and cloven morion before old Greysteel's head will fall," said Dundee, with a sigh; and, without another word, he sprang to his feet, and leaning against a tree, gazed with knitted brows and compressed lips towards the high towers and dark castle of the beleaguered town.

Tall, handsome, and sunburnt, with pointed moustaches, a broad manly brow and magnificent black eyes, the Earl of Dundee presented a perfect picture of manly grace and beauty.

He was attired in a coat of scarlet, richly laced, and which was worn open the better to display his corselet of bright steel, which was inlaid with gold. His heavy military wig escaped from beneath his plumed helmet, the visor of which was raised, and flowed in long curls over his shoulders.

His companions were the Earl of Dumbarton and Sir Andrew Douglas; the former a splendidly armed cavalier, glittering with military orders, the latter a gallant-looking young officer, in the rich uniform of the Scottish Life Guards, his bright steel helmet being surmounted by a plume of white horsehair.

The sword and gauntlets of this latter personage lay on the ground by his side, a heavy cloak or roquelaure of scarlet cloth draped his figure; and, while he leaned against the trunk of a felled tree, his lips rested in a half smile, and his hand played inadvertently with the richly-inlaid stock of a pistol which protruded from his belt.

"What art thou pondering on, Douglas?" said the Earl gaily; "is it love or war that makes you so oblivious of the present, and so dull a companion? Here is Viscount Dundee, as though struck dumb, leaning on his sword like a statue hewn from marble, while his gracious Majesty's dashing guardsman, ever ready for frolic or adventure, wears the air of a Puritan Divine, and seems more disposed to howl in the Conventicle than to sing a jovial camp song. Come, rouse thee, man, for friendship's sake, or I shall begin to think myself among the spirits of the departed, instead of with fellow beings of bone and blood."

"Your pardon, noble Earl!" said the young cavalier, in a low musical voice, "I was lost in thought. What said you?"

"That which is not worth repeating," replied the Earl. "Lost in thought, say you? I would sooner be lost in a fog. On what wert thou pondering, most doughty knight—on matters of love or war—on past events or present?"

"On both," was the reply.

"As if the present were not sufficient to engross all thy ideas," said the Earl. "By the mass, these greasy citizens of Carlisle have given us enough to think of, and the news of last night is not calculated to encourage or cheer our cause."

"My lord, let not Viscount Dundee hear thee!" said Douglas. "The merest allusion to the massacre of Ipswich fills him with the fury of a madman. He is calmer this evening; but if Carlisle falls into our hands, fearful will be his vengeance on the bloodthirsty followers of the Stadtholder, for he has sworn to put to the sword every man capable of bearing arms in the place," and, as he spoke, the young soldier glanced towards the spot where Dundee had stationed himself.

The great leader of the Royal army still stood calm and motionless a few yards distant from them, the moonlight revealing the swarthy pallor of his face, and the kindling fire of his dark eyes, which were directed towards the gates of Carlisle.

"He will keep his vow, Douglas," said Dumbarton, with a grim smile. "When did John Grahame of Claverhouse forget the hour of vengeance? To-morrow midnight will see the downfall of Carlisle, and, once within its walls, we can laugh at Duke Schomberg and the Stadtholder to boot. Ah! what is that?"

Gliding gently around a bend in the river, about a quarter of a mile up the stream, her white sail glittering in the moonlight, and her sharp prow scattering the water on each side like showers of pearls, appeared a small boat, steering directly towards the spot where the three cavaliers were grouped.

Before Lord Dumbarton and Sir Andrew had recovered from their surprise, Dundee also perceived the strange craft, and exclaimed hurriedly—

"A boat from Carlisle, by the saints! Dumbarton and Douglas, get ye quickly under shadow of the withies, or its occupants will see the glint of our armour, and take alarm. They must be spies from within the walls, and if we can capture them, we may make them of some service to the good cause."

As he spoke, he screened himself behind some low bushes that skirted the margin of the river, and Douglas and the Earl quickly followed his example.

Meanwhile, on came the boat, silently and swiftly gliding towards them.

As it approached nearer, Sir Andrew started on perceiving that its sole occupant was a woman, who stood upright in the stern, and, with one hand on the tiller, guided the bark on its course.

She was apparently young and beautiful, the graceful costume of the period showing to advantage her elegantly-proportioned figure. Her hair was long and black as jet, her face pale, and her full, flashing eyes seemed to be fixed alternately upon the sail and the course of the stream beyond.

The fairy-like bark was in the middle of the stream, within a stone's throw of the three cavaliers, who appeared to be spell-bound by the wondrous beauty of its occupant.

The next moment, yielding to a sudden gust of wind, it was bounding quickly past, when a grating noise was heard, followed by a shrill cry, and Sir Andrew sprang to his feet on beholding the boat upset, and the beautiful girl it had contained left struggling amidst the waters.

He saw her long black hair floating on the stream, her eyes raised to heaven, and her lips parted as if in terror.

Anticipating the Earl of Dumbarton and Viscount Dundee, who were quickly throwing off some of their mail to swim lighter to the rescue, Sir Andrew rushed down the bank, and, speedily divesting himself of his cloak, sprang, heavily armed as he was, into the river, and struck out out towards the drowning girl.

As he neared her, she uttered another cry, threw her white arms above the waves, and then sank beneath their surface.

"She is lost!" exclaimed Dundee, from the bank; and with the words on his lips, he also plunged into the stream.

Meanwhile Douglas had dived after the fair stranger, and in another moment he reappeared on the surface, sustaining her afloat with one arm, while with the other he struck out for the shore.

Now, however, the weight of his corslet, back-plate, and helmet began to tell; faint and exhausted, his strokes grew short and feeble, and had not Dundee swum towards him and relieved him of his only half-conscious burden, he would never have regained the bank.

At length, however, he felt some one drag him out of the stream and up the ascent beyond.

Opening his eyes, he recognised in his deliverer the Earl of Dumbarton, and upon looking around perceived the rescued girl sitting on the river's bank, rapidly recovering, while the Viscount Dundee, who had wrapped his heavy cloak around her wet clothing, was rubbing her hands to restore their warmth.

"Thank Heaven, she is saved!" fervently ejaculated the young Life Guardsman, as he approached and knelt by her side.

She heard the words, and turning round, with a bright smile on her countenance, said—

"I have to thank you brave gentlemen for my rescue from a watery grave. I shall ever be deeply grateful for the services of this hour. Would that I could reward my preservers better than by thanks."

"The consciousness of having done you a service, fair lady, is sufficient reward in itself. To win a smile from one so fair, what danger would not be worth encountering?"

So spoke the gallant Dundee, but Sir Andrew remained silent, for he was both enchanted and awe-struck by the wondrous beauty of the fair girl at his side.

And beautiful indeed she was.

Slightly above the middle height, the proportions of her form were perfect.

Her hair, dark and luxuriant, hung, heavy with the water of the river, around her neck and shoulders; it was parted on the forehead, and bound by a fillet of gold.

Her full liquid eyes were of the darkest hazel, and full of spiritual expression, with long, drooping lashes, and brows perfect as though an artist had pencilled them.

Her complexion was brunette, but of that transparent tint peculiar to the women of Southern Italy; and her arms, which were exposed to the elbow by the loose open sleeves, were charmingly rounded, and as white as new-fallen snow.

She smiled at the gay Dundee's high-flown speech, and replied to the young Guardsman's mute glance of admiration by a burning blush that suffused her cheek and neck with the hue of the rose.

Then, as Douglas essayed to dry the heavy masses of her hair with his embroidered scarf, she turned deadly pale, and a shiver ran through her delicately proportioned frame.

"There is no time to be lost, Dundee," whispered the Earl of Dumbarton in his ear. "If the poor girl does not quickly change her wet garments the consequences may be fatal. The best plan is to mount her on horseback, and send her under escort as far as the gates of Carlisle. The boat has foundered, and a rapid ride will prevent her taking a chill."

"Well thought of, Dumbarton!" said the Viscount. "As Scottish cavaliers, the laws of chivalry will prevent our detaining her a captive or questioning her as to what fanciful freak induced her to sail so far down the Eden at such a time as the present. So we will e'en mount her and send her home again. Sir Andrew Douglas," he continued, turning to the Life Guardsman, "you are a true knight errant and a squire of dames. Assemble a score of horsemen with all speed, and escort this lady to Carlisle."

## CHAPTER II.

### AN INTERESTING RIDE.

Does Baxter say right, that a bodice laced tight,
Should never be seen by the sun or the light?
Like stars from a wood, shine under that hood
Eyes that are sparkling though pious and good.
Surely this waist was by Providence placed
By a true lover's arm to be often embraced.

FIVE minutes after the scene recorded in our last chapter, Sir Andrew Douglas, at the head of a score of mounted Life Guardsmen, rode down the gentle slope towards the river.

In one hand he held the rein of a milk white steed, whose brilliant trappings glittered in the moonlight.

Springing from the saddle, as he reined up beside his two companions and the lady, who had now risen to her feet, he bowed low and said—

"A steed awaits you, madam; is it your will to mount?"

She answered with a smile, and bidding the Viscount and the Earl adieu, allowed the Life Guardsman to assist her to the saddle; then vaulting on his own charger, Sir Andrew gave the signal to march.

For some minutes they rode on without speaking, and no sounds broke the silence of night save the dull echo of their horses' hoofs on the sward, and the rattling of swords and accoutrements, as the mounted escort, all heavily armed, trotted in front and rear.

At length the lady said—

"Will you take me to the eastern gate, sir cavalier? I know the sentries who are on guard there, and, with your permission, let us ride faster, for I feel deadly cold."

"Your wishes shall be obeyed, lady," he replied, and urging their horses to a gallop, they approached the town.

"Will you take my cloak?" he said, presently, to his fair companion, "it will keep you warmer; we still have more than a mile to ride."

"Nay, sir cavalier, that will be performed in a very short time, and I have already the loan of one mantle. But tell me who were those gallants, your companions? Methought that I recognised the features of the younger."

"They were the Captain-General of the forces, Lord Viscount Dundee, and his second in command, the Earl of Dumbarton."

The lady started, and then, after a short pause, exclaimed—

"Who, then, are you? I would fain remember the name of my preserver, of him to whom I owe my life."

"Alas, lady," said he, "I am but a lieutenant in the King's Life Guards, a humble scion of the once great house of Douglas, and a soldier of fortune, whose whole worldly possessions are on his back. My life has been spent in the noisy camp, my only friends have been my sword and charger, and I have but seldom listened to woman's voice, or beheld woman's smile. May I be excused for, in turn, asking your name, that I may ever whisper it to myself when I recall the events of this night?"

Sir Andrew spoke low and earnestly. The lovely stranger perceived that his voice faltered as he concluded, and turning towards him a sad smile, she said—

"And why do you wish to learn my name, or remember the incidents just past?"

"Because the latter will never be forgotten," he replied; "and I would fain know your name, for the reason that I shall ever hold it dear. While life remains, there will dwell in my heart a longing to see you again, for your presence has thrown a bright halo across the monotonous course of my existence, as yon bright moon sheds its effulgence on the dark waters of the river."

"Your language is poetical, sir knight," said the lady; "you speak as a lover."

"Oh, fair one," replied he, "would that you could regard me as one."

Whilst speaking, he had brought his horse so close to the white palfrey as to be able to lay his hand on that of his companion.

She exhibited no surprise; but turning her full lustrous eyes towards the excited face of the young royalist, said, softly,—

"Do you mean what you say, sir knight?"

"Aye, verily I do, beautiful lady," was the rejoinder. "By the Holy Virgin, and all the blessed saints, I swear it; I love you already, with my whole existence, my whole soul."

"Your affection has grown very quickly then," returned the gay girl, with a ringing laugh; "what wonders are you ready to perform to convince me of the truth of your attachment?"

"Anything you may ask me; my life is at your service," he replied; and carried away by his enthusiasm, and the sudden passion with which love had inspired him, he raised her little white hand to his lips, and kissed it fervently.

"What a proper gallant!" she exclaimed, hastily withdrawing her hand; "but I will put your love to the test. I am not about to ask you to go and kill Saracens before Jerusalem, or to unhorse a score of knights in joust or tourney, as did the fair dames of the olden time, but only to answer two questions, will you do so?"

"Yes, lady, willingly and truthfully," he replied.

"Then, they are these," said she. "What is the precise force of the royal army? and when does the Viscount Dundee intend to assault the city?"

Sir Andrew's cheek turned pale as marble in the moonlight; for a moment he remained silent, and then said hurriedly, "I am a soldier of King James, lady, and as such dare not reply to either of those questions."

"Not even to win my love, sir cavalier?" said the young girl.

"Not even to win that priceless boon can I forfeit my honour; but ask aught else, and at the peril of my life I will serve you."

"No, I will ask no more. I desire not to put your devotion to the test a second time," she replied, coldly. "Let us part as we met; see, we are close to the gate."

"But your name, lady? Tell me at least that," urged Sir Andrew.

"Not now; soon, perhaps, you may learn all. Meanwhile, accept of this ring as a souvenir of the service you have rendered me this night. Should you be taken prisoner during your contemplated rash assault on Carlisle, it may prove a talisman of safety to you. But we must now say farewell."

She was about to give the ring to Sir Andrew, when the sharp report of a musket was audible, and a bullet carried away a portion of the knight's plume, and then buried itself with a dull "ping" in a turf bank a few yards in their rear.

The lady uttered a ringing laugh, and observed,—

"We are within range, and you have no flag of truce flying. I see that our sentries keep sure guard, and we have some deadly shots in the gate-tower."

As she spoke, another bullet was fired, and flattened itself against the steel cuirass of one of the Lifeguardsmen, who sat motionless as a statue on his coal-black charger close beside Sir Andrew.

The soldier merely regarded the incident with a grim smile, and our hero quickly unsheathing his long sword, drew a richly laced handkerchief from his scarf, and tying it to the bright glittering blade, held it aloft in token of a peaceful mission.

In reply a white flag presently floated from an outwork of the city wall, and with a smile, the lady again turned towards her companion.

"The danger is over," said she; "again I ask you to accept the ring, sir cavalier, and with it my gratitude and thanks. I feel that we are shortly destined to meet again. To-night I cannot ask you to escort me further. To-morrow I will see that both palfrey and cloak are returned to Viscount Dundee. Farewell."

Sir Andrew accepted the ring, placed it carefully in the lappet of his scarf, again kissed the proffered hand of the beautiful girl, and quick as a flash of light she swept down the hill-side, urged the white palfrey over the lowered drawbridge, and the next moment vanished from sight beneath the dark frowning archway of the gate-tower.

Sir Andrew waited until he heard the harsh crash of the gate as it was again closed, and the creak of chains and pulleys as the drawbridge was raised, and then shouting—"Fall in, my men, to the right by threes, wheel, trot!" he dashed the spurs into his grey charger's flanks and led the way back to the camp.

## CHAPTER III.

### "GOD AND THE KING."

We'll shake their red roofs with our echoing hoofs,  
And flutter the dust from their tapestry woofs;  
Their old minster shall ring with our "God save the King,"  
And our horses shall drink at St. Christopher's spring.  
We shall welcome the meat and the wine will taste sweet,  
When our boots are flung off and as brothers we greet.

The pale light of early dawn was breaking in the east, the faint rays of the October sun shone glimmeringly upon the motionless waters of the Eden, on the grey walls of Carlisle, and on the white canvas tents of the royal army that surrounded the beleagured town on three sides.

Sir Andrew Douglas was roused from a troubled and broken slumber by the shrill blast of trumpets, and the quick hoarse roll of the drum.

Springing to his feet, he hastily armed and quitted his tent.

The morning was cold and chilly, and a grey mist hung over the distant hill sides.

Rain had but lately fallen, and the earth was soft and spongy, whilst the thickly-dotted tents were glittering with crystal drops.

As he glanced towards the town he perceived that the besieged were busy on the walls; the steel caps of the Puritan pikemen and the plumed bonnets of the Scotch pistoliers were conspicuous amid the outworks, while the blue standard charged with the white *fesse*, the banner of the States of Holland, floated from the high Norman keep of the old castle—that same grim fortress, built by William Rufus, wherein, 121 years previously to the date of our narrative, Mary of Scotland, Mary the pious and the beautiful, experienced the first traits of Elizabeth of England's inhospitality and dark guile.

Around him on all sides arose the tumult of a camp.

Soldiers were hurrying about in all directions, armour was being cleaned, and chargers groomed.

There was the clatter of mail, the neighing and whinnying of impatient steeds, the creaking of tent ropes, and the confused murmur of many voices, while in the distance, wafted towards him by the fresh morning breeze, came the sound of music, the swell of the clarion, the clash of the cymbal, and the hoarse brattle of brass drums.

As Sir Andrew was walking thoughtfully on towards the distant pickets of Northbrigg, a cavalier, richly attired, rode up to his side, and exclaimed, as he reined in his roan charger—

"Sir Andrew, I have been sent to seek you. Dundee is about to hold a council of war in his tent, anent an immediate assault on the town, and he desires your presence.

"And how soon, Laird of Lundin, does the council meet?" asked Douglas.

"Half an hour from the present, Sir Andrew."

"Then tell the Viscount that I will not fail to be there. Where ride you now?"

"To summon Dalyel and Montgomerie, who have pitched their tents at Holsterlee," replied the Laird of Lundin; and whistling a joyous air, the light-hearted soldier again spurred on his course.

. . . . . . . . . . .

Within the gorgeous tent of Dundee a glittering assembly are met.

All the lords, the barons, and the distinguished leaders of the Scottish royalist army are there.

The brave, reckless, and remorseless Earl of Dumbarton, with the same cynical and dark smile that ever dwelt upon his handsome mouth, the same deep, flashing eyes, and long curling Ramilies wig; the tall, slender, and graceful Napier, with his finely-cut aquiline features and deep blue eyes, clad in the vivid scarlet uniform, and polished steel morion cuirass and gorgee of the "Royals;" and near him the youthful Baldock, as much a scholar as a soldier, too reckless to think, but ever ready to act, a hero proved in war, who ever felt most at home when in his armour, and the gaiety and merriment of whose disposition was ever most conspicuous on the eve of battle, or even amid the fury of actual strife.

Other members there were amongst that assembled conclave equally worthy of mention, the venerable Sir Thomas Dalyel, attired in his antique buff coat, steel cap, and long boots, and whose grey beard reached to his belt; the brave Laird of Lundin, master of the ordnance, and the ill-fated D'Arley, afterwards beheaded on Tower-hill.

At the head of the long table, which was covered with wine cups, leather bottles, papers, parchments, plans, swords, pistols, gauntlets, and a host of other miscellanea, sat Dundee, the first cavalier in Scotland, apparelled in the rich uniform of the Scots Greys, his raised visor revealing the manly beauty of the face it shaded, and his cheek flushed, and dark eyes flashing with the ardour of enthusiasm, and a desperate longing to avenge the treason of the nation in general, in the hot blood of Carlisle's burgher garrison.

. . . . . . . . . . .

There was a murmured greeting as Sir Andrew Douglas entered the tent.

The young knight bowed low in reply, and took his seat beside Sir Thomas Dalyel.

"You are late to attend council, Douglas," observed Dumbarton, with his usual reckless laugh, from the opposite side of the table. "Your adventures with a certain fair lady last evening have caused you to oversleep yourself, I imagine; or did you spend the night within the gates of Carlisle?"

The blood mounted to Sir Andrew's cheek, and he was about to reply to Dumbarton's somewhat equivocal remark, when Sir Thomas Dalyel called attention to the subject more immediately in hand by saying—

"Well, Viscount, what, then, is our decision regarding this attack on the town? When is it to come off? Methinks we are idling our time here when the King is in such pressing need of our services elsewhere. Therefore, what is to be done had best be done quickly."

"Let us unfurl the Royal standard, and assault the place at once. It must and will fall. Not for a moment can the greasy burghers or the Williamite soldiers of Carlisle stop our course. Hurrah! God and the King!"

It was the youthful Baldock who spoke, and, as he concluded, he waved his drawn sword above his head.

No answering enthusiasm, however, met his, and the chivalrous Napier said—

"We have granted the besieged three days' truce; then how can we violate our promise? To-morrow night the time will have expired—why not wait until then? and we shall be able to rush to the assault with ready swords and clear consciences."

From a few voices there was a faint murmur of assent to this proposition, but the majority of the council remained moodily silent.

At this moment the sound of galloping hoofs was heard without; a knight, heavily accoutred, and splashed with mud from head to heel, reined up his panting and foamed-flecked charger, and, dismounting, hurriedly presented himself to the assembly.

His visor was raised, and every eye recognized

the Lord of Eversham, aide-de-camp to the King.

"What tidings, sir?" asked Dundee, hurriedly. "You appear to have ridden fast and far."

"I have been on the spur since midnight," was the reply. "Carlisle must fall within twenty-four hours, or all is lost. Mareschal Frederick, Duc de Schomberg and Mynheer Goderdt van Baron de Ginckle are already on their way to relieve it. To-night their vanguard of Swart Ruylers will not be twenty miles distant. To-morrow at mid-day they will raise the siege."

"There shall be no siege to raise, Eversham," said Dundee, "for, ere daybreak, the Scottish lion and St. Andrew's cross shall float on the walls, and every stone in Carlisle shall be sprinkled with Puritan or Dutch blood. Comrades, our course is now clear. Two hours before next dawn we must carry the town, or leave our dead bodies, and all hopes of the Stuart cause, before its gates; for there is no stronghold on English soil, and yet so near to the territory of his faithful Scots, as Carlisle, and I am assured that directly we hold it our King will seek refuge therein, for he dares not quit England, lest it may be made out that he has thereby forfeited the throne."

Then, as he finished speaking, Dundee rose from his seat, and, drawing his sword, exclaimed, solemnly—

"I swear never to sheath this blade until Carlisle is ours, and King James is safely within its walls."

When he had said this, the council to a man sprang to their feet, and imitated their leader's example by throwing away their scabbards and returning their bare blades to their belts, while, carried away by their enthusiasm, cheer after cheer rang through the tent, and being quickly caught up by Dumbarton's Royals, who were on duty outside, it rolled along the camp, until the hoarse shout of ten thousand voices, swelling every moment higher and higher, awoke the echoes of the broad valley of the Eden, and provoked a faint reply from the beleaguered garrison of Carlisle.

"Let the council be now dissolved, knights and gentlemen," said Dundee, "but at midnight we meet again, for I will then explain the plan of the assault, and carve out ample work for each of you. Baron, you will stay and take a cup of wine with me; and, Sir Andrew Douglas, I wish a few words with you also."

Then, after the nobles and cavaliers who had assisted at the council had bowed, and quitted the tent, Dundee drew Sir Andrew aside, and asked,—

"What about the lady whom you escorted back to the city last night, Sir Andrew? She was very beautiful! Did you learn her name or rank?"

"No, Viscount, she would avow neither."

"Nor how she came to be sailing alone down the river at so late an hour?"

"We did not once refer to the river during the ride," replied Sir Andrew.

"By the saints, Douglas, you must have used your tongue to advantage," rejoined Dundee, in a half-vexed tone, "but, perhaps you were discussing softer subjects, eh?"

"I do not know by what right you ask that question, general," said Douglas, with a flushed cheek; "suffice it to say that our ride was, to me at least, a short and pleasant one, and that I left the lady at the eastern gate."

"Pardon me, Sir Andrew; I meant nothing impertinent by my last remark," said Dundee, with a smile; "but I have a great wish to know who this stranger is, and I half regret that I let her slip through our fingers so easily."

"Wherefore?" asked Sir Andrew.

"Because I am convinced that she is a spy in the service of William of Orange," said the Viscount.

Sir Andrew started; the two questions which the lady had asked him concerning the force of the Royal army, and when they proposed to attack the city, recurred to his mind, but, turning to Dundee, he inquired, "What grounds have you for your suspicions, Viscount?"

"A sealed packet, which must have dropped from her dress, and which I found amongst the reeds a few minutes after you left us, and a prisoner whom some of d'Arcourt's Fusiliers captured an hour later in a fisherman's hut a mile below Northbrigg."

"Explain yourself, Viscount; I do not clearly understand."

"Well, then," said Dundee, "the letter was addressed to Mynheer Goderdt van Baron de Ginckle, the same wretch on whom the usurper hath dared to bestow the Earldom of Athlone, and contained an earnest prayer that he would march to the relief of Carlisle, with all speed. It stated that the town, owing to the great number of troops quartered therein, was running short of provisions, and could only hold out a few days longer.

"This letter was directed to be given to one Herbert Hastings, who was to be awaiting it three miles down the river, in a small hut that stands close beside the stream, and he was to bear it on the spur to Ipswich, and deliver it either into the hands of this de Ginckle, or those of the Duc de Schomberg.

"With this clue, I immediately dispatched half a dozen men-at-arms to capture him, and within an hour they brought him a prisoner to the camp.

"He then confessed that he was a spy in the service of the Stadtholder, and that he, that evening, had expected to receive an important packet from a lady, with whom he was in the habit of communicating, and that she had more than once sailed down the river leaving secret despatches from old Greysteel, to be taken on by him, to one of the Williamite generals I have mentioned."

"And did he reveal her name?" asked our hero.

"No, neither threats nor persuasions could draw that from him," replied Dundee, "but I have no doubt but that she is the fair damsel whom we fished out of the river yesternight. He confessed that from her the rebel leaders had received a full account of our proceedings before the walls, with even a tolerably correct statement of our force and position."

"But what can we do, Viscount?" asked Douglas. "It is doubtless these despatches which have caused the Dutch leaders so promptly to lead their forces northwards in order to raise the siege. I do not see what we can do now;

the mischief is already caused and cannot be undone."

"I think otherwise, my young comrade, or at all events that we can prevent mischief in the future," replied Dundee. "My commands, therefore, are that an hour after sunset you take a dozen men, and with them lie in ambush by the bank of the river, and at about the same spot where we had the romantic adventure last night. If a boat passes, capture its inmates at all hazards and bring him, her, or them, whichever it may be, quickly to my tent; for even though we cannot alter the past we may make our pretty spy show us some secret way of entering the town or gather from her some other information of almost equal importance."

Sir Andrew bowed in silent acquiescence.

"And hark ye," continued Dundee, "you may await her until four in the morning, when, if nothing happens, you will march back and rejoin us, for at that hour we move on to the assault," and waving his hand to prevent reply, he bowed Sir Andrew from the tent.

## CHAPTER IV.

### THE SECOND MEETING.

Love rules the camp, the court, the grove,
And men below and saints above;
For love is Heaven, and Heaven is love.

THE sun had long set; the camp had once more sunk into comparative silence, for in consideration of the early morning muster the Captain-General had permitted the troops to turn in early and get as much rest as they could.

The winding river had changed from a light blue to a muddy brown, and then again glanced white as crystal; for the full moon, half screened by clouds of gauzy mist, rose from behind the keep of Carlisle's grey castle, and shed its mellow light on city and on tent.

Under shadow of some thick withies that grew on the border of the stream were six troopers of Sir Andrew Douglas's regiment; they were all lying or sitting on the ground and talking in low tones amongst themselves, whilst a seventh form, whose burnished steel morion and black cuirass and gorget, studded with gold embroidered sword-belt and crimson scarf, terminated with golden tassels, betokened him to occupy the rank of lieutenant, paced up and down the bank at a few rods' distance, his visor lifted and his eyes bent on the ground as though in deep meditation.

It was Sir Andrew Douglas, and he was in no amiable mood, for enraged at the taunts of the Earl of Dumbarton, and annoyed by Viscount Dundee's suspicions of the lovely girl, whose charms had so completely fascinated him, even while he himself doubted her motives for so late and lonely a voyage, he was now entrusted with the painful duty of watching for her reappearance, and if she did appear again, his duty would oblige him to arrest her, and take her as a captive to Dundee's tent.

Foiled in her intentions the night before the chances were that if she was a spy she would again attempt the descent of the stream that evening on the same mission; and although the young knight longed with all the ardour of a lover to behold her face again, he nevertheless grew pale, and his heart beat, at the mere thought of the steps which his loyalty to the King would oblige him to take, were she indeed to sail that way.

It would be hard, therefore, to decide whether his feelings and emotions were of a pleasing nature or otherwise, when, after an hour's anxious pacing up and down, he beheld a snow white sail again sweep into sight around a bend of the river, and, with quick perception, perceived that a female form stood in the stern, grasping the painted tiller.

The bow of the boat was pointed towards the shore, and it was evidently the passenger's intention to land on the southern side of the river, about fifty yards below the spot where he had placed his men in ambush,

Hastily concealing himself in the rear of the withies, Sir Andrew nervously awaited the approach of the boat, nor had he long to exercise his patience, for a minute later it touched the bank, and the lady sprang lightly ashore.

In one hand she held a slender cord, which was attached to the bow, and she secured her light skiff by tying the other end to the stem of a stunted pollard.

She next walked up and down by the margin of the stream, as though looking for something amidst the bushes.

Sir Andrew immediately thought of the lost letter to Mynheer de Ginckle, and not doubting the object of her search, he signalled to his men to remain silent, and rising to his feet, advanced towards her.

She did not observe his approach, for her back was towards him; but she started as she perceived his shadow on the grass, and with a cry strove to regain her boat; but the cavalier arrested her flight by laying his hand gently on her arm, and saying,—

"Why, do you fly from me lady? We have met before."

Tremblingly she looked up, and her expression of terror changed into a blush and smile as she recognised the features and white plume of her previous night's deliverer.

"Sir Andrew!" she exclaimed, in her low silvery voice. "What brings you here?"

"I was about to ask you the same question, fair lady," replied Douglas, his love returning and his suspicions forgotten after one glance at the spiritual countenance of the fair being by his side.

"And what if I do not choose to answer you, sir?"

"Then, lady, I must enforce an answer."

"*Enforce* an answer!—and from me! What mean you?"

"This" said Sir Andrew, solemnly. "That Viscount Dundee ordered me to arrest you, and bring you as a prisoner to his tent."

"Wherefore?" she asked.

"Because he holds proofs that you are a spy in the service of William of Orange," replied Sir Andrew.

"What proofs?" she demanded eagerly.

"A letter addressed to Mynheer von Baron de Ginckle, and the testimony of one, Herbert Hastings, who is already in our power."

"Ah! then the letter I lost has fallen into the hands of your Captain-General, and its contents have led to poor Hastings's capture!" she exclaimed. "You are commissioned to arrest me, also?"

"Alas! I am," he replied.

"And will you obey Dundee's commands?" she asked.

Sir Andrew paused: he gazed at the half-terrified countenance and tearful eyes of the beautiful spy, who in her anxiety, had placed her hand on his arm. He felt that hand tremble, and his fortitude and sense of duty were overcome, as he pressed it fondly in his own, and replied,—

"Never, dear one! I would die on the block rather than cause you pain. Take you prisoner before Dundee! No, rather would I yield myself into the hands of the bloodthirsty Duc de Schomberg."

"Thanks, Sir Andrew. I had scarcely a right to expect this kindness," she replied, softly; then, as her gaze rested on her last night's gift, the diamond ring, which was attached to the cavalier's gorgetband, she added,—

"Perchance, ere long, I may have it in my power to serve thee also."

"Nay, I trust not, fair one—at least in the way you appear to apprehend. But will you not *now* tell me your name?"

"No, not yet," she replied, with a ringing laugh, "at least not all of it; my christian name is Flora."

"Thanks, lady, for yonr disclosure," rejoined the cavalier; "I will henceforth love that name, as I shall ever love to remember her who bears it."

"Then in return, I hope you will now call me Flora, and not by the vague term, 'lady,' as you have hitherto done."

"With pleasure! Oh, how kind of you to permit me to do so, dear Flora! If you only knew how I have thought of you since our parting last night; how, in short, I love you with my whole heart and soul——"

"Hush!" she said, interrupting him. "When I asked you to call me by my christian name, I did not grant you permission to talk nonsense at the same time."

"Dear one," said he; "I call the saints to bear witness that my professions are sincere."

"Well, then, Sir Andrew, for pity's sake, say no more, for at present I dare not listen to such assurances. Time flies, and I must return to Carlisle."

"To Carlisle!" he repeated.

"Yes!" said Flora, "why do you start?"

Sir Andrew's manner was agitated and his voice trembled as he replied, "Flora, I beg and entreat of you not to return to-night. My tent is at your service, and to-morrow you shall be guarded safely to the walls; but for Heaven's sake seek not to re-enter Carlisle before daybreak."

"Sir cavalier, why do you urge this? Some strange meaning seems to be couched in your words."

"There is, dear one; I could tell thee much, but dare not. I warn thee of a danger that threatens thy city and its inmates—a danger which you cannot avert, but may avoid. Oh! I beseech thee and pray thee to stay in our camp this night.

"I cannot, Sir Andrew," she replied, sadly, but firmly; for I have an old father within yon walls who is anxiously awaiting my return. I am his only hope and joy, for all other affections are buried in my mother's grave. If danger threatens, so much the more is it my duty to be with him this night, and sooner would I suffer the death of an early Christian martyr than be absent from his side when his grey hairs are in peril, and destruction threatens my native city."

As she spoke, the young girl drew herself up to her full height, and her dark brown eyes flashed with the ardour of enthusiasm. Beautiful, indeed, she appeared, as filled with the holy sentiment of love and filial duty, she raised those liquid orbs to the blue vault of heaven as though to invoke a blessing on her aged parent and his cause.

Then, she again laid her soft hand on that of the cavalier, and said,—

"Farewell! I feel persuaded that this is not our last meeting. I depart with a spell of gratitude and interest twined around my heart that makes it thine for ever."

'Ere Sir Andrew Douglas had recovered his self-possession and presence of mind, Flora, with the velocity of light, had regained her skiff, cut the cord which secured it to the shore, and was sailing up the river with a fair breeze towards Carlisle.

---

## CHAPTER V.

### FATHER AND DAUGHTER.

> It was about the noon of a lovely day in June,
> That we saw their banners dance and their cuirasses shine;
> And the man of blood was there, with his long essencep hair.
> And Astley, and Sir Marmaduke, and Rupert of the Rhine.

About the time that Flora quitted Sir Andrew on the bank of the river, on her return to Carlisle, an old weather-beaten warrior stood, with arms folded, at one of the narrow windows of the castle, gazing pensively out into the night.

He was plainly accoutred in an unlaced buff coat and black iron cuirass, over which hung the glittering order of St. Vladimir. On his head was a plain velvet skull cap, but beneath it beamed a round and pleasant face, with a short beard and moustaches, silvery grey hair cut close to the head, and a visage browned by continual exposure to all weathers.

His hands were thrust into the pockets of his voluminous trunk hose, and he was whistling a low monotonous tune, while his gaze rested alternately on the sparkling river, and on the thickly-dotted tents of the Scottish army, whose white canvas shone like snow in the moonlight.

As he distinguished the glittering pavilion of Viscount Dundee, and the commingling folds of the rampant lioned and saltire crossed banners that waved above it, his brow grew stern; and turning again towards the river, his face brightened as he saw the dark hull and flashing sail of a small boat rapidly nearing the castle.

"My daughter, my brave daughter," muttered the old man, turning round as he caught sight of a graceful figure standing in the stern waving a kerchief towards him, and Sir Stephen Macclesfield, the Presbyterian Commandant of Carlisle, better known to the cavaliers under the pseudonym of "Old Greysteel," hurriedly quitted the room.

"Here, Obadiah, Malachi," he shouted, as his long spurs clinked along the stone passage without, "Hasten, ye knaves, and open the water-gate!"

. . . . . . . .

Meanwhile, the light bark rapidly neared the walls, gliding under the shadow of the Rufus tower; it emerged again for a moment into the moonlight, and then a harsh grating noise was heard as the huge water-gates rolled open and disclosed a canal running apparently under the portcullis.

Into this black aperture the beautiful girl guided her skiff; the gates crashed home behind her, the glare of torches shone around instead of the mellow moonlight. She heard the hum of voices, and stepping from her boat on to some stone steps, she felt herself clasped in the arms of her father.

"Well, my dearest child, what tidings do you bring us?" asked Macclesfield, when a few minutes later he and his daughter found themselves alone in the room which a short time previously he had quitted to receive her. "Have you seen Hastings?"

"Alas! dear father, I have not!" she replied "for he is a prisoner in the power of the Jacobites."

"A prisoner!" exclaimed the commandant. "How came he to be captured?"

"The letter which I lost yesternight fell into the hands of Viscount Dundee, and led to his discovery."

"Then your mission has been unaccomplished Flora," said her father; "and yet how came you to learn all this?"

"Because I also have been a captive," she replied.

"You, my dear child?" exclaimed the old man, in accents of horror. "What mean you?"

"That the Jacobite commander set some soldiers to guard the river above Northbrigg, and upon landing, I fell into their hands."

The old man's cheek grew pale, and his lips quivered as he asked, "How did you escape? How did you break from their custody?"

"Through the generosity of a young and kind-hearted cavalier, dear father, the same who rescued me from the river only yesternight, and escorted me to the eastern gate. He said that he should disregard the injunctions of the Captain-General respecting my arrest, and suffer me to depart as I came, free and unquestioned."

"God's blessing be upon his head," said the Commandant, "but you shall no more take such perilous journeys, my darling; you know that my wishes have always been against it, and that with terror and anxiety I ever await your return, fearing lest some evil, or mishap, may have overtaken you."

"And yet, you have more than once owned, dear father, that it was for the best," said Flora. "Had one of the garrison been captured in those expeditions, he would have been hung by the Jacobites as a spy; or had he escaped such a fate, it would only have been by turning traitor to our oppressed Church and to King William, its champion and saviour. Now, although full of danger, my course had been a prudent one. A chivalrous cavalier like Dundee, were he to suspect my motives, would scarcely punish me for them, and even if he had put me to torture, I would have been true to the cause, and not a word should have been wrung from my lips prejudicial to the Orange succession."

As she spoke, her cheek flushed with the kindling enthusiasm of her nature, and the old Commandant's eyes sparkled with the honest pride that he felt in his daughter's courage and beauty, but he replied,—

"You must not risk your life any more, notwithstanding, for I would sooner that our cause were lost than that you should constantly run such peril."

Flora threw her arms around her father's neck, and kissed him tenderly.

"There is no need that I go again, dear father, for 'ere daybreak the Scottish troops will attack us."

"Ah! say you so!" exclaimed the old knight, with a start. "How learned you that?"

"From the same young cavalier who refused to detain me a prisoner, Sir Andrew Douglas, he is called. He did not tell me so in plain words, but he spoke in such a manner that I could not doubt his meaning."

"But how came he to reveal so important a matter to thee, my child?"

"He wished me to stay in the Scottish camp until the place was carried," replied Flora. "He said that there I should be out of danger. But I declined his offer, and when he, out of kindness, would have detained me by force, I evaded him and regained my boat."

Flora blushed crimson as she spoke, but her father heeded it not, for he was too busy pondering over her last communication. At length he said,—

"There is no time to lose. It is now nearly midnight, and they may already be preparing for the assault. Did you hear aught, Flora, of the movements of De Ginckle, or of the Duc de Schomberg?"

"Not a word, dear father," she replied.

"Then, we must e'en trust to ourselves," said Macclesfield, and pacing to the window he looked out.

"The night is as dark as need be," he exclaimed, after a pause; "heavy clouds have obscured the moon. I hear no sounds from the direction of the camp; but let them come; in half an hour we will be well prepared."

Then, with a smile, he kissed his daughter, as she stood by his side, and said,—

"Go to bed, child, and get some rest. On your way to the 'ladies tower,' see Randolph, the steward, and send him to seek Sir Edward Hamilton, and Van Zuylestein, my captain of ordnance, and bid them attend me here with all speed."

. . . . .

Shortly after Flora had quitted her father's presence, the tramp of armed feet was heard in the corrider without; the arras at the end of the apartment was raised, and two soldier-like looking men made their appearance.

One of them was tall and dark, and equipped in a plain suit of buff and steel, his back and breastplate being curiously inlaid with quaint devices, and his gilt helmet was surmounted by a plume of black feathers. His companion, who was shorter by a head, wore a helmet and corslet of unpolished iron as black as his long jack-boots, and his yellow coat heavily cuffed, and his looped skirts proclaimed him to be a Dutchman

This latter individual was Van Zuylestein, captain of the ordnance, and his six foot companion was Sir Edward Hamilton, colonel of Swart Ruyters, also in the service of the Stadtholder.

The Commandant received his visitors with a bow, and then said,—

"I have summoned you, gentlemen, that I may give you instructions concerning the defence of the town, for within an hour the enemy may be upon us."

Van Zuylestein received this information with stoical indifference; but Hamilton's eyes flashed with exultant pride as he answered,—

"Let them come, Sir Stephen, we are ready!"

"Be not too rash, brave Hamilton," said the Commandant, with a smile. "Is the new barricade raised by Sir Andrew's gate?"

"It is, Sir Stephen, and similar ones are erected at the northern and western entrances to the town; the fascines are filled with earth, and the sentries doubled at every gate and tower."

"And the defences of the castle and walls?" said the Commandant; "does aught remain to be done in order to perfect them?"

"Naught, Sir Stephen; the drawbridges are up, the portcullis down, and hackbuts, falconets and cannon-royal are double shotted," replied Zuylestein.

The Commandant laughed, and said, "You have both of you done well; I thank you for your combined zeal, energy, and precaution, which I think will enable Carlisle to hold her own."

"And if the enemy pass the walls, their course through the town will be hotly contested, for every house is fortified, and every wall is loopholed for musketry. They will be shot down in the streets by a foe whom they connot attack in turn—shot down and decimated."

"That also is well," said Macclesfield. "Now listen to me. Rouse the troops as quickly and silently as possible, and ere a quarter of an hour be over let every man stand to his arms. Station your musketeers and artillerymen so that they may be available at any instant. See, also, that the garrison of the castle are up and doing, and do thou, Sir Edward, summon the Swart Ruyters of Arnold Joost van Keppel to the saddle, tell the Mynheer that he must form them in the great square, and there await further orders. Bein Tonk's heavy horse will await there also."

The tall Hamilton bowed in silence.

"Then off, and be speedy, man, and when you have done all that I have told you to do, return to me. You will find me on horseback in the Bastion Court. Even now, methinks, I hear a faint stir in the direction of the camp. If so, there is no time to be lost; but let not a drum beat, or fife sound. I want not Dundee to know that we are on the alert."

The two officers with a stiff military salute then quitted the room, the clank of their spurs sounding on the stone staircase, and then, as Stephen Macclesfield advanced again to the window and gazed into the darkness without, he heard in the distance a dull rumbling sound like the roar of a wintry sea; but he knew that it was the echo of twice ten thousand feet marching against his devoted city.

## CHAPTER VI

### IN BATTLE ARRAY.

Carabine slung, stirrup well hung,
Flaggon at saddle-bow merrily swung;
Toss up the ale—for our flag like a sail,
Struggles and swells on the July gale;
Colours fling out and then give them a shout,
We are the gallants to put them to rout.

"Welcome back to camp, Douglas. You are the first man I have met who does not appear to be in a hurry."

Sir Andrew started from his reverie, and looking up, met the frank laughing gaze of the Earl of Dumbarton.

"I was not aware that there was any need of haste, my lord," said the Life-Guardsman. "Are the troops ready to march yet?"

"Some are, by this time, on the road," replied Dumbarton; "others are only awaiting their leaders."

"Then they shall not have long to wait for one," retorted Douglas. "Farewell, noble Earl," he added. "When next we meet I trust it will be within the walls of Carlisle;" and so they parted.

. . . . .

Meanwhile, in the Scottish camp, every tent had been struck. Quickly and silently the troops had been aroused from sleep, and formed in heavy marching order around their standards. The colours slowly unfolded to the chill morning breeze, and obeying the dull roll of the muffled kettledrums, company after company of helmed and corsletted infantry fell into rank, with the more lightly-armed Grenadiers covering each flank.

Mounted on his dark grey charger, and clad in his full uniform of bright scarlet and flashing steel, his white horse-hair plume floating above his helmet, and his visor closed, Sir Andrew Douglas passed down the dark serried lines of infantry to the spot where the dense masses of heavy horse were awaiting the order to march.

The glittering squadrons of cavalry comprising the horse grenadiers of Clermistonlee, Michael Fenton's regiment of red-coated lancers, the Earl of Dunmore's dragoons, the Scots Greys in their janissary caps, buff coats, and iron panoply, and Claverhouse's Life Guardsman in their polished plate armour, were drawn up in the neighbourhood of two bright camp-fires, and the ruddy flames shed a rich glow on burnished helms and nodding plumes, on velvet and cloth of gold, on gleaming weapons and glancing mail; revealing the rolling folds of the large silken standards, and the prancing and curvetting of proud chargers.

"Better late than never, Sir Andrew!" shouted the commanding officer of the Life Guards. "I suppose you serve with us to-day as a volunteer? Your company of the regiment is at Chester, I think?"

As he spoke the grey-bearded Dalzel rode up, and shook Sir Andrew warmly by the hand.

"No, they are at Ipswich, and I am the only officer of my company present before Carlisle, so that I shall accept your invitation to charge with you, and consider it an honour to follow so brave a leader."

"This is not the place for courtly speeches, my young friend, which I always estimate at their proper worth," said Sir Thomas; "but if you will strike with us, so good a sword will be welcome. You shall ride beside me in the front, an' it so please you."

Douglas bowed, whilst a gleam of fierce joy lighted up his dark eyes. Then he exclaimed, suddenly, "Ah, here comes the Captain-General."

Mounted on a superb charger, white as the driven snow, Lord Viscount Dundee, surrounded by his staff of splendidly-equipped and superbly-mounted cavaliers, passed rapidly down the line, giving orders to the different captains of companies as he rode along.

In another minute the vanguard of foot, Dumbarton's Royals, was in motion. The shouldered pikes and Sweyne feathers (a kind of weapon resembling the demi-halberd). The gleaming morions and the bright scarlet coats gleamed in the firelight as they marched by; and then Sir Thomas Dalyel, drawing his enormous Andre Ferrah, gave the words rapidly, as became a soldier of spirit, Cavaliers and Gentlemen of the Life Guards, draw sabres, to the left wheel, trot."

As he spoke, the colours bent forward to the breeze, a thousand bright blades flashed in the moonlight, which at this moment burst out from between two heavy masses of jagged cloud; and without beat of drum or blare of trumpet, the Guards, 'mid the neigh of steeds, the clank of armour, and the waving of plumes and standards, swept down the hill side towards the clear waters of the Eden, and the dark walls of beleaguered Carlisle.

Side by side with Sir Thomas Dalyel rode Sir Andrew Douglas, his visor closed, his lips compressed, his eyes fixed on the distant walls, and his thoughts centered on her he loved— the beautiful Flora Macclesfield.

---

## CHAPTER VII.

### THE ATTACK ON CARLISLE.

See, black on each roof, at the sound of our hoof  
The Puritan's gateer, but keep them aloof;  
Their muskets are long and they aim at a throng,  
But woe to the weak when they challenge the strong.  
Butt-end to the door—one hammer more,  
Our pike-men rush in and the struggle is o'er.

"By Heaven! there must be ten thousand men marching against us!" muttered Sir Stephen Macclesfield, as the sudden burst of moonlight revealed the dark masses of armed troops that were rolling like ocean billows towards the outworks; then, turning to the musketeers and pikemen who lay crouched behind the parapets of the wall, he shouted,—

"Hurrah! my brave hearts! the foe are upon us. They have sworn to drive us from the city, and make of Carlisle a vast shamble-house; but we are strong enough to hold our own; they will fall before our walls, and the first man who passes them shall do so over my body. Hurrah; for King William and the reformed religion!"

Aware that the moonlight must already have enable the besieged to discover their approach, the troops of Dundee pressed on with tumultuous shouts; their standards waving and their hoarse drums beating, while their advanced skirmishers fired at every gleaming morion that showed itself above the walls.

The intention of the royalist general appeared to be to direct all his efforts against one point, and that point was evidently the Eastern gate and its outworks, for his whole army was heading towards this entrance to the city, utterly regardless of, and almost uninjured by, the ill-directed fire from the hackbuts and falconets on the walls.

A heavily armed regiment of foot, the Scots Fusilier Guards, clad in coats, breeches, and stockings, all of bright scarlet, with white scarfs and long feathers, the officers marching with half pikes, and the soldiers with lighted matches, poured along the road, and heedless of a heavy fire of cannon and musketry from the walls, advanced resolutely to storm and destroy the thick palisades which protected the outside of the wet ditch, while two companies of matchlock men took up their position on a little knoll to the left, and kept up a rattling fire at the soldiers on the walls, and at every head that showed itself through the loopholes of the embattled tower that rose above the gate.

Conspicuous amongst the defenders stood the aged Commandant, his armour glancing, his black plume waving, the mark of a hundred bullets, which he regarded no more than if they had been pebbles.

The old man's visor was closed, but with voice and hand he encouraged his men, often shouting,—

"Well done, stout cannoneers! well shot brave musketeers, hackbut and falconet, matchlock and fusil, fire slowly and fire sure. Let every bullet send a Jacobite to the shades! Hurrah! the kirk and King William!"

By his side stood Mynheer Van Zuylestein, the master of the ordnance, his countenance calm and stolid, as a Dutchman's invariably is, and his voice ringing loud and clear as he superintended the handling and working of the cannon.

The scene had become animated and exciting to the utmost degree, for while on the left the Earl of Dumbarton, with a strong body of infantry, was diverting the attention of the besieged by throwing a bridge of planks across the Eden, as though with the intention of storming the outworks of the castle, and on the right Dundee, in person, was manœuvring a thousand heavy cavalry, nearly within matchlock range, the contest before the gate had waxed fiercer and fiercer.

In spite of the heavy fire rained down upon them, the besiegers had hewn down the wooden palisades with their axes, and planted their ladders against the walls. Twice they were overthrown and again raised, while regardless of bullet and grenade, the Fusilier Guards swarmed up them, their swords, axes, and armour glancing in the now unclouded moonlight.

"The King! The King! hurrah! down with the crop-eared rebels!" they cried; but while the words were on their lips heavy cannon balls, grenades, bar and chain shot were hurled down on their devoted heads, and back again fell the ladders into the ditch with the soldiers grovelling under them, bruised and beaten; while loud and shrilly answered the triumphant shouts of the besieged, "Down with the followers of Belial—smite them both hip and thigh. Hurrah! The Kirk and King William!"

Dismayed by the fall of the ladders, the stormers paused irresolute; but at this moment loud cheers was heard in the rear. Nearer and nearer

THE DOOR OPENED MID THE GLARING OF FLAMBEAUX AND CLATTERING OF ARMS.

moved Dumbarton's Royals towards the walls; they halted exactly opposite the eastern gate.

The Earl received a few hurried commands from an aide-de-camp, who now galloped up to the head of the column, and then the latter rode away towards a body of lightly armed horsemen who were drawn up on the brow of a gentle eminence to the right.

There were two hundred volunteer cavalry, under the command of Roger St. George, a brave young borderer, who figured conspicuously throughout the campaign.

As they slowly walked their horses down the slope nearer to the scene of action, their leader drew a white kerchief from his scarf, and attaching it to his sword waved it above his helmet.

In quick reply a flag was run up from the battlements of the gate tower, and to the astonishment of both besiegers and besieged, the drawbridge was lowered and the portcullis raised.

"Treason! treason!" cried the troops on the walls; and loud above the surrounding din, thundered the manly voice of the aged Commandant, as he shouted,—

"To the gates—to the gates! forward pikemen, and matchlock-men, or the foe will pass the barrier. We have traitors amongst us. Van Zuylestein, haste thee, and bid Hamilton bring up his Swart Ruyters, or the outworks are lost."

As he spoke, Sir Stephen glanced hastily round, and to his surprise, discovered that the master of the ordnance had suddenly vanished.

He stamped his foot impatiently as he again shouted, "Every pikeman to the gate, cut down all who oppose you, and up with the drawbridge before the enemy can cross!"

The men-at- arms answered with loud cheers, and with pike, sword, and axe, rushed tumultously towards the point of danger.

But it was to late, for the instant that the drawbridge was lowered, the Earl of Dumbarton drew his sword, and changing from line into close column, the heavily-armed Royals made a dash at the gate, and entered the city at the double, the earth resounding to the regular tramp of their feet, and the moonlight flashing on their gleaming morions and levelled pikes.

As at their head the Earl passed beneath the dark arch of the gate tower; a soldier, in black rusty armour, approached his charger, and laying one hand on the rein, said in a low voice, "All is well, Lord Dumbarton, I have kept my word, Carlisle is fired in three places. Captain Van Zuylestein holds the gate tower for King James. Now for the gold pieces you wot of."

"'Tis well, traitor!" answered the Cavalier Earl, disdainfully. "Here is thy reward. Now go, or 'twill be the worse for thee, for here come those thou hast betrayed."

With wild cries, and in a disorderly mob, down poured a large body of armed rebels towards the gate.

"Close in! close in! shouted Dumbarton. "Level your pikes, and forward! Down with this scurril mob. Forward, my brave hearts! forward! charge!"

"The King! the King! Death to the Roundheads!" they shouted.

And, like a huge wave on a frail bark, the Royals dashed at the advancing foe, who gave way on all sides, while, above the rush of men and the clash of steel, rang the yells and battle cries of the combatants, mingled with the groans and shrieks of the wounded and dying.

A mounted aide-de-camp at this moment swept up a side street at gallop.

"Stand firm, men of Carlisle!" he cried, as he dashed past the wavering and disorganized citizens. "In an instant Hamilton's Swart Ruyters will support you, and Mossue de Rouvigny's Protestant Battle-axe Guards are fast coming up."

This encouagement was of little avail, for the pikemen had already given way; a few were fighting in detached groups, others were seeking safety in flight, and the victorious Royals were sweeping up Castle Street towards the Cathedral, bearing everything before them, when their advance was again checked by Rouvigny's Frenchmen, who were advancing at a run, their long pointed battle-axes at the "charge" and glittering in one unbroken line of steel from helm to waist-belt.

"Stand firm and close, my iron crabs! receive them like a wall of granite," cried the gallant Dumbarton.

And, as he spoke, with a concussion like that of two heavily-charged thunder clouds, pikemen and battle-axe guards crushed together.

Then ensued a dogged fight, of several minutes' duration, neither side yielding an inch of ground to the other.

In numbers they were equally matched, but the long pointed spear and axe halbered of the French was a far more formidable weapon than the short pike of the King's troops, who were harrassed, moreover, by unceasing discharges of fusils and matchlocks from the upper windows on each side of the street.

It is impossible to say which side would have been victorious, had not, at this critical juncture of affairs, a squadron of horse swept up a side street, and unexpectedly falling on the left flank of Dumbarton's Royals, broken their firm array in an instant.

In vain their brave leader strove to restore order and confidence; in vain he waved his sword, and called on his men to stand firm; the flashing blades of the rebel cavalry were commiting sad havoc amid his ranks, while the swinging axes of the Frenchmen were opening terrible lanes in their closely packed columns.

A minute later, and all traces of order had vanished; they had changed into a flying disorderly mob, and were driven back upon the leading columns of Dunmore's dragoons, who, after cutting to pieces a desperate stand of Puritan pikes that, under the personal command of the veteran Commandant, had defended the narrow passage of the East Port, now galloped up to the relief of Dumbarton.

"Hold hard, you white livered cowards! Force your way on to the next street, or you will break our ranks, and we shall have to spear you with the rebels," shouted Dunmore, their colonel; but he might as well have spared his breath, for back the Royals were still borne; back, back, until horse and foot were mingled together in one confused melée; a disorganized, struggling mass of men and horses, swinging from side to side like ocean billows, while the red glare of burning houses (for the city had been set on fire at three points by traitors within the walls) shed a lurid glow on a sea of upturned, scowling faces, on the gleaming mail of the combatants, the undulating banners, and a waving forest of tossing plumes, pennoned spears, and wildly-whirling and gore-clotted swords and battle-axes.

## CHAPTER VIII.

### A CHARGE OF THE LIFE GUARDS.

Their heads all stooping low, their points all in a row,
Like a whirlwind 'mong the trees, like a deluge on the dykes;
Our Cuirassiers have burst on the ranks of the accurst,
And with a shock have scattered the forest of his pikes.

MEANWHILE, the heavily armed Life Guards, of Claverhouse, numbering a thousand sabres, led on by Sir Thomas Dalyel and Sir Andrew Douglas, formed in squadrons, and with their steady advance, uncheered by blast of trumpet or roll of drum, moved through the city by a circuitous route towards the cathedral, before which it was understood that more of the reserve troops of the Statholder were drawn up.

Before, however, they had got half way to the Cathedral Close, the sharp bray of horns was heard approaching, and round the corner of a street appeared a strong body of foot, marching in close column, and peculiar in appearance from their yellow uniforms, and the colour of their corslets and morions, which were of a dull, deep black.

Perceiving the approach of the King's cavalry, their commanding officer brought them to a halt, and forming across the whole breadth of the street, with the front rank kneeling, the butts of their pikes resting against their feet, the second stooping, while those behind presented their spears over their heads, they offered such a resistance to the rapid advance of the Life Guards as the hedgehog offers to the eager terrier.

But their resolute front made no impression on the panoplied masses of Dalyel; the words of command flew from rank to rank with lightning rapidity.

"Gallop! Charge!" was the cry, and with the blast of trumpet, and amid the crash of kettle-drum and cymbal, on swept the mailed chivalry like a whirlwind.

The streets and houses fairly shook before the rush of their galloping squadrons, as, with flashing swords and floating plumes, they dashed at the foe.

Then there was a rattling fire of musketry, a momentary check, a crashing of wood, as the Life Guards thundered down on the walls of Puritan pikes, a rasping of steel against steel as their flashing sabres cut a way through the compact mass of steady English valour that was opposed to them; their grey horses' heads, and broad buffeting shoulders rising and sinking, and rising again, as, with terrible slaughter to the foe, they swept through their ranks, and rode on once more towards the Cathedral Close.

The entrance to this they soon gained, and in its broad area, by the lurid glow of the burning city, beheld heavy masses of horse drawn up in battle array, their long lances sloping over their shoulders, evidently only awaiting the signal for onslaught.

These were the reserved squadrons of Sir Edward Hamilton's Swart Ruyters, who, conspicuous by his sombre mail, sat on his black Flemish charger at their head; and in their rear were many of the Duke of Manchester's Protestant Pistoliers, scaled like armadilloes in steel and brass.

"There are the crop-eared followers of the Dutch Pretender; the Praise God Barebones spawn of Old Noll. Let us show them what the loyal cavaliers of Dundee can do," cried Dalyel, hoarsely. "Follow me, gentlemen of the Scottish Life Guards, hurrah! God and King James!"

"God and our King! Form troops, form squadron!—march! trot! gallop! charge!" echoed Sir Andrew Douglas, waving his sword.

A wild cheer rang through the ranks, a thousand trenchant blades flashed above a thousand plumed helms, and spurring, holster to holster, and knee to knee, like a mighty 'avalanche they dashed at the sombre Puritan chivalry.

"Level lances! rest lances! goad flanks! forward! charge! Gluck! gluck! Vivat Wilhelm!" shouted the astonished Hamilton; but ere his large Dutch troops could get into motion, with all the advantage of a heavy impetus the Life Guards were upon them.

Pouring on in a steady line of at least a thousand cavalry, with bridles and bits, stirrups and spurs clanking, horses champing and tossing the white foam from their steaming nostrils, brandished swords glittering, and plumes waving—it was a splendid sight to look upon, that steady advance of the Scottish Life Guards, as with the venerable Dalyel and the youthful Douglas leading them on at full speed, with the rush of a whirlwind they charged through and through the ranks of the Swart Ruyters.

It was a fearful shock; a hundred saddles were emptied in a minute; down went men, horses, and standards. There was a clashing of steel as the Dutch spears shattered against Scottish helm and corslet, and then the broken shafts were thrown aside, and swords and pistols handled in their stead, for the Swart Ruyters were game to the backbone, and a storm of shouts and cries arose to the luried heavens as the combatants engaged hand to hand, and the wounded fell groaning and shrieking to the earth.

"Close in, close in—hack, hew, and spare not," cried Sir Andrew Douglas, as, with his heavy sword reeking with blood, he attacked a tall horseman, who was animating the Swart Ruyters to further resistance.

This worthy's reply was a heavy blow from his long straight sword, which our hero with difficulty guarded; but spurring his charger forward so as to bring his ponderous chest full on the counter of his adversary, he bore both horse and man to the ground.

At the same moment he was, however, himself felled to the earth by a blow from a pistol butt, and, with a groan, fell prostrate over the body of his late antagonist.

By this time the dense masses of the Stadtholder's horse had been totally routed. The Scottish Guards had thrice charged forth and back through their ranks, riding them down like a field of ripe corn, until, weakened and dismayed, they turned to fly.

Loud cheers then again broke from the Royalist cavalry. "On—on! the Saints smile on us! victory is ours! spur after those flying traitors, and cut them down."

So shouted Sir Thomas Dalyel, whose towering plume, and waving white beard had been ever conspicuous amidst the the thickest of the melée.

His spirited and gallant followers were right willing to obey his behest, and harrass the retreat of the panic-stricken foe, who were now madly spurring out of the vast Cathedral Close.

At this moment, however, wild and shrill above the roar of the burning city, the rattle of musketry, and the clash of steel, echoed the prolonged blare of the recal trumpet, and Dundee, in person, attended by only two cavaliers of his staff, was seen rapidly crossing the open towards them.

Reining in his foam-flecked steed beside Sir Thomas Dalyel, Dundee exclaimed, hastily—

"Dress your ranks, Sir Thomas; the enemy are not yet beaten. A large body of infantry are even now marching down the next street; and unless the Life Guards can scatter them, the day may yet be a black one for us; for all my other troops have scattered themselves in quest of riot and pillage."

Even as he spoke, the dull roll of the drum and the clash of cymbals echoed in the distance; then rang forth the harsh tooting of horns, clearly audible above the tramp of hurrying feet, the clattering of weapons, and the sharp hissing sound of the destroying flames that were rapidly spreading from house to house, licking around the quaintly carved chimney- tops and hiding the pale moon and star-spangled firmament with a dense lurid canopy of smoke and fire.

That red unearthly glow flashed on the iron mail of a dense body of infantry, who, with colours flying, and shouldered pikes gleaming, debouched from a neighbouring street into the Cathedral Close, and also on the waving sword of Dalyel, who shouted at the top of his stentorian voice—

"Cavaliers and gentlemen of the Guards, behold the last stand of the crop-heads and their Dutch allies. One blow more, and victory is indeed ours. Viscount Dundee, does it please you to lead us on?"

"Nay, brave Dalyel, not I," replied Dundee; "maintain the command that you are so worthy to wield. I will fight by your side, but not supplant you.

Then, turning to the fierce troopers, he said, "Gentlemen, in this charge I am not your general, but your comrade, e'en as I was in the olden time; a simple volunteer, under Sir Thomas, ready to smite once more for the good cause. This is our last charge—let your rallying shout be 'Victory!' Dalyel, give the order to advance."

The words of command once more ran along the line. "Charge!" was again the cry, and knee to knee, bridle to bridle, a living avalanche of men and horses, the Life Guards swept upon the advancing foe.

Their onset was so rapid that Sir Stephen Macclesfield, the veteran commandant, had barely time to throw back the flanks of his infantry with a triple stand of pikes in front, ere, like an iron torrent, the heavily-armed Scots surged against them.

"Victory! victory! Cut them down! The King! the King!" was shouted on one side; and loud above the surrounding discord rang the clear voice of the old commandant, who, with his head bare, and his long silver hair floating in the wind, was encouraging his men with word and gesture.

"Stand firm," he cried, "stand firm, and receive them like a wall of granite. Behind you the city is on fire. Retreat, therefore, is impossible; so better die than give way. William and the Kirk!"

His words were the next moment drowned by the shock of the charge, and in an instant the human rampart was hurled back before the irrepressible sweep of horse and man—hurled back, but not broken.

For once the ranks of the rebel pikemen stood firm, and the glittering squadrons of horse recoiled from the steady volley and the forest of steel points like a crested wave from a rock.

Aware that to give way was death, and rendered desperate by the heat of the fire in their rear, even the craven heart now grew bold, and shoulder to shoulder, silently and sternly, with lowering brows and compressed lips, they kept their ranks.

But the gallant Life Guards were not to be so easily daunted; ever in the van, conspicuous by their waving plumes and brilliant uniforms, on went and home went Dalyel and Dundee.

Charge after charge they made upon the enemy, bearing back the mass of desperate men once more into the narrow street from whence they had only a few minutes previously emerged. Back—back further and further still, until breathless, begrimed with gore and smoke, by sweat and dust, the roar of the raging fire again surrounded them, and clouds of wreathing smoke rolled over and around, madly whirling swords, and dinted spear points, and a tumultuous ocean of undulating morions and waving plumes.

Yet still the line of Puritan infantry remained unbroken, and every moment the horses of the cavalry, frightened by the smoke and flames, the blazing of roofs, and the fall of burning beams and rafters, were becoming more and more restive and unmanageable.

At this moment, above the roar of the contest and the flames, there arose another sound, the wild bellowing of infuriated beasts; and down a side street, with lowered horns and panting nostrils, maddened by darts and arrows rankling in their flesh, with flaming tar-pots bound to their legs and necks, and pursued by a disorganised and yelling rabble, firing guns, and waving torches and pitched flambeaux, close in their rear, came a herd of bulls, flying wildly from their pursuers.

"Face round, my men; fall back, or your ranks are broken," cried Dalyel, seeing the full extent of the new danger that threatened them.

But it was too late; in another second the bulls were amongst them, breaking in their right flank, while an immense flaming rafter falling from a neighbouring house at the same time in their midst rendered the confusion irretrievable; their firm array was converted into a disorganized mass of rearing and surging horses, while the Puritan pikemen, seizing the opportunity, quitted the defensive, and moved down upon them like living wall, slaying without mercy.

A scene of the most frightful carnage ensued; in a few minutes four hundred brave cavaliers lay dead and dying in their steel harness in that single street. They all perished sword in hand, around the waving plumes of Sir Thomas Dalyel and the gallant Dundee, who at length convinced, even against their will, that further resistance was worse than useless, reluctantly gave the command to fall back.

"Not so fast, my gay gallant," shouted a voice at his elbow, and glancing round, Dundee found himself face to face with the commandant of the city, Sir Stephen Macclesfield.

Their blades crossed; but the old man was weakened by fatigue, and after a few cuts and thrusts, his sword was dashed from his grasp, and he stood defenceless before the Royalist General.

"Strike!" he cried, "I ask no quarter, I die for England, and England's reformed Faith!"

But lowering his sword point, Dundee replied,—

"Nay, live, Sir Stephen, still to hold that city which you have to-day so gallantly defended. James Claverhouse [Claverhouse and Viscount Dundee are one and the same person] can well afford to spare so brave a foe;" and with a courtly bow, he galloped after his men.

It was but a small party of that heroic regiment, who, fighting their way to one of the city gates, quitted the once happy and picturesque city of Carlisle, leaving five thousand dead within its walls, and wiping their dripping blades in their horses' manes, rode southward with Dundee, and the grey-bearded Dalyel, still at their head.

And Sir Andrew Douglas,—Where was he? wounded and insensible, lying amongst a heap of dead in the Cathedral Close, the hilt of his broken sword still grasped, however, tightly in his red right hand.

---

## CHAPTER IX.

### A FRIEND IN NEED.

Ho comrades scour the plain, and ere you strip the slain,
First give another stab to make your search secure;
Then shake from their sleeves and pockets their broad pieces and their lockets,
The tokens of the wanton, and the plunder of the poor.

THE morning sun shone high in the heavens when Sir Andrew Douglas awoke from the death-like trance caused by the heavy blow of his adversary's pistol butt.

On opening his eyes, he beheld a graceful youth, in the uniform of a Dutch musqueteer, with the vizor of his steel morion drawn over his face, bending over him, until his bright yellow plume mingled with the blood-bedabbled horsehair that surmounted his own battered helmet.

While Sir Andrew gazed wonderingly at his strange visitor, uncertain whether he looked upon friend or foe, the unknown knelt by his side, and whispered in his ear—

"Sir Cavalier, it is I—it is Flora Macclesfield who speaks, and she is come to repay the debt of life, that she still owes to her gallant preserver."

As she spoke, an ungauntletted snow-white hand raised the barred morier, and disclosed thereby her luxuriant black hair, her sparkling eyes, and exquisitely-moulded features.

Her face was pale, but a sweet smile rose to her lips, and her cheeks flushed as she perceived the effect her words produced upon the wounded officer, whose eyes sparkled, and whose brow relaxed as he regarded the almost holy beauty of the still girlish face that was bending over him.

Then, in a weak voice, he murmured,—

"Dear lady, why are you here, standing amid this plain of blood? Can it be for my sake that you have braved all the horrors of such a field of carnage?"

His hand sought hers as he spoke, and, with unaffected simplicity, she laid her taper fingers within his buff gauntlet, saying, as she did so,—

"I *am* come for your sake, to urge you to fly; for, if discovered by our soldiers, your doom will be death. Once in the hands of the Council, not even I can save you. Are you wounded?"

"I scarcely know," replied Sir Andrew, faintly. "I fancy I am more stunned than hurt. I feel almost suffocated by the closeness of my helmet, and oppressed as though by a heavy weight lying on my cuirass."

"No wonder, Sir Cavalier," said Flora; "my trusty servitors, Hob and Hackett, found a dead charger stretched across your body, and the vizor of your helmet closed, while your face was turned to the ground. Had it not been for your uniform, I should have failed to recognise you; but now all is well. Take a sip from this flask; it will refresh you."

As she spoke, Flora placed the lip of a small phial to Sir Andrew's mouth.

He sipped it eagerly, and the effect was instantaneous.

A colour again rose to his cheek, and, almost without an effort, he sprang to his feet.

"Now, how feel you?" asked Flora, with a smile.

"Once more myself," was the reply. "Oh, lady, how much I am indebted to you. You have saved my life."

"And have you not preserved mine, also?" said Flora. "No, Sir Andrew, I am still your debtor, for I have scarcely run any peril to serve you, whereas you risked your own life to save me. But this is no time to spend in idle talk; you must quit Carlisle, and that speedily."

"Our cause is lost, then? the Stadtholder's troops still hold the city? Dundee is defeated?" questioned the cavalier, in a tone of anxious inquiry.

"Yes, Carlisle has not changed hands; we were able to hold our own," replied Flora, proudly. "But we can converse as we walk along, for now we must hasten."

Then, turning to her two servitors, she said—

"Hob, give this gentleman the cloak you carry on your arm; and do you, Hackett, bring hither the helmet of yonder dead Hollander, the one lying across the brass-mounted saddle, with the black helmet of Hamilton's Swart Ruyters."

Then, resuming her conversation with Sir Andrew, she said—

"You must for once suffer yourself to take another's place, and don the orange cockade of King William. Let me remove your helmet."

With a smile, Flora unbuckled the steel clasp, and lifting the dented head-piece from the closely curling locks of Sir Andrew, let it drop to the ground.

In another moment one of her attendants had replaced it with the plain steel helmet of the dead Swart Ruyter, while the other threw a heavy red cloak across the Cavalier's shoulders, thus making the disguise complete.

As Sir Andrew's eye rested on the orange cockade, the badge of William and the rebel Puritans, he was about to tear it from his breast; but Flora laid her hand on his, exclaiming—

"Do not, Sir Andrew, I pray you, it is your badge of safety."

"Not even to preserve my life and liberty will I wear the colours of that vile man who calls himself England's King," replied the knight with a clouded brow.

Fora's eyes flashed; she paused with indecision, but still keeping her hand on the Cavalier's gauntlet, she said, while the colour mounted to her cheek,—

"O, Sir Andrew, if not for your own sake, condescend to wear it for mine. Twice have you said that you loved me. If your professions are true tear not off these colours. Your life depends on your compliance."

The cloud passed from the Cavalier's brow, and clasping the young girl's hand within his own, he said,—

"And do you really feel such an interest in my safety, dear one? When you owned yourself to be the daughter of the proud Governor Macclesfield, I deemed that my hopes were for ever crushed. Can you love me in sincerity?"

This dialogue had been carried on in so low a tone as to be inaudible to the two servitors who stood near; and in the same accents the gentle Flora replied,—

"How would you have me answer you save by silence? Enough that I feel an interest in your safety. In happier times we may meet again; now there are other matters to think of, which, I fear, we have delayed too long. Ah! what is that?"

As Flora spoke, the sounds of music, and the tramp of hurrying feet were heard in the distance, and dropping her voice, she said,—

"Come on, Sir Andrew. It is the city guard searching for the Jacobite wounded. Follow me," and with the armed servitors a few paces in their rear, they crossed the Cathedral Close in the direction of the outer walls.

The lovers pursued their way over ground strewed with the bodies of men and horses, and slippery with blood.

They passed the dark frowning walls of the Cathedral, even then grey with age, then into a narrow street beyond, filled with the débris of fallen roofs and chimneys, where the houses on each side were still smouldering with the expiring fire, the thick columns of smoke issuing from window and doorway, and curling upwards until their wreathy folds were dissolved in the blue ether above, until they found themselves at the spot where a few hours before the Life Guards had ridden down the pikemen of the Stadtholder.

These brave soldiers lay as they had fallen, line on line, their dull black corslets and morions gleaming in the sunlight, and in many places tinted with a richer dye, marking the spot where the life-blood from their undaunted hearts had oozed forth from the narrow slit or broad gash made by the remorseless lance thrust or sword cut.

Several times on the road had Flora trembled, and her cheek blanched as she gazed upon the many appalling shapes of the grim phantom, Death; and now she uttered a shrill cry, for in passing that group of ghastly slain, she accidentally stepped upon the arm of a dying trooper, who uttered a low groan of pain.

Although faint and giddy, Sir Andrew sprang to her side, and said, tenderly,

"Dearest Flora, what scenes of horror your kindness to me has led you into! You are too young and tender-hearted to traverse this great field of death without acute pain."

"Never mind, Sir Andrew," she replied, with a faint smile, "a daughter of Carlisle should not fear the sight of blood, and I would fain be as brave as the noble hearts who have fought within her walls; but we are close to the Eastern Gate, the chief point of danger; the watchword is 'Keep and guard.' You go out in the character of an aide-de-camp of the Commandant, bearing despatches to the army of the Duc de Schomberg, so no questions will be asked. Hob, bring out the black charger," she continued, turning to that worthy servitor, who, for the last five minutes, had kept a profound silence, merely pricking up his ears to catch all he could of the conversation carried on in front, though to his great dissatisfaction, the only part audible was the command addressed to himself.

In reply he darted through an open doorway to the right, and a moment afterwards reappeared, leading by the bridle a magnificent steed, richly caparisoned, and black as the raven's wing.

"Now, mount and away," said Flora, hurriedly, "for round the corner of yon street stands the Eastern Gate, and the sooner you are outside the walls the better. Remember the password. In happier times of peace we may meet again."

"Adieu, then, since it must be so. May God and his holy saints have you in their keeping, dearest one! Right glad shall I be to see the grey walls of Carlisle again, if you remain within them," and with a lingering fond clasp of the hand, Sir Andrew mounted, and rode slowly away.

---

## CHAPTER X.

DISCOVERY.—THE DUNGEON.—ANOTHER FRIEND.

O, evil was the root, and bitter was the fruit,
And crimson was the juice of the vintage that she trod;
For ye trampled on the throng of the haugthy and the strong,
Who sate in the high places and slew the saints of God.

Sir Andrew Douglas had only quitted Flora a few minutes, ere he reined in his horse before the Eastern Gate, and looking upwards, saw, spiked on the battlements of the tower that rose darkly above it, a human head.

The eyes were protruding and bloodshot; the pale face was dappled with blood; and the red elf-locks, that floated in the wind, betokened it as belonging to the traitor master of the ordnance, Van Zuylestein, whom an offer of two hundred golden crowns had bribed to lower the drawbridge, and open the gates for the Royalists to enter the city on the preceding night.

The clash of arms close by roused Sir Andrew from the reverie into which the grim aspect of Van Zuylestein's head had for the moment cast him, and a man-at-arms advancing from the shadow of the gate-house, laid his hand on the bridle, as he demanded,—

"Where ride you, sir courier, and on what errand?"

"What is that to thee, fellow?" exclaimed Sir Andrew; "take thy hand from my rein, and lower the drawbridge."

"That will I not do, my dainty gallant, without knowing wherefore," said the man. "Deliver the password."

"Keep and guard," replied Sir Andrew, rapidly losing his patience.

The man then let go his hold on the bridle, and asked more respectfully, "and wherefore do you ride forth? Pardon me, sir courier, but our orders are strict."

"I am an aide-de-camp of Sir Stephen Macclesfield, bearing despatches to his Grace the Duc de Schomberg."

The man-at-arms, as though satisfied with this answer, stepped back, made a military salute, and commanded two subordinates to lower the bridge.

This was speedily done; the chains rattled, and the bridge began to drop, but ere it touched the ground a loud voice shouted—

"Stop, guards, you are relieved;" and with spurs clanking, and plume waving, an officer, equipped in sombre mail, stepped before the

Life Guardsman's charger, and, with a haughty bow, said,—

"It is an unusual honour for one of my Swart Ruyters to be be selected to bear despatches to the Duc de Schomberg, and still more remarkable for one of them to be able to speak such excellent English. Up with thy visor, man, that I may see thee, *rara avis* that thou art, and produce thy missive to his Grace."

"I am no trooper of thine, but am clad thus in disguise for a special purpose. I am simply a gentleman volunteer, therefore will I not raise my visor at thy bidding, nor show my despatches, which I have strict orders to deliver into no other hands than the Duke's. I command thee to let me pass, for I ride in haste."

"Not until I have seen thy face, my gay esquire, and know why thou wearest the helmet and cloak of one of my Swart Ruyters. I bid the again to raise thy visor, or it will be the worse for thee. Until I am fully satisfied the drawbridge will not be lowered."

Sir Andrew bit his lip with rage and vexation; his position was critical; had the bridge been fairly down, he could with ease have dashed past his pertinacious questioner, and effected an escape, but there it hung suspended by the great iron chains, only half lowered, and retreat that way was therefore impossible.

Twelve black corsletted, yellow uninformed Dutchmen were drawn up his rear, their burnished pikes glittering in the sunlight. They had quietly emerged from the gate-house only a minute previously, and in obedience to a mute sign from their commanding officer, had quickly surrounded the young Royalist.

For an instant Sir Andrew thought of drawing his sword, of cutting his way through these sturdy foot soldiers, and trusting to a better chance of leaving the city by some other outlet.

Then he reflected that his features were doubtless unknown to the knight, who was so haughtily interrogating him; and that by assuming a bold and straightforward mien, he might still allay his suspicions, and obtain a free passage.

He was, therefore, about to throw up his visor, when approaching footsteps were audible, and a young officer, booted and spurred, his visor closed, and followed by two musqueteers, made his way through the state guard, without opposition, and stood by his side.

"Sir Edward Hamilton," said the new comer, "the Commandant requires your presence in the Council Chamber immediately. You are to leave the charge of the gate to your next in command."

Then turning to Sir Andrew, he continued, "I think I have the honour of addressing Colonel Morton, aide-de-camp to his Grace the Duc de Schomberg?"

Sir Andrew bowed acquiescence, and his heart beat tumultuously, for he immediately knew both by the figure, the costume, and the richly-toned voice of the speaker, that it was Flora who again stood between him and death.

"I am charged, Colonel, to entrust to your care this second packet, to be given into the hands of King William himself, immediately you reach the royal camp," she continued. "Sir Stephen Macclesfield did not remember it until you had left the castle. It contains mention of those brave soldiers who distinguished themselves the most conspicuously in the defence of the city, and the list of our killed and wounded. Men at arms, lower the drawbridge! Colonel. God speed you.

Sir Andrew took the packet from Flora's hand, thanked her by a mute glance of affection through the bars of his visor, and gathered up his reins to get his horse well in hand ere he crossed the bridge, which by this time was lowered, for all Sir Edward Hamilton's suspicions were at length allayed, when, as ill luck would have it, a powerful gust of wind swept through the gateway, and blowing his cloak, which he had loosened in order to place the mock missive within his pocket, over his shoulders, disclosed to view on the broad silk scarf that crossed his gleaningcuirass, the white cockade of the house of Stuart.

In vain did Sir Andrew strive again to draw his cloak over the tell-tale badge, and spur his noble charger towards the bridge.

In an instant twenty rough hands were laid on his steed's reins, and helped to tear him from the saddle.

Before he could draw his sword, or take any measures of self-defence, his arms were bound together with strong cords, and he found himself helpless in the power of his foes.

"How long has a lewd soldier of the papistical James Stuart been the aide-de-camp of his Grace the Duc de Schomberg, and quitted the service of Belial to join the army of William the Good?" asked the dark-browed Hamilton with a sneer.

"Close round this fellow, guards; to the castle dungeons with him! Another reptile of the Jacobite brood to glut the sword of retribution. Secure the young traitor, too, who sought to aid him to escape, and his two followers wearing the badges of the Commandant. They are all Jacobites in disguise," he added, fiercely.

Willingly would the gate-guard have carried out their chief's commands, but amid the confusion and excitement attending the capture of the young Life Guardsman, the three connivers at his escape had disappeared.

Hamilton bit his lip with disappointment and rage at the discovery, but turning again to his myrmidons, he exclaimed,—

"Ten of you will remain to keep the gate! and on peril of your lives see that you allow none to pass without giving the new watchwords, 'WITH FAITH.' Denton and Tyler, you will help me guard the prisoner to the castle, and the other five of you start on the track of the three runaways. I will give twelve golden crowns for the capture of each; they cannot be far off. Now then, my gay Scot, we are at your service."

"Dastardly rebel, is it thus that you treat an officer of King James's Scottish Guard?" exclaimed Sir Andrew, angrily. "Had I but five minutes freedom, a few yards of clear ground, and my good sword in my hand, I would make you answer for these insults."

"Very probably," sneered Hamilton; "but as you have not, you will be spared the exertion. It will be a long while before a few yards of clear ground will be again at your service, though if the same space of clear air will suffice, that, ere many days are over, I may be able to procure you."

"What mean you, dog?" exclaimed Sir Andrew; "I am unused to buffoonery."

"A tall gallows and a short rope, my friend," replied Hamilton. "We follow thy King's example, who ever exalts his favourites to high places," and with a hoarse laugh, at his own jest, Sir Edward paced on in front.

Aware that resistance was useless, Sir Andrew walked passively between his guards, who, with shouldered pikes, and lowering brows, strode moodily by his side.

In this manner they passed along the same streets which a short time before he had traversed with Flora Macclesfield, and ere many minutes had elapsed, they paused before the walls of the castle.

In reply to Hamilton's bugle, the postern gate was thrown open, and Sir Andrew found himself within the bastion court of that strong Norman fortress.

"I want the key of the lower dungeon, Andrew?" said Sir Edward, to a gruff-looking servitor, who was crossing the yard.

In reply, the man drew a ponderous iron instrument from his pocket, shaped like a cross, and green and mouldy with age and damp.

"Where are you about to take me?" asked Sir Andrew, as they were parading some of the inner corridors of the castle.

"To the dungeons, as you might have learned without questioning had you but kept your ears open when I asked Andrew for the key," replied Hamilton.

"Sir Stephen Macclesfield is the only man in Carlisle who has the right or power to condemn me to durance so vile," said Sir Andrew, "and before him I demand to be immediately led."

"Ah! ah! does the lamb, struggling in the claws of the lion, demand his freedom so imperiously? Yet, methinks, the cases are parallel. Sir Stephen has, perhaps, the sole *right* to punish, but I who hold you have the *power*, and I shall follow the course I consider most likely to please King William and gratify my own tastes," said Hamilton; and once more the fierce warrior strode on in front.

Along more gloomy corridors wherein their footsteps appeared to wake a thousand weird and prolonged echoes, then, with lighted torches, through a trap door, and down a long flight of stone steps, green and moss-grown with slimy damp, they arrived at a low arched doorway, apparently composed of solid oak, and studded with immense iron nails and clasps.

With an effort, the huge cross-shaped key turned in the rusty lock, the door swung open, and Sir Andrew Douglas was roughly pushed by his guard into the midst of the gloom within.

By the ruddy glare of the torches, he perceived that the floor of his cell consisted of damp earth, in many parts of which pools had been formed by the dropping of water from the roof, which was about eight feet overhead, and was merely a natural dome of wet unhewn and crumbling sandstone rock.

Window, there was none, and the only furniture consisted of an old iron bedstead, and the decayed tattered remnant of a mat.

It took but a moment to survey his future home, and the young Royalist shuddered as he saw the heads, and glaring eyes of water-rats, emerge from the red shallow pools that dotted the dungeon floor, and heard the pattering of water from above that fell thick as a shower of summer rain on the wet ground. The scene was, indeed an awful one, and with fury at his heart, Sir Andrew turned upon Hamilton, exclaiming,—

"Craven hound, is this my prison? Let me but once cross the threshold of that door, and bitterly shalt thou rue the courtesy thou hast shown me this day."

"When thou cross it next, my blythe comrade, 'twill be to march to the gibbet," said Hamilton. "Meanwhile dream not of escape. This door contains three strong bolts on the outside, in addition to lock and chain; the wall facing inwards is composed of stone and iron, on the other three sides you might dig a passage through the world without finding the surface. The only possible means of exit is through the roof, for there is only a few feet of earth between that and the bed of the river. It is of soft crumbling stone; so if you can drive a hole through it, you may possibly escape the gallows by being drowned—Farewell."

With a low chuckling laugh, Hamilton then closed the door, and the next moment Sir Andrew found himself in profound darkness.

He heard the heavy bolts crash back into their securers, the receding steps of the men at arms, and then all became as still as death.

He was alone with his own thoughts, and no living things near by to hear or see him save the rats.

In an agony of despair and horror, he flung himself on the rusty iron bedstead, striving to collect his thoughts, and assure himself that it was not all a hideous dream.

Suddenly he sprang to his feet, for again footsteps were audible traversing the passage without. Once more a gleam of light streamed beneath his dungeon door.

Then a loud altercation was heard, amid which he could distinguish the angry tones of Hamilton. When it ceased his prison door again rolled open, and, 'mid the glaring of flambeaux, and clatter of arms, a dozen sturdy troopers rushed in.

## CHAPTER XI.

### WHAT OCCURRED IN THE LADIES' TOWER.

Love rules the camp, the court, the grove,
And men below and saints above,
For love is Heaven, and Heaven is love.

"Guards, I persist that you have no right to interfere in this matter; the prisoner is mine. I am responsible for my actions to King William alone," muttered Sir Edward Hamilton, who, with frowning brows and folded arms, stood in the background.

"And I tell you, once for all, Sir Edward Hamilton, that I acknowledge no authority but that of Sir Stephen Macclesfield. He has commanded me to bring the prisoner before him immediately and I shall do so. Prevent me at your peril!" exclaimed a fine, handsome, and richly-armed officer, in reply.

And, turning to the young Royalist, with the sharp blade of his sword he cut the cords that bound his arms, and then said, politely—

"You must permit me to guard you to the council-chamber, sir Cavalier, where the Commandant awaits you. Guards close around the prisoner."

In another minute, Sir Andrew found himself again traversing the gloomy subterranean passages, while the torchlight flashed on the shouldered pikes and glittering morions of his guards, as they tramped on silently before and behind him.

Ere long he stood in the council-chamber, face to face with Sir Stephen Macclesfield and his daughter, while, in the background stood the ruthless Hamilton.

A deep flush crossed Sir Andrew's cheek, as his gaze rested upon the face of the lovely girl, who once more attired in the garb of her sex, stood by her father's side.

She advanced towards him and held out her hand.

"Sir Cavalier," she said, "I am sorry to see as a prisoner, in my father's presence, one to whom I owe more than life, and who is entitled to my most sincere gratitude and friendship. Father," she continued, turning to the grey-haired Commandant, "this is the brave officer who saved me from drowning in the river, and of whom I have spoken to you before."

Sir Andrew bowed, and the Commandant, rising from his chair, also advanced towards him, and in turn grasping his hand, said—

"Sir Andrew Douglas, I am glad to have an opportunity of personally thanking you for your gallant rescue of my daughter. I have heard the particulars thereof more than once. And yet, on the other hand, right sorry am I that you stand now before me as a captive. While here, my whole castle is at your service, regard yourself as merely a prisoner on parole. My daughter will do her best to make the temporary durance light; and, ere long, I trust I may have the power to restore you to full liberty. I was apprized of your capture, but how came it that you were consigned to the dungeon?"

"I have to thank Sir Edward Hamilton for being consigned to such quarter," said the Life Guardsman, glancing threateningly towards that worthy, who returned the look with a sneer of scorn; "and I only await the time when I may repay with the sword the insults he has heaped upon me. In your presence, noble Commandant, and in yours, fair lady, I proclaim Sir Edward Hamilton to be a felon knight, and a false-hearted coward, and thus challenge him to mortal combat."

As he spoke the royalist hurled the buff gauntlet which he had hitherto held loosely in his hand at Hamilton's feet.

For an instant the latter stood as if irresolute, then taking up the gage of battle, he fastened it to his morion, saying,—

"If you escape axe and gallows, I will not refuse you a death by sword or pistol. Once at liberty, Sir Andrew, and I am at your service; quite ready to make you retract the words you have just uttered with a rapier point at your throat."

Then turning to the aged Commandant, he continued,—

"Sir Stephen, you are responsible for the safe custody of this soldier of Belial. If you allow him to depart without the judgment of the Council, or in any way interfere with that judgment, I shall force you to answer for it to King William."

"I am quite aware of my responsibility, and the proper course to be taken in the matter, without your tutoring," returned Macclesfield haughtily. "Neither do I longer require your attendance; you may retire."

The knight, however, remained doggedly still; and presently the Commandant exclaimed, losing all patience at his obduracy,—

"Do you hear my words sirrah? I am unaccustomed to speak my wishes twice. Retire, or I will command my guards to remove you under arrest."

"Sith that is your intention, I will save them the trouble, Sir Stephen," retorted Hamilton. "Adieu, wield your uncertain power while you can! To-day I obey: to morrow I may command;" and with a muttered curse, he turned on his heel and quitted the room.

"Now, guards, you may depart also," said Sir Stephen, and a minute later our hero was left alone with father and daughter.

"Use this castle as your own, but on no account leave its walls, they are the boundaries of your prison. Duty necessitates my now making my rounds; in my absence, Flora will do her best to entertain you. Adieu!" And so saying, Sir Stephen also took his departure, leaving the lovers together.

A few days after the scenes recorded above, Sir Andrew Douglas and Flora Macclesfield were sitting alone in one of the private apartments of the Ladies' Tower.

They were conversing low and earnestly, the lady's head resting against her lover's shoulder, while her glossy tresses fell over the silken sash, and were reflected in the bright steel cuirass of the young guardsman.

Their conversation was carried on in that low earnest tone that betokens real feeling, or its imitation, and the voice of Sir Andrew trembled as he said,—

"This morning, you say, the Stadtholder and his Queen enter Carlisle. Ah! my dear one, I fear me that soon we shall be torn asunder."

"Never anticipate evil, Sir Andrew," returned Flora. "Why do you fancy so?"

"For many reasons," he replied; "from the hatred of this unnatural daughter to every follower of her royal father; from the fearful vengeance her husband has sworn to take on all who are allied with the name and fame of Dundee; and lastly, from the designs of Sir Edward Hamilton, whom common report sets down to be a favourite officer of Mary's."

"Hamilton is a reckless and remorseless soldier of fortune, who may be crushed like a painted wasp," said Flora. "Besides, think you that my father cannot protect you? No, Sir Andrew, the danger that threatens is but a shadow; you have naught to fear."

"Fear for myself I know not," replied Sir Andrew, proudly; "all I dread is the chance of being separated from you. O! Flora, it is you who have taught me the happiness of life, and that there is something more to live for than mere glory."

And with a smile he put back her glossy curls, and kissed her smooth, white brow.

"I hear that King James will be brought to Carlisle, to yield up his crown to his son-in-law," she said, suddenly, after a prolonged pause.

"How, dear one?" exclaimed Sir Andrew, "I knew not that his Majesty was captured."

"He is, then," replied Flora; "or at least so said a pursuivant who rode into town this morning. He was taken prisoner at Faversham only a few days ago, and is now a captive at Whitehall, and while some state his future place of confinement to be Rochester, others fancy that he will be brought here."

"My poor King!" murmured Sir Andrew; "the saints smiled not on thy cause, and while others are still struggling to uphold thee on thy throne, my sword lies idly in its scabbard. Ah! what would I not give to behold one more fair battle field, to ride in one more headlong charge for thy crown and sceptre."

"'Tis a vain wish, Sir Andrew, for all hopes of James's cause are lost," replied Flora, "Dundee and Dalyel are by this time fugitives amid the mountains of Scotland, and the Earls of Dunmore and Mar, Colonel Wauchop, and the Laird of Lundin are captives. Not a hundred men throughout broad England would now gather round the banner of King James, were it again unfurled. The prayer of the whole nation is for religious freedom, and that privilege we will have."

"And then, Flora," said Sir Andrew, tenderly, "you will be my own wife, will you not, and leave this for bonnie Scotland?"

Flora replied by a loving glance from her bright hazel eyes.

And a smile dwelt upon her cherry lips as Sir Andrew pressed her fondly to his heart, and kissed her glowing cheek again and again, with all the enthusiasm of an ardent, youthful affection.

---

## CHAPTER XII.

### A ROYAL PROCESSION.

O! wherefore come ye forth, in triumph from the North,
With your hands, and your feet, and your raiment all red?
And wherefore doth your rout send forth a joyous shout?
And whence be the grapes of the wine-press which ye tread?

THEY were interrupted in their pleasant love-dream by the loud flourish of trumpets in the distance.

And rising from the couch on which they had been sitting, the lovers advanced to the narrow iron-barred window, and looked out.

Overlooking the outer walls of the bastion court, this embrasure commanded a fine view of Castle Hill-street, which was crowded on each side with human heads, the centre being kept open by the partisans of the City Guard, and far a-down it echoed the crash of music, every moment sounding nearer.

It was a magnificent morning.

The sun shone brightly upon field and meadow, upon the wild beauty of the surrounding country, and on the walls and ramparts of the city.

The tall tower of the Cathedral rose darkly up against the bright blue sky, its pinnacles and Gothic fretwork glittering in the sunshine, and flags and banners of many colours waving from its sides.

Similar banners hung from windows and house-tops, mingled with wreaths of flowers and evergreens.

Triumphal arches were erected in street and close.

The fountains spouted water and wine at intervals, while hundreds of citizens and country people, attired in every variety of costume, were hurrying up and down, and struggling lustily to obtain favourable places from which to view the approaching cortége.

All things wore the air of jollity and rejoicing, but every here and there, like dark shadows of the past, rose the charred and blackened walls of burnt houses, in some places running along an entire street, and presenting the only outward tokens of the late siege.

At this moment the massive bells of the Cathedral crashed out a responsive answer to the roaring kettledrums and clashing cymbals, an a wild buzz of human voices rose from the street below as the head of the procession appeared in sight.

At a rapid trot, a troop of light cavalry, with their long slender lances and red and white pennons glistening in the sun, rode by.

They were succeeded by twelve trumpeters splendidly attired in crimson and cloth of gold, and then at a slower pace, by a strong body of heavy horse, the dusky Swart Ruyters of Mynheer Goderdt van Baron de Ginckle, who were conspicuous by their helmets and corslets of unpolished iron, their long jack-boots, and their yellow coats, heavily cuffed, and with looped skirts.

"William and Mary! William and Mary!—God bless our good King and Queen!" was shouted from many thousand throats, and surrounded by a glittering cavalcade of horsemen, beneath a broad canopy of Genoa velvet and cloth of gold, which was upheld on each side by eight youthful nobles, on the points of their lances, appeared William of Orange and his Queen.

The latter was mounted on a cream-coloured steed, whose gorgeous trappings almost swept the ground. Dark and swarthy of complexion, she was nevertheless handsome, with full flashing black eyes, and an exquisitely proportioned figure, which was shown to advantage by a closely fitting velvet habit, the body whereof was slashed with cloth of silver.

The Prince of Orange rode a coal-black charger, and was attired in the uniform of a colonel of a Dutch cavalry regiment. His visorless morion revealed the phlegmatic cast of his features, and the dull meaningless smile that perpetually hovered on his lips.

Amid the groups of nobles, courtiers and soldiers, who surrounded the usurpers, two were pre-eminently conspicuous, for on the right of the Stadtholder, with his grey hair floating from beneath his unadorned steel morion, rode Sir Stephen Macclesfield; while beside Mary and so close to her bridle-rein that his slighest whisper would have been audible, hovered another form, whose bright yellow uniform and sable plume betokened him to be Sir Edward Hamilton, captain of Swart Ruyters.

As they arrived opposite the window at which the lovers stood, both the Queen and Sir Edward looked up, and Flora perceived a sneer cross

Hamilton's ill-omened countenance as he leant over towards his royal mistress and whispered something in her ear.

In reply, she gave one more hasty glance towards the Ladies' Tower, and amid a wild whirl of prancing and curvetting steeds, of glancing armour and nodding plumes, passed on to the Cathedral, where thanksgivings were to be offered up according to the ritual of the reformed faith for the defeat of the unhappy King, her father, and the restoration of the Protestant religion.

A few companies of foot soldiers brought up the rear, for the bulk of the Stadtholder's army was following the royal cortége at their leisure, and amid the renewed cheers of the populace they passed on their way, the music sounding fainter and fainter in the distance until the crash of bells ceased and every sound was hushed as their Majesties dismounted at the great door of the Cathedral, and followed by a glittering crowd, entered the sacred edifice.

## CHAPTER XIII.

### AN UNWELCOME VISITOR.

Saddle my roan, his back is a throne,
Better than velvet or gold you will own;
Look to your match, for some harm you may catch,
For treason has even some mischief to hatch.
And Oliver's out with all Hazlerigg's rout,
So I'm told by this shivering white-livered scout.

ABOUT an hour after the scene just described, Flora sat alone within her apartment in the Ladies' Tower.

Sir Andrew had only left her a few minutes, promising to return speedily.

Hearing a footstep in the outer passage, and a gentle tap at the door, she bade the applicant enter, thinking it was him, but started with mingled surprise and anger upon recognising in her visitor Sir Edward Hamilton.

The visor of the knight's morion was raised, and his swarthy countenance beamed with an expression of triumphant malice, as closing the door behind him, he said,—

"Flora, my visit appears to be unwelcome."

"The presence of Sir Edward Hamilton is ever unwelcome," was the curt reply.

"And yet of late I have seldom visited you, seldom recurred to the subject with which I now again venture to address you," returned the knight. "Flora, can you still remain cold to all my prayers? Are you resolved to crush every hope within my breast? O, relent! On my knees let me beseech your mercy. None love you so truly as I do. Can you not return the feeling at least in some degree?"

As he spoke, he knelt before her and essayed to take her hand.

"You know full well that I cannot, Sir Edward," she replied, haughtily. "You have had your answer before to the same question. I freely confess that my affections are already engaged; so your bride I can never be."

"Then it is vain for me longer to entreat?" cried Sir Edward.

"I have said so," was the calm reply.

The knight sprang to his feet, and his eyes flashed as he exclaimed,—

"If so, it is now time to command. Girl, you mistake! You will be mine! You are in my power, and I will bend you to my will. Refuse, and I can crush you like a worm."

Flora turned pale at his words, a thousand conflicting thoughts rose to her mind; yet she replied firmly,—

"Sir knight—I understand you not?"

"I will speedily explain then," said he. "Your father is no longer Governor of Carlisle. Here is the document that appoints me to that important office in his stead."

Drawing from beneath his cuirass a piece of vellum, he waved it before the eyes of the dismayed daughter, and continued—

"Within an hour, Sir Stephen Macclesfield will be arrested on the charge of treason and concealment of Jacobite officers, and I shall be sworn in to fill the vacant governorship. I have a warrant, also, for the immediate trial of your guest, Sir Andrew Douglas, which will be put in force at once. The lives of both father and lover are in my hands."

"'Tis false, monster!" exclaimed Flora. "My father will disprove all the vile charges brought against him, and establish his innocence. As for Sir Andrew Douglas, he only fought for his King in the open field; he is but a prisoner of war; and the war being over, and all hopes of his cause lost, he will, of course be set at liberty. The King will, without hesitation, acquit both. I am not to be terrified by mere threats."

"Brought before King William, those you love would, perhaps, be safe; but his Majesty leaves Carlisle immediately, and his weak-minded consort I can bend to my will in all things," retorted Sir Edward. "As Governor of the city, I shall be entitled to select their judges, and I will take heed that they be such as shall echo my own wishes in such matters as I bring before them. Maiden, I say again, that both father's and lover's lives are in my hands; you alone can save them, and I have pointed out to you the way. Again I ask, therefore, will you be mine?"

"My answer is the same — never!" replied Flora. "I entrust my father's and Sir Andrew's safety to the care of God, who will save them from your power, and cause the vengeance of the unjust to recoil on their own heads."

Sir Edward stamped his foot in anger, and said, savagely,—

"Believe it not, foolish one. Providence is not wont to interfere in such matters; but a third life depends on your decision—*your own!* Refuse my hand, and my love shall be turned into hatred. I have abundant proof against you —the midnight cruises down the river; the two interviews without the walls with the chief officers of the Jacobite army, one of them Viscount Dundee himself; and still later, your assisting in the frustrated escape of the prisoner, Sir Andrew Douglas; the coined story invented for the sake of deceiving the gate guard—all will tell against you. Choose, therefore, between marriage and death."

"The choice is made, false traitor; for I prefer the latter," replied Flora, bravely.

Her outward expression showed no sign of fear, though in truth her heart sank, and her brain appeared to whirl, more at the thought of the danger surrounding her father and her lover than at the peril which threatened herself.

The dark-browed Swart Ruyter remained a

minute silent; but as Flora appeared resolved in her course of action, and did not deign further answer, he again stamped his foot on the floor, and exclaimed, fiercely—

"My persuasions appear idle. I left the Cathedral ere the service was half over to seek this interview. I now go to rejoin the King and Queen. I entreat no more; your pride and disdain I will soon crush. Perish in your folly! dragging both father and lover to the same doom. When next you behold me, 'twill be as a judge, not as a suitor."

He was about to leave the room, when a new thought appeared to strike him, and turning round suddenly, he exclaimed—

"One kiss I will have before we part; for one moment you shall be mine, whether you will or not."

Advancing towards her, he would have clasped her in his arms, but quickly eluding his grasp, Flora sprang from her seat, rushed across the room, and gaining the passage, locked the door on the outside, before Sir Edward could prevent her.

Running down the steep staircase of the tower, she then proceeded hurriedly towards the guard-room, expecting there to find her lover.

She met him, however, in one of the corridors, and observing her flushed face and excited manner, he anxiously inquired whether she was ill.

"No, Sir Andrew," replied the lovely girl, placing her white hand in his, "but I was seeking you. We must fly, and that speedily."

"Wherefore, dearest?" he asked.

"Because Sir Edward Hamilton is come to arrest you," she replied. "He is appointed Governor of the city in my father's stead; so even this castle affords you no longer a place of safety. Once, now, in his hands, and you are lost. Come with me."

"You speak in riddles, dearest," said Sir Andrew. "Why is your father supplanted so suddenly in his office?"

"I scarcely know," she answered, "and there is no time to explain. Hark to those sounds! To favour your escape, I have Sir Edward under lock and key. He is kicking the door, and calling aloud for the castle guard to release him quickly. We must act, and again yon must don disguise."

Ere she had concluded, they had reached the armoury.

Quickly throwing a horseman's cloak over Sir Andrew's uniform, she handed him a silver morion, surmounted by a high crimson plume, saying, as she did so—

"This is the same as those worn by one of King William's regiments of Dutch horse. To-day all the gates are thrown open, so that any one who lists may either enter or leave the city. Your only danger is pursuit. Here are sword and pistols. Now to the stables."

"But Flora, my darling, are you not risking your own safety by aiding me to escape?" said Sir Andrew. "O! if this infernal Hamilton were to vent his anger and resentment upon you!"

"Never fear, Sir Andrew, I am safe; the Queen will protect me," she replied, in a tone of assumed confidence, for well she knew that were she to hint of the danger threatening herself, the young royalist would remain, and brave death at her side.

A few minutes later, and they stood in the Bastion Court.

Sir Andrew's arm was thrown over his charger's neck, his right hand clasped that of his companion.

"Oh, Flora!" said he, "I tremble at leaving you behind, in the power of this new governor. You say that you are safe, that the Queen will protect you; but are you certain that she will? Why not fly with me? At the first convent or abbey we reach, some holy preacher will unite us in the sacred bonds of wedlock, and then we can ride on the spur to my own castle in the Highlands, where I have a strong garrison of free retainers. Once there, and we shall be safe. Oh, ponder on my words!"

Flora's cheek flushed; for a moment the combat of the soul was strong.

On one side lay escape, safety, a union with one whom the truly and fondly loved; on the other persecution, trial, death—death by the headsman's axe.

But her irresolution was of short duration, and her eyes flashed, and her breast heaved, as she replied—

"No, dear Sir Andrew, it may not be. Return to me in happier times. I assure you again that I am quite safe. It is my duty to stay beside my old father, and nothing will induce me to leave him in this sore strait."

Her cheek turned pale as she uttered the necessary falsehood, yet it was for her lover's sake. Then she faltered,—

"Now leave me. You know the way to the walls. Adieu! God and His holy saints guide and protect you."

"Farewell, Flora," responded her lover; "may the Blessed Virgin have you in her keeping. We shall soon meet again."

He kissed the long glossy tresses that draped her delicate throat, and fell in heavy luxuriance over her snow-white and rounded shoulders; he kissed her pale brow; and lastly, their lips met in one long and passionate embrace.

Flora felt that it was their last, and, though she endeavoured to repress her feelings, her eyes filled with tears, and she leant against a doorway for support, as Sir Andrew let fall the umvrier of his morion, and, vaulting lightly into the saddle, dashed out of the court at a gallop.

---

## CHAPTER XIV.

### A RACE AND A SINGLE COMBAT.

No jockey nor groom, wears so draggled a plume,
As this that's just drenched in the swift flowing Froom.
Red grew the tide, ere we reached the steep side,
And steaming the hair of old Barbary's hide.
But for branch of that oak, that saved me a stroke,
I had sunk there like herring in pickle to soak.

Sir Andrew had scarcely disappeared from view, when tumultous cries, and the rush of many feet were heard close by, and, looking up, Flora, to her horror, beheld Sir Edward Hamilton, at the head of about a score of Swart Ruyters, issuing from the low arched Norman gateway of the castle into the yard.

"To the stables! to the stables!" he shouted. "Mount and pursue, he has only this minute

AT THE FOOT OF THE SCAFFOLD.

quitted the court; I hear his charger's hoof-strokes in the street. Out with the horses! I will give a hundred crowns to whomsoever brings me his head. Hasten! hasten!

Then, perceiving Flora, he crossed the yard, and gripping her left shoulder as with a vice of iron, cried in a voice hoarse with passion, "I will teach thee not to brave me, my gay damsel; which way has he flown?"

Flora showed no signs of emotion, no expression of pain, though, when the fierce knight withdrew his hand from her shoulder, the impression of his heavy steel gauntlet was imprinted in purple marks upon the soft white flesh.

"The thumb-screw, the wheel, nor the rack, should force me to answer your question," she replied.

"We will see what the torture can effect when it is applied," returned Sir Edward. "We can find the traitor without thee, and, ere many hours are over, I will send his head as a companion to solace thy imprisonment."

Pushing her rudely aside, he sprang on his charger, and followed by the Swart Ruyters, dashed out of the bastion court, on the track of the fugitive.

With flashing eyes and throbbing brain, Flora sought her chamber; she felt not the pain of her bruise; she scarcely knew that the impression of the fierce knight's hand was still imprinted on her lovely skin; but, falling on her knees by her bedside, she forgot her own sorrow and danger in praying for the safety and preservation of her lover and her father.

Meanwhile, Sir Andrew had trotted quickly along the streets of the city; but it was not until he neared the eastern gate-tower, that he was aroused by the rattle of hoofs, and the sound of voices behind.

On looking back, he beheld a disorderly body of horsemen brandishing their swords, and madly spurring in his rear.

Rightly conjecturing that he was the object of pursuit, he increased his speed to a gallop; and the next minute, rising darkly in his front, he beheld the frowning archway of the gate-tower, with the bleached skull of the traitor Zuylestein still spiked upon the battlements.

"Up with the drawbridge, guards," shouted a dozen voices; and, in obedience to the cry, two soldiers rushed from the gate-house to carry the command into execution.

Sir Andrew saw that not a moment was to be lost. Again he dashed the spurs into his horse's flanks, and "swift as arrow from the Tartar's bow," the noble animal bounded forward.

There was a creak of wheels and a rattle of chains, the drawbridge trembled on the rise; loud exulting cheers rang closely in his rear; another moment and he would be too late.

Again sink the spurs, rowel deep, in the black charger's sides; she obeys the call by one furious bound that brings horse and rider under the shadow of the gate tower.

The Life Guardsman's long sword glances from its scabbard; it hisses through the air, and —cloven through morion, skull, and gorget band, to the very collar bone—the man who was winding up the bridge fell to the earth a hideous corpse.

His comrade, who advanced with the intention of hamstringing the galloping steed in its course, owing to a slip of the foot, came in collision with the charger's shoulder, and was hurled back, stunned and insensible, against the sharp coping stone of the gateway.

Then with tightened rein and unchecked speed, Sir Andrew thundered across the iron drawbridge, which was slightly raised, and landing safely on the other side the drop, found himself outside the walls, and dashing along the banks of the river in the direction of Northbrigg.

Curses and imprecations rang in his rear.

He heard the clatter of the bridge as it was again hastily lowered across the chasm, and then the disorderly mob of horsemen in pursuit appeared in view, with plumes waving, swords glittering, and their armour and steel scabbards clanking and jingling, as at full speed they dashed on in pursuit.

Owing to the delay at the bridge, the enemy were now some five hundred yards distant, and a smile, as of derision, flitted across the handsome countenance of the young royalist as, drawing his horse suddenly up, he sprang to the ground, and with wonderful dexterity divested it of all the heavy trappings that encumbered its head, neck, and breast, together with its massive gold and velvet saddle cloth.

He next loosened the long steel curb in its mouth, and turning its head to the wind, carefully wiped its nostrils with the ends of his richly-laced scarf; and then patting the noble charger's swelling crest he sprang once more to the saddle and gathered up the reins.

By this time his pursuers were close upon him, all keeping together in a compact body, Sir Edward Hamilton taking the lead by about three lengths.

Their cries and shouts rang shrilly on the morning air; but turning in his saddle, Sir Andrew shook his gauntlet at them in defiance, and quickly wheeling his horse round again, urged him to the gallop.

With head bent, so that his long drooping plume mingled with the flowing mane, the reins sufficiently strained so as to feel gently his charger's [illegible], and both hands dropped below the peaked pommel of his saddle, with one knee and leg planted closely to the black steed's sides, and his heels well dropped, Sir Andrew presented the very *beau ideal* of an accomplished equestrian.

Contenting himself with keeping about fifty yards ahead of his pursuers, he held his steed well in hand, easing the strain by keeping its head slightly turned to the wind, and urging it onwards more by words of encouragement than by the spur.

Thus, on they went. Quitting the river's side by Northbrigg, Sir Andrew headed to the left, crossing a steep hill-side diagonally, in the direction of Tupsley, rightly judging that he should thus leave some of the foe behind in the deep clay soil of the newly-ploughed fields.

Nor was he mistaken.

Already blown by hard and injudicious riding, heavily mounted by men armed in a massive panoply of iron, the chargers of the Swart Ruyters sank knee deep at every step in the yielding soil; and when, after leaping lightly over a turf fence, and skirting for half a mile the margin of a thick coppice wood, Sir Andrew galloped lightly down again into the verdant pasture-land beyond, he saw upon looking back that more than half of his pursuers were floundering onwards nearly a mile in his rear, while his own brave steed, by its regular breathing and steady pace, showed itself to be almost as fresh as ever.

Still however, the fierce Hamilton, and about half a dozen more, hung perseveringly upon his trail, while about the same number were following irregularly only a field or two behind.

No longer did they cheer and encourage the chase with whoop or halloo, but in dogged and stern silence followed like sleuth-hounds on the trail.

After crossing the valley for about two miles, Sir Andrew again made a sharp detour to the right, and heading towards a high copsewood fence, with a stream of water on the other side, cleared it at a bound.

It was a desperate leap, and a loud curse burst from Hamilton's lips as he prepared to follow; but the magnificent animal which he bestrode answered the call nobly; crashing through the top branches of the hazel hedge, it cleared the broad stream beyond with dry fetlocks,

The success of the other horsemen was not so marked; four or five refused the leap altogether, and rode round to discover a better crossing; two other chargers fell back on their riders, on the wrong side; and another heavy Flemish mare caught her fore-legs in a hazel branch, and fell on her head in the water, immersing her rider in its muddy depths, from which the weight of his armour prevented his escaping with life.

When the fugitive again glanced round, the number of his pursuers had diminished to three, of whom Sir Edward was still the leader.

Obeying a sudden thought, he now once more turned towards the river, shouting, as he did so—

"A hundred Jacobuses to thy brainless skull, Sir Edward, that I am on the opposite side of the Eden first."

Hamilton replied not, save by another thrust of his spurs, and again, like lightning, on swept pursuers and pursued, the three knights still keeping close together, though Sir Andrew knew by the panting of their steeds, which was plainly audible, though he was a clear hundred yards ahead, that their race was nearly run.

On, still on, over the level common, down a slight declivity, and, glistening in the sunlight, like a stream of molten silver, flowed the calm waters of the Eden.

In another moment Sir Andrew had leaped his horse from the bank, and in spite of a strong current, was swimming lightly across towards the opposite shore.

Scrambling up the bank, he drew rein to breathe his charger, and watch his pursuers.

The three Swart Ruyters leaped their steeds from the bank almost simultaneously, but to two of them that leap was fatal.

Heavily mounted, and already exhausted, one charger sank to the bottom like a stone, dragging its rider, who could not extricate his feet from the stirrups, down with it. A second was too weak to battle against the current, and was borne away on its side by the strength of the stream, leaving its master to struggle alone; and, as he could not swim, his struggles were short.

With a loud cry for help, he disappeared beneath the waves; and while the wretch's drowning shriek yet rang in his ears, the young royalist found himself face to face with only one foe, but one whom he thirsted to meet—the fierce favourite of the Queen, the ferocious Hamilton.

"At last we are alone, villain! The river has saved thee for my vengeance," said Sir Andrew, with flashing eyes.

"Say rather, fool, that it has preserved thee for mine," was the reply.

Without another word, with drawn swords, they advanced upon each other.

The conflict was short, but decisive.

Impelled by mutual hatred, they fought with savage ferocity.

In a few minutes, Sir Andrew's sword was broken, but seizing the heavy scabbard, he guarded the descending blow that his antagonist intended should prove fatal, and ere Hamilton could recover his guard, with a side swing of this novel weapon he felled him from his saddle.

Leaping lightly to the ground, Sir Andrew pressed his knee on his opponent's cuirass, and drawing a long poignard from its sheath, held the sharp point within the open slits of his foeman's visor, saying,—

"Now, hound, crave pardon for the past; or, by the light of Heaven, thou diest."

"I crave mercy, Sir Andrew. Spare me, I am already dying," faintly responded the wounded man, with a deep groan.

The Royalist's eyes flashed as he raised the glittering poignard for the fatal stab; but ere it descended, his better nature prevailed. Instead of burying it in his victim's brawny throat as he had intended, he returned it to its sheath, and in a calmer voice, said,—

"If thou art mortally wounded, false traitor, I will not hasten thy doom. Die, if thou can'st in peace! Thy life is spared to thee; if thou livest learn to mend it."

Without waiting for a reply, he remounted, and trotted leisurely on in the direction of Scotland.

We must now return to the fortunes of Flora Macclesfield, whom we left seeking refuge in prayer within the precincts of her chamber.

Long had she knelt in silent devotion, her lips moving, and yet emitting no sound, for the still voice that the heart speaks is loud enough for God to hear.

An hour passed by, then another; but she moved not until the sound of music, the tramp of passing feet, and the hubbub of many voices, made her start from her knees, and rush towards the window.

## CHAPTER XV.

### TWO GREAT CAPTIVES.

Where are your tongues that late mocked at heaven, and
hell, and fate,
And the fingers that once were so busy with your blades;
Your perfumed satin clothes, your catches and your oaths,
Your stage plays and your soncets, your diamonds and
your spades?

FLORA'S heart beat wildly, and her brain appeared to whirl, as she heard a tumult of oaths, yells, and hootings rise from the street below, and beheld, amid a crowd of men and women, and surrounded by the glittering pikes of a detachment of the city guard, two mounted cavaliers with their heads uncovered, and their arms and wrists secured by massive iron chains, being borne along by their captors.

A whisper at the heart first told her that one of these was her lover, but as they drew near, she perceived that she was mistaken; for in the long, silvery hair, and open, placid countenance of the one she recognized the venerable Sir Thomas Dalyel, and in the long cavalier locks, the flashing eyes and dark complexion of his companion, the handsome, brave, and chivalrous commander of the Scots Royals, the Earl of Dumbarton.

Slowly they passed along, amid the jeers, the hisses, and execrations of the fierce mob, who were only prevented from tearing them in pieces on the spot by the threatening pikes of the guard, and the knowledge that, in all probability, they were reserved for a still more fearful fate.

Meanwhile, widely different was the demeanour of the two captives,

The carriage of the elder knight was lofty and proud; not a muscle of his face moved; not a single sign of emotion crossed his countenance as the yells of the rabble smote upon his ear.

He wore more the air of a mighty general marching to victory, than that of a prisoner being led to captivity.

The Earl of Dumbarton, on the other hand, bore on his countenance a forced expression of hilarity and mirth.

His eyes appeared to flash with fun and good humour.

His lips frequently curled in a smile, and he acknowledged the insults of the populace as though they had been welcomes, by repeated bows and nods.

As they arrived opposite the Ladies' Tower, the Earl looked upwards, and recognising Flora, bowed, with a gay smile.

She replied by waving her kerchief, and forgetting her own sorrows she wept in the contemplation of the terrible fate that hung suspended as by a single thread over the heads of the brave men, who were now, in all probability, being led to their last prison.

She was, however, not allowed long to ponder on the sorrows of others, for the tumult of the mob had scarcely ceased to be audible in the distance, when hurried steps re-echoed in the corridor without; the room door was thrown open, and half a dozen Dutch soldiers, wearing the bulbous corslets and black morions of Hamilton's Swart Ruyters rushed into the room.

"I bear a warrant from the governer, Sir Edward Hamilton, for your arrest, lady, on the charge of treason to King William, and the reformed religion!" said the officer in command; "you will be pleased to accompany us to the Western Tower."

"First take me to my father!" said Flora.

"I dare not," was the reply; "he is himself a captive, and there are strict orders issued that no one be allowed to communicate with him. Guards, surround your prisoner. March!"

Without opposition, Flora was then conducted by Sir Edward Hamilton's myrmidons along the dark and gloomy passages and corridors of the old castle towards the grim prison rooms in the Western Tower.

## CHAPTER XVI.

### CONDEMNED TO DEATH.

We now pass over the space of one short month.

During that time many important political events had taken place within the realm of England.

The unhappy King had been deposed, and his unnatural son-in-law and daughter crowned in his stead.

The streets of Carlisle had been stained with blood—the blood of martyrs.

The first sacrifice to the fierce thirst for vengeance was the brave and chivalrous Earl of Dunmore, who walked to the place of doom with the same firm step and stout heart with which he had often marched to victory.

The same composed half smile on his lips as he usually wore, when, as one of the chief favourites of England's rightful monarch, he trod the halls of the royal palace, and the same white cockade on his gleaming cuirass that he had so often perilled his heart's best blood to guard, the badge of his generous, but unfortunate, prince.

He it was, who, on ascending the scaffold, pointed to the grim cross-tree, fifty feet above his head, with the exclamation, "Higher in death than in life," and as the executioner wreathed the noose around his neck, said, "I die for my King! I esteem this rough collar a greater honour than my circlet of knighthood. God bless King James!"

Four days later Lord Evandale, of Tiviotside, suffered a similar fate with equal courage and firmness.

. . . . . ,

The thirst for blood has not yet sated.

Again the solemn tribunal are assembled, presided over by the Queen Consort in person, and again the sentence of death has gone forth.

This time the doomed victim is a woman!

Standing apart from all, guarded on each side by a sturdy pikeman, her arms folded across her bosom, she shows no sign of surprise upon hearing her sentence.

A dead silence falls upon the court, and then the prisoner's voice rings clearly forth in reply, not loudly, but so musically sweet, and each word pronounced with such distinctness, that it is audible in every part of that large gloomy hall.

"My Queen, judges, and fellow citizens," she said, "you have found me guilty of high treason, and sentenced me to death—the death of the axe. While I deny the truth of the charge, I stoop not to petition for my life, neither do I condescend to explain my actions, knowing that were I to prove myself innocent, it would, before *this tribunal*, avail me nought. I am in your power; if my life is required of me, take it. Many times, O, Queen, have I perilled it for your husband's cause and the welfare of the reformed religion! in my native city will I now yield it up, calling God to attest my innocence of all with which I am accused, and to have mercy on my soul!"

She ceased, and, with flashing eyes and heaving bosom, confronted her accusers.

Most lovely did she then look.

Her finely proportioned and rounded form was drawn up to its full height, and her long glossy hair thrown back from her fair white brow, hung around the pure white neck, and over the full snowy shoulders, even to the waist.

Her full dark hazel eyes flashed, and her lips curled with pride and disdain, while her cheeks and as much as was visible of her neck and bosom, were flushed with the delicate tint of the rose.

Her words, however, had no effect upon her judges.

An officer, brilliantly uniformed and accoutred, whose head was swathed in thick bandages leaned over the back of the Queen's chair, and whispered in her ear.

In reply her Majesty said,—

"You speak well, my trusty Hamilton," and then turning towards the lovely captive, she continued,—

"Guards, remove the prisoner, and bring before us her father, our late governor, Sir Stephen Macclesfield!"

There was a moment's silence; then a voice at the lower end of the vast hall shouted,—

"The command is vain, Sir Stephen Macclesfield has escaped!"

Both Sir Edward and the Queen started.

Search was made for the speaker, but he could not be found, and ere many minutes had elapsed, the guards returned with the information that Sir Stephen Macclesfield had, indeed, disappeared.

## CHAPTER XVII.

### THE CAPTIVE AND HIS VISITOR.

It was the evening of the day on which the preceding events had occured, that a cavilier, richly armed, passed down the eastern transept of Carlisle Cathedral towards the Lady Chapel.

His long spurs jingled on the paved floor, and his uplifted visor revealed the open and singularly handsome countenance of a man to all appearance about forty years of age.

Entering the chapel, he advanced to where, a year previously, the Virgin's altar with its gorgeous decorations and flowers had stood, and touching what looked like a black spot on the wall with the pommel of his poignard, a concealed door flew open and gave admission to a small apartment apparently excavated it the thickness of the outer wall.

Carefully the cavilier secured this door behind him, and lighting a small lamp that he held in his hand, proceeded to look around.

Presently his eyes rested on the figure of an old man, who, with arms folded, stood in the midst of the ill-paved floor with his gaze fixed on the ground, quite unconscious of the intruder's approach.

The cavalier advanced towards him quickly.

"A good evening to you, Sir Stephen," said he, "am I not to my word?"

The old man started, and in broken accents faltered—

"My daughter! my daughter! What is the sentence?"

"Death!" was the reply, "as I foretold you it would be."

The father sighed deeply as he said,—

"And how did she bear up against it?"

"Like a heroine of romance," was the reply. "She wore more the air of a Queen than of a criminal, and when the sentence was passed, by neither word nor sign did she show the inner emotions of her heart!"

"My brave child," exclaimed the old man. "It is like her, she would sooner perish than show fear."

"The execution is fixed for to-morrow at noon," continued the cavalier. "The block is to be erected in the Cathedral Yard."

What further was said was uttered in so low a tone as to be scarcely audible. In reply, Sir Stephen, for it was he, grasped the stranger's hand, saying,—

"O! sir, can you really do all that you say? You speak as one having authority; yet you are sure that you do not overrate your power? I already owe you my freedom, but to-morrow!—ah! that will be a far more difficult matter to execute, and if we fail——"

"Well, if we fail?" said the unknown.

"Then I will fight my way to the block, and perish by her side," replied the old man. "But you?"

"I will do as you do," was the reply.

"Brave man!" said Sir Stephen, "peril not your life so rashly. I am old; love for my child nerves my arm; but you are young, and 'tis only sympathy or love of desperate enterprise that urges you to risk your life in our cause. Ponder, I beseech you, on the step you are about to take."

"I have done so, Sir Stephen," he replied; "your daughter I will save, or perish in the attempt. God will strengthen my arm in a right cause, and enable me to save the innocent, and in time, I trust, to punish the guilty. Sooner would I lose my coronet, and——"

The stranger stopped short in some confusion, and Sir Stephen said,—

"Your coronet? Heavens! then you are—"

"It matters not who I am at present. When I have kept my promise, I will reveal all. But I must now be gone. Farewell!" and turning on his heel, the stranger quitted the dungeon.

## CHAPTER XVIII.

### THE DESTROYER AND HIS VICTIM.

At the same hour wherein the strange cavalier had sought the deposed Commandant of Carlisle in his place of concealment, another interview took place within the walls of the castle.

Fatigued and wearied with the exciting events of the day, to her the last of existence, Flora, without undressing, had thrown herself on her bed, to endeavour to gain a little sleep, which she felt she much needed, and which hoped would enable her better to bear the doom that awaited her on the morrow.

Rest, however, was not permitted her; and as she watched with aching eyes and throbbing brain the faint flicker of the oil lamp that stood on the rough hewn table opposite, the harsh creek of a door caused her to look round, and as she she did so her eyes rested on a dark figure that was standing by her side.

With a cry she sprang to her feet, for in the pale, haggard face, the bandaged head, and crimson robes of the midnight visitor, she recognized her remorseless prosecutor, Sir Edward Hamilton.

"Lady," said he, in accents low and sad, "I see that my presence is still distasteful to you, it is my last visit."

"Then I am indeed thankful," she replied, 'even to the block and executioner shall I be grateful, for they at least will prevent you persecuting me further."

"I am aware that my conduct towards you has been cruel," said Hamilton, "but it was the madness of disdained love that caused it."

"The love I could pardon," said Flora, "but not the misery it has entailed on many. Yours has been the phantasy of a madman; for because I could not return your affection, you have sought to compass the ruin, dishonour, and death of myself, and of those whom I hold dear."

"I have done so," he replied; "but it was because your coldness and indifference maddened me; because I resolved to humble your pride, and bend you to my will; but I who can do can undo; I can yet save your father and yourself."

"I suppose you forget that my father has escaped," said Flora, "and that I am now the only victim left."

Sir Edward bit his lip ere he replied—

"I have not forgotten it; nor am I ignorant of where he is now concealed; his recapture is certain; but I can secure pardon for you both if you will be mine."

Flora uttered a scornful laugh.

"Thine!" said she, "never!"

"Oh, say not so," returned Sir Edward, "there is another life besides thine at stake—thy father's."

"I commend his and my own safety into the hands of God," said Flora, "and I reject thy offers as though they were the temptations of the Evil One. Begone!"

"Naught, then, will induce thee to revoke thy determination?" said he.

"Nothing," she replied.

"Then there is but one way left," he retorted. "Flora you shall be mine, in spite of God or man. These walls are thick, there is no one near to aid you; you are in my power."

As he spoke he advanced with open arms towards his victim.

Flora uttered no cry, but as he drew near she drew a small poignard from the folds of her dress, and holding the point to her breast said,—

"Keep back, false traitor! I may be powerless, but nevertheless I can save myself from you. Touch me not for you will embrace a corpse."

The words were calmly spoken, but there was such an air of majesty in her manner that Sir Edward quailed before her, and paused irresolute.

"Leave me," continued Flora; "the daughter of Sir Stephen Macclesfield can guard her own honour, even if she cannot avenge herself on her persecutor. This is our last meeting. 'Ere to-morrow's sun is high in the heavens I will try to learn to forgive you also."

Sir Edward Hamilton was for once awed, and by a woman.

He knew that the proud and beautiful girl who stood before him would not permit him to clasp her in his arms alive.

Her flashing eyes and expanded nostrils told of a fixed determination to die by her own hand rather than submit to his embraces.

So with an inward admiration that even the darkest and most hardened heart ever feels for a noble nature, he turned and left the room.

## CHAPTER XIX.

### THE CHAMBER OF THE QUEEN CONSORT.

Fool, your doublet shone like gold, and your heart was gay and bold,
When you kissed your lily hand to your leman to-day;
But to-morrow shall the fox from her chambers in the rocks,
Send forth her tawny cubs to howl above her prey.

HALF an hour later, as Queen Mary reclined on a luxurious couch, in one of the rooms which had been carefully fitted up for her use while at Carlisle, a tap was heard at the door, and in obedience to a permission given to enter, the arras was raised, and with a low bow Sir Edward Hamilton entered the apartment.

"Welcome, brave governor, ever welcome! I expected you before," said the Queen Consort languidly.

"Duty detained me, most sovereign lady," replied the knight, as he knelt to kiss the royal hand, and then in obedience to a mute sign he seated himself by her side.

Sir Edward was attired in a magnificent uniform covered with gold lace. On his head, and covering as much as possible of the bandage that swathed the wound delivered him by Sir Andrew Douglas, he wore a black velvet skull-cap having a long silver tassel.

The Queen Consort was habited in a dress of cloth of gold covered with rich lace, and her jet black glossy hair was intertwined with strings of pearls.

Said Mary after a short pause,—

"Will you attend the execution to-morrow, Sir Edward?"

"Yes," replied the knight starting, "why does your Majesty ask? As the governor of the city, it will be my bounden duty to do so."

"And at what hour does it take place?" inquired the Queen.

"Ten in the morning, sovereign lady," he replied.

"I wish when we are alone, Edward, you would spare me the tedium of always addressing me by my title," said Mary. "Can you not in such cases learn to treat me as a——" She paused, but, after a moment's hesitation, concluded, "as a friend?"

She accompanied the words with a flashing glance of her full dark eyes, and laid one jewelled hand on that of her companion.

He returned the pressure as though abstractedly, and said,

"As you command, I will obey, lady; but it is not every one who can or dare treat his Queen with the grace and gallantry of a Van Keppel."

Mary started, and her dark cheek flushed, for she understood the taunt, and then quickly changing the subject, she said,—

"Are you certain, Edward, that this maiden is really guilty of all wherewith she is charged? Her manner showed no token of her guilt."

"There can be no doubt upon the matter," was the reply; "both father and daughter are dangerous offenders, and both are equally deserving of death."

"Well, I take your word for it," said the Queen, "though I thought that, at the trial, some of the charges were but lamely supported and proven. The old man has escaped, it appears."

"He has," said Sir Edward," but I feel sure that he is yet within the city. If so, before another sun has set, he shall again be in our power."

"That is well, let it be so," said the Queen. "Who takes the command of the troops who immediately surround the block?"

"I do so, myself, my liege. Your Majesty will, of course, witness the sight?"

"I have given orders for my pavilion to be erected immediately opposite the block," replied the Queen. "I would fain see how this maiden suffers; for, by my faith, if her conduct to-morrow be as firm and undaunted as it was in the hall of judgment, she is not an ordinary woman, but a heroine."

Sir Edward smiled grimly in reply, though he felt a pang at his heart, as the Queen talked so carelessly of the horrors of the morrow, and, after an awkward pause, he said, abruptly,—

"Adieu! I am very weary and would fain seek rest."

"What, leave so soon?" said Mary. "There was a time when my presence did not so easily tire."

"The pain of my wound must excuse me," was the reply, and, lifting the Queen's hand to his lips, he kissed it.

"Farewell, then," she said, "if it must be so. But come to me to-morrow early, for I wish to speak to you on other matters."

With a sigh she then again sank back into the yielding pillows of her gorgeous couch, and, bowing reverentially, the Commandant quitted the room, muttering to himself, as he gained the passage,—

"Ever meet her half way; that is the safest plan. Royalty soon tires of its favourites; of that we have had many examples, and now the silly

THERE WAS A MIGHTY SHOCK, AND THE RESCUERS SWEPT THROUGH THE DUTCH RANKS.

moth, Van Keppel, hovers around the flame that ere long will consume him. O, silly Queen! thy love shall be my herald to ambition, as it is now my instrument of vengeance, but nought more," and with heavy and thoughtful steps, he strode on to his own rooms.

## CHAPTER XX.

### THE PLACE OF DOOM.

EARLY the following morning, strange sounds floated upwards in the still breezeless air, from every close, street, and wynd of the ancient city of Carlisle.

It sounded like the murmur of distant waves, or the howling of the wind among the rustling foliage of a forest.

It was, however, neither of these, but the tramp of human feet, and the buzz of human voices, as the inhabitants of Carlisle, the country people from the adjoining villages, and the armed soldiery of the Stadtholder, crowded from all quarters towards one spot—the Cathedral Close—*the place of doom.*

It was a bright clear morning, and in that large square thousands of eyes were already anxiously and expectantly directed towards the raised wooden platform, and the crape-covered block, that stood in front of the great doorway to the cathedral.

The windows, and even the stone roofs and chimney-tops of the surrounding houses were crowded with spectators, who looked down at their ease upon the sea of heads beneath, and listened

The windows, and even the stone roofs and chimney-tops of the surrounding houses were crowded with spectators, who looked down at their ease upon the sea of heads beneath, and listened to the confused hum of their myriad voices, mingled often with loud laughter and scraps of song, or sometimes echoing a frightened cry, or fierce imprecation, as, amid the clink of steel, and the clatter of iron hoofs, the glittering horsemen of the Dutch Guard rode up and down, keeping the dark line of sightseers within bounds, and preserving an open road for the Royal *cortége*, and the dignitaries of the city, to pass on to their respective seats or pavilions.

A space of fifty yards around the block was kept clear of the mob by the halberds of the City Guard.

Within this area were drawn up a company of a regiment, then only designated the "Oxford Blues," but now better known as the "Horse Guards Blue." They were all mounted on jet black horses, and were under the temporary command of Sir Edward Hamilton, who, once more equipped in his handsome Swart Ruyter uniform, with the visor of his plain steel morion concealing his face, sat motionless on his fine grey charger, close to the raised platform, whereon stood the block.

At length the dread hour of ten rang forth in thundering monotones from the great tower of the cathedral.

As the echo of the last boom died away, the crash of music was heard close by, and, amid the waving of banners and plumes, the clatter of arms, and the prolonged flourish of trumpets, Queen Mary, surrounded by a glittering cavalcade of officers, and the chief dignitaries of the city, swept on to the gorgeous scarlet and gold pavilion, that stood immediately facing the place of execution.

They had scarcely taken their places, when another procession was seen approaching from the direction of the castle, and every heart leaped, and every eye dilated, upon beholding the victim of the day, surrounded by her guards, slowly coming on towards the scaffold.

A low murmur for a minute ran through the crowd, then all was hushed; every eye was fixed upon the solemn procession, and the stillness was so intense, that even the distant tramp of the Guard was clearly audible.

First came twelve Sweyne-feathermen, clad in dark grey uniforms, and marching in double file, their glittering weapons sloped to the morning sunshine.

Then followed seven magistrates of the city, in their robes of office, attended by the sword and mace bearers.

Next came several clergymen of the Reformed Church, bare-headed, and clad in long black Geneva gowns, their eyes bent on the ground and each of them holding an open Bible in his hands.

Close in their rear walked the prisoner, with a firm and free step, attended, on one side by a clergyman, on the other by her executioner, who was dressed in scarlet, with a black half mask covering the upper part of his face, and bearing in one hand a huge axe, the instrument of death.

A few halberdiers, clad in richly-laced doublets, slashed with crimson, brought up the rear, and terminated the procession.

Another murmur rose from the crowd as Flora, still attended by chaplain and headsman, ascended the platform and gazed calmly around; but it died quickly away, for the whole multitude appeared to be frozen with pity and horror at the terrible fate which hung over one so lovely and so young in years.

She was attired in a tunic of light blue silk, and her luxuriant hair fell in glossy tresses over her shoulders.

There was no haggard expression in her face, no sign of emotion in her dark clear eyes, whose full and spiritual expression already appeared illumined with the light of another world; but there was a slight flush on her cheek, and a smile on her half parted lips as she calmly looked around on the thousands of human faces, whose countless eyes were fixed on her alone, and read in all one universal expression of sorrow for her untimely death.

Poor Flora! amid that vast assemblage, in one spot alone did she fail to encounter glances of pity and commiseration, and that was beneath the scarlet and gold canopy of the royal pavilion.

The Queen Consort's brow was stern and dark, and the officers of the city, most of them newly chosen by the unscrupulous Governor, together with the surrounding nobles and officers, like ready courtiers, wore the same expression.

The prisoner sighed as the feeling rose to her heart that for these people's sakes she had so often risked life and liberty—that for their cause her father had so long held the city, and so bravely defended it to the last; and yet now, without crime or fault, he was an outcast and a fugitive, and she was a criminal standing beside the block.

These ideas she quickly banished from her mind, however, for she had but five minutes to prepare for death.

Turning her attention, therefore, to the exhortations of the clergyman, her lips moved in silent prayer.

Hovering between two lives, she seemed already as though crowned with the glory of another and a brighter sphere.

As the eyes of that vast multitude gazed upon her, her youth, beauty, and meek resignation moved their hearts.

Many wept, some prayed, and the older citizens who were present whispered to each other of her many acts of charity and kindness, of her heroism during the siege, and of her brave father, who had fought long and nobly in the defence of their city and their homes.

Still that weird and awful silence prevailed.

Flora and the aged clergyman were kneeling side by side, and clearly the old man's voice could be heard as in low and tremulous tones he repeated the prayers for the dying, whilst the lovely martyr, with head bowed, faintly murmured the responses, with her white hands humbly crossed upon her pure and stainless breast.

And still the bright sunshine streamed down upon that open square, and its breathless excited multitudes—upon the horsemen who guarded vicinity of the block, and who sat motionless in their saddles, like figures hewn from marble—upon the roofs of the adjoining houses, and on the square and massive tower of the cathedral that rose darkly upwards in the clear blue sky, throwing its heavy shadow across the square below and casting in partial shade the crape-covered block—the kneeling victim beside it—the stern ferocious headsman—the black-robed clergy—and in still deeper gloom the heavy folds of the royal pavilion and the glittering assembly that sat within.

The prayers were soon over, but Flora still remained on her knees.

The executioner, after carefully rolling up his

sleeves to the elbow, drew his thumb twice across the blade of his axe to test its keenness, and then laying it across the block, stooped forward and whispered in her ear.

In reply, Flora rose to her feet, her countenance still calm, and not a trace of emotion visible therein.

Again she glanced round on the spectators, but her lips slightly trembled, and her cheek for a moment paled as her gaze met that of Sir Edward Hamilton, who had backed his horse close up to the block, and thrown open the visor of his helmet.

His face was ghastly pale, his eyes were bloodshot; and, as he met his victim's glance, he said, in a hollow voice,—

"Flora, it is not yet too late; I have still power to save you."

But she turned proudly away from him, and her dark eyes lighted up, and her cheek again flushed, as, facing the Royal Pavilion, she exclaimed.—

"Fellow citizens, I am innocent of the crime imputed to me. I am the victim, not of public justice, but of private veangeance. I die, however, forgiving all my enemies, as I trust that my Heavenly Father will forgive me."

The words were so clearly spoken that they were audible throughout that vast Close; and, when she ceased speaking, a murmur like that of a summer wind amid the foliage of a cork wood, again rose from the crowd.

The Queen Consort thereupon made an impatient sign to hasten the execution; and the headsman bluffly bade the passive victim "prepare, for the Court waited."

Then the clergyman, who had been in attendance on her, closed his Bible, and covered his face with his hands; the headsman took up the instrument of death, and threw the crape covering from off the block.

*The dreadful moment had arrived!*

---

## CHAPTER XXI.

### THE RESCUE.—ONE BLADE AGAINST A THOUSAND.

Now look to your buff, for steel is the stuff
To slash your brown jerkins with crimson enough;
There burst a flash; I heard their drums crash;
To horse! now for race over moorland and plash,
Ere the stars glimmer out, we will wake with a shout
The true men of York, who will welcome our rout.

ONCE more Flora Macclesfield looked round, and then with firm hands she unfastened the top buttons of her tunic, and bared her throat for the stroke.

In doing so, she exposed to view a handsome gold and pearl necklace, and she was about to take that off also, when the headsman, fearing that he should lose it as a perquisite, tore it roughly from her neck.

She then again knelt down, and while a slight shudder ran through her frame, placed her head on the block.

The executioner laid his hand on her beautiful long hair, moved it away from her ivory throat, and pulling her dress further down from her snow-white neck, so that no obstacle should stay the force of the blow, raised his gleaming weapon above his head.

Again, however, he lowered it, for he had not balanced it properly.

The excitement of the multitude was by this time intense; but at this moment a cry was heard amongst the bystanders, and an armed cavalier, like a flashing meteor of scarlet and gold, leapt his horse clear over the heads of the foot guards, who kept the open ground around the platform, and dashing up to the block, before the astounded cavalry could intercept him, he cut down the headsman from skull to collarbone, with one stroke of his heavy sword.

Then springing from the saddle, he raised Flora from the ground, and throwing his left arm around her slender form, brandished his reeking blade in his right hand, shouting,—

"A Douglas! a Douglas! Come on, ye craven hounds, and try the strength of a leal Scottish blade."

"Flora," he continued, turning towards the now half-fainting girl, "I heard nought of this until yesterday, but I have travelled night and day to save, or else to perish with you."

He could say no more.

Around him on all sides there arose the confusion of Babel.

Some of the crowd cheered, and the contagion spread.

Interest for Flora was combined with admiration at the bravery of the lover, and thousands of voices rang forth on the clear morning air in sympathy and approval.

But there arose other sounds also—the shrill blast of the trumpet, and roll of the drum, calling to horse, and Sir Andrew was alone—*one blade against a thousand!*

"On, soldiers! 'tis a Jacobite officer," thundered a hoarse voice close by, and spurring towards the lovers, Sir Edward Hamilton, with a curse, again crossed blades with his rival and hated foe.

The swords clashed together; but, at the third pass, Sir Andrew ran his weapon up to the very hilt through Hamilton's body, and with a deep groan, the fierce knight fell back over the body of the headsman.

"O! Andrew, would to heaven you were not here," said Flora. "You will sacrifice your own life without saving mine."

"If I cannot save you, I can both avenge and die with you," he replied. "Let one, let all come on, I am ready."

But the foe in his immediate vicinity did not move.

The troopers of the slain Hamilton still sat motionless in their saddles; the battle-axe guards stood to their arms; and though trumpets sounded, and the clash of arms echoed in the distance, though glittering horsemen were spurring towards the spot from the direction of the Royal Pavilion, the troops who surrounded the block showed no wish to accept the challenge, or to cross cross blades with the young royalist.

At this critical juncture of affairs, a small body of horsemen galloped up from the direction of the Cathedral, the sunlight glancing gaily on their burnished armour and waving plumes.

"Flora, beloved Flora," exclaimed Sir Andrew, as the glittering horsemen drew near, "it is only left me to show how a Douglas can fight and die! Farewell! ere many minutes are passed, we may meet in another world."

As he spoke, he gently disengaged himself from her frightened clasp, for, fearless of the danger surrounding herself, the noble girl trembled at the peril threatening her lover, and placing himself before her, with his hand on his sword hilt, he resolved to sell his life dearly.

On came the cavalry! they were within the area, within twenty yards of the block. With compressed lips, and the visor of his bright morion closed, Sir Andrew grimly awaited them.

Then one of the foremost of the advancing troops shouted,—

"To the saddle, Sir Andrew! Mount the lady behind you, and ride, for life and death, towards the northern gate. We are friends, and will aid you."

"Quickly, Douglas!" cried the other voice. "The trumpets are everywhere sounding to horse, and, by the saints, yonder come a troop of Dutch cavalry!"

For a moment, the young Life Guardsman was astounded; those whom he took to be enemies were friends; how they were so, he did not stop to inquire; 'twas no time for explanations.

Raising Flora to her feet, for she had again, through faintness, sank down besides the block, he leapt on his horse, which with the docility of a well-trained charger, had stood motionless by the platform, and lifting her up he hastily tied her to him with his scarf, and with his left arm around her waist, the bridle between his teeth, and his still reeking sword in his right hand, turned his horse's head towards the north.

"Good angels smile upon us," he said, gaily, in order to disperse the fears of the fair girl, whose white arms clasped his waist. "We have friends even here; all may yet be well, we will leave the event to the fates."

"To Providence!" was the gentle rebuke, and the next moment surrounded by their gallant band of rescuers, they were sweeping on, twelve abreast, up the North Wynd, knocking over everything that obstructed their course, towards that gate of the old city which faced the hills of bonnie Scotland.

Surprised and appalled by the rapidity of events, Queen Mary, and her courtiers, the soldiery and the multitude, stood as if paralysed.

"To the gate! to the gate! or they will escape! Mount and pursue!" shouted several officers of the Stadtholder; but the roar of voices and wild tumult of that vast assembly, drowned all other sounds.

A strong body of Dutch Dragoons, were, however, posted near the northern gate, and in obedience to the command of a mounted aide-de-camp, who had just galloped up from the royal pavilion, they threw themselves across the road.

In numbers they doubled their assailants; but hearing the gallop of another body of horse in their rear, the brave band of rescuers never stopped to draw rein; but with crests stooped, and bare swords flashing in the sunlight, rode right at them.

There was a mighty shock, a crash of steel, and the white plumes of the rescuers swept like a vision through the Dutch ranks, and spurring, plunging, and fighting, every inch of the way, they hewed them down on every side, and cutting half their number to pieces, dashed through the great gate, which was fortunately open, and gained the open country beyond, leaving the old city of Carlisle with its disappointed Queen Consort, and its dismayed and astonished multitudes in the rear.

Only five of their number were missing.

A sword thrust had wounded Sir Andrew in the shoulder, but the hurt was slight; and a slashing cut delivered by a Dutch officer had shred the plume from his morion.

Spurring up the steep hills that lie to the north of the city, they crossed the green fields of Lugwardine, swept past the frowning woods of Holme, and then all danger of pursuit and recapture being over, the two cavaliers who had headed the expedition wheeled their horses round and approaching Sir Andrew Douglas, threw up the visors of their gleaming morions, and he immediately discovered, with a thrill of joy, that they were Viscount Dundee and the Earl of Dunbarton.

---

## CHAPTER XXII.

### A DRY CHAPTER; BUT ONE THAT MUST NOT BE SKIPPED.

Down, down, for ever down with the mitre and the crown,
With the Belial of the court and the Mammon of the Pope;
Their is woe in Oxford halls, there is wail in Durham's stalls,
The Jesuit smites his bosom, the bishop rends his cope.

PERHAPS a few words relating to the historical events that have taken place between the commencement and the present point of our narrative may not be here out of place.

King James, who possessed no small share of courage and military skill, had upon the actual landing of his treacherous son-in-law in his dominions, thrown himself entirely on his army, which he had spent so many anxious years in fostering, training, and disciplining.

He despatched his son, the famous Duke of Berwick, to take possession of Portsmouth, and prevent the inhabitants declaring for the invader who was then on the march for Exeter.

Meanwhile, he hurried to Salisbury Plain, and placed himself at the head of twenty battalions of infantry, and thirty squadrons of cavalry, with a resolution to defend his crown to the death.

But alas! the spirit of disaffection, disloyalty, and ingratitude, had already manifested itself in the camp.

The desertions were numerous and alarming, while sullen discontent and open mutiny so greatly marked the conduct of those who remained that save a few of the Scottish regiments, James found none on whom he could rely.

Lord Colchester, son of the Earl of Rivers, with many of his regiment, were among the first who deserted to the standard of the invader. Lord Cornbury, son of the Earl of Clarendon, followed with three regiments of horse.

Lord Churchill, afterwards the celebrated Marlborough, who, from the position of a page, had been raised by James to the peerage, and a high military command, also betrayed the blackest ingratitude by forming a plot to seize his royal benefactor and deliver him as a bondsman to the Prince of Orange.

Failing in this, he deserted with several troops of cavalry, and took with him the Duke of Grafton, a son of the late King.

Many officers also of distinction informed the Earl of Faversham, their General, that they could not in conscience fight against the Prince of Orange, and thus hourly the whole English army fell to pieces.

The spirit of disaffection soon spread into the Scottish ranks. Their perfidious General, Archibald Douglas, with his own regiment of Red Dragoons, openly marched off to William with the Scottish standard displayed, and kettledrums beating, a circumstance which deeply affected James, for this was a corps on which he had particularly relied; but the treason of Douglas was ultimately avenged by a cannon shot on the banks of the Boyne.

James was a Stuart, and naturally founded his hopes on the soldiers of the nation from whence he drew his blood.

A battalion of Scots foot-guards next revolted under a corporal named Kempt.

And then every regiment went over in succession, under their several standards, save a troop of Dundee's Life Guards, a corps of Dragoons, and the Scots Royals, fifteen hundred strong, which as yet remained loyal and true.

These repaired to Reading, where the gallant Viscount Dundee, after the repulse at Carlisle, had ridden on the spur, and where, by exerting all his energies, he re-mustered ten thousand men in ten days.

With these small forces he offered to attack a Dutch army of forty thousand men, and, by a more than Spartan example of heroism and rashness to shame their faithless allies.

Meanwhile the Dutch drums beat merrily up for recruits, which poured in to the banner of the invader on all sides.

And horses were brought to mount the cavalry, and drag the artillery, with great speed and expedition.

All was lost!

By this time King James had fled from Whitehall, and, under an escort of Dutch troops, was —nobody knew where.

William was in possession of his palace, from whence he issued orders to the troops, and proclamations to the people, with all the air of a conqueror and authority of a king.

The entire forces of Great Britain joined him, except the Earl of Dumbarton's regiment of Scots Royals, who set out on their return to Scotland with drums beating and colours flying, fifteen hundred strong, and sixty gentlemen of the Scottish Life Guards, and twelve of the Scots Greys, who also turned their horses' heads homewards, under Viscount Dundee in person.

Dumbarton's regiment of foot was pursued by four entire regiments of Dutch cavalry, and whilst yet many hundred miles distant from bonnie Scotland, was surrounded, and, after a desperate contest, forced to yield to overpowering numbers.

The Earl and Sir Thomas Dalyel were thereupon sent as prisoners to Carlisle, and the other officers and privates to London, where the Stadtholder was intent on revenging, by lash and bullet, this signal instance of resistance to his authority.

Dundee, on the other hand, had succeeded in leading the whole of his little force of seventy-two horsemen through almost the entire length of hostile England, and had arrived at Carlisle, not only in time to save the Earl of Dumbarton and Sir Thomas Dalyel from execution, but also to rescue Sir Andrew Douglas and his betrothed from certain death.

The reader has already been informed how the latter feat was accomplised, but the way in which Dundee, at the risk of his own life, singly and unaided, released his illustrious *confrères*, Dumbarton and Dalyel, as well as the aged Commandant, Sir Stephen Macclesfield, from their dungeons beneath the old castle of William Rufus, will be narrated in a future chapter.

## CHAPTER XXIII.

### THE CAVALIERS OF DUNDEE.

There are hills beyond Pentland, and friths beyond Forth,
If there's lords in the south, there are chiefs in the north;
There are brave Duinne wassals three thousand times three,
Will cry "hey for the bonnets of bonnie Dundee."

Return we now to the little band of fugitives from Carlisle.

For some distance they rode at a brisk gallop, for pursuit was almost certain, and they were yet in the midst of a hostile territory, and many miles away from the blue hills of Scotland.

At last, however, they slackened their headlong pace, to relieve their horses, and then conversation became possible.

Dundee rode near Sir Andrew Douglas, and he now hastened to assure the pale and still frightened Flora of her father's safety, which information gave her intense delight.

"You will have to leave your pretty charge in some place of safety at the earliest opportunity, Sir Andrew," said the Viscount, at length. "King James—God bless him—cannot spare one leal Scottish blade at an hour like this. The goddess of love may not yet awhile shake your allegiance to the god of war."

"Noble Dundee, to victory or the grave, to the field or the scaffold, I will follow thee; and in that hour when I fail in my duty or allegiance to King James, may woe betide me, and dishonour blot my name; but whither go you, my lord?"

"Wherever the shade of Montrose shall direct me," was the thoughtful and poetical reply.

For a few moments he seemed to sink into a profound reverie, then his eyes suddenly flashed fire, and striking his gloved hand upon his gauntleted breast he exclaimed—

"Yes, I will hazard life and limb, estate and title, name and fame; yea, I would peril even my salvation, were it possible, in the cause of my honour and allegiance, and if I cannot save the throne of King James, at least I will not survive its fall, so the will of God be done."

There was something sublime in his aspect as he spoke, his dark and lustrous eyes were full of fire; his face, the manly beauty of which few have equalled, and none surpassed, was suffused with a warm glow; and the proud curl of his moustached lip showed the high spirit of achievement that burned within him.

"I am resolved, like you, Viscount, to fight to the last gasp for king and country," said the Earl of Dumbarton, who at this moment rode up at Dundee's bridle hand. "Yet much I fear that the white banner of the Stuarts has fallen to rise no more."

"Believe it not, my gallant comrade," answered Dundee, fiercely. "In the wilds of the pathless north, ten thousand claymores will flash from their scabbards at the call of Dundee. The loyal and gallant clans have not yet forgotten the glories of Alford, Inverlochy, and Auldern, when the standard of James Grahame of Claverhouse was never unfurled but to victory. Again will I lead them against this Dutch usurper, and scatter his armies of traitors and hirelings to the winds."

"My lord, a strong body of cavalry are in our front," exclaimed a vedette, at this moment riding in upon the main body of Dundee's little troop with this anything but welcome intelligence.

"My lord, a squadron of light horse are moving on our left flank," said another trooper, dashing up at a gallop.

Dundee, Dumbarton, and Douglas exchanged glances of uneasiness and surprise.

"Cut off, hemmed in at last," hissed Dundee, between his clenched teeth; but bah! it cannot be; our sixty berry-brown blades shall cleave us a way back to Scotland, though the clouds rained Dutch troopers as thick as hailstones all the way in our faces."

Then, turning to his little band of Life Guardsmen, he drew his good sword, and cried in a voice of thunder,—

"Fear not, my good and gallant comrades, though fifty times our number of scurvy traitors and ten-breetcher Hollanders bar our retreat to Scottish heathen; for by the blessing of God, by the holy consecration of our standard, by the strength of our hands, the valour of our hearts, and the justice of our cause, we will cut our way through them, and ten thousand other obstacles, and reach the far off highlands, where the loyal clans are all in arms, and wait but the appearance of Dumbarton and myself to sweep like a whirlwind down on the lowlands and across the border."

A loud shout from the gallant sixty greeted this soul-stirring address. Every blade leapt from its scabbard, and they loudly demanded to be led against the foe.

"Nay, let your courage be tempered with prudence, for we must not forget that we are the last hope of King James, and this being the case we must be chary of our persons. We must avoid the foe, and give them the slip if possible, though if hard blows are inevitable, I am sure our swords will give a good account of themselves," said Dundee with a gay laugh, and away dashed the Life Guardsmen to attempt by a flank movement to pass between the two opposing forces of cavalry diagonally before they could unite and hem them in.

---

## CHAPTER XXIV.

### A SKIRMISH WITH DUTCH DRAGOONS.

Pistolet crack, flashed bright on our track,
And even the foam of the water turned black;
They were twenty to one, our poor rapier to gun,
But we charged up the bank, and we only lost one.
So I saved the old flag, though it was but a rag,
And the sword in my hand was snapped off to a jagg.

THE quick eye of Dundee now saw that by quitting the open ground, and galloping down a rough road that led between two wooded hills, both of the large cavalry forces that were hovering in their front, and on their left flank, might be avoided.

The command was given with lightning rapidity, and turning as if on a pivot, the Life Guards swept down the slope, and in another minute were galloping through the narrow defile, amid a cloud of dust that almost hid them from sight.

Suddenly, however, upon turning a sharp corner, they beheld a body of horse riding leisurely up the narrow pass towards them. A collision was inevitable.

The blue standard with the white *fesse* that fluttered above the black unpolished helmets of the opposing force, declared them to be Dutch, and their large heavily jointed horses looked as phlegmatic in aspect as did their riders.

They were about two hundred and fifty in number, and at their head rode an officer of vast rotundity, cased in a capacious cuirass of polished steel, which gave him the aspect of a mighty tortoise, or some great bulb, of which the gilt helmet formed the apex. An enormous basket-hilted sword swung on one side of him, and a brass blunderbuss on the other, while a great tin speaking trumpet was grasped in his right hand, as though it had been the baton of a field-marshal.

Directly this worthy caught sight of the glancing helms, the gleaming cuirasses, and the flashing sword-blades of the Scottish Life Guards, he raised his trumpet to his lips, and, puffing out his cheeks, bellowed a command in a voice of thunder to his troops to form in a line across the pass.

This they did as though mechanically, without evincing any surprise at the presence of their opponents, moving inertly, phlegmatically, and as though half asleep.

The manœuvre effected, horses and riders stood still, motionless as a line of stone statues; not a jingle of a bit, the rattle of a sword-scabbard, or the murmur of a single voice was heard amidst their apparently lifeless array.

Their bulbous commander then yawned leisurely, stretched himself in his saddle, as though just aroused from a pleasant nap, and then again, slowly raising his tin trumpet to his lips, bellowed out, this time addressing the impatient Scots—

"Vat cabalry is zat, in ze debil's name?"

Dundee had long ago brought his little force to a halt, and now he rode a few yards in advance of his men, and replied in his clear ringing voice that required no speaking trumpet to render it audible—

"A troop of the Scottish Life Guards, in the service of King James."

"Ach tuyfel, zare is no zuch King. Scots horse, der tuyfel! You are our brisoners, or we cut you into den towsand bieces. Yield brisoners at vonce," shouted back the Dutchman.

"Gluck! gluck! Vivat Wilhelm!" cried his black dragoons, apparently dropping off to sleep again directly they had given utterance to the guttural battle cry.

"Gentlemen of the Scottish Guard, prepare to charge," cried Dundee. "Uncase the standard! sound trumpet!"

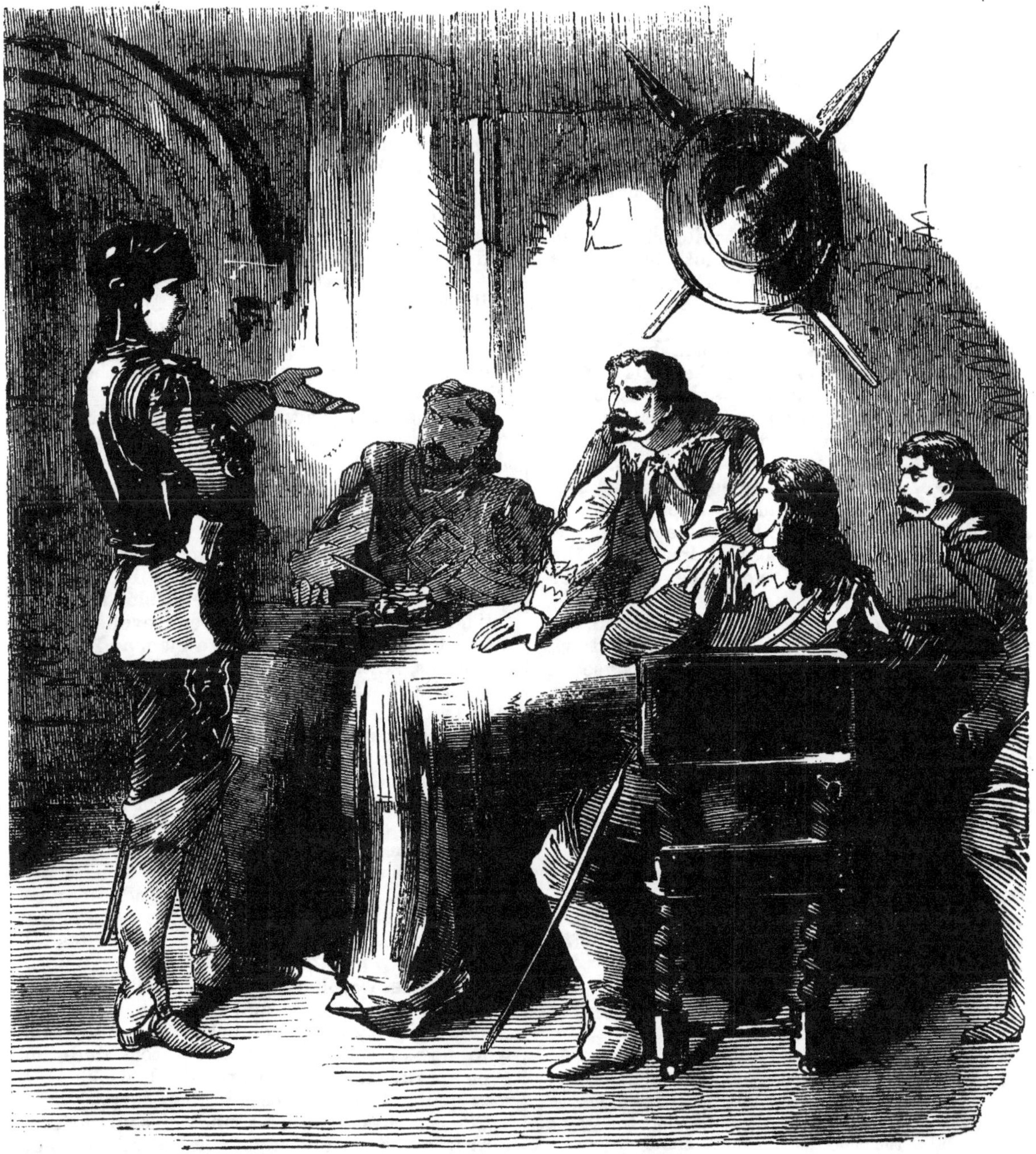

THE CONSPIRATORS IN COUNCIL.

The snow-white bannerol was unfurled, a solitary trumpet sounded, a single kettledrum ruffled, but each brave Scot set his teeth firm and gathered up his reins in mad anxiety for the charge.

Then Dundee dashed out a couple of lengths in advance, and wheeling round his snorting horse, that pawed the air in its fiery impatience, he drew his long bright rapier, and, while his dusky eyes gleamed with fire, he gave the deep and distinct order—

"Cavaliers of the Life Guards—Gentlemen of the Scots Greys, forward! charge!"

"Hurrah! down with the Stadtholder—to the devil with his hirelings!" cried the reckless troopers, and with their white plumes waving in the breeze, and their uplifted rapiers flashing in the sunshine, sixty Scots spurred their matchless black horses forward, and with the force of a whirlwind, bridle to bridle, and boot to boot, rushed with wild valour to the onset.

The Dutch were as four to one, but they could not withstand the fury of that charge.

"Unsling carbines! blow matches! fire! towsand tuyfels, no, traw swords. Got tam, hold firm," cried their commanding officer, through his great trumpet.

In vain the commands, for the front rank of his dragoons had already recoiled in confusion on the rear.

There was a tremendous shock, a flashing of swords as their keen edges rang on tempered helmets, and corslets of proof, a furious spurring of horses, and high above all other sounds Dundee's shrill slogan of—

"Claverhouse to the rescue! A Grahame, a Grahame!"

"A Grahame, a Grahame! God for Scotland and James VII. To the devil with the Stadtholder. Hurrah!" echoed his fierce troopers, as they rode down their heavy Dutch opponents as though they had been so many unwieldy turtles.

And there was Dundee, a spear's length in front of them all, with his sword brandished aloft, and hiswhite ostrich feathers streaming behindhim, his cheek glowing, and his wild dark eyes flashing with that supernatural brightness which was the true index of his fierce and heroic spirit.

The Earl of Dumbarton's white charger was neck and neck with the Viscount's black steed, and the sword of that brave Scottish noble did good service in his royal master's cause that day.

Sir Andrew Douglas, on the other hand, having one more dear to him than his own life to protect, kept pretty well in the centre of the charging troop, and amid the plunges of his steed and the descending strokes of his trenchant blade, he found time occasionally to address a cheering word to his companion, whose body he guarded even to the neglect of his own.

Presently, he found himself opposed to the rotund Dutch officer, who had evidently selected himself as a special foe, possibly imagining that hampered as he was he would be easily overcome.

"Come on, old gorbelly, hand to hand, and point to point, for here's a skewer that will truss thee like a turkey," cried our hero, seeing the contest was not to be avoided.

In a trice his rapier was through the Dutchman's protuberance, up to the very hilt, by a clever thrust just under the corslet. The hot blood spurted out over the young Royalist's hand and arm, and at the same moment a ringing cheer proclaimed that the cordon was broken through, and the Dutch ranks pierced.

With a loss of only one man the sixty Scots had cut through at least two hundred and fifty Dutch dragoons, and once more the pathway towards Scotland was clear and open before them.

## CHAPTER XXV.

### THE REVOLUTION IN EDINBURGH.

See black on each roof at the sound of our hoof.
The Puritans gather but keep them aloof;
Their muskets are long, and they aim at a throng,
But woe to the weak when they challenge the strong.
Butt-end to the door—one hammer more,
Our pikemen rush in and the battle is oe'r.

PASS we over another fortnight and shift we the scene to Scotland's capital, the princely city of Edinburgh.

The Lords of Convention are met in the high court of justiciary, to depose their rightful monarch, James the VII. of Scotland, and II. of England, and to draw up a servile address, inviting William, the Stadtholder, to accept the crown.

The vast hall was dimly lighted, and the forms of the assembled conclave were but indistinctly visible, yet amongst them might have been distinguished the weak and servile Melville, the crafty and fanatical Stair, and the no less crafty and unscrupulons Duke of Hamilton, names ever to be associated with Scotland's disgrace.

There, too, were Sir John Lanier, and Lieutenant-General Sir Hugh Mackay, of Scoury, commander-in-chief of the Scottish forces, both of them brave and gallant soldiers, and, perhaps, rather more honest rogues than their colleagues.

The sound of their voices seemed to die hollowly away amid the great beams and rafters high overhead, and some of the conspirators spoke hesitatingly and in hoarse whispers, as traitors often do, whilst a few of the weaker-minded would occasionally start and handle their sword-hilts, for even the dark corners of the old hall seemed to inspire them with nameless terrors.

And while this swarm of hornets deliberated and plotted, and hatched treason in their secure but gloomy nest, the whole city was a vast amphitheatre of rapine, murder, and bloodshed.

Edinburgh was in the power of a mad and lawless rabble, who rendered furious by bigotry and drunkenness, were committing the most frightful atrocities.

The houses of every known Catholic and episcopalian were being given to the flames, and their inmates put to the sword.

The shrieks of unoffending women and children, the howls of their destroyers, and the crash of falling masonry made night hideous.

The streets were full of smoke, the air was sheeted with flames, but redder still in every quarter gleamed the horrid hue of blood.

The Jesuit college had first been levelled to the dust, the priests massacred to a man, and crosses and relics, statues, pictures, and vestments were now being borne along the streets by drunken men and women, amid yells of rage and derison.

The ordinary custodians of public law and order had cast aside their uniforms and joined the mob, and preachers, in their long black gowns were borne on the shoulders of the rabble, often with an open Bible in one hand and a sword in the other, exciting the wretches to still greater acts of atrocity.

"On, on, to the good work and prosper. Smite and slay! smite and slay! lest the curses that befel Saul for sparing the Amalekites fall upon ye."

Thus these wolves in sheep's clothing urged on the work of death, and excited to a state of religious frenzy the people who listened to them, who hewed their victims limb from limb, not even sparing the bodies of the dead, which they mangled and tore to pieces in their fury.

At last these mingled sounds of soul-thrilling horror reached the ears of the assembled councillors in the House of Convention, and Lieutenant-General Mackay, interrupting the maudlin speech of a half intoxicated noble, said bluntly,

"It strikes me that our good citizens are carrying matters a little too far; had I not better let some of my lambs check their ardour? I hear the screech of women."

"Your lambs will remain in barracks, Mackay, what matters it if some women are slain; they are but prelatists and papists, and if spared may become the dams of whelps of the same breed," said the President of the Council.

In reply the Lieutenant-General shrugged his shoulders and was silent.

Then a dwarfish mis-shapen figure, clad in senatorial robes, but with wig awry and face bloated and pimpled, leapt on to the table, and unfolding a sealed document with his trembling hands steadied himself with an effort and read as follows—

"My lords and gentlemen,—I move that for sae mickle as the vile and bloody papistical James,

Duke of Albany and York, having assumed the regal sceptre without the oath required for due maintenance of religion, and having altered the ancient constitution of the kingdom by ane exertion of tyrannous and arbitrary power, has forfeited all richt to the crown of Scotland now and for ever; that it be forthwith settled on the Stadtholder William, and Mary his spouse; that there be made ane list of grievances to be redressed, and a new law framit anent witchcraft, papacy, prelacy, and ither abominations."

"I second the motion of Lord Mersington, and move as an amendment that an address, writ as nearly as possible in the same words, be signed by us all, and at once be forwarded to King William at London," said the Duke of Hamilton.

"Here, then, is just such an address ready, my lord," said Stair, with a laugh, as he threw a roll of parchment on the table; "you will find it, word for word, my lords, accord with Lord Mersington's motion, so let us all sign it, and despatch it by a sure messenger to Whitehall within the hour."

There was a hurried dipping of quill pens into inkhorns, and each one of the traitor council signed the document in turn.

Sir Hugh Mackay was the last to affix his signature.

As he threw down his pen, he exclaimed, with a laugh—

"A neat hempen collar each one of us has fitted to his throat by this act, if King James ever enjoys his own again."

"A silken collar in my case, for as a noble of Scotland I shall stand out for the privilege due to my rank," sneered Hamilton.

"And I shall turn sides again in time to avoid all risks of scragging, take my word for it," muttered Mersington.

"Hell's furies! what is that?" cried Sir John Lanier, at this moment. "The scurril mob are, indeed, carrying the license of the hour to rather a high degree. If they dare to invade the Parliament yard, while we, the High Court of Convention, are in the midst of our deliberations——"

"Bah! the *leaders* of a revolution are ever the *servants of the mob*, not its masters," said Mackay; but let us see the farce that is about to be enacted; our position, at all events, secures us good places from whence to behold the play."

By this time, the dark and gloomy Hall of Convention was as well lighted as though twenty suns had been pouring their rays through its groined roof, but it was by the glare of fire.

Hundreds of torches gleamed redly in the great square without, and with drums beating, horns blowing, and kettles, frying pans, and cleavers clattering, a dense mass of ragged, squalid, and insane-looking men and women poured in, and nearly filled it in every part.

Begrimed with smoke, filth, and blood; maddened by intoxication and slaughter, their yells, shouts, and execrations sounded like those of fiends from the very depths of hell.

Conspicuous above them all, raised on the bare, brawny shoulders of two women, into each of whose fat white heaving bosoms he had plunged one of his great bony hands, the better to steady himself on his uncertain perch, was seated a man whose sad-coloured garments and starched bands announced him to be a preacher.

His long hair of raven hue waved around a face flushed with passion, drink, and lust, whilst his large black eyes glowed like those of a tiger with fury

"Bring forth these troublers of Israel, these scarlet women of Babylon," he shrieked; "bring forth these foul lemans of the persecutors of God's saints, and let them be stoned to death."

This rhapsody was responded to with yells of delight, and two nuns, who, in trying to escape from their burning convent, had been seized by the mob, were dragged into the middle of the square by their brutal custodians.

They were both young and both beautiful, but they were as pale as death, and their clothing torn in strips.

Neither their beauty nor their helplessness secured them any favour, however, in the sight of that foul mob; and the drunken preacher, withdrawing a hand from the hot throbbing bosom in which it had so long been buried, pointed his skinny forefinger towards them, exclaiming in his shrill nasal twang,—

"Oh! thou daughters of Babylon, know that this night there is a sword upon the inhabitants of Babel, and upon her princes and her mighty men, for it is the load of graven images, and they are mad upon their idols. Verily, ye shall be stripped of the raiment of the scarlet women, ye shall be beaten with many stripes, and scourged and stoned to death."

"Malediction! can they not be rescued?" exclaimed Sir John Lanier, who, with the other Councillors, beheld this painful scene from the windows of the Hall of Convention. "They are both noble ladies; one is the daughter of the Earl of Belcarris, the other is Mistress Lilian MacAlister of Holm Lea."

"No; I have taken the precaution to lock the doors, and the keys are in my doublet pocket. I will not surrender those keys but with my life. S'death, man; you would turn the wrath of the multitude upon ourselves," growled the Duke of Hamilton.

"But, my lord," urged Sir John, "would you countenance such a deed as this?"

"Bah! they are but papists; what matters it?" was the retort.

"Besides my dear friend, what could we do against such numbers; we might sacrifice ourselves, but could not serve these unfortunate ladies one whit," said Sir Hugh Mackay.

At this moment the preacher's voice sounded shrilly above the surrounding din, as he shrieked,

"Off with the devil's uniform that they wear. Strip them to the waist, bind them back to back, and then scourge them with their own beads and crosses, until their skins are as black as that of the foul fiend, their master. Nay, don't so many of you get about the work, or none of us will see the sight; two will suffice."

For a minute there was a fight amongst a group of men as to who should obey the preacher's behest, seeing which, two strapping frowzy wenches from the Netherport, strong and muscular as dragoons, sprang forward, and seized hold of the passive victims, exclaiming with a laugh,—

"What should men know of tirewomen's work? Faith, we will do the matter properly. Come, no resistance, minions."

Their great fleshy arms were bare to their

shoulders, and already covered with blood; their hair fluttered in tangled masses around their flushed faces; no mercy was to be expected from them.

With oaths and mocking laughter, they pulled the monastic habits from the persons of their victims, and then with nails and teeth, tore their underclothing to shreds. In a second, as it were, both the young nuns stood nude to the waist before the populace.

Neither of them could have been more than eighteen years of age, and the sight of their exquisite lovely forms seemed to work the two female furies up to madness.

"Here's fat shoulders, and dimpled backs, and rounded arms," exclaimed one, giving a sledge-hammer blow with her great fist at each lovely charm she apostrophised. "They speak of penance, and discipline and mortification, don't they?"

"And here's a skin white as snow, and soft as velvet, and not a bone to be felt. Precious little fasting you've done, my lady, and taken a bath of milk every morning for your complexion, I'll be bound," screamed the other harpy, seizing an alabaster arm with such a passionate grip that its owner shrieked aloud.

"Ah! you feel that, do you? I thought 'twas fine to be a martyr; but put your arms behind your back, for I mean to mark you with the emblem that you are so fond of—come, obey, or twill be the worse for you?"

Frightened into compliance, the young girl clasped her hands behind her back, and this movement made her grandly developed chest and swelling bosom expand into their full beauty. She looked like a lovely statue imbued with the warm colouring of life.

Then her inhuman tormentor crooked her fingers like the talons of a bird of prey, and burying her five long nails into her victim's white chest, drew them quickly down her body between her breasts, even to the waist, leaving five little red lines of blood in their course.

Then she quickly transferred her claws to her victim's left side, and drew them quickly around her body to the same point on her right side, thus forming a perfect cross.

How the poor girl throbbed and quivered with the pain, and her companion had to endure the same torture from her persecutor, the device being hailed as original and worthy of imitation.

They were then bound back to back with ropes that cut deep into their delicate flesh, being thrice thrown down in the operation, and their lovely bodies scratched and bruised against the hard gravel.

Then the mob took up stones and bricks and other missiles wherewith to stone them, uttering wild yells of satisfaction.

The two young nuns threw round a glance of hopeless agony; there was no hope of escape from their appalling fate, and now their souls sank at the prospect of so cruel and painful a death.

Battered out of all human shape, before life was quite extinct, they would be crushed into one scarcely distinguishable mass of flesh and bone.

Was it for this that they had been so exquisitely formed and proportioned by the wondrous and Almighty architect in his own image?

A stone was at last thrown, and it hit the youngest on her wildly throbbing chest with a dull thud.

She uttered a stifled sobbing gasp, it was answered by a dreadful yell from the populace; but the next instant a fierce wild cry rang even above the voices of these inhuman fiends.

Then there was a flashing of sword-blades in the torchlight, the glitter of burnished helmets, the waving of snowy plumes, while high above all other sounds one terrible voice rang loud and clear, shouting,—

"Claverhouse to the rescue! A Grahame! a Grahame!"

It was Dundee, the gallant—"the terrible Claver'se, that man-fiend," as the surperstitious Covenanters thought him, whom all deemed six hundred miles away, a prisoner in England.

This splendid cavalier was a good three lengths in front of his troop of Royal Life Guards, who with their bright arms flashing in the red light of the waving torches were hewing and trampling down the scurril mob like a field of rye.

"Close up, fall on, gentlemen! No quarter to the knaves!" exclaimed Dundee, upon whom all eyes were centred, for there was no mistaking the splendour of his armour, the nobility of his air, or the ferocity of his purpose.

Those who saw him spurring down upon them like the avenging archangel, seemed to be fascinated to the spot as birds are by the glitter of a serpent. They were too terrified to fly.

Standing erect in his stirrups he showered his blows on every side, his white plume rising and falling in unison with his trenchant rapier.

"Hey for King James! Ho for the cavaliers! Down with the rebels!" cried Sir Andrew Douglas on his right.

"Down with the Whigamores! Death to the traitor knaves! Long live James VII. of Scotland," shouted the Earl of Dumbarton on his left.

As the brilliant array of royalist cavaliers pressed forward, the rabble were trampled in the dust beneath the tremendous rush of their heavy horses, and their riders in steel and buff.

With one stroke of his sword Sir Andrew cleft the half-mad, half-drunken, preacher from crown to chine.

He fell to the ground, together with the two lusty damsels, upon whose broad shoulders he had sat as on a throne, whose bodies were the next instant crushed under foot, and spurned by the steel hoofs of the cavaliers' rushing steeds.

Then he dashed up to the spot where the two poor nuns stood still lashed back to back; in a second the Earl of Dumbarton was at his side. With their sharp sword blades they quickly severed the cruelly strained cords, and each lifting one of the beautiful, and by this time only half-conscious sufferers before him on to the saddle, awaited the next command of Dundee.

By this time the Parliament yard was cleared of the rabble. The sixty Life Guards had made more than three thousand rioters melt away before them like mist, leaving at least two hundred of their number dead or wounded on the ground, whilst they had not lost a single man.

Dundee threw up the visor of his helmet, and

riding up to the Earl of Dumbarton and Sir Andrew, said—

"Take with you thirty men, and convey these two ladies to the castle, which I have just learnt his Grace the Duke of Gordon still holds for King James with a strong garrison of Catholic soldiers; there they will at least be safe."

"And whence go you, my lord?" asked Dumbarton.

"Into the High Court of Justiciary to read my Lords of Convention a lesson," was the proud reply.

"Alone, my lord?" exclaimed Sir Andrew.

"Alone," answered Dundee, whilst his dark eyes filled with a dusky fire. "Is not one loyal cavalier a match for a hundred psalm-singing, snivelling, canting hypocrites like these Lords of Convention? By the mass, when a pack of foxes dare show their teeth at a tiger, let them 'ware his claws."

"But you will at least have some of your men within your call, Viscount," urged Dumbarton.

"The thirty men you leave behind will keep their saddles in front of the great door. Should they hear the slogan of Dundee they will know what to do, but I anticipate no danger," was the reply. Then, after a moment's pause, he said, hurriedly—

"Away with you; carry those two poor young girls as tenderly as possible, and convey them to the castle with all speed. Tell his Grace of Gordon that I will be with him within an hour. Adieu. Now for my Lords of Convention."

He lowered the point of his sword in parting salutation, and then sent it back clattering into its sheath.

A minute later, the Earl of Dumbarton and Sir Andrew Douglas, each bearing one of the rescued nuns before him on his saddle, and followed by thirty troopers, dashed out of the Parliament yard and directed their course towards the castle, while Dundee, at the head of his thirty remaining Life Guards, rode leisurely towards the great outer door of the High Court of Justiciary, where dismounting, he threw the reins of his charger to a trooper, and entered the gloomy portal alone.

## CHAPTER XXVI.

### BEARDING THE LORDS OF CONVENTION.

To the Lords of Convention 'twas Claverhouse spoke,
Ere the King's crown go down there are crowns must be broke;
Then each cavalier who loves honour and me,
Let him follow the bonnets of Bonnie Dundee!

As the concluding scene described in our last chapter was being enacted in the Parliament-yard, the illegally constituted Lords of Convention remained terrified and panic-stricken spectators of its every incident.

It seemed to them nothing less than a miracle that Lord Dundee could have traversed the whole of hostile England, and the equally hostile Lowlands, and though menaced on every hand, the whole way, by great bodies of troops, have at last reached his native capital in safety, bringing with him not only sixty of his troopers, but also Lord Dumbarton, whom they had thought was a prisoner in the Tower of London.

The presence of these two great Catholic nobles and zealous adherents of the fallen dynasty with their little handful of followers, strangely disconcerted them. The prestige of one terrible name had made cowards of them all, their minds had suddenly become a chaos.

And as the rioters fled with their torches and resinous pine wood flambeaux, so the square without, and the grim hall from whose windows they gazed, darkened, as did their own souls; and a kind of gloomy and unnatural horror seemed to oppress them.

"Candles, more candles here; one would think that these crystal lustres were filled with farthing rushlights. By the blessed kirk, we can scarcely see each other's faces," cried Sir Hugh Mackay.

"Aye, summon the varlets hither, they must be replenished. My Lord of Mersington, will you touch the gong?" said Lord Stair.

A tremendous boom startled the silence as the request was complied with, but no varlets answered the call, for while their masters were in consultation, they had some of them joined the rioters, whilst others had found greater attractions in larders and wine cellars, and were by this time hopelessly gorged or drunk.

Presently, however, one footstep was heard ascending the stone turnpike stair without, and the jingle of spurs, and clatter of a sword scabbard accompanied them.

"Surely no swaggering trooper of the bloody Claver'se would dare to enter our very council chamber?" exclaimed Mersington, with a start.

"No fear of that, my lord; he and his handful of Life Guards have by this time taken refuge behind the ramparts of the castle, the only wasp's nest in bonnie Scotland left us to destroy," laughed Sir John Lanier.

But almost ere he had ceased speaking, the door of the council chamber was burst violently open, and a tall, stalwart form, glittering in bright scarlet and steel, stood on the threshold.

On the silk scarf that crossed his glittering cuirass, gleamed the white cockade of the House of Stuart; and such was the panic that his sudden presence created, that every Lord of Convention, with the exception of Sir Hugh Mackay and Sir John Lanier, tore from his breast the orange rosette of the Stadtholder William, and hastily threw it under the table.

Not quick enough, however, for the act to escape Dundee's eagle glance, who, with a bitter smile, observed—

"My sudden arrival seems to have disconcerted you, my lords; has no one here a word of welcome for James Grahame of Claverhouse?"

He advanced some paces further into the room, and folding his arms on his chest, surveyed the traitor council calmly, but scrutinisingly.

Seeing that he was alone, some of them grew bolder, and though none yet dared to speak, hostile looks became common.

"How is this, my lords?" exclaimed Dundee. "Have I returned unfaithful to my trust? Three months ago you sent me into England to fight for his sacred Majesty King James, against the Stadtholder of Holland. I have obeyed your instructions, and am the only one of your generals who has not turned traitor. My regiment alone has preserved its standard too, and brought it back undefiled to Scotland."

"Viscount Dundee, do not feign to misunderstand matters; times have changed," growled Sir Hugh Mackay.

"Have men's hearts changed with them," asked the royalist, sternly.

"Well, where the de'il drives, ye ken that—" began Mersington.

"Wherefore beat about the bush, my Lord of Mersington? Dundee has asked a plain question, and I will give him a plain answer; men's hearts *have* changed with the times," interposed Sir Hugh Mackay.

"Then ye are all an assemblage of traitors, I presume?"

"Traitors!" exclaimed the Duke of Hamilton, Chief Lord of the Council, springing from his canopied chair, and laying a hand on the jewelled hilt of his sword. "How dare you, my lord, apply that epithet to us?"

"By the right that every man has to speak the truth, my lord. I see the braw orange favours that most of you have cast under the table, and I understand their significancy. You have sold King James as you once sold King Charles, aye, and as you would sell King William in turn, if it suited your purpose. By the mass, I wonder that ye are not ashamed to look a loyal cavalier in the face," retorted Dundee, in mocking sarcasm.

Few Scottish nobles could brook language like this, and many sprang to their feet, and began to handle their swords and daggers.

"Ah, you resent my plain words, my Lords of Convention, do you? Well, what my tongue has spoken, my sword can defend. If any of ye will pick up that gauntlet, let him do so in the foul fiend's name!" said Dundee, with a bitter laugh.

As he concluded he pulled the heavy leather gauntlet from his right hand and flung it on the floor.

Then he drew his good sword, still red with the blood of the rabble, and stood on guard.

But so majestic did he look, with his towering stature, his cold, stern, unimpassioned face, and all his flashing accoutrements, that not one of those traitor lords, brave men though many of them were, dared to pick up his gage of battle, or cross blades with him in so bad a cause.

"Take up thy gauntlet, Viscount," said Lord Stair at length. "It would ill become any one of the Lords of Convention to make their common council chamber the scene of a gladiatorial combat."

Dundee dashed his sword back into its scabbard with a clatter that made the very rooftree ring.

He then picked up his gauntlet, but instead of replacing it on his hand, fastened it to the basnet of his helmet, exclaiming—

"My lords and gentlemen, I came here as a peer of the realm to serve his Majesty James VII., and the Parliament of Scotland. I find the latter dissolved, and an illegal assembly, calling itself 'A Convention of the Estates,' established in its place. To it I owe no service, no fealty, and I announce myself the personal foe of every man here present. Whoever amongst you cares to accept my challenge I will meet hand to hand, and sword point to sword point, at any place he may name within the hour."

He waited an instant for some one to reply to him, but not one of the assembled senators uttered a word.

"Farewell, sirs," then said Dundee, with a smile of pride and scorn. "When again I appear before you, it will be to command, and may it be to punish. My trumpets will now sound to horse, and I shall journey northwards—to the country of the clans — where the hills are as steep, the woods as pathless, the glens as deep, and the rivers as rapid, as in the days of the Romans. In less than a week, from the wild Highlands shall the whole tide of Celtic war roll on the traitor Lowlands, as in the days of the great Montrose. When again you hear the voice of Dundee, my self-elected Lords of Convention, *tremble*!"

He dropped the visor of steel morion, and with armour clanking strode out of the room.

As the jangle of his sword and spear descending the stone stairs died away, a deep silence pervaded the dusky hall, for the threats of this chivalric soldier, when united to their foreknowledge of his dauntless courage, his unflinching loyalty, his loftiness of mind, and intense ferocity threw a complete chill upon these coldblooded and calculating revolutionists.

But soon the gallant blare of the trumpet, the stirring battle of a brass kettledrum, the clang of iron hoofs, and jingle of steel scabbards and chain bridles, awakening all the echoes of the great Parliament squares, announced the departure of the man they dreaded, and of the few brave gentlemen, who of all his once numerous and fondly-cherished army now alone remained stanch to the hapless James.

---

## CHAPTER XXVII.

### A TERRIBLE PREDICAMENT.

Come fill up my cup, come fill up my can
Come, saddle my horses and call out my men,
Unhook the west port, and let us gae free,
For it's up with the bonnets of Bonnie Dundee.

Riot, pillage, incendiarism, and murder, still held high revel in the city, and as Dundee and his thirty cavaliers rode along the streets in the direction of the castle, they beheld sights and heard sounds that made their hearts swell within them with anger and indignation.

Dundee, however, did not forget that he and his little band were the last hope of his King in this hotbed of presbytery and rebellion; so he resolved to be economical of his trooper's lives, and not expose them to more risk than necessary by encountering the mad burghers and drunken saints who were making night hideous by their blood-orgies and blasphemy.

They had scarcely gained the steep Leith Wynd when they were met by the Earl of Dumbarton and the other half of their small force.

Fearing that Dundee and his thirty troopers might be attacked and overcome by the mob, they had, after depositing the two young nuns in safety within the castle walls, returned on the spur to rejoin their great leader, in case their aid might be needed.

On their way, Sir Andrew Douglas had learnt with a thrill of horror that the mansion of the Earl of Perth, in which, on their arrival in Edinburgh, he had left Flora Macclesfield, as being a sure place of safety, was attacked by the populace, who were swearing to put every inmate to the sword.

"Viscount," he now said, addressing Dundee.

"Can you not spare a dozen men for me to attempt a rescue?"

"Impossible," was the stern reioinder. "I cannot spare a man; the King is my only thought, Though of course, if anyone not strictly belonging to my regiment likes to join you, I will not say aught to dissuade him."

"Then I am with thee, brave Douglas," said the Earl of Dumbarton, giving our hero his hand.

"And I!—and I!—and I!—and I!" shouted the four Scots Greys, who were attached to the troop, though simply as volunteers.

"My friends, how can I thank you?" exclaimed Sir Andrew; "but let us hasten, for we have no time to spare. Lord Viscount we will rejoin you at the castle within the hour?"

"I hope so," answered Dundee, solemnly, "and I trust that you may be successful in your enterprise; but I pray you be chary of your lives, for the good cause has very few such choice spirits to spare."

The little troop of rescuers replied to this caution with a joyous shout, and dashing the spurs into their horse's flanks, they quitted their companions, the Life Guards, at a gallop.

The latter then made their way direct to the castle, while Sir Andrew and his friends, describing a detour down one narrow wynd, and up another, so as to avoid those streets wherein the rioters were gathered most thickly, at last reached the mansion they were in quest of.

It was a lofty edifice, with turrets at the angles, steep roofs, and great stacks of chimneys. It stood a little way back from the street, and had a row of tall Dutch poplars before it.

Beneath these poplars, and, indeed, filling the whole open space in front, were thousands of the unkempt, unwashed, and brutal mob, forming a confused forest of fierce faces, uplifted hands and weapons—swords, pikes, staves, and halberds.

These flashed incessantly in the glare of hundreds of brandished torches, while gaudy banners of orange and blue fluttered in the red light, the former being the colour of the Revolutionists, the latter of the Covenanters.

Hundreds of these worthies, too drunk to stand, wallowed like pigs in the kennels, and around them lay staved casks of nut-brown ale, and ruddy wine, which, in some places, flooded the gutters to such an extent as to drown their prostrate votaries outright, whilst many others were crushed to death by the feet of the mighty host that kept sweeping to and fro over them.

The yells of these demons resounded between the solid walls of the narrow streets that lay around, like the cries of veritable fiends.

The din of hammers, too, rang like thunder against the strong oaken door of the mansion, and many guns were being discharged by the mob at the windows, which were securely grated.

Sir Andrew and his five friends, who, from the deep shadow of a neighbouring church, surveyed this scene without being perceived in turn, beheld with anxiety the sturdy wielders of sledge-hammers, who were thundering away at the outer door.

Nor was this anxiety unnatural, for the whole house resounded under the energy of the blows; and though the barrier as yet refused to yield, it was rapidly falling into splinters, and a very few minutes would evidently suffice to effect an entry.

"We must get inside before we can render any assistance to the besieged," said the Earl of Dumbarton, at length.

"But how can we do so? My God! I don't see a way in which we can be of any service, and yet it is torture to remain here inactive, while the lives of those we love are in such deadly peril," exclaimed Sir Andrew Douglas, wildly.

At that instant a face appeared at one of the upper windows; a female face of rare beauty, clearly revealed against the glass by the red unearthly glare without.

"Heavens! 'tis she," exclaimed the lover, wildly. "I must save her, or perish in the attempt."

He was about to spur single-handed amidst the mob, but the Earl of Dumbarton seized his rein in time to stop him.

"Stay," he said, peremptorily, "the act you contemplate is madness. Let us get round to the back of the house; perchance an entrance unperceived by the mob may be effected from the gardens."

They set spurs to their horses, and dashing up a narrow lane, presently gained the rear of the mansion.

Before them was a high stone wall, and through a great wooden gate they could perceive a stately garden, together with the dark buttresses, the square tower, the deep ribbed doorway and tall lancet windows of the beautiful church of the Sancta Crucis beyond, which were all bathed in a blood-red hue by the flaring sheets of flame that ascended from many a burning house in their vicinity.

"There, you see, we can enter the house, as I said, at the rear. The rioters have never thought of surrounding it, for all here is still as the grave," remarked the Earl of Dumbarton.

"But what has hindered the whole household from escaping this way? A free road lay open to them, without let or hindrance," suggested one of the Scots Greys.

"I know not, indeed I cannot guess; but I am certain that I saw *her* face at the window. There is some terrible mystery about the matter. Blow this old lock to atoms with your carbine, Hab Helshender, and let us hasten," exclaimed Sir Andrew, impatiently.

The Scots Grey addressed unslung his carbine, placed the muzzle to the great lock of the old garden gate, and pulled the trigger.

The lock was blown to atoms, the gate rolled open, and dismounting, and securing their horses to the gate, they ran up the garden, across velvet lawns, trim flower beds, and neat gravel pathways, and presently gained the rear of the house.

Three doors were tried in succession, but each was found to be firmly locked. Sir Andrew, however, discovered a half open window on the ground floor, and throwing up the sash he leapt through it.

He was quickly followed by his five friends, but as it was as dark as the grave inside the room which they had just entered, they could not for some minutes find the door leading thereout into the other parts of the house.

While searching for it, they could hear the hootings of the vile rabble in the front street, and the banging of the sledge-hammers against the strong oak portal, which the sharp splintering of wood informed them was being battered into fragments.

Not a moment was to be lost, and Sir Andrew's impatience and anxiety were increased by the shrill shriek of a woman within the house itself. He could almost swear that it was Flora's voice.

An instant later he had discovered the door. It was unlocked, and he tore it open, rushing out into the passage, sword in hand, followed closely by Dumbarton and the four Scots Greys.

They now found themselves in the great hall of the mansion, opposite the main entrance door, which still thrilled and quivered with the strokes of the rioters. Though made of massive oak holes and fissures were already visible in many parts, and great iron nails had been started out of the wood, and lay scattered over the tesselated pavement in every direction.

Sir Andrew saw that its powers of resistance were limited to a very few minutes, when it would fall in with a great crash, and thousands of the mob surge through the arched portal, intent on bloodshed, pillage, and rapine.

"On! on! brave hearts! not an instant is to be lost," he shouted, as he bounded up the wide turnpike stairs three steps at a time, crying as he went, "Flora, Flora, where are you? I am here to save you from the populace. Speak, say where we are to find you."

No voice answered him, the house appeared to be empty.

Corridor after corridor, the royalists traversed, room after room they entered, but no one could they discover.

At last, however, a low indistinct moaning struck their ears.

They came to a closed door, and essayed to open it, but it was locked on the inside.

The moaning sounds they had heard proceeded evidently however from its interior, and so with a hearty kick, Sir Andrew dashed it open, and bounded into the room.

A terrible sight met his gaze.

It was a bed chamber, and on a snowy couch lay the form of her he so fondly loved.

She had evidently retired for the night, but had been aroused by the mob, and had resumed a portion of her clothing. Thus the lower part of her person was draped in a robe of dark velvet, but the upper was only covered by a loose night dress, which being unfastened in front, disclosed her glowing bust from throat to waist.

In one spot her white skin was stained with blood, merely a few specks, but there was a little round hole in the centre of these, just under her right breast, as though made by a stiletto. She was evidently bleeding inwardly, perhaps to the death.

"Who can have done this vile deed?" exclaimed Sir Andrew.

"She has done it herself to save her honour," said the Earl of Dumbarton. "See, she holds the weapon still in her clenched fist."

With some difficulty, her fingers were unclasped, and a small stiletto, sharp as a needle, and with a blade of about an inch in length, fell from her hand.

"By heavens! she still lives. she breathes," cried Sir Andrew at this moment, joyfully.

"Better were she dead, for hark! it is all over with us all. The oak portal has given way, the mob are upon us," rejoined Dumbarton.

It was indeed too true, the great door had fallen in with a tremendous crash, and hundreds of footsteps already resounded on the stairs, mingled with yells, curses, and loud shouts of triumph.

The six royalists gazed at each other in mute consternation.

Dumbarton rushed to the window, and after a momentary survey uttered a cry of joy, for he had made a great discovery.

"Hasten, hasten, there is yet hope! Here is a balcony and a flight of wooden stairs leading down into the garden, at the end of which are our horses. Wrap the lady in a blanket and bring her along quickly," he cried.

He was obeyed with lightning rapidity, but by this time the rioters had gained the upper rooms, and everywhere they could be heard hammering at the panels, and slitting tapestry window hangings in search of concealed royalists.

"They are coming this way, hasten, Sir Andrew. Away with the lady, and Jock Haselton, Walter Tyndale, and myself can hold this narrow doorway against a hundred of these rascals, until you gain the garden, when we will fall back and rejoin you," said a Scots Grey.

There was no time to thank the chivalrous proposer of this desperate feat save by a mute glance, and then, Sir Andrew bearing her shoulders, and a Scots Grey her feet, the still unconscious Flora was carried out of the room on to the balcony, down the steep wooden stairs, and into the garden.

They had scarcely reached it, when the clash of steel was heard in the chamber they had just quitted, mingled with shots, cries, and inhuman yells; but high above all rang the voices of the three gallant Scots Greys who had been left behind to hold the doorway, shouting,—

"Ho for King James! Hey for the Cavaliers! Down with the Whigamores!"

A minute later the horses were reached. Dumbarton and Douglas mounted, and the Scots Grey who accompanied them lifted Flora on the saddle in front of the latter.

"Now let me return and die with my three comrades," said the Scots Grey sadly.

"Nay, man, one extra sword will be of little avail," rejoined the Earl; "I fear me that a hundred would arrive too late to save them."

"I can but do my best, my lord; but if I cannot save them, I may at least be able to avenge one of them. Farewell! in five minutes we will all come back together, or be lying dead in our steel harness side by side."

He was off before either Dumbarton or Douglas could do aught to detain him. They waited some minutes for his reappearance, but neither he or his comrades came; and then, as Flora's wound had begun to bleed, and immediate surgical aid was of vital consequence, they reluctantly abandoned the four Scots Greys to their fate, set spurs to their horses, and, after encountering many perils, at last reached the castle, above whose proud keep still floated the banner of the House of Stuart, and where they were warmly welcomed by the Duke of Gordon, Dundee, and many cavaliers who yet remained true to the fallen dynasty.

## CHAPTER XXVIII.

### THE COUNCIL OF WAR IN EDINBURGH CASTLE.

Come fill up my cup, come fill up my can,
Come saddle my horses and call out my men,
Unhook the west port and let us gang free,
For it's "Hey for the bonnets of Bonnie Dundee."

CARCELY had Sir Andrew Douglas secured comortable quarters within the castle for the terried and exhausted Flora Macclesfield, and atendants to wait on her, than he was summoned o attend a council of war that was about to be eld in the great banqueting hall.

Thither he immediately proceeded, and there e found already assembled the Duke of Gordon, ord Viscount Dundee, the Earl of Dumbarton, he Duke of Perth, the Earl of Belcarris, Sir eorge Mackenzie, and Sir William Wallace, vith a few other nobles and officers, who yet reained true to the falling dynasty.

They were all in battle harness, and the red lare of a hundred torches held aloft in the ands of a hundred athletic highlanders, ranged quidistantly, fifty on each side of the vast apartnent, was reflected from plumed morions, glitering curiasses, huge jackboots, and the gleamng hilts of swords and daggers.

Every cheek was flushed, every brow was tern, the chief actors in the scene spoke little, ut they thought much between their brief peeches. They were evidently bent upon acts, ot words, and some even held their drawn weaons in their hands whilst they conversed, as hough it were unbecoming, whilst the cause hey supported was in such peril, to return them o their scabbards, even for a moment.

And whilst this small band of noble but desperate men discussed their position, and what ast course was to be adopted, the roar of he drunken, howling bloodthirsty mob, who were still desolating the city, rose fitfully to heir ears, and the tall narrow lancet windows n each side of them every now and then flashed redly with the reflection of some new conflagration.

"Well gentlemen," said his Grace of Gordon, at length. "I must confess that my Lord of Dundee is right. The last hope of King James rests with the highland clans; but fifty miles of hostile country have yet to be traversed before the hardy mountaineers of the north can be roused to arms. Now, I cannot spare one of my small garrison to proceed thither, for this is the only fortalice in Great Britain over which the white flag of the house of Stuart yet floats."

"But, your Grace, surely a few men might be spared," urged the Earl of Belcarris. "Well I wot that our walls are strong."

"Aye, but they are also extensive. A thousand men are none too many to hold the place, and I have barely nine hundred in garrison, whilst I hourly expect Sir John Lanier with at least ten thousand troops, and Heaven alone knows how many pieces of cannon, to invest me closely. Again I repeat that I cannot spare a man."

"It is not needed, brave Gordon," said Dundee, dashing the point of his ponderous sword into the oaken floor, in his fiery enthusiasm; "I and my sixty Life Guards have already traversed three hundred miles of hostile country with adverse armies in front, flank, and rear. Another fifty or sixty miles ITY. ... bagatelle to us, and though the legions of hell bar our path, we will cut through them, to the wilds of the pathless north, where, in less than a month, ten thousand claymores shall flash from their scabbards for Dundee and King James. What says your Grace, is my offer accepted?"

"Aye, that is it, Lord Viscount, and with every faith of its being performed successfully. James Grahame of Claverhouse has never yet undertaken what he has not achieved," replied the Duke of Gordon, clasping Dundee's hand.

"Thanks for those words, Gordon; my trumpeter shall sound to boot and saddle at once. We will leave the city under cover of the darkness. Sir Andrew Douglas, of course you are with us?"

"To the death, Viscount," retorted our hero.

"You, my Lord of Dumbarton, will I suppose, remain here?" continued Dundee, turning to that noble.

"Faith, not I! After your risking your own life to save mine at Carlisle, ill would it become one of my name and lineage to suffer thee to depart on this dangerous mission alone. No, I insist in riding in my troop as a simple volunteer."

"I cannot gainsay thee, old friend," answered Dundee, whilst a tear dimmed his eye. Then, turning to our hero he continued, "Douglas, proceed to the Bastion Court, and get our men to horse with all speed; in half an hour we must be on our way."

"Dundee," exclaimed the Duke of Gordon, "whilst King James has one such soldier as you remaining to him, his cause is not utterly lost. Go on your desperate enterprise; you will carry it out, I feel convinced. I will hold this castle till the blood of my last soldier stains its ramparts, and, perhaps, in less than a week, a French fleet will have anchored in the Firth of Forth, and an Irish army have landed on the shores of Cheshire. Then, my lord, it will be your turn to swoop down on the traitor lowlands, like an eagle on its prey, and the King will soon have his own again."

The council was then dismissed, and while the Duke of Gordon and some of his officers went to visit the walls, and see that the sentries were properly posted, Dundee, Dumbarton, and Douglas hastily prepared for their night march northward; the two former, by making a hearty supper; the latter by paying a farewell interview to Flora Macclesfield.

---

## CHAPTER XXIX.

### HEY FOR THE HIGHLANDS!

Dundee, he is mounted, he gangs up the street;
The bells they ring backwards, the drums they are beat;
But the provost, douce man, says "Just e'en let him be,
For the town is well rid of this de'il of Dundee."

IN less than an hour after the scenes recorded in our last chapter, the gallant blare of the trumpet, the stirring brattle of the brass kettledrums, the clang of iron hoofs and jingle of steel scabbards and chain bridles, awaking all the echoes of the great Cathedral, and the hollow arcades of the dark Parliament Square, announced the march northwards of Dundee's Life Guards; those sixty brave gentlemen who, of all his once numerous [illegible] cherished army, now alone remained stanch to the hapless James.

Twelve guns were fired from the ramparts of the castle as a parting salute, when the steel morions and glittering accoutrements of the little body of cavalry were seen ascending the steep hill towards the Netherbow Port, and Dundee's trumpets rang out a shrill and martial response as the troops disappeared under the dark archway, leaving burning, howling, blaspheming Edinburgh behind them.

Then the multitudes, thousands of whom had witnessed the departure of the Life Guards, and had heard the hoarse thunder of the cannon from the castle, fled to Parliament House, and reported to the still assembled Lords of Convention, that "There was a coalition and general insurrection of the adherents of the bloody Claver'se," and thereupon a dreadful panic ensued.

The city drums beat the point of war; the Duke of Hamilton, and other Revolutionists, who had for weeks past been secretly bringing great bands of their vassals into Edinburgh, where they were concealed in cellars and garrets, now rushed to arms.

The members of Convention, confined in their hall, were terrified and put to their wits' end by the uproar.

It is related that Lord Mersington, one of their number, exchanged his senatorial robe and wig "for ane auld wife's mutch and plaid," fled to his lodging, and appeared no more that day.

But their fears were causeless, for Dundee and the devoted cavaliers who accompanied him in his chilvarous, but next to hopeless enterprise, were then passing the woods and morasses of Corstorphine, on their route to the land of the Gaël.

At a hand-gallop they soon flanked the grey rocks and pine-covered summits of those beautiful hills, and a sequestered village lay before them, with the morning smoke curling from its moss-roofed cottages, its broad lake swollen by the melting snows, but calm as a mirror save where the swan and dusky water-ouzel squattered its shining surface; the ancient kirk peeped above a grove of venerable sycamores, and to the south stood the castle of the old hereditary Foresters of Corstorphine.

Avoiding this village, the Life Guards spurred along the edge of the moor that bounded it on the left, and had almost crossed its wide expanse when they perceived at the bottom of a little hollow an overturned carriage surrounded by a crowd of some five hundred people.

It was an elaborately carved and richly gilt and painted vehicle, and four beautifully caparisoned horses were struggling and shrieking on the ground; their legs covered with blood showed that they had been hamstrung.

Two postilions clad in purple and white, with a servant or two in handsome liveries, stood shuddering and terrified prisoners amidst the lawless rabble, and a portion of another form habited in rich vestments could be seen dangling from the branch of a wide spreading oak-tree.

"On—on, loyal cavaliers!" exclaimed Dundee, spurring his horse to a gallop, "some work of hell is being enacted here;" and at a headlong pace the little troop of horse bore down upon the rabble, though the latter outnumbered them by nearly ten to one and were most of them armed with pikes, scythes, or clubs.

## CHAPTER XXX

### SCOTTISH JUSTICE AND SCOTTISH HOSPITALITY.

Down on your knees, you villains in frieze;
A draught to King James, or a swing from those trees;
Blow off this stiff lock, for 'tis useless to knock,
The ladies will pardon the noise and the shock;
From this bright dewy cheek, might I venture to speak,
I could kiss off the tears, though she wept for a week.

With loud cries of "Down with the Whigamores!—down with the Cropheads! no quarter! slay, slay," the Life Guards charged the unkempt, unshaven mob, who scattered before them like chaff before the flail of the thresher.

"Murder and sacrilege! murder and sacrilege! a priest of God has been hung in the very vestments of his office by these rascals," thundered the voice of Dundee. "Hack, hew, and spare not."

With every word his great black charger reared and plunged, and trampled a blaspheming reviling wretch under its iron hoofs, while the bright keen blade of its rider swept around —right, left, cut, thrust, like a flash of blue lightning—cleaving heads, arms, and shoulders, or plunging deep into broad chests or brawny throats, the next instant to be drawn blood red and dropping gouts of gore upon the good steed's sable coat.

In a minute that bloodthirsty mob of five hundred armed men were flying terror-stricken, before Dundee's sixty troopers, who pursued them for a mile, cutting them down like so many unresisting sheep.

Then they returned with about a dozen pale quivering prisoners, who knew well enough to what fate they were destined.

The dangling body of the churchman had long since been cut down, but life was previously extinct.

He had been hung with a strong leathern sash, and his face and body bore tokens of previous buffettings and ill-usage at the hands of his assailants.

"By the mass, 'tis the good canon of the church of Sancta Crucis," exclaimed Dundee, gazing sadly and sternly at the pale, calm, rigid features of the dead priest. "Tell me, ye infernal villains, why did ye this evil deed?"

He had turned fiercely upon the dozen prisoners to ask the question; and one of them, a tall, lank, sallow-faced Puritan, rejoined, in a harsh, nasal twang—

"That the curse that fell upon Jeroboam should fall upon him in turn. He was a priest of Baal, and we have but sent him howling to his false gods that the Scripture might be fulfilled which saith—"

"Hold thy impious blasphemy, wretch. On thy carcass, foul kite, will I avenge this slaughter of the Lord's anointed!" cried Sir Andrew Douglas, as, with one blow of his sword, he cleft the mad enthusiast from skull to collarbone.

A deep groan escaped from the other prisoners, upon each of whose countenances in turn the dark eagle glance of Dundee was momentarily bent.

Suddenly he started and beckoned one of their number to approach him. The man obeyed, and stood before the loyalist cavalier, with his arms crossed upon his chest but his eyes bent on the ground.

"Randolf Lisle, my cousin and boyhood's playmate, how came you amongst this infamous rabble?" asked Dundee, gravely.

"Because their cause is mine, their faith is mine, and their feelings are mine, James Grahame," was the calm reply.

"And do you expect me to spare you, because you are of my own kith and kin? If so, your hope is a vain one. Many men have accused Dundee of harshness and cruelty, not one of injustice. Were you my own brother, you would share the fate of the other prisoners. What hast thou to urge that I should not hang thee from a branch of this very tree?"

"That I am of gentle blood," answered Randolf Lisle, boldly, "a lesser baron of coat armour by twelve descents. I am ready to die, but do not sentence me to the death of a dog."

"I grant thee the boon," replied Dundee; "thou shalt die by the hand of one who loves thee as a brother, by the hand of a near kinsman, aye and what is better, thou shalt have the honour of perishing by the hand of the first cavalier in Scotland. Place thy arms behind thy back—so. Art thou ready?"

"I am ready, Grahame—God grant that you may never stand in the same position that I do now, give fire!" exclaimed Randolf Lisle, as he obeyed Dundee's directions.

"God grant that I may never deserve to!" was the proud reply. "Now then, may Heaven receive thy soul!" and with the last word yet on his lips, Dundee plucked a pistol from his belt, and almost without taking aim, hastly fired.

The bullet passed through his cousin's brain and sank deep into the trunk of the old oak tree immediately in his rear.

The body sank prostrate on the turf, quivered for a moment, and then lay still and stiffening, with upturned eyes and relaxed jaws.

"Now, is there any other amongst ye deserving of death at my hands? for what I have granted to a kinsman, I will not refuse to a stranger," said Dundee, turning towards the other prisoners.

"I am a Writer to the Signet, in the good city of Edinburgh, and therefore a gentleman by Act of Parliament," said one of them; "as such, I would beg you to shoot me, or rather to let me off altogether, as I am a very harmless person, and only here in the character of a looker-on."

## CHAPTER XXXI.

### THE WAY THE LIFE GUARDS LEVIED BLACK MAIL.

Storm through the gate, batter the plate,  
Cram the red crucible into the grate,  
Saddle-bags fill, Bob, Jenkin, and Will,  
And spice the staved wine that runs out like a rill.  
That maiden shall ride all day long at my side,  
Those ribbons are fitting a cavalier's bride.

"A VERY harmless person would not countenance such an atrocity by his presence, and thou art an oppressor of the poor, the fatherless, and the unfortunate, I'll be bound, like others of thy race. No, the noose is plenty good enough for thee," was Dundee's sneering retort.

Then turning to his troopers he exclaimed—"Twelve of you dismount and convert your bridles into halters. We must string up these fellows with all speed, and resume our march again."

He was promptly obeyed. In less than five minutes the eleven remaining prisoners were swinging from the same stout branch of the old oak whereon they had hung the canon of Sancta Crucis. Within ten they were all cut down again, and their extemporary halters reconverted to their accustomed uses. Then Dundee, turning to the frightened servants of the dead canon, said—

"You had better get a litter and convey your master's body to Edinburgh. Some of my troopers should form an escort befitting the dignity of the deceased, but we ride on the King's service, and I cannot spare a man," said Dundee, regretfully.

"Gentlemen of the Scottish Guard, to horse! Sling carbines, forward—trot!" he exclaimed the next moment, turning to his troopers, and away they rode in silence, leaving the cold remains of the dead lying on the grassy sward."

"What mansion is that, with its vanes and turrets showing above the gorse yonder?" asked Dundee of Sir Andrew Douglas, after another hour's brisk ride.

"'Tis a country chateau of the Duke of Hamilton, my lord."

"What? does it belong to that canting psalm-singing traitor, that human weathercock, who turns with the wind, whichever way it may list to blow? By heavens, we will visit it, and by all the devils, if his Grace returned there this morning, after the council broke up, I will hang him from his own roof-tree, peer of Scotland though he be."

"A right good resolve, Viscount, for this crafty Duke's name heads the address of welcome sent by the turncoat council to Dutch William. Besides, he or his steward must pay us riding-money for the King's service. We have good right to insist on this, and, by the saints, I vote that we make him shell out handsomely."

So replied the Earl of Dumbarton; but Dundee merely nodded a retort, and then gave the order to increase the pace from a trot to a gallop, into which the little troop immediately broke.

Riding in single file along the muddy and rough bridle path that led across a kind of morass they at last reached the gate of an outflanking tower, for like most country houses in that unsettled time, the country seat of the Duke of Hamilton was half mansion half fortalice.

They encircled the barbican wall, which was built partly on fragments of low rock, without being able to find an entrance, the great gate being securely fastened, whilst the stillness of the place seemed to imply that it was uninhabited.

"Trumpeter, sound a parley," cried Dundee, impatiently.

The shrill blare awoke the echoes of hill and dale, but it elicited no response from within the walls.

"Open your gates, in the King's name, or we will force our way in," shouted Dundee, in a voice of thunder.

Still all was silent as the grave.

"Would that we had a petard. This gate is

as strong as an iron wall," observed the Earl of Dumbarton.

"Unsling your carbines, gentlemen," shouted Dundee; "a volley at the lock will soon settle it. Give fire."

Twenty or thirty carbines poured a concentrated volley upon the lock; it was torn to fragments, and then the gates were thrown open, and the troopers spurred through into a large court-yard.

At this moment a musket flashed through a loophole in the outer wall, and a bullet struck Dundee's cuirass, glancing off and falling harmlessly to the ground.

One of the troopers sprang from the saddle, and picked it up, exclaiming with a laugh, "They take you for the foul fiend, sure enough, my lord, the ball is of silver."

"I will make the superstitious idiot who fired it swallow it as a pill, if I can catch him; but let us force our way in, or he may try his hand again, with better success," replied the Viscount.

In a minute the Life Guards were close under the walls, the outer windows of which were all barred, and far from the ground.

An iron gate closed the inner portal or archway, and beyond it the cavaliers could see ten or twelve sinister-looking ruffians, clad in a sort of livery, and armed with black cross-belts, musquetoons, or sweyne-feathers.

"Rascals," exclaimed Dundee, "open the barrier and give us instant admission, or it may fare the worse with your lord, to whom we must speak, and without delay."

An aged porter, who fairly trembled with fear, slowly undid the bolts and chains, imploring that his life might be spared.

"Spared, dotard, of what use is your life to us?" said Sir Andrew, with a laugh.

"Now, which of ye dared to fire at James Grahame, of Claverhouse, and by whose order?" demanded Dundee, laying his hand on his sword-hilt, and surveying the dozen fierce-looking servitors with a stern haughty glance.

"My lord, not one of us levelled musquetoon or petronel at you; the deed was none of ours," said one of them, doffing his plumed cap.

"Who was it, then? faith you must all know well enough who fired the shot. Will ye answer, or shall my troopers force the truth out of some of you at the sword's point?" demanded Dundee.

"Well, then, my lord, it was the Duke himself who has only just returned from Edinburgh, and who aimed at you from the little lancet window in the turret yonder. He has this instant passed back into the house, with the muzzle of his piece still smoking," answered one.

"By heaven, then, the courtesy shall cost him dear, or I am not — but bah! let us perform, not threaten. Lead on to your lord's presence, worthy porter," said Dundee.

Ascending a staircase of stone, the stained-glass windows of which were illumined by the bright flush of the early morning sun, the cavaliers found themselve in an ancient hall, decorated in a quaint style of architecture. Lighted by four large windows, which overlooked heath and forest, its roof was arched with stone, rudely carved, supported by twelve massive pillars, whose timeworn, mutilated forms bespoke their great antiquity. The walls were adorned with sylvan trophies and sombre paintings, from which grim faces of old Scottish knights and older saints looked forth, whilst numerous weapons of various dates still further adorned the lofty walls.

"'Tis long since I stood in such a noble old hall as this," said Dundee, throwing himself into a gilt fauteuil, "pity it should belong to a traitor."

"Traitor indeed, and of the blackest dye. Ha! what have we here?" and as he spoke the Earl of Dumbarton snatched from a marble slab the long envelope of some official communication which had just caught his eye.

It was addressed to "His Grace the Duke of Hamilton, Lord High Chancellor of Scotland, Parliament House, Edinburgh," and endorsed in the corner "Schomberg, Général de Division."

Tearing it open, Dumbarton uttered an exclamation of angry surprise, and exclaimed fiercely, "'Tis a document offering a reward of a thousand pounds to Scots, for your body, dead or alive, my lord of Dundee, and half that amount for mine; verily, these Dutch hounds seem disposed to set a higher value upon our deeds than we rate them at ourselves."

"Hand it here, Dumbarton. Ha, it is sealed with the Royal Arms of England, and—but, behold, here comes our host," said Dundee, rising from his seat, and thrusting the letter into his long glove.

As he spoke there entered the hall a tall man of powerful frame and most forbidding aspect, attired in the full dress of the old school, his black Ramilies wig flowing over his shoulders, his shirt ruffled at the wrists and bosom, a wide skirted coat and blue satin knee breeches with buckles; but the courtly air which this costume was calculated to impart to the wearer rather heightened than diminished the repulsive appearance of this traitor lord.

He was past the meridian of life, and his countenance was rendered yet more forbidding by a hideous cicatrix, the gash of a sword cut received at the battle of Bothwell Brig, which grew purple and black by turns.

He was followed by half a dozen armed servitors, and when within some dozon yards of the royal cavaliers he halted, and bowing to them with frigid hauteur, exclaimed—

"My lords Dundee and Dumbarton, in what character do ye thus force yourselves upon my privity, unwelcomed and uninvited?"

"As officers in the service of his Britannic Majesty King James II. Our purpose is to levy contributions, at the sword's point if necessary, for the maintenance of his cause," answered Dundee.

"And to force you, vile traitor, to apologise on your knees for firing upon us, like an Italian bravo, from behind your stone walls," added Dumbarton.

"By the ancient laws of Scotland, I may defend my residence against all men, and as for treason, I care little whether James or William is ruler of these realms, so that I am no loser by the change of dynasty," retorted Hamilton.

"These paltry excuses will not serve your turn," sneered Dumbarton.

"Then I've a sword by my side that will, and if Lord Viscount Dundee, against whom I especially aimed the bullet, wishes to avenge the

THE BLADES OF THE TWO SWORDSMEN CLASHED TOGETHER.

shot, why, I am at his service," answered the Duke.

"I thank you for the offer, but recollect that as a cavalier of birth and honour, I would scorn to put my life in the scale with a traitor's," was the haughty retort of the Viscount.

"How know ye that I am a traitor?" exclaimed Hamilton, starting.

Dundee plucked from his gauntlet, and held before his eyes, the precious document that Dumbarton had discovered, and the Duke changed colour beneath the cold sarcrastic smile of the royalist cavalier.

"I had resolved to make thee swallow thy silver bullet and thereafter to force this letter down thy throat with my dagger point, yet if one of my troop will condescend to give thee a soldier's death, I will not gainsay him. Which of you will cross blades with His Grace of Hamilton?" continued Dundee, turning to his troopers.

"I claim that privilege, Lord Viscount," said Sir Andrew Douglas, stepping forward and drawing his trenchant blade.

"What indignity is this that you would put on me," exclaimed Hamilton, hoarsely. "Is a peer of Scotland to be made cross blades with a nameless trooper, a beardless boy?"

"My troopers are all gentlemen of coat armour, and many of them lairds or lesser barons. He who has offered to fight thee is their captain, a scion of the great house of Douglas, and as such thy equal in every way, even wert thou a loyal peer instead of a false and perjured one," answered Dundee, calmly. "Wilt accept death at his hands?"

"Aye, if he can bestow it, but if I slay him I shall expect thee and thy men to withdraw and leave my poor house in peace. Is that a compact?" asked Hamilton, drawing his sword in turn.

"If thou defeatest Sir Andrew, we will, after a good meal on the best thy larder and cellar affords, and on receipt of a thousand crowns or their equivalent towards the King's cause, leave thy house in peace," answered Viscount Dundee.

"These are harsh terms, my lord."

"In my opinion they are mild ones; anyhow, they are better than you deserve. Now to the combat at once, for we have little time to waste."

"I am loth to cross swords with your Grace, for I am scaled like an armadillo, whereas you wear no defensive armour; the fight would scarcely be a fair one," interposed our hero, at this juncture.

"You mistake, good youth, you will find me better armed than you imagine," answered Hamilton, with a diabolical leer, "therefore have at thee," and as he spoke the two blades crashed together.

Each swordsman remained a moment with his head drawn back, the right leg thrown forward, and his eyes glaring on his antagonist, while steel was heavily pressed against steel.

Sir Andrew was ten years younger than his adversary, whom he presently discovered to be a skilled swordsman. He accordingly fenced with caution, but in endeavouring to pass his point and close, received a slight wound on the hand, which kindled him into a terrible fury.

But Hamilton parried all his cuts and thrusts with admirable coolness, until perceiving that the royalist's impetuosity bagan to flag, he pressed him hard in turn, the ferocity that sparkled in his eyes and blanched his nether lip revealing the bitterness of his intention.

At last, however, Sir Andrew passed his antagonist's guard, and inflicted a cut on his left shoulder, which would have shred off his arm.

But to his surprise, his swordblade rang as though it had met with resisting steel, and half turned in his hand.

The Duke laughed a haughty defiance.

"You will have it then, come on, plated varlet, and look well to guard and parry, for I am the best swordsman north of the Clyde, and wear an inner coat of impenetrable Spanish mail," he cried.

Sir Andrew's cuirass rang with a slash from his assailant, who fell furiously to work, lunging like a madman, and exclaiming every time the fire sparkled from their clanging blades—

"Bravo! excellent! come on again, Mr. Malapert, and I will teach thee to measure swords with a Scottish peer. Cock's nails, but thou art no tyro in the art of fencing. D—— me, what a thrust! but I was equal to the parry, was I not? Now, may the devil seize thee, how came that about?"

The Life Guardsman's sword by one lucky parry had broken the Duke's sword off at the hilt, the next instant he had struck him down on the oaken floor, with his sword hand under him.

Rage had deprived Sir Andrew of all government over himself; in an instant his knee was on the Duke's breast, and his weapon shortened in his hand, with the intention of running him through the heart, for the guardsman's blood was now up, and all the devil was stirred within him.

He felt the deep chest of his powerful adversary heaving beneath him with suppressed passion and fury, and at last he gasped forth—

"Beware thee, villain. I am a Lord of the Privy Council. If you dare to slay me bitterly shall I be avenged."

"Were you King William himself, I would run you through the heart, for applying such an epithet to a cadet of the House of Douglas," was the angry retort. "Die, traitor, regicide, hound that thou art!"

The sword was raised, but ere it could fall, the hand that wielded it was seized by a convulsive clutch, and an arm, rounded as that of a statue, white as snow, and bare from wrist to shoulder, interposed between him and his victim.

"Spare him! O for God's sake, spare him, he is my father!"

Such was the appeal of a beautiful young girl, who, scantily clad in but one garment of fine linen, had leapt from her couch, and rushed into the presence of the fierce soldiery, intent only upon saving her parent.

Her long tresses, black as the raven's plumage, flowed around her divine form, contrasting charmingly with her pale, but intellectual face and deep grey eyes, and still more so, with her creamy shoulders, and exquisitely lovely back, chest, and bosoms, which were all revealed by her disordered and scanty attire.

Sir Andrew was rendered powerless by this sudden apparition.

She had clutched his sword blade, and in her agony of apprehension, was grasping it so tightly that drops of blood were falling from her lacerated palm upon her snowy linen, and equally white skin, whilst kneeling by her father's side, she leant over, so as to protect his body with her own.

"Lady for God sake relax your hold on my weapon, or your hand will be cut to the bone," gasped Sir Andrew, at length.

"Spare my father's life, then?" she urged.

"Nay, he may live for all that I care to the contrary, though his life is justly forfeited for his treason. You must proffer your request to Vicount Dundee yonder, for your father's fate is in his hands, not mine," answered Sir Andrew, in a kindly tone.

Then the fair petitioner raised her lovely eyes, in mute appeal, to the first cavalier in Scotland; her lips parted, her fair broad chest and rounded bosoms throbbing wildly with doubt, hope, and anxiety, yet she could not utter a word.

"Lady, I cannot resist your silent prayer. Your father is free. Retire to your room; I pledge you my word that he shall be spared," said the Viscount, and, advancing towards her, he threw his vast red cloak around her half-naked body, and begged of her to return to her chamber.

She kissed his hand, with a look of deep gratitude, then pressed her lips to her father's cold brow, and darted out of the grim banqueting hall, like the vision of light and beauty that she was.

. . . . . . . .

Meanwhile the unscrupulous cavaliers were ranging over the entire household, breaking open every press, cabinet, and panel, with the butts and balls of their carbines in search of wine vivres, or anything else that suited their fancies, or was of service to *the* cause.

A full larder was happily discovered, and its contents furnished an ample breakfast even for their sixty hungry stomachs.

Several whole cheeses, a cask of ale, and a thirty gallon runlet or two of canary were trundled into the hall as supplemental cheer.

A hearty repast, with the usual military accompaniments of mirth and laughter, was enjoyed by the devil-may-care troopers, whose appetites a night in their saddles and a ride in the keen air of a winter's morning had sufficiently whetted.

Then they crowded round the great wood fire that was roaring in the vast archway, which spanned one side of the apartment, joked and toyed with the half-pleased and half-frightened maids, and compelled the indignant housekeeper to join them in the chorus of the famous camp song, with which they made the oak rafters ring,—

"Dumbarton's drums beat bonnie, O!"

to the great envy of the luckless male servitors of the Duke of Hamilton, all of whom they had imprisoned in the barbican tower, through whose narrow windows they could witness all the hilarity and good cheer which they were debarred from joining in or partaking of.

Then another violent and unscrupulous search was made for concealed valuables.

Every curtain, bed, and panel was pierced by swords and daggers.

Every press, cupboard, and bunker, the turrets, and all the innumerable nooks and corners of the old house searched, every lockfast place being blown open by carbine balls, and their contents scattered promiscuously around.

Pale and dignified, with his arms folded on his chest, and his broken sword lying at his feet, the Duke of Hamilton stood on the dais of his vast banqueting hall, listening to the uproar that rang through all the stone vaults, wainscoted chambers, and long corridors of his mansion, and regarding Dundee, Douglas, Dumbarton, who were conversing at the lower end of the hall, with glances of pride and hostility.

His daughter, now fully dressed as became her rank, stood by his side, endeavouring to console him, though apparently with very little effect, for he answered her not save by impatient gestures.

A large quantity of plate was found, but very little money. Intent upon raising the thousand crowns for the King's cause, Dundee ordered that the whole of this should be broken up and cast into a crucible, in order to be melted down for more convenient carriage.

The fire in the great chimney of the servants' hall was therefore replenished, the gold and silver plate, all covered with the emblazoned arms of the House of Hamilton, broken up with axes and hammers, a vast crucible thrust into the red flames, and the fractured pieces thrown in pell mell.

One trooper, with a rusty pike, stirred round the seething, hissing mass, while others kept up the fierce heat by fanning the flames, or else piling on fresh fuel.

All this while, some of the troopers were filing their saddle-bags with miscellaneous valuables, and others were spicing and quaffing huge goblets of wine, that flowed freely from the staved casks, to the health of King James and the destruction of his enemies; while a half-dozen or so were making love to the maids, aud that in no very timid or gentle way either.

Suddenly, however, the quick ruffle of drums, the blare of trumpets, and the rattle of arms without, recalled every one to his sober senses, and the next instant one of the sentries rushed into the hall, exclaiming,—

"The place is surrounded by at least a thousand horse, it is a regiment of Dutch dragoons. Escape is impossible!"

---

## CHAPTER XXXII.

### STANDING A SIEGE.

Now loop me this scarf round the broken pike staff,
'Twill do for a flag though the cropheads may laugh;
Who was it blew? Give a halloo,
And hang out the pennon of crimson and blue.
A volley of shot is welcoming hot—
It cannot be troop of the murdering Scot.

"In the foul fiend's name, who stood as sentinel at the southern gate?" cried Dundee angrily, as he strode in amongst the troopers.

"It was I, my lord," answered a young guardsman, hesitatingly.

"Then see that you amply retrieve your blindness by some conspicuous act of valour in the contest that is about to ensue, or you will be either hung or shot directly it is over," said the Viscount sternly. "Now, my men, let us to work with all speed."

In five minutes the little party were thoroughly prepared to defend the place to the last gasp. Every door, window, and aperture were strongly barred and barricaded; piles of furniture, statues, cushions, ottomans, massive tomes from the library, and everything suitable, were pressed into the service, forming barriers in the passages and on staircases in case of an assault.

Then then the Life Guardsmen were so posted that the different approaches to the house were completely enfiladed, whilst that by the Bastion Court would be exposed to a deadly cross-fire from three windows. Sir Andrew Douglas commanded one wing of the mansion, the Earl of Dumbarton the other, while Dundee in person occupied the centre.

In this order they awaited the attack—sixty to a thousand.

By this time the Dutch Dragoons were close under the walls, looking a superb body of heavy cavalry, in their yellow coats and black unpolished helmets, cuirasses, and backplates. They were mounted on fine bay chargers, and moved with great precision.

Presently their commanding officer raised a tremendous speaking trumpet to his lips, and bellowed through it,—

"Whosesoever house this may be, there are hidden therein three vile traitors, called respectively the Earl of Dumbarton, Viscount Dundee, and Sir Andrew Douglas, of that ilk. Unless these same, with sixty of their followers, are delivered into our hands, we shall assault the place, and perchance, in the prosecution of our duty, even proceed to the burning of it down."

"Trumpeter, sound the alert!" cried Dundee, to a boy trooper at his side; and the sharp blast of his brass instrument awoke every echo of the great mansion.

There was a clatter of accoutrements, a brief jingle of sword blades being loosened in their scabbards, and ramrods sending home their charges, and all became silent as the grave.

Then Dundee, in all his glittering accoutrements of scarlet and gold, stepped out upon the raised terrace outside the great banquet hall, and in his clear bell-like voice, that required no speaking-trumpet to make it audible, answered the captain of Dragoons thus:—

"This is the country residence of his Grace the Duke of Hamilton, but it is now held in the name of King James, by me, Viscount Dundee, who, with my loyal sixty cavaliers, will defend it while we have a drop of blood left in our veins, against every Dutchman in the Stadtholder's armies."

Thereupon the colonel of the Dutch regiment, not condescending to reply to this speech, wheeled his horse round, and galloping away, rejoined his other officers.

The Dutch troopers were then observed to dismount, and having piquetted their horses to divide into two bodies—one to assault the house in front, the other in flank. Their heavy tramp and the clink of their long spurs were plainly audible as they drew near.

As the outer defence of the mansion, the great gate in the barbican wall, had been forced by the Life Guardsmen themselves to effect an entry, it of course now offered no obstruction to their foes, but six iron wickets leading to the lawn and garden formed the defenders' first barrier against the enemy, who had advanced within a few yards of it before Dundee ordered his trumpeter to sound again.

At the first note, a volley which the assailants had little expected was poured upon them, throwing them into the utmost confusion, and driving them back with slaughter.

They rallied, however, and replied with promptitude, and one of his men fell dead at Dundee's side.

"Keep up your hearts, my Trojans!" he shouted while brandishing his sabre, and hurrying from post to post to animate their resistance. "Level low, and fire where they are thickest."

Then for a few minutes the roar of the carbines stirred all the echoes of the vast resounding building, whose long corridors, lofty saloons, and domed ceilings gave back the reports with redoubled force. Every place was filled with smoke within and without; every window and aperture was streaked with fire bristling with gleaming steel, and swarming with dark fierce faces.

The fire of the besieged made frightful havoc amongst the Dragoons, though it did not dispel their courage in the least, and their yells of rage and defiance were like those of wild beasts or savages.

Onwards they again and again rushed to batter down and break through one of the main doors of the mansion, but each time they were repulsed, leaving the terrace walk or the court of the quadrangle strewed with killed and wounded.

"Gluck! gluck! Vivat Wilhelm," cried a terrible voice at this juncture. It was that of the Dutch colonel bellowing through his trumpet as he came on heading a fifth attack in person.

A strong party had by this time made a lodgement under the portico, and assailed the grand entrance with crowbars and levers that they had found in various outhouses.

The colonnade protected them from the fire of the Life Guardsmen, and the massive framework of the door was fast yielding to the blows from the pickaxes and hammers which they had also discovered on the premises.

At last a tremendous shout announced that an aperture was made, upon which the barricades within the vestibule itself were hastily strengthened and lined by a double rank of troopers under Sir Andrew Douglas.

The fire of the besiegers had already struck five men from Dundee's little muster roll, and his anxiety for the ultimate fate of the fray increased painfully with the wounds and deaths around him.

The whole terrace on the land side was lined with marksmen, who knelt behind the stone balusters and fired between them with excellent precision at the large upper windows, through which the scarlet uniforms and gay trappings of the Life Guards were at intervals plainly visible as one or other sprang up to discharge his piece.

Dundee dreaded the continuation of this deadly fire more than a close assault; and to increase his anxiety, Sir Andrew Douglas presently hallooed out that their ammunition was nearly spent.

"All is lost, then," exclaimed Dumbarton, in wild despair.

"All is never lost," answered Dundee, half angrily. "We must sally forth, and trust to our good swords, and our horses' speed."

"Impossible! to reach the stables we have to cross the great court; every man of us would be shot down ere we were in the saddle," answered Sir Andrew Douglas, gnawing his lip with rage.

"Nay, there is another way to the stables, which I have discovered, direct from the main building. The horses must be led into the great banqueting hall. On one side its three windows reach to the ground, and through those windows we must charge, disdaining alike glass and sashes: 'tis our only way of escape, gentlemen," said Dundee.

But his strange proposition was received by his reckless, devil-may-care troopers with yells of delight. "Out with the horses! but quickly, or 'twill be too late," was the general cry, and five minutes later forty-five brave steeds dinted the oaken floor of the grand old hall, as they pawed it in eager impatience to be gone.

Then the Life Guardsmen hastily relinquished their posts of defence, and rushed to the hall.

In an instant they were in the saddle, and only awaited their great leader's command to charge through the three windows, upon the Dutch soldiers outside.

At length Dundee gave the word, and not an instant too soon, for the immense hall door fell in, just as he uttered the command.

There was a shivering of glass and wood as the Life Guards dashed at the window, and burst through them on to the broad terrace walk without, like three solid wedges of steel.

A simultaneous yell of anger, surprise, and dismay broke from the Dutch Dragoons, and was answered by a shout of reckless defiance from the Life Guards, who, driving their spurs rowel deep into their fleet horses, compelled them to clear the high balustraded terrace at a flying leap.

Meanwhile, the long sword of Dundee flashed in the sunlight, a good three lengths in front of any of his troop, as he slashed right and left, crying—"Hey for King James! Ho for the cavaliers! King and High Kirk for ever!"

Thus did the first cavalier of Scotland cut a passage through the phlegmatic mass of Germans, escaping bullet and steel, as though he really possessed the charmed life that the country people gave him credit for, and behind him thundered his forty-four surviving troopers, like a living avalanche of men and horses.

They cut and slashed away through the Dutch ranks, but their retreat is now known to the Dragoons who invest the other side of the mansion; trumpets are sounding to horse, presently they will have eight hundred well-mounted horsemen thundering on their track! Can they escape such fearful odds?

## CHAPTER XXXIII.

A CHASE.—THE REFUGE IN KINROSS CHURCH.

Fire the old mill on the brow of the hill;
Break down the plank that runs over the rill;
Bar the town gate—if the burghers debate,
Shoot some to death—for the villains must wait.
Rip up the lead from the roofing o'erhead,
And melt it for bullets, or we shall be sped.

AWAY at the top of their speed dash the Scottish Life Guards, with an irregular line of Dutch Dragoons in their rear, spurring on pell mell in pursuit.

Every minute the latter body increases, however, in number and compactness, until the wounded and the dead alone lay around and within the grim old country mansion of the Duke of Hamilton.

Over the broad common at a spanking gallop, up the steep slopes of Brutisfield, and slantingly across the yellow gorse-clad undulations of Scarrigdell, and yet the Dutch Dragoons held perseveringly on their track, not gaining ground evidently, but just as certainly not losing an inch of way; and now the cavaliers' horses, subjected as they had been to overwork and irregular feed for many weeks, began to show symptoms of distress that were not to be mistaken.

"By Heaven, my lord of Dundee, many of our steeds I observe flagging, and they are nearly all in a lather of sweat, whereas the chargers of yonder infernal Dragoons have scarcely a hair turned," exclaimed Sir Andrew Douglas at length.

"Aye, we shall be worsted in this race, our horses are knocked to pieces, they will be dropping one by one within an hour as they gallop on," echoed the Earl of Dumbarton, with an oath.

"I know it," answered Dundee; "but there is a river hereabouts, and a fragile bridge crossing it that will only give passage to two horsemen abreast. If we can find it, get the other side, and smash up the frail structure in our rear, we may yet escape these bloodhounds."

"Ah! and there is the river and the bridge, too, as I live, down the hollow yonder, scarcely a quarter of a mile distant, shouted Sir Andrew, waving his sword above his head in fierce glee.

Down the slope they swept like an avalanche, then reined in and gingerly, two at a time, crossed the trembling ricketty wooden bridge.

Dundee was the last to cross, and scarcely had his good steed touched *terra firma* on the opposite side when the foremost of the Dutch Dragoons topped the ridge in their rear, and the royalists could hear their cries of anger and dismay at the discovery that their prey might after all elude them.

"Now then, my men, dismount, and set to work with carbine and sabre. We have but five minutes to destroy the bridge in," cried Dundee.

Quickly was he obeyed; the timbers were but united together by ropes and such other weak fastenings. In less time than it has taken us to describe the incident, planks, beams, and uprights fell crashing into the boiling stream.

"My lord, there is a ford not a hundred yards up, dangerous I allow, but practicable; the landing place this side is right under the old mill yonder," cried Douglas, who had ridden a few furlongs up and down the river to inspect its banks.

"Take three men and fire it then, 'twill flare up in a minute, and no horse will cross the stream directly in the face of the conflagration. O, thank you, for the discovery, 'tis an important one," said Dundee, calmly.

The command was immediately acted upon, and by the time the Dutch Dragoons had reached the opposite bank of the river, which was here about a hundred yards wide, every vestige of the bridge had been swept away, while the tarred sides of the old mill were wrapt in one broad sheet of flame, rendering the passage by the ford impossible.

They levelled their carbines, however, and with their invariable war cry of "Gluck! gluck! Vivat Wilhelm!" treated the cavaliers to a rattling fusilade, which emptied two or three saddles and made many a dint on helm and corslet in addition.

"To horse! we have done all that we can do. To horse, and away!" cried Dundee, to those troopers who had not yet had time to mount, and returning the Dutch fire with one hasty volley, they dashed up the slope, and were soon out of range of their opponents.

On, and still on, for another half dozen miles, and the roofs and church spires of a town appeared before them.

"What place is that yonder?" asked Dundee of Sir Andrew Douglas, whom he knew to be a native of those parts.

"Kinross, a town of seven hundred inhabitants, but walled and fortified as though 'twere a city," answered our hero, with difficulty holding up now his staggering and reeling charger.

"Well, then, we must enter it, and requisition the townsfolk for food, money, and fresh nags; particularly the latter, for ours will not hold on for a mile further," answered the Viscount.

In a few minutes the wall that encircled the little town was gained. One of the gates stood invitingly open. No sentinels were on duty, and the cavaliers rode into the street without challenge or question.

"Close that gate and two of you stand sentry thereat. We have fully half an hour's work before us here, and the Dutch Dragoons may, by some chance, come up before it is well over," said Dundee.

He was immediately obeyed, and then with the rest of his troops he rode to the old market-house, and by blast of trumpet and ruffle of drum proclaimed King James at the Burgh cross.

The mayor was then summoned to the spot and ordered to provide a cold collation for forty-five troopers in a quarter of an hour, and within the half hour to have forty-five sound staunch fleet horses piquetted in the market square, and a hundred silver crowns ready to be paid down, all for the King's service.

But by this time the whole population of the place, the males nearly all of them armed, though many in a very barbarous fashion, had repaired to the spot, and the mayor began to think it absurd that some three hundred resolute men should *nolens volens* have to obey the commands of a handful of troopers.

After, therefore, glancing twice or thrice around him, and feeling sure that he should meet with ample support in the course he was about to adopt, he flatly refused to comply with Dundee's commands.

"That is as you choose, master mayor, but I can assure you that forty-five of your townsmen's lives will be forfeited, if horses and dinners are not forthcoming in the time I have named; and even if you procure the horses, for every worthless animal amongst them, and I am a pretty good judge of horseflesh, one man's life will pay the forfeit, yours of course being the first taken," answered Dundee, sternly.

"And what graceless loon of a trooper are ye that speak to the Mayor of Kinross in this style?" asked that functionary, indignantly.

"James Grahame, of Claverhouse, Lord Viscount Dundee, very much at your service," replied the noble, with an ironical bow.

"God sain us, 'tis the bluidy Claver'se, sure enow," was the general cry, as Dundee threw up the visor of his helmet and glared defiantly around.

## CHAPTER XXXIV.

### A CHASE.—THE REFUGE IN KINROSS CHURCH.

Fire the old mill on the brow of the hill;
Break down the plank that runs over the rill;
Bar the town gate—if the burghers debate,
Shoot some to death—for the villains must wait.
Rip up the lead from the roofing o'erhead,
And melt it for bullets, or we shall be sped.

SOME fell on their knees and begged and besought for mercy, and amongst them was the hitherto valiant mayor, but a few of the populace quailed not, and presently a shot was fired and striking the Viscount's morion glanced off, and embedded itself in a wall in his rear.

Instantly, however, the perpetrator of the outrage was discovered, and shot down by one of the Guardsmen. A riot would then doubtless have ensued had not Dundee shouted in a voice of thunder—

"Secure a dozen of the miscreants, and shoot them as a warning to the rest. Shall the Scottish Life Guards of King James submit to the insults of a base-born rabble?"

Then the troopers charged the mob, riding them down like a field of poppies, and having taken the requisite number of prisoners by grappling them by collar or belt, and throwing them across their holster flaps by mere strength of arm, they ranged them with their faces to the neighbouring wall, and shot them down without mercy.

"Now, men of Kinross, are you willing to obey my behests? Mayor, you will be amongst the next batch of condemned. Five minutes have already been lost. By Heaven, if my commands are not complied with, I will leave of your town but a heap of ashes!"

Mayor, aldermen, and townsmen were now civil enough, and within a very few minutes a meal was laid for the hungry troopers that would have done credit to the King's kitchen.

They partook of it great haste, however, and ere it was fully ended, a long line of horses were led up for the cavaliers to choose from, for so awed were the townsfolk by Dundee's acts and threats, that rather than incur the suspicion of keeping back their best nags for their own use, they drove up for his approval every animal that was to be found within the walls.

Selection was speedily made; rugs, saddles, holsters, chain-bridles, and other military accoutrements, were transferred from the exhausted chargers to their hastily-obtained substitutes, and huge trusses of hay and other provender slung up behind.

The hundred silver crowns, all duly forthcoming from the now servile and cringing mayor, were next counted out, and poured into numerous greasy pouches, and then the trumpet blared, the kettle drum ruffled, and the forty-five cavaliers loosed their swords in their scabbards, gathered up their reins, and awaited the order to march.

"Mayor, we only borrow these horses, recollect; we leave our own in their places, and right sorrowfully too, for a soldier's charger is his nearest and dearest friend. See that they are well used, therefore, or bitterly will you rue it when we come back to reclaim them," said Dundee.

Then turning to his troopers, he continued, sternly, "Gentlemen of the Life Guards, once more we direct our course northwards. Unfurl the standard, sound the trumpet, march!"

Silently the little band closed around their beloved commander; the blue and crimson silk standard, the regimental colour, fluttered in the light breeze, riddled by bullets though it was, and 'mid the hoarse clangour of trumpets and roll of drum, they moved on towards the northern gate.

But what is that roar of music, of voices, of hoof-strokes and clanging accoutrements, that suddenly salutes their ears from right to left, in front and in rear?

Why do the townspeople suddenly lose their cringing humility and look of fear?

It is because the hireling soldiery of Holland are moving down upon the town from east and west and north and south, and they know that Dundee and his little band are caged like rats in a trap.

THE DESTRUCTION OF THE SACRED VESSELS OF THE CHURCH.

The great general learns it, too, soon enough, partly by the sound of the different martial instruments, partly by instinct.

He reins in his horse, and glares round for an instant, like a tiger at bay.

Then he shouts, "To the right! by threes, wheel; we must into the old kirk yonder, horses and all, and hold it to the last man."

His followers raised a gallant shout, and swept up the steep street, towards the promised haven, at a gallop, hurling to the right and left the few who attempted to bar their course.

The church was soon reached; luckily the great door was open.

The troopers dashed into the sacred building without dismounting, and then closed, locked, and barricaded the door with all speed.

They picquetted their horses to the stunted pillars, loosened cheek-straps and girths, watered them from the stone font, and then made a tour of inspection, to see whether there was any door or low window through which their foes could effect an easy entrance.

They found none, and placing a few sentries in different parts of the church below, Dundee, Dumbarton, and Douglas, with the rest of their followers, mounted to the summit of the tower, from whence a good view could be obtained of the whole country round.

The kirk stood upon the summit of a hill which rose in the centre of the town, and from the top of the tower the royalists could not only see the town itself, but also the surrounding walls, and beyond them hill and dale, plain and wood, for a radius of many miles.

Four strong bodies of troops were approaching the town from four different directions.

On the south the regiment of Dutch dragoons from whom they had so long been flying.

On the east a regiment of foot which Dundee recognized as the Coldstream Guards.

On the west a squadron of scarlet-coated horse, whom Sir Andrew declared with an oath to be the Red Dragoons of his perfidious kinsman, Sir Archibald Douglas, and on the north the well-known regiment of Scotch Greys, in their janissary caps, buff coats, and black iron panoply.

"And all these four thousand foreigners and traitors are sent to entrap and capture half a hundred leal Scottish gentlemen," exclaimed Dundee, bitterly, as he regarded the advancing hordes. "Well, it is the seventh net of the kind that has been set for us, and time will prove whether its meshes are stronger than those of its predecessors."

"Does it please you that we display our colours, Lord Viscount?" asked Sir Andrew Douglas of his chief.

"Aye, man, that does it," was the hearty retort, "while a rag of silk remains on the staff, we will flaunt it in the faces of these renegades, and let them win it from us if they can; but well I trow that to do that they must come in stronger force than at present, although they do outnumber us by eighty to one."

"The standard was then fixed at an angle of the tower, and carbines, swords, and pistols were hastily examined.

"Heavens! we have not three rounds of ball cartridge left," exclaimed the Earl of Dumbarton suddenly.

"That is, indeed, a mishap," answered Dundee, gloomily, "however, lead must be got, and bullets made speedily. On to the roof, some of you, in Heaven's name, and tear off the leaden spouts and drains, others rush down and light a fire in the vestry, it is no fun to be shot at without being able to reply. If we can't get ammunition our race is well nigh run."

The troopers obeyed their great leader's mandates like lightning; some scrambled down off the tower on the great sloping roof, and cut off large strips of lead with their swords and daggers. These they threw through one of the tower windows to companions within, who carried them down to the great fire that had already been kindled in the vestry for melting purposes, and by the time that the enemy had closely invested the building the besieged had ammunition enough to last them a week.

---

## CHAPTER XXXV.

### A TERRIBLE SIEGE.—ARRIVAL OF THE CLANS.

Ring the bell back, though the sexton looks black,
Defiance to knaves who are hot on our track.
"Murder and fire!" shout louder and higher;
Remember Edge Hill, and the red-dabbled mire,
When our steeds we shall stall in the Parliament hall,
And shake the old nest till the roof-tree shall fall.

"Thank God they have no cannon amongst them," said Dundee, fervently," and their muskets will do little harm to us, especially as night is drawing on, sheltered as we shall be behind the parapet of the tower."

"No, my lord, but unhappily morn will follow night, and even if our position is impregnable yet we can expect no succour, and in the end we must yield or starve," answered Dumbarton, with a sigh.

"Behold, my lords, an officer rides towards the tower, with a white handkerchief borne aloft upon his sword; he wishes to treat with us," observed Sir Andrew Douglas, at this juncture.

It was indeed the case; a stalwart Scots Grey, mounted upon a magnificent charger, curvetted towards them, and reining in immediately under the tower, courteously saluted the officers grouped upon its summit, and announced that he wished to treat with Lord Viscount Dundee.

"I am he," answered Claverhouse, looking over the battlement.

"I come to urge your lordship to surrender; if you resist us further you will but sacrifice yourself and your few followers, without one good object to be gained. Your capture or death is certain. We have drawn a cordon around you which it is impossible to break through," said the officer, earnestly.

"And what are the terms of surrender?" asked Dundee, calmly.

"Unconditional. You and your men must throw yourselves upon the King's mercy, I can only promise that, for a time, all officers shall be allowed to retain their swords, no other favour am I privileged to accord," was the reply.

"Well I wot that the extent of King William's mercy would be the block on Tower Hill, or the salt mines of Holland, neither of which boons do I care to accept at his hands. If any of my officers or followers choose to yield, I shall urge naught to prevent their doing so; as for myself, I mean to die sword in hand, in the service of King James," said Dundee.

"That being the case, my lord, I must address myself to your next in command, the Earl of Dumbarton."

"There is no need to do that," shouted back that chivalrous noble, "as my intention to die at my post is as thoroughly rooted as that of the Viscount; nor do I think your persuasions will have better success with our troopers. Cavaliers of the Life Guards, whoever is in favour of surrender, let him speak, or, if he prefers it, leave us in peace."

The latter part of the Earl's speech was addressed to the troopers, who replied, in a unanimous chorus,—

"We don't mean to surrender; let us fight to the death, that is all we ask. God bless King James! and down with all Dutchmen and traitors!"

"You see, sir, the spirit that still inspires our hearts; I think you will perceive from it that your mission is a bootless one," said Dundee, saluting the envoy with his sword.

"My lord, I am convinced on that point, and I almost envy you and your followers the death of glory and the page in history that awaits you. Farewell!" and the Scots Grey, bowing until his white plume mingled with the mane of his gallant charger, wheeled round, and darted away at a gallop.

Five minutes later, there was a crash of martial music, a hoarse cheering, that seemed to revolve in a circle, and then, still closer and closer up to the red walls of the old kirk, moved the cordon of four thousand men, whose arduous task it was to capture or kill the last forty-five cavaliers who remained loyal to the House of Stuart.

The sun had by this time set. Masses of dull clouds covered the whole sky, which gradually became streaked with crimson and gold to the westward, where the rays of the departed sun yet illumined and coloured the huge mountains of vapour, although his light was fast leaving the earth to the grim shadows of approaching night.

The appearance of the sky and aspect of the scenery were wonderful and glorious. The whole landscape was covered with a red hue, as if it had been deluged by a red shower. The mountain streamlet wound through the valley below, like a long gilded snake, towards the base of a dark mountain, where appeared a reach of the Clackmannan, gleaming like a river of liquid fire.

Beautiful as the scene was, the cavaliers of Dundee were too much occupied with their own stirring thoughts to admire it, or to survey any part with anxiety save that which, by gradually assuming a more sombre hue, announced the approach of night. It was not easy for them to regard a landscape with artists' eyes whilst placed in a predicament so desperate.

The enemy had already assumed the offensive; shots were being fired, and bullets were flying around the tops of the old tower like hailstones; but Dundee and his followers crouched behind the breast-high battlements, and so escaped hurt, though balls frequently flattened themselves against the tall spire above, and fell with a dull thud on their morions or backplates, causing a momentary tingling, or stunning sensation, that was all.

The great door of the church was also attacked with desperate energy, but Dundee knew that it was of solid oak, four inches in thickness, and strengthened by immense iron bands and nails, so that there was no probability of its giving way for many hours.

Shots were, however, being fired hap-hazard through the windows; and the clatter of bullets against pillars and walls, the crash of falling tablets, and sometimes the half-cry, half-moan of a wounded horse, were plainly audible.

Meanwhile, the sky grew darker and darker, and the clouds, in black and copper-coloured masses, descended on every side, and like gloomy curtains shut out the pale rising moon from view, while the wind that blew around the old tower seemed like the very breath of hell.

Then a few rain-drops began to fall, large and round, splashing heavily on the battlements of the tower, and on the leaden roof far below.

The valley, the distant mountain peaks, the town below, the very tower whereon the bold defenders stood, were presently hidden from sight, and then the long-gathering storm descended in all its fury.

An ocean of rain poured down upon the earth with such violence that it was a wonder the crazy old tower was not levelled beneath it like a house of cards.

The thunder peals grew grand and sublime, louder and louder than a thousand broadsides; they roared as if heaven and earth were coming together, until the quick irregular flying of the enemy, and the furious hammering they maintained upon the great door, ceased to be audible, save amidst occasional lulls in the tempest.

Meanwhile, the Scottish cavaliers could do naught but crouch under the battlements and watch the elemental war, gazing with mingled awe and fiery excitement upon the bright streaks of forked lightning, as they darted through the sky, lighting up church and town, the mountain tops, the deep valley, and the swollen river, displaying them vividly, tinging them all over with a pale sulphurous blue, and causing the whole scene, including the thousands of armed men below, to assume a wild and ghastly appearance, as though an army of spectres were besieging a phantom fortalice.

Then again the thunder would roar and die away, and naught could be heard but the howling wind, the rain rushing fiercely down from the parted clouds, scattered shots, the rattle of arms, and the continued hammering against the old church door.

But at last the thunder-storm passed over, and between occasional rifts in the clouds the moon peered out.

Then hundreds of torches sparkled into light, and by their radiance a terrible fusillade was directed upon the tower.

A Life Guardsman fell at Dundee's side, mortally wounded, but with his last breath he cried, "God save King James!" as he waved his bright sword above his head.

"Thus to avenge thee, Hugh M'Ivor, for verily thou were the best swordsman in my troop," said Dundee, and seizing the dying man's carbine, he levelled it over the stone parapet, and covering a richly-uniformed officer of Douglas's Red Dragoons, pulled the trigger.

The soldier fell from his saddle, and neither moved nor stirred, and then dropping the carbine, and brandishing his sword, Dundee cried, hoarsely,

"Level low, my gallant cavaliers, and fire where they are the thickest. Each bullet will kill double. Down with the false Whigamores!"

The roar of forty carbines stirred all the echoes of the old tower, and every shot told with dire effect in the compact masses of the enemy.

These returned the volley with interest, but carbine bullets were of no avail against stone walls, and no casualty occurred amongst Dundee's little band, who continued to reload and discharge their weapons, until the foe could count their dead by hundreds.

Indeed the Coldstream Guards at last fairly wavered before the continuous fire of the besieged, a fire they could not return, and they were only rallied by their commanding officer continually shouting—

"Stand firm, my men, we will have cannon here within an hour."

"Cannon!" echoed Dumbarton, as he exchanged glances with Dundee, "then we are indeed lost."

"Nothing is lost while life remains. We will fight until roof and rafters, column, tower, and spire fall in ruins around us, and crush the last hope of King James's cause beneath them," answered Dundee, sternly.

Again a cloud passed over the face of the moon involving the scene in comparative darkness.

But it was soon to be illuminated in a manner that the besieged little expected.

There flashed forth a sudden glare light, revealing the sea of ferocious visages and glancing arms of the enemy, the kirk-yard, heaped with dead, the dark walls of the old church, and the thatched roofs of the cottages that at some distance surrounded it.

A lurid glare shone over everything, and a soldier advanced close up to the walls, holding aloft a round, strange-looking wheel, whose outer circle was of fire.

Its yellow blaze fell full upon the face of the bearer, and Sir Andrew Douglas snatched a carbine from the hands of a trooper in order to shoot him down.

But, ere he could discharge it, the man had cast the fiery missile from his hand and disappeared.

This terrible instrument of destruction tore through a window of the church, and, plunging about inside the building, as if instinct with life, set fire to everything inflammatory within its reach.

From its size and weight, and the formation of its sides, which were bristling with spikes, it finally stuck fast to the flooring of the church, where its powers of combustion increased every instant, and a succession of reports burst from it as its fire-balls flew off in all directions.

The four sentinels who had been posted in different parts of the church fled in dismay to their comrades in the tower, to avoid being blown up by the sparks falling into their pouches, scorched to death by remaining in its vicinity, shot by its bullets, or stabbed by the spikes which it shot forth incessantly, like quills from a fretful porcupine.

The poor horses neighed, and shrieked, and moaned, as the diabolical engine bounded, roared, and hissed, like a very devil, killing or maiming them by dozens with its missiles, and in three minutes the church was in flames.

"Let them burn their kirk, if they will, for if this tower hath a good stout inner wall, the flames cannot hurt us," laughed Dundee. "Faith my hands are cold, and the blazing roof will soon warm them."

"But, see, a worse danger is at hand, for yonder come two field pieces at a gallop!" exclaimed the Earl of Dumbarton, seizing his chief's arm.

Up they dashed, and, in an instant, the drivers were out of their saddles, the guns unlimbered, shotted home, and their muzzles pointed at the little arched doorway that gave admittance to the basement of the tower.

The discharge was simultaneous.

Two round shots passed through the air, which fell clattering inwards, for one had destroyed the lock.

And, with triumphant shouts and yells, the Coldstreams, with the glittering moon pouring its cold, white light upon their glazed caps and bristling pikes, made a dash at the breach.

"Gentlemen of the Life Guard, a hand-to-hand fight now awaits us. Our forty leal Scottish blades have to defend this tower against nearly four thousand men. Well, the feat is not impossible, for not more than two can ascend this spiral staircase abreast, and so two will be ample to oppose them. Let the first couple slay until their hands are weary of smiting, and then give way for two of their comrades, until each brace of heroes have slain their score or so of men, when the two who went in first will be rested and able to renew the strife," said Dundee.

A loud cheer was the fitting response to his words, and the cavaliers, drawing their swords, rushed to defend the tower staircase.

Already the heavy tread of the Coldstream Guards was heard ascending the first flight, amid the clatter of their firelocks and accoutrements.

"We must meet them below the belfry, or they may set fire to the flooring thereof, and burn us out," said Sir Andrew Douglas, hastily.

"A good thought, my friend. Come, let us hasten," answered Dumbarton.

"Yes, onwards!" cried Dundee, his dark eyes flashing with a strange fire. "Dumbarton, will you take the first round with me, and help send a score of those crop-eared roundheads to the shades before us?"

"Aye, willingly, my lord; my sword is thirsty, and in sore need of a drink of warm blood. To the front!" was the exultant retort.

And down they all went with as light hearts as though it had been to a wedding breakfast, instead of to a carnival of blood, in which all their lives must, ere the end came, be sacrificed.

The belfry, a dark, square room, whose only furniture was the six thick bell ropes hanging down through holes in the ceiling above, was soon reached.

At its extreme end a low-arched door opened upon another long fight of narrow stone spiral steps, and this was the point to be defended to the last grasp.

Dundee and Dumbarton, sword in hand, were about to take their position at the head of the stairs, when Sir Andrew Douglas and another trooper sprang in front, the former cavalier exclaiming,—

"Excuse us, my lords, for our lives are of little value but to ourselves. Yours belong to our King and country, and may yet be of priceless worth to both. Now, Hubert, draw and strike in."

Two Coldstreamers, with their pikes at the charge, were upon them; but Sir Andrew, with a fierce lunge, thrust his sword into the breast of the one up to the very hilt, and his companion sliced the other's head down as though it had been a ripe melon.

The two dead soldiers fell heavily back against their comrades.

They were, however, speedily trodden under foot, and undeterred by their fate, their comrades charged up over their bodies, and two more came within reach of the Scots' flashing weapons.

Down, however, they were hurled in like manner, one with a slash across the face, the other pierced through the heart.

For nearly a minute their comrades stood irresolute, and were only encouraged again to the attack by one of their officers shouting a long way in the rear, "There are less than half-a-hundred of them, and I will give a sovereign to every soldier who slays his man, and fifty pounds for the capture of each of the officers alive."

Then another rush forward was made; but Sir Andrew Douglas and his brother cavalier were fully equal to the occasion.

Down went the two front Coldstreams as their predecessors had done, and bending over their bodies, which could not fall because of those pressing up behind, the cavaliers sheathed their swords deep in the breasts of the two rear rank men, and thus those behind had now to force an ascent against the weight of four of their own dead.

It was an impossible task, though they essayed bravely to perform it; but at last they were obliged to recoil headlong down the staircase, pursued by the pistol bullets of the still undaunted cavaliers, who greeted their retreat with boisterous cries and cheers.

The tower was now evacuated, and the guns again brought to bear upon it, this time being pointed against the brick walls, not the smashed-in door.

"By Heaven! a few shots will bring us and the tower down together," remarked Dundee, looking out through a narrow eyelet slit in the wall upon the movements of the besiegers.

A ball was rammed home in each of the field pieces, and discharged point blank against one side of the tower.

A big mass of brick and mortar fell from the wall, and a hearty cheer thereupon arose from the beleaguering host, for they saw that less than half-an-hour's judicious pounding would bring the whole structure toppling down, and the intrepid cavaliers with it.

"A precious predicament, truly, to be placed iu," exclaimed the Earl of Dumbarton; "and the worst of it is, that I do not see a way out of the scrape. Ah! what is that?"

"What, my lord Earl?" asked Sir Andrew Douglas, eagerly.

"That sound? 'tis music in the distance, 'tis the skirl of the Highland bagpipe. My God! if it should be the loyal clans of Glengarry, Maclean, Clanronald, or Lochiel, advancing southwards!" answered the Earl.

"If it should be, then is the siege of Kinross church as good as raised," said Sir Andrew Douglas, with a faint smile; "but I hear no music, my lord, and I fear that we are not yet far enough north by twenty miles, at the least, to hope for succour from any of the clans."

"I know not that, Douglas," broke in Dundee, who had been intently listening for some seconds; "I know not that, for, by the blessed mass, *it is* the skirl of the bagpipe that we hear, and what is it more, 'tis the pibroch of the gay Gordons, I would swear to it amongst a thousand."

"Hurrah then, there is yet hope. Six of you to the belfry. Ring the bells backwards as a signal of our distress, they will know the token. How bonnily the church blazes below, 'tis good as a beacon fire. Hurrah for the gay Gordon, the Cock of the North! Shout a loud defiance at these hirelings of the Stadtholder who surround us. We will thrash them yet, aye, and whip them across the border, too, in another month," exclaimed the Earl of Dumbarton, in wild enthusiasm.

"By the holy rood we must keep picking off those artillerymen with our carbines, though, or there will not be left of this tower one brick upon another by the time the Highlanders come up," said Dundee, calmly.

Then while the loud crash of the bells sounded even above the rattle of the musketry and the roar of the flames, which shot high up above the roof of the burning church, in which forty-five noble horses were groaning, neighing, and kicking in the agonies of death, the surviving cavaliers of Dundee knelt in a row under shelter of the tower parapet, intent only upon shooting down the artillerymen who worked the two six-pounder field pieces, for upon their success in this feat, perhaps, depended their lives.

"You and I are fair shots, I know," said Dundee, picking up the carbines of the only two cavaliers who had yet been slain, and tossing one of them to the Earl; "let us pay devoted attention to the bombardiers—it strikes me we can pick them off like muir cocks. Gentlemen, do with the other artillerymen what you will, but leave the bombardiers to us."

And so true was the aim of these two nobles, that for more than a quarter of an hour not a cannon was fired, for directly a bombardier moved his lighted match towards the vent-hole of his gun he fell, shot through the head by one or other of the splendid marksmen.

During that time they had slain fully a dozen men each, whilst thrice that number of artillerymen had been knocked over by the other cavaliers.

At length the two field pieces were run back out of carbine range, and again opened fire; but now the damage they effected to the wall was not quite so great, and Dundee began to entertain hopes that the Highlanders would yet come up in time to save them.

At this juncture of affairs day dawn brightened the eastern horizon, and the wild melody of the pipes was plainly distinguishable to the holders of the tower, though it did not appear as though the enemy below had yet heard them.

"'Tis the wild skirl of the '*piob mhor*,'" said Sir Andrew Douglas, "and behold, yonder come the clansmen, descending the mountain side."

He pointed to a hill about a mile away, which a long array of skilled warriors were descending towards the plain. The rising sun shone on their gleaming sword blades and brass-bossed targets, which flashed and glittered between the trunks of the trees at every step. Even the ribbons fluttering from the drones on the three pipers' shoulders could be discerned, and the heart-stirring strains they were blowing came floating towards them on the fitful wind.

"They are the clan Gordon, and they are marching straight towards us," said Sir Andrew, "God grant that they be in force enough to effect a rescue."

"There are two thousand of them at the least, and look away to the left, for there another clan is debouching through a narrow pass. Now those fellows, from their small green and black tartans, and the red feathers in their bonnets, must be Glengarry men. By my fay, the siege will be raised in gallant style," exclaimed Dundee, half wild with enthusiasm.

All this while, however, the soldiers of the Stadtholder, from their less elevated position, saw nought of the approaching clansmen, nor did they even hear the wild music of the bagpipes. Their whole attention was directed, their whole interest absorbed, in the levelling of the grim old church tower, and the consequent destruction of the loyal gentlemen who had sought refuge therein

The cannoneers, now out of carbine range, worked at their pieces steadily and perseveringly, ball after ball was fired at the tower, each shot knocking away abundance of bricks, and undermining its strength wondrously. At last the old structure would shake and quiver as each ponderous missile struck it, and every moment, besiegers as well as besieged, expected it would fall over with a crash.

Cheer after cheer rang through the rebel army at every discharge of the cannon, and hundreds of eyes were anxiously directed to the battlements, wondering if in this moment of terrible peril the loyal cavaliers would hoist a white flag or show any signs of a desire to surrender. If they hoped for such an event, they were sadly disappointed.

To Dundee and his brave companions death was preferable to dishonour; like the French Old Guard, on the field of Waterloo, they knew how to die, but they did not know how to yield.

Their courage and endurance was at length rewarded, for the wild pibroch of the Highlanders was at last audible even to dull Southern ears. Out piquets and videttes came galloping in with the intelligence that an army of barelegged mountaineers was advancing upon them, almost with the speed of cavalry. The consternation was tremendous. Dundee and his heroic little band were at once forgotten; the guns were limbered up, the horses put too, and the whole investing force formed hastily in order of battle to resist the approaching foe.

They soon came in sight, a forest of plumed bonnets, bare broadswords, waving scarfs and kilts, and bossed shields; no sounds cheered their steady advance but the sonorous drone of their great war pipes, and the regular tramp of their heavy feet, but there was no lack of bravery amidst that stern array, who unlike the lowlanders, ever faithful to their legitimate line of kings, were now on the march from their mountain homes with the full intention to retake Edinburgh.

## CHAPTER XXXVI.

### THE BATTLE OF KINROSS.

Here is a dint from the jagg of a flint,
Thrown by a Puritan, just as a hint; [rough,
But this stab through the buff was a warning more
When Coventry city arose in a huff;
And I met with this gash, as we rode with a crash
Into Noll's pikes on the banks of the Ash.

THE number, discipline, and order of the Stadtholder's troops would have struck terror and dismay into the breasts of any other volunteers than Highlanders, a race whose hearts have never known fear, and who had long been accustomed to rout both horse and foot with equal speed and success.

Arrayed in the picturesque tartans of their respective tribes, they formed in close ranks with their filleadhbegs belted about them, their brass studded targets, long claymores, ponderous pole-axes, and long-barrelled Spanish rifles, shining in the morning sun.

They brandished their weapons and clan standards, and the fierce notes of war and defiance rang among the neighbouring hills, as the pipes struck up their various pibrochs.

The warlike challenge was replied to by the rattle of drums, and the blare of trumpet and bugle, as the Southerners formed in battalions of foot and squadrons of horse, to receive them, for well these latter knew that the impatient Highlanders would commence the attack.

The clansmen surveyed with unflinching courage the measured steadiness and precision of the Lowland soldiers, whose silken standard fluttered gaily above their moving masses of polished helms, screwed bayonets, and long pikes, that flashed like silver in the sun.

Like greyhounds in the slip straining upon the start, their leaders could scarcely restrain them until the right moment.

At last the signal was given, and while the Glengarry men divided into two bodies, the one attacking the Scots Greys on the rebel right, and the other Archibald Douglas's Red Dragoons, on the left, the Clan Gordon made a dash at the Coldstream Guards, who formed the enemy's centre.

Like a cloud of battle, the race of old Selma rushed down upon the foe.

Reserving their fire until within a pike's length of King William's troops, the Highlanders poured upon them a deadly volley, and throwing down their muskets, drew their claymores, and under cover of the smoke charged with the fury of an avalanche, striking up the levelled bayonets with their studded targets and hewing with sword and axe, routed the Lowland infantry in an instant.

In like manner the Stadholder's horse were driven in on both flanks, one of their standards captured, their artillery utterly routed and both field pieces taken.

In a mass of disorder, horse and foot, musketeers, pikemen, and cavalry, the soldiers of the Stadtholder were driven like a flock of frightened sheep through the streets of Kinross, while the fierce clansmen, swaying with both hands axe and claymour, cut them down like a field of ripe poppies as they ran.

"Now, God be praised! the rascals fly," said Dundee, when he saw the Southeners give way on all sides before the clansmen. "Gentlemen of the Scottish Guard, let us sally forth and join our preservers."

They descended the tower staircase over the dead bodies of the foemen they had slain, and then made the best of their way after the pursuing Gordons, whom they soon overtook.

Dundee, Dumbarton, Douglas, and their devoted followers, were received with rapture by the Highland chiefs, who declared that their presence was as good as an army of ten thousand men. After the enemy were utterly routed, a great feast and council of war was held, at which Dundee was nominated Captain-General of the loyal clans, and the whole conduct of the approaching campaign left to his control.

. . . . . . . . .

With this troop of loyal cavaliers, Dundee continued to wander from place to place in the Highlands, until the beginning of May, 1669, when he appeared at the head of about three thousand clansmen, the greatest number of followers that he conld gather round his banner, and these were respectively led by Sir Donald Macdonald, and the chiefs of Glengarry, Maclean, Lochiel, and Clanronald, all names ever associated with the purest ideas of chivalry, generosity, and valour.

He had, also, a force of about a hundred and twenty horses; but they were composed entirely

DUNDEE'S VICTORY AT KILLYCRANKIE.

of gentlemen, and led by our hero, Sir Andrew Douglas, in person.

The revolution might be said to be now fully achieved; for save Dundee, Dumbarton, Belcarris, and a few other Catholic peers, with their immediate followers, all Scotland, save the remote highlands, had submitted to the new sovereign, whom those loyal nobles would rather have died than acknowledged.

Viscount Dundee had been required by trumpet to return to the Convention; he treated the summons with scorn, and was thereupon branded as an outlaw and traitor, and stigmatised with every epithet that Presbyterian rancour, heightened by the remembrance of his former military prestige, could heap upon him.

Colin, Earl of Belcarris, the High Treasurer, was captured and thrown into a dungeon. The weak and servile Melville, the crafty and fanatical Stair (the Scottish Talleyrand), and the not less crafty Duke of Hamilton were now at the head of the Government, and these, though all staunch Presbyterians, were by King William united in council with a few of the high-church nobles, an intermixture which inflamed the animosities of both parties and sowed the seeds of hatred, discord, and confusion.

Lieutenant-General Hugh Mackay, of Scoury, now Commander-in-Chief of the Scottish forces, Colonel-commandant of the Scottish Brigade, and Privy Councillor of Scotland, was at length despatched against Dundee and the loyal tribes, at the head of five thousand foot and two regiments of cavalry.

Neither the fall of Edinburgh castle, which Sir John Lanier captured after a desperate defence by the Duke of Gordon, nor the disappointment of assistance from Ireland which King James had thrice promised him, had damped the ardour of the brave Dundee.

Deficiency of provisions had compelled him to shift his quarters frequently, and his devoted followers had endured the most severe privations, but under these they disdained to complain when they knew that their beloved leader shared them all.

Like Montrose, Dundee was eminently calculated for a Highland leader. In his buff coat and plain steel head-piece, he would march on foot, now by the side of one clan, and anon by the ranks of another, addressing the soldiers in their native Gaelic, flattering their long genealogies, and animating the fierce rivalry of clanship by reciting the deeds of their forefathers, and the sonorous verses of their ancient bards.

It was one of his maxims that no general should command an irregular army in the field without becoming acquainted with every man under his baton.

## CHAPTER XXXVII.

### THE NIGHT BEFORE THE BATTLE OF KILLYCRANKIE.

Now, whatever may hap, this rusty steel cap
Will keep out full many a pestilent rap;
This buff, though it's old and not larded with gold,
Will guard me from rapier as well as from cold;
This scarf, rent and torn, though its colour is worn,
Shone gay as a page's but yesterday morn.

On the evening of the 16th June, 1689, Dundee marched to defend the Pass of Killycrankie, where on the morrow one of the most decisive battles in Scottish history was to be bravely fought, and, alas! fruitlessly won.

The setting sun was brightening the hills of Athole, and the purple summer heather, the long yellow broom, the wild briar and honeysuckle, that clambered among the basaltic cliffs, loaded the air with a rich perfume, while through the savage and stupendous gorge of Killycrankie the setting sun poured a flood of golden lustre, bringing forward in strong light the wooded acclivities of those sublime hills that heave up to heaven their scaured and wooded sides, involving in dark shadow the deep rocky chasms through which the foaming Garry rushes to mingle its waters with the rapid Tummel—chasms so profound, and so hidden by the overhanging foliage that the roar only of the unseen water was audible, awakening the echoes of the dewy woods and shining rocks.

Nothing in nature can surpass the wild grandeur and imposing sublimity of this mountain gorge, the frowning terrors of which, in after years, so impressed a brigade of Hessians in the war waged by the Chevalier de St. George, to regain his grandfather's throne, that they refused to penetrate what appeared to them to be the termination of the habitable globe,

Save the mountain torrent foaming down from the lofty hills, appearing one moment to hurl its spray against the shining rocks and urge masses of earth and stones along with it, and disappearing the next as it plunged into the bosky woodlands, all was still as death in that Highland solitude, when in steadiness and order Dundee drew up his little host at its northern verge, admirably posted on well chosen ground, two miles from the mouth of the pass, the only road to his position being the ancient pathway that wound along the face of the precipitous cliffs, where the least false step threatened instant destruction, even to the most wary passenger.

Dundee's band, for it was nothing more, though named an army, was only three thousand strong, and was composed of various little parties which were but the nucleus of the corps he had expected to form. On the right was the *soi-disant* regiment of Sir John Macdonald and a small body of the clans under the illustrious chiefs of Lochiel, Glengarry and Clanronald; the Athole men under Ballechin, Sir Andrew Douglas's troop of horse and a corps of three hundred half-clad, and miserably accoutred Irishmen, formed the main body, while Dundee's old troop, in which rode the Earl of Dumbarton, his officers and several Highland gentleman, composed the reserve of cavalry, and were about fifty strong.

The gloaming had scarcely come on when the roll of distant drums became more and more audible, and at length increased, until the hoarse and sharp reverberations of the martial music rang between the steep stupendous rocks of the long mountain pass, through which the foe were about to attempt to force a passage.

Anon the whole Southern host came in sight, and the Scottish standards, the red lion with the silver cross, and one with that of St. George (borne by Hastings' regiment) with the yellow banners of the Scot's Brigade, appeared at intervals of time, and weapons were seen flashing through the openings of the chasmed rocks and sable woods of drooping pine.

Onwards they came, nearer and nearer still, but presently the rattle of the Southern drums and the blare of trumpet and bugle sounded a halt, and the army of Mackay debouched from its windings on to the open plain, above which the fierce and impatient Highlanders were drawn up in battle array, and began forming their camp for the night.

. . . . . .

An hour later a council of war was held in Dundee's tent, every leader and chief of note being present.

The plan of the morrow's battle was warmly discussed, and every heart was full of ardour, and flushed with the hope of victory.

"What a pity 'tis that we are so short of cavalry. Even if we beat the enemy the victory will be a barren one, because, for want of horses, we cannot gall his retreat," said the Earl of Dumbarton.

"How many, think you, we have in our force who, if they had horses, could act efficiently as cavalry?" asked Sir Andrew Douglas.

"Five hundred at least," answered Dundee, "and could we but mount them their services would be invaluable."

"Then the animals shall be forthcoming my lord. I will engage with fifty of my troop to bring you five hundred chargers, all saddled and harnessed before midnight," said our hero, confidently

"And where on earth will you procure them, my friend?"

"From the enemy. My false namesake's Red Dragoons are camped on the extreme right of Mackay's position; their chargers are picketed to stakes fastened in the ground, and are ready at a minute's notice. Twelve horses are attached to each stake, but merely by their slip bridles, and are watched over but by some half-dozen sleepy sentries. A bold dash, and the horses are captured and driven up the hills to our camp."

"A bold proposition, truly, and I think a feasible one. Anyhow, I give you permission to attempt it, Sir Andrew," said Dundee gravely.

. . . . .

An hour later, at the head of his fifty troopers, all equipped in light marching order, Sir Andrew Douglas cautiously descended the steep slopes towards the right of the enemy's position.

Their horse's iron shoes had been removed, and others of leather covered with velvet and felt substituted, whilst steel bits, curb chains, sword scabbards, and every other accoutrement likely to make a jingling noise, had been muffled in some soft substance.

Even conversing in the ranks, save by an occasional whisper, was forbidden, and the little company of daring and desperate men glided down the steep slopes towards the plain, more like a troop of spectres than of armed men.

Both camps were by this time wrapped in profound repose, for both Dundee, and Sir John Mackay were experienced enough to know the immense importance of a good night's rest to troops about to engage on the morrow in deadly strife.

The night was very dark, but the watch fires of the Southern army gleamed redly at fixed intervals through the gloom, and as the Scottish horsemen approached nearer, they could see indistinctly the outlines of tents and baggage waggons, guns and tumbrils, and could distinguish the forms of the sentries, as they paced to and fro, beside their watch-fires.

"Yonder is the camping ground of the Red Dragoons," whispered Sir Andrew to his lieutenant. "We must make a detour to the left, we have scarcely a quarter of a mile further to ride. Didst ever make a night raid on a Lowland farm?"

"Aye, often," was the low response, "and driven the fat beves for a score of miles with prick of spear, though the whole country was on our heels."

"Well this night's work will be very similar. Imagine yon camp to be a Lowland farm, and the chargers we are in quest of fat oxen that you are about to levy black mail on. We must drive them off in the same way, remember."

"Ah, 'twill be fine sport, such as well pleases a Highland heart, but hush, we are close upon them. Shall we make a dash, Sir Andrew?"

The whole party reined up, and in silence surveyed the scene before them.

Dozens of mobs of horses, all standing ready accoutred, were dotted over the plains before them, forming little rings thereon, a few yards distance from each other. In their rear gleamed three camp fires, before each of which paced two dragoons, their brass helmets, long scarlet cloaks, heavy Jack boots, and drawn swords, gleaming in the ruddy light.

Then Sir Andrew whispered his instructions to his troop, to form into two parties, spur forward in a circle to right and left, meet in the rear of the horses they wished to capture, slay the sentinels if necessary, and then expanding, in the shape of a crescent, to drive the frightened steeds before them with shout, hallo, and pistol shot, up the mountains and right into their own camp.

The ruse was a clever, and bold one, and succeeded admirably. Twenty-five cavaliers made a dash to the right, as many to the left, unfixing picket stakes as they galloped. In less than three minutes, they had met in the rear of the frightened, trembling chargers they had come to capture, cut or shot down the six astounded sentries, well nigh trampled their fires out with the hoof-strokes of their rearing, plunging steeds; and then expanding like a fan, they overlapped the captured horses on each flank, and urged them to a wild gallop.

But by this time the alarm was given, and the whole right wing of the Southern army was in commotion. Trumpets sounded to "boot and saddle," drums beat the "assembly," and a troop of cavalry were speedily thundering in pursuit of the adventurous Scotch.

On went the latter, like the wind, driving their frightened captives before them, with whoop and hallo, and pricking those that lagged behind with the points of their long rapiers. The plain was soon crossed and the steep ascent leading to the pass of Killycrankie gained, but by this time a troop of the enemy's light cavalry was close upon their heels.

Sir Andrew glanced back and knew by their coats of spotless buff and helmets of polished steel, that they belonged to the calavry corps of the Marquis of Annandale, the *èlite* of the Southern cavalry.

"Twenty of us must face round and hold these fellows in check," whispered Sir Andrew, hoarsely to his lieutenant. "Do you and the remainder of our force drive the captured horses on with all speed to the camp."

A score of the Life Guardsmen accordingly wheeled round and with wild cries of "Hurrah for King James! Down with the followers of the Stadtholder," charged right at the Annandale troopers, though the latter out-numbered them by at least four to one.

There was a shock, like to the concussion of two heavily charged thunder clouds—a flash of swords, as their keen edges rang on tempered helmets and corslets of proof—a furious spurring of horses, and then Sir Andrew felt himself forced somewhat out of the melée, and found himself opposed to a horseman who was deliberately pointing a long brass-barelled pistol at his head between his horse's ears.

Our hero saw that he was fairly covered, and his gaze fastened with painful acuteness upon the little black muzzle, and the stern grey eye, that through a slit in the closed visor, glared along the barrel.

He fired, and the bullet grazed the cheek plate of Sir Andrew's morion, who never winced, but felt his heart tingle with rage and exultation, as in turn he levelled his long horse-pistol at the Williamite trooper, who was reloading with the utmost coolness and *sang froid.*

The Life Guardsman then fired, and with a loud snort, a strange cry, and a terrific bound, the strong Flemish charger of his adversary sank to the earth and tore up the turf with its hoofs. Its brain had been pierced.

The rider lost his pistol by the plunge, but adroitly disengaging himself from the twisted stirrups, high saddle, and convulsed legs of the fallen steed, he unsheathed his long sword and brandished it, crying,—

"Vivat Wilhelm! Come on again, Papist dog!"

Disdaining to take advantage of his antagonist's being dismounted, Sir Andrew sprang from his horse, drew his bright sword, and rushed to the encounter, and sparks of fire flashed from the crossed blades.

The Williamite trooper, swaying his sword with both hands, attacked Sir Andrew with great fury and undisguised ferocity.

This courage was, however, well met by the young Life Guardsman's address, but his bodily strength and weight of weapon were far superior, and he pressed on pell-mell, until a deep gash in the right cheek reminded him of the necessity of coolness, and that the cautious game was the best.

Without the least advantage being gained on either side, the combat continued for three or four minutes, during which time the greatest skill in swordsmanship was exhibited by both antagonists in their efforts to pass each other's points, until a smooth pebble caught Sir Andrew's heel, and he was thrown to the earth with great force.

Ere he could draw breath, his opponent sprang upon him like a tiger, and with his sword shortened in his hand, and his knee pressed upon his breast, he exclaimed in a fierce whisper, through his clenched teeth,—

"Ah! you thought that I was brushed from your path for ever, but you see that I am still alive and that *my turn* is now come. Behold, I am Sir Edward Hamilton."

He threw up his visor with one hand, and our hero recognised the ci-devant captain of Swart Ruyters, whom he thought he had slain many months before, on the morning whereon he had saved Flora Macclesfield from her doom.

He felt half stifled as his corslet was compressed beneath the heavy knee of his conqueror, and made an ineffectual effort to grasp his poignard, but he could not, for it lay under him.

"Die, dog," shouted Hamilton, and raised his shortened sword, which he grasped by the blade, to deliver the final *coup-de-grace*, but at this instant, loud cries of "God and King James! They fly! they fly! Down with the Whigamores!" rang on the cold night air, Sir Edward was hurled backwards by a charger's shoulder, and when our hero sprang to his feet, he beheld the white garbed horsemen of Annandale in full retreat, and a body of Scots horse, headed by Dundee in person, thundering close in pursuit. He looked around for Hamilton, but he was gone, so he strolled back to camp, which he discovered his charger had reached before him, as well as his comrades, with all the captured horses

---

## CHAPTER XXXVIII.

### THE BATTLE OF KILLYCRANKIE.

No, by my word, there never shook sword
Better than this in the clutch of a lord.
The blue streaks that run are as bright as the sun,
As the veins on the brow of that lovliest one;
No deep light of the sky, when the twilight is nigh,
Glitters more bright than this blade to the eye.

THE sun rose redly on the following morning, as ominous of the tint with which even the grass and the brattling waters of the rivulet would be dyed ere he set.

It was the morning of a battle, and as dawn brightened the hills of Athole, Sir Andrew Douglas, who had lain down to rest with his head pillowed on his charger's flank, awoke from a feverish slumber, cold, hungry, and his left arm stiff and sore from a pistol shot wound he had received in the skirmish of the preceding evening.

The war drums of the Saxons were beating the "point of war" on the plain below, answered by the blare of trumpet and bugle, and the neighing of battle steeds, the clatter of arms, the tramp of feet, the hum of voices, and the confused medley of sounds rang with a thousand reverberations between the old bluffs of that tremendous gorge.

The enemy were forming battalions prepatory to a grand attack, each regiment mustering under its respective colours, and Sir Andrew could distinguish the bright scarlet uniforms of Sir James Hastings' heavy English foot, and the Scotch brigades of Levan, and Mackay, and on the left the battalions of Balfour, Ramsey, and Kenmore, with their black iron caps, scarlet hose, and yellow coats faced with purple.

On the left of the infantry were the cavalry corps of the Marquis of Annandale, clad in coats of spotless buff, and caps of polished steel; on their right the heavy horse of Lord Belhaven, in light blue uniforms and brass helmets, whilst in the rear appeared sombre masses of Swart Ruyters, motionless as though they had been a squadron of bronze statues.

Meanwhile the Highland army of Dundee was not idle. Clan after clan formed in array of battle, and the spirit-stirring strain of the bagpipes roused the kilted warriors to a degree of valour and enthusiasm that was in itself dangerous, because almost uncontrollable.

Clad in his rich scarlet uniform, with his cuirass, gorget, and helmet gleaming in the sunshine, and his snowy plume of white ostrich feathers floating in the wind, his fine features full of animation, and his fierce black eyes flashing with valour and enthusiasm, Viscount Dundee galloped to and fro, from clan to clan, inspiring them by every exertion of graceful gesture and military eloquence to add that day to the fame of their forefathers.

At last he rode up to the spot where Sir Andrew Douglas sat motionless on his black charger at the head of the forty bronzed, scarred, and veteran Life Guardsmen, the heroes of a hundred fights.

Dundee bowed to his handful of brave men, some of whom had been his companions for a score of years, until his floating plume mingled with the mane of his gallant war-horse. He was received with vociferous cheers and the waving of swordblades in the air.

Then shaking hands with Sir Andrew Douglas, he said, with a smile, "I hear that you were completely successful in your last night's undertaking, and I thank you, both in the King's name and my own."

Douglas pointed to a mass of horsemen, clad in a diversity of uniforms, who were drawn up a little way to the right, and replied,—

"Three hundred horses we brought clear away, and at the sacrifice of only three lives. You see, my lord, that they are mounted by men who know well how to sit and control them and if the uniforms were not so motley, they would make a very respectable appearance, as cavalry."

"But think you they will act well together?" asked Dundee, anxiously.

"Yes, my lord; for every man amongst them has served, at one time of his life or another, as a cavalry trooper. I manœuvred them myself, for more than an hour in the bright moonlight, and they do the evolutions very creditably, I assure you," answered Douglas.

"Well if we win the day and drive Mackay back, they will be invaluable. A victory is next to worthless, unless the enemy is harrassed and cut up by cavalry during their retreat. I will reserve this patchwork squadron for that purpose. Who commands them?"

"Sir William Wallace, a young soldier of lofty courage and daring."

"It is good. They could not have a braver leader, I know him well; but, Douglas, I depend on thee and thy handful of my own dear old regiment, for services during the coming fray, that may, perchance, require thy own life and that of thy last man. The enemy have cannon, which must be captured at all risk and turned by us against them, for we have not a single piece of ordnance, and without artillery I feel convinced that the day is lost."

"The last drop of our blood shall be shed like water at thy word, O, noble Dundee. Say I right, my men?" answered Sir Andrew Douglas, flourishing his sword and turning to his stern troopers.

"Death or victory!—a Dundee! a Dundee! A Douglas! a Douglas!" was the answering shout, that rolled down the pass like thunder.

At this moment a mounted aide-de-camp dashed up to uniform the Viscount that Sir James Hastings' regiment of scarlet clad English foot were making a flank movement on the Scottish right.

"Let the Camerons of Lochiel advance to oppose them, supported by the hardy mountaineers of Glengarry," said the Viscount, and away galloped the aide-de camp to convey the General's commands to the respective chieftains.

It is recorded in history, that at this juncture, Dundee hastily repaired to his head-quarters, a deserted Highland hut or shieldihg, standing nearly in the centre of his position, and exchanged his scarlet coat for one of buff, richly laced with silver, and that over it he tied a scarf of *green*, which caused great grief and consternation to the Highlanders when they beheld it, as it was a colour considered by them ominous of evil.

Meanwhile, the Camerons had descended the steep slope like a mountain avalanche upon the red columns of the advancing infantry.

Forcibly did they depict Scott's glowing description of a Highland charge,—

> Like wave with crest of sparkling foam,
> Right onward doth clan Alpine come.
> Above each helm each broadsword bright
> Is brandishing like gleam of light,
> Each targe is dark below,
> While like the ocean's mighty swing
> When hurtling on the tempest's wing,
> She hurled them on the foe.

For, pouring upon the English a deadly volley when within about fifty yards of them, they cast their muskets to the ground, and drawing their great basket-hilted swords, charged right on, under cover of the smoke, guarding the bayonet thrusts of their foes on their bossed and studded targets, and hewing down both musketeers, and Sweyne-feather men as though they had been merely a field of red poppies.

In less than five minutes, Hastings' Englishmen were cut to pieces and forced to retreat pell-mell behind the legions of Leven and Mackay, who being Scotchmen, were better calculated to withstand successfully the wild torrent of Celtic warfare that was surging up against them.

Dundee, with lightning glance, surveyed the field; and turning to the Earl of Dumbarton, who stood beside him, he said, sternly,—

"We have struck the first blow successfully. Lochiel and Glengarry can hold their own against Mackay and Leven, but, nevertheless, let Sir John Macdonald move down his regiment to their support, if needed. Ah!" he continued, the next moment, "the Southeners are about to assume the offensive on a grand scale; their whole line of battle is in motion. Behold."

As he spoke a simultaneous volley ran from flank to flank along the English line, and the roar of musketry and the heavy boon of the cannon rang from peak to peak, and rebellowed along the sky and among the hills like thunder, with a thousand echoes.

Half a dozen mounted aides-de-camp immediately surrounded the great royalist General, waiting for his orders.

They were speedily given,—

"Sir John Gordon, let the chieftains of Clanronold and McIvor oppose with their Highlanders the battalions of Balfour, Ramsay, and Kenmore, who are advancing on our centre. Sir Wentworth Scott, command Ballechin to lead his Atholemen against the cavalry corps of the Marquis of Annandale and Lord Belhaven, who are sweeping up on our left, and bid Colonel Ormond lead on his three hundred Irishmen, as a supporting column; and do thou, Lord Dumbarton, ride to Sir Andrew Douglas, and tell him to capture yonder battery that threatens to sweep a clan or two from the face of the earth unless quickly silenced. Aye, to capture it, though he lose his last man in the attempt."

Away went the three messengers at a gallop, and presently the whole line of Scottish battle was also in motion, rushing down to meet the foe.

"Douglas, my boy, you are to ride into the very jaws of hell yonder, and bring away that battery of twelve field-pieces from under the noses of the thousand Swart Ruyters who are drawn up close in their rear," said the Earl of Dumbarton, as he drew rein at our hero's side.

"We will capture and spike them, noble Earl, but there will not be one of us left alive to bring them away," answered Douglas, firmly, but sadly.

"We must attempt it, my lad, for such are Dundee's commands. Let the trumpeter sound the charge, I will accompany you," said Dumbarton.

"Nay, noble Earl, death has no need of you. Consider, that if aught should happen to Dundee, you are the King's only hope," urged Douglas, seizing his rein.

"I cannot help it, I must have my own way for once. This is the last charge that the Scottish Life Guards will ever ride, and I would sooner loose my Earldom than not strike a blow in their ranks. Let us on, not a moment may be lost."

Douglas saw that the Earl would yield to neither persuasion or entreaty. He, therefore, waved his sword, and the trumpet peel rang wildly forth.

Ere its last note ceased to echo in the gloomy mountain gorges, the little troop were descending the hill side at a gallop, boot to boot, like a solid wedge of glittering steel.

But as Sir Andrew Douglas dashed down into the valley of death, at the head of his devoted troopers, he thought not of the desperate perils that surrounded him, for the dear image of Flora Macclesfield was in his heart and mind. Since he had so abruptly quitted her in Edinburgh, now many months ago, he had never even heard of or from her. How long the time had seemed. The gentle expression of her face now came powerfully to his recollection, with all the vigour of a deeply impressed vision, and recollection summoned the tones of her sweet voice to his heart, like the memory of some old familiar air, and all the gushing tenderness of his soul was awakened. But with these remembrances came the conviction of bitterness and despair that he would never see her more; that in a minute or two, at most he would sink a corpse on that gory field, and that, perhaps, she would never learn his fate, and deem that he was still alive, though unfaithful.

He was aroused from this reverie by a cannon-ball, which passed so close to his ear that the wind nearly knocked him out of the saddle. In an instant he was himself again, and, with bent brows, compressed lips, and a heart on fire with heroic courage, dashed onwards towards the foe.

Thus they rode on, exposed to the full fire of the guns they were bent on capturing, for a considerable distance, with no squadron to support them, no aid to be expected from any quarter.

As they neared the battery, regiments of foot, both on their right and on their left, opened fire on them with volleys of musketry.

But the band of forty heroes swept proudly past, glittering in the noonday sun in all the pride and splendour of war.

They were going to charge an army in position, their valour knew no bounds—they advanced in two tiny squadrons—quickening their pace as they neared the death-dealing cannon.

A more fearful and yet a grander spectacle was never witnessed. They were rushing into the very jaws of the grave.

When within three dozen yards of the battery, the twelve field-pieces composing it belched forth a flood of smoke and flame, through which hissed the deadly balls.

Their flight was marked with instant gaps in the Life Guard's ranks, by dead men and horses, by steeds flying wounded and riderless across the plain.

The first line was broken, it was joined by the second. They never halted or checked their speed for an instant; to have done so would have been annihilation.

With diminished ranks thinned by the guns which the artillerymen had laid with the most deadly accuracy, with a halo of flashing steel above their heads, and with a cheer which was many a noble fellow's death cry, they flew into the smoke of the batteries; but ere they were lost to view the plain was strewed with their bodies and the carcases of their horses.

Through the clouds of smoke and dust, Dundee could still see their sabres flashing as they rode up to the guns, and dashed between them, cutting down the cannoneers as they stood.

Douglas and Dumbarton saw at a glance that to attempt to take the cannon away would be madness; but they spiked them most effectually, though they lost a dozen men in effecting the important service.

By this time there were but twenty of them left, and they were surrounded and hemned in by the enemies' Swart Ruyters.

But with a desperate courage they reformed and dashed at the investing cordon, cutting through it and scattering the Swart Ruyters to right and left like chaff, aye, without the loss of a single man.

Then they found themselves opposed to Lord Belhaven's heavy dragoons, five hundred dashing horsemen, the pride of the Midland Counties.

The space between them was only a few hundred yards, it was scarce enough to let the horses gather way, not had the men quite space enough for the full play of their sword-arms.

But with only eighteen men at their backs, eighteen as opposed to five hundred, on went, and home went Douglas and Dumbarton, with a cheer that thrilled every heart; and at the same instant the wild shouts of the Swart Ruyters who had reformed and were thundering in their rear rose through the air. But the Life Guards looked not back; but as lightning flashes through a cloud, they pierced through the glittering masses of the English horse.

There was a clash of steel and the light play of the sword-blades in the air, and they disappeared in the midst of the shaking and quivering columns.

In another moment they emerged and dashed on, now only nine in number, and many of them wounded sorely, and scarcely able to sit their horses through mingled fatigue and loss of blood.

These nine reeling, swaying riders, a body of Annandale horse, fully fifty in number, who were retreating from a bloody contest with Ballechin's Atholmen, in which they had been terribly worsted, thought it a fine thing to attack; but the nine bleeding heroes nerved themselves for a last desperate effort, and boldly stood the onslaught.

In the melée Sir Andrew Douglas encountered the standard-bearer of the light horse, and after a brief contest, drove his sword through his corslet, and spurning him with his foot and stirrup bore off the trophy.

Then holding the great yellow bullion-fringed Dutch banner aloft, he fought his way out of the press, and spurred up the heights towards the Scotch army.

He heard a horseman in his rear, and drawing rein, was presently joined by the Earl of Dumbarton, who grasped in his red left hand the bullet-torn, sword-slashed banner of his own regiment.

"Thank God you have saved it, Dumbarton, but, heavens! where are our men? has not one of them, except ourselves, escaped?" gasped our hero.

"All but ourselves have found a bed of glory. Of Dundee's Life Guards, that marched into England twelve months ago a thousand strong only one man remains, and that man is thyself, Sir Andrew; but they will live in history, and 'twere vain to regret them. Let us hasten to Dundee, for yonder he sits on his black charger like an equestrian statue hewn from marble."

Carrying aloft the two banners, Douglas and Dumbarton rode towards Dundee, who was speaking to the great chief of Lochiel, who stood by his side, with his right hand resting on his bridle rein.

As they cantered along, their hearts glowed with fierce exultation and pride, for a mere glance at the field showed them that the Southerners were giving way on every side. Maclean's Highlanders had cut their left wing to pieces, and hurled it back onthe centre, while the Camerons and Macdonalds had met with equal success on the right, and in the front the battalions of Balfour, Ramsay, and Kenmore were in a state of panic and confusion, which might be turned into a precipitate flight at any instant, pressed closely as they were by the fierce followers of Clanronald and McIvor.

"Now, God be praised, I ne'er thought that you would have come out that terrible fray alive," said Dundee, as Douglas and Dumbarton drew rein at his side; then his eyes lighted up with joy as he continued—"Ah! and you have saved the old flag, too; and what is more, captured one from the foe, that is as it should be. But tell me, have all fallen?"

"All, Lord Viscount," answered our hero, solemnly.

Dundee's face grew grave, then he hastily brushed a tear from his eye with his richly-laced cuff, and said in a voice husky with emotion—"Well, they have died the death of brave men, they have died for their King and country, as I hope I shall have the honour of doing when my time comes. Ah! Heaven, *'tis already come*," he grasped, as he dropped his sword and clapped his hand to his left side.

Both Dumbarton and Douglas sprang towards him and lifted him from the saddle, a deadly pallor had overspread his beautiful features and it was discovered that a bullet had pierced his buff coat above the coarselet, and buried itself in his shoulder under the left arm.

"Let me be, let me be, my time is come, but I care not, for I feel that my mission is achieved, the day is won; the enemy, doubling us in numbers, fly before our conquering legions. I die, but O! how happily, for I die in the arms of victory. Noble Dumbarton, you will take the command of the army; Douglas you will harras the enemy's retreat with every horseman you can muster. Let me kiss the old standard of my regiment. John Graham of Claverhouse will ne'er wield sword beneath its rustling folds again."

Douglas held the bullet-torn flag close to the dying chief's lips, which he pressed to it fervently. Then he said in an altered tone, which told how intense were the torments he suffered. "Now let me be borne to my head-quarters and propped up in a chair against the outer wall, from whence I can watch the retreating foe for miles, aye until death shall close my eyes never to be opened again on scenes of war and bloodshed. Dumbarton and Lochiel will perform this service for me; Douglas, thou must not stay an instant, to horse and away, follow the fleeing rabble like sleuth-hounds, on the trail; hack, hew, and spare not. Hurrah! God and the King!"

Douglas had no option but to comply with this request, he accordingly bent over and kissed his beloved leader's cold hand, then vaulted into his saddle, and galloped away to where the three hundred motley horsemen were drawn up under shelter of a low ridge of rock anxiously awaiting the moment when they should be permitted to take some part in the fray.

No sooner had he taken his departure than Dumbarton, Lochiel, and two strong Highlanders raised Dundee and bore him to the spot whither he had desired to be carried.

. . . . . . . . .

We will conclude our brief sketch of the battle in the words of an old Scottish Chronicler (Blackadden) who, speaking of the close of the fray, says,—

"In a mass of disorder, horse and foot, musketeers, pikemen, and cavalry, the army of General Mackay was driven like a flock of frightened sheep down the narrow pass, while the fierce clansmen, swaying with both hands axe and claymore, cut down both officers and soldiers through skull and neck to the very breast; others had their skulls cut off above their ears like nightcaps; some had their bodies and crossbelts cut through at one blow; pikes and swords were severed like willows, and whoever doubts this may consult still living witnesses of the tragedy.

"Thanks to the military genius of Dundee and the valour of his troops, never was there a more decisive victory won. Mackay lost his tents, baggage, artillery, provisions, and his standards; he had two thousand men slain, and five hundred taken prisoners, mostly during the pursuit.

"Such was the battle of Killycrankie, or *Rinn Ruaradh*, as it is still named by the peasantry, who attribute the ultimately fatal effects of the victory to the circumstance of Dundee wearing *green*, a colour still esteemed ominous to his surname. A rude obelisk of stone still marks the exact place where the death shot struck him, and is pointed out by the mountaineers with respect and regret as *Tombh Claver'se*."

. . . . . . . . .

It was now evening, and the sun had verged to the north-west, but from between gathered masses of saffron clouds, streams of dazzling light were radiating, and the setting rays, as they poured aslant on the mountain sides, made the deep pass seem darker as it receded beyond them.

The grief and consternation spread through the Highland ranks on learning the fall of their beloved leader, had already dimmed the ardour of the clansmen, and prevented their following so eagerly in pursuit as they would otherwise have done.

Had it not been so, few of the foe would ever have reached the southern mouth of that terrible pass.

"Dundee hath assuredly been slain," General Mackay is reported to have remarked, as he reined in his exhausted charger two miles from the field, and at the further extremity of the gorge. "I am convinced of it, otherwise we should have lost a quarter of our force before we had got thus far."

Sir Andrew Douglas, however, pressed hard upon the enemy's rear with his three hundred cavalry—pressed on until the broad round moon had risen above the dark ridge of the far-off mountains, and poured its cold lustre into the very depths of that hideous pass, and on the distorted visages of the writhing wounded, and more ghastly features of the pallid dead, more than two thousand of whom laid therein.

The retreat of the English army was covered by a miscellaneous body of cavalry, themselves almost as disorganised as the rest, but more than thrice outnumbering Sir Andrew's little regiment, which came up with them just as they had gained the southern mouth of the pass.

"Charge!" was the cry, and with Douglas at their head, the gallant force of cavaliers rushed on, and hurled themselves like a thunderbolt against the masses of the foe.

A fire, innocuous from the terror and confusion with which it was directed, was opened upon their advancing line; but ere swords were crossed, the English cavalry, with the exception of one small body, turned the rein and fled.

The Scottish cavaliers thundered on their flank and rear; men and horses rolled ever together, and foremost in the fight, wherever a show of resistance was made, waved the long bright sword of the Life Guardsman, the sole representative of a lost regiment.

On they rushed, pursuer and pursued, over the plain, over the hill; down went steel jack and buff coat and iron morion.

Some turned at last to strike one stroke for life, but still the fiery spur of Douglas was behind them, and Killycrankie field was far away when he first drew rein, and cried,—

"Halt! Sound to the standard; we have ridden perhaps too far."

With swords dyed in gore, and arms weary with smiting, the little troop wheeled round, and spurred headlong back towards the pass, and as they rode, some of his officers perceived that Sir Andrew wavered somewhat in his saddle, and that a stream of blood was trickling down his scarf from his left shoulder.

Spurring up to his side, his lieutenant, a cadet of the House of Argyll, said,—

"You are wounded, sir; you are badly wounded. Let me——"

But at that moment our hero interrupted him with,—

"Is this a time to talk of wounds? Look up the pass; our retreat is cut off, for yonder come the Swart Ruyters, a thousand strong, while we have not a hundred men who can keep the saddle. They cut us off from our army, they perceive us; their trumpets sound the advance. Now, gentlemen, for a death-bed of glory and a page in history. Charge!"

With undaunted courage, they spurred towards the foe, but the Swart Ruyters, with their long lances in the rest, bore down upon them with the swoop of an eagle on its prey. They outnumbered the Scots by ten to one, and though Sir Andrew would have scorned such odds had he been leading on his veteran Life Guards, he dreaded them now that he could only oppose to that stern compact array a troop of mere volunteers.

## CHAPTER XXXIX.

### THE PURSUIT.—AN OLD FOE TO THE FRONT.

The water was churned as we wheeled and we turned,
And the dry brake, to scare out the vermin, we burned;
We gave our halloo, and our trumpet we blew;
Of all their stout fifty we left them but two;
With a mock and a laugh, won their banner and staff,
And trod down their cornets as threshers do chaff.

OUR hero's fears were justified by the result, his men fought bravely, resolutely, doggedly, but they were overpowered, cut down, and slain, and in less than a quarter of an hour, out of the troop of three hundred horse that he had raised the night before, barely three dozen wounded, wearied, and despairing prisoners remained, the rest lay dead or wounded on the plain.

Then a tall stately horseman rode up to the spot the Swart Ruyters making way for him as he approached, and demanded the name of the senior officer amongst the captive Scots.

"I, Sir Andrew Douglas, late captain of King James's Scottish Life Guards, am he," answered our hero, sternly.

"Ah, is it so? Then I am Sir Edward Hamilton, a colonel of Swart Ruyters, in King William's service; perhaps you have heard my name before," rejoined his questioner, with a reckless laugh, and throwing up the visor of his helmet, the moonlight shone on the pale, stern, and vindictive countenance of his deadliest foe.

"I told you that we should meet again," laughed Hamilton, "and I am sorry that it is upon an occasion when my duty to my king will oblige me to hang you as a rebel and a spy."

"Hound, I have never sworn allegiance to thy Dutch King, therefore I cannot be a rebel, and the part of a spy I would scorn to play."

"Nay, thy memory is treacherous, for thou art already condemned to death for having played that very character at Carlisle, eighteen months since," answered Sir Edward Hamilton, with a scornful laugh. "Now wilt thou kneel to me and beg me to forget this old decision against thee?"

"Never, do thy worst; he whose head is in the wolf's mouth knows that 'tis vain to expect mercy, but I would that my hands were free, rascal, if only for a minute, for I would pull thee out of the saddle and strangle thee."

Hamilton's eyes glared with rage, he spurred forward and struck the young Scot a heavy blow on the mouth with the hilt of his sword, causing the blood to spurt forth in a torrent. Then turning to his men, he exclaimed, "Make the rascal Scots dismount and walk by the sides of their horses, or rather of ours, for they are the chargers that were stolen from our camp last night. We must up the pass again, and keep an eye upon the movements of the rebel army of Dundee, for tomorrow will Mackay return with powerful reinforcements, and sweep it from off the face of the earth. The first tree we come to, we will string these three dozen prisoners on its boughs, as scarecrows to frighten other traitors."

The Scots were then gagged, and each man's arms were confined to his sides, by a long trail-rope, the other end of which was attached to the belt of a mounted Swart Ruyter.

Sir Andrew was separated from the other prisoners, and the end of the rope that bound him was attached to the saddle of a fierce old trooper who frequently accelerated his speed by jerking him nearly off his feet, or pricking him savagely with his lance point.

After an hour's hard walking, he became so exhausted that he felt hardly able to proceed, for he was weak from loss of blood; and walking so far, in his heavy jack-boots, was no easy task.

At last, thoroughly exhausted, he threw himself on the ground, and signified by signs, for the Dutchman who guarded him could not speak a word of English, that unless he were permitted to remount he could not proceed a step further.

After some hesitation, the man grunted a refusal, but intimated that he should take off his boots, which our hero gladly did, thinking that he could manage better without them, on the smooth grass where there was no stones; but he soon discovered his error, for he found that there were innumerable little hard lumps of earth and brambles that caused him the most fearful agony, and he was again compelled to throw himself down.

His strength was now exhausted, and he signalled that if they wished him to proceed, he must do so on horseback.

He closed his eyes, and throwing his head back begged earnestly that he might be allowed some, if only ten minutes' repose.

He had just begun to think that his fierce custodian had granted him this petition, when he was suddenly made to start up, by the most fearful dart of pain through his feet. To his rage and horror, he then perceived that two ruffians had dismounted, ignited some tinder, and were carefully applying it to the soles of his feet.

They now explained to him, by signs, that unless he arose and went on, they would continue their pleasing operation until he did.

For a moment he tried to bear the pain and lie still, but the agony became too intense, and he was forced to stand up.

Once fairly upright, the Ruyter, to whom he was bound, put his horse to a trot, and actually dragged him along by main force.

He felt that he was gradually losing consciousness, his eyelids closed, his head swam, a sort of buzzing noise filled his ears, and he became indifferent as to what was happening, only feeling an occasional pang from his feet, now naked, bruised, and bleeding.

Suddenly he became alive to the fact that the whole party had halted, and by a great effort he recovered himself sufficently to notice that they were overshadowed by an immense beech tree, whose heavy moss-covered branches swept the ground, and formed a complete curtain around.

Nearly fifty Swart Ruyters were congregated in the circle beneath the huge leafy dome, but to Sir Andrew's horror, he perceived that at least three dozen dead bodies were swinging in the breeze, from the great boughs overhead, and that they were those of his captured comrades.

An imposingly beautiful spot was that; no poet could have dreamed or desired a lovelier. Above, the huge vault, with its natural frettings and arches; below, the greenest, freshest grass; around, an eternal half light, streaked and varied, and radiant as a rainbow. Why had man turned a heaven into a hell, by a deed of cruelty, atrocity, and bloodshed?

It was now discovered that there was not a rope amongst the whole troop, long enough to hang Sir Andrew in due form.

But two short pieces of cord were at last found, and several of the Swart Ruyters dismounting, threw it over one of the lowermost branches. Then uniting the two ends, they formed them into a strong noose, which was left dangling from the bough, the simple preparation was soon completed.

Sir Andrew was now forced to mount his horse, for the rope was too short to hang him standing, and having done so, one of the Swart Ruyters passed the noose round his neck, another bound his eyes, a third drew his feet out of the stirrups, whilst a fourth stepped behind his horse armed with a heavy riding whip.

All was done in the deepest silence; not a word was breathed, not a footfall heard on the soft yielding turf. There was something awful and impressive in the profound stillness that reigned in that vast enclosure, yet, with hundreds of steel-clad horsemen, grouped like spectres around.

The whip fell, and the horse gave a spring forwards. Sir Andrew made an involuntary clutch at the bridle, but missed it, and the next instant he was dangling in the air, swinging to and fro, with his feet a good yard above the ground, like the pendulum of a clock.

But simultaneously with his being swung off, a loud Gaelic war cry rang amongst the surrounding hills, and hundreds of kilted warriors swept down into the plain. In a panic, the Dutch Ruyters sprang into their saddles, and galloped as fast as their heavy Flemish horses could carry them, nor did they look back or draw rein, before the camp-fires of General Mackay's army loomed redly before them.

A cavalier clad in a glittering uniform, pushed through the mob of Highlanders, to the tree whereon Sir Andrew hung suspended, and with one stroke of his bright sword, cut him down; then while his whole frame trembled with eagerness and excitement, he strove to unfasten the noose.

"Brandy! brandy! has nobody any brandy?" he cried, impatiently.

One of the Highlanders sprang forward with a whiskey flask, another supported the body, and a third the feet, of the half-hanged Life Guardsman, while the cavalier poured a few drops of the spirit into his mouth. Then to the joy of all, he opened his eyes and gazed vacantly around him. Luckily the leather stock encircling his throat, which had not been removed, had prevented his neck being broken by the sudden jerk, as well as strangulation afterwards, and in a few minutes not only was he able to converse, but also to rise to his feet.

"Dumbarton," he gasped, "I owe you my life; had you arrived a minute later, it had been sped. But tell me, what of Dundee, is there hope?"

"Of his living, none," answered the cavalier Earl. "The great chieftain, whom we so love, will be gathered to his fathers ere the midnight hour. Naught but my anxiety for thy fate would have induced me to quit him even, for an instant."

"Alas, I have lost every man entrusted to me for the pursuit of the foe; you may behold the last three dozen hanging like acorns above our heads, strung there by the rascally Dutch, whom may Heaven confound; but for all that, every trooper of them slew three of the foe; for two miles we cut the fleeing foe down like poppies, in riding through the pass," said Sir Andrew, bitterly.

"Douglas, 'tis well, what would you wish more? but tell me are you strong enough to ride to Dundee's head-quarters, 'tis only a mile and a half distant, and he would be glad to see us both before he dies, I'll dare swear."

"For such a purpose I would find strength, were I in ten times worse a case," said Sir Andrew, and his horse having been caught by a Highlander, he permitted himself to be lifted thereon, and surrounded by the hardy clansmen, Dumbarton and Douglas slowly rode back to the pass.

They noted not the brilliant moonlight, as it flooded the narrow fissure between the mountains, they noted not the dead or dying upon whose pale faces it gleamed, they felt not their own wounds, fatigue, or sorrow, for their thoughts were all centred upon their great leader, but at the same time, their beloved friend and comrade, Dundee, the peerless, the unequalled.

## CHAPTER XL.

### THE DEATH-BED OF DUNDEE.

Weep Albin to death and captivity led,
Weep, weep, but thy tears shall not number the dead;
For a merciless sword o'er Kilcrankie shall wave,
Kilcrankie that reeks with the blood of the brave.

INTRODUCE we our readers to a little wainscoted chamber, within a small mud-built cottage, known as the "house of Urrard."

Four long candles flare in the brazen branch, and illumine a low truckle bed, whereupon lies, in the agonies of death, the great Dundee.

He breathes slowly and painfully, his beautiful features were sharpened, pale and ghastly, his Ramillies wig was laid aside, and his natural raven tresses, long and glossy as those of a woman, flowed over his shoulders and the snowy pillow, forming a strong contrast with the deadly pallor of his skin.

His blood-stained buff coat, his sword and helmet, together with the ominous green scarf, lay upon a chair near him, and the whole of his dying energies seemed concentrated on the accomplishment of one object, the penning of a despatch to his King; for a low table was drawn up to his bed's side, and on it stood a desk with a sheet of foolscap paper stretched open thereon, which he was rapidly covering with strong nervous and blotchy writing.

It contained an account of the glories he had gained in that King's cause, and the long career of service that he had sealed with his own gallant blood, and though every muscle of his face was at times contracted with the torture he suffered, as he stretched from the bed to write, he finished the letter,* with an effort signed his name, and then fell back, utterly exhausted on his pillow, closing his eyes as if in death.

It was at this moment that the Earl of Dumbarton and Sir Andrew Douglas entered the room, the former covered with dust and dew, the rich uniform of the latter slashed and ripped up by sword blades, and in many places stained with both his own and his foeman's blood.

They gazed first on the dying noble and then on the assembled chieftains, who consisted of Sir Evan of Lochiel, Glengarry, Clanronald, Grant of Glenmorriston, Sir John Macdonald, Sir William Wallace, Ballechin, Colonel Ormond, and a few other men of note, who leaned on their ponderous broad-swords, and either conversed in low whispers or watched in grim, and in one or two instances, tear-dimmed silence, the ebbing life of the first cavalier and the truest heart in Scotland.

Nearest to the bedside stood David Grahame, the only brother of the deceased, who was sheathed in steel, *à la cuirassier*. (This brother afterwards assumed his title, but died in great obscurity in France in 1700.) He held in his hand the riddled standard of the Scottish Life Guards, Dundee's own old regiment, and also the Dutch colours, that Sir Andrew had that morning taken from the enemy.

"Is he dead?" asked Dumbarton, in a harsh whisper, of the stern Lochiel, as he entered the room; "has the great soul really flown from the worn-out casket?"

"Not yet, not yet," was the agitated response, "but it cannot abide therein for long—accursed be the green scarf that wrought this evil work to Scotland and to us!"

Two regimental surgeons at this minute entered the humble chamber, and approached the bed to minister to the dying chief, but he opened his eyes, and with a smile, bade them desist, saying,—

"It is all over, gentlemen; you cannot prolong my life, best let me then die in peace." Then, recognizing the Earl of Dumbarton and Sir Andrew Douglas, he beckoned to them to approach, and said to the latter,—

"Ah! so you have returned from the pursuit, tell me what thou hast done."

Our hero briefly related the events of the evening, and then Dundee resumed,—

"Noble Dumbarton, to you I leave my batôn, and if thou should'st fall, I would that you would bequeath it in turn to Colonel Cannon. Douglas, you will pardon me, that I have entrusted to my brother, Colonel Graham, the banner you took from the foe this morning, together with my last dispatch, to convey to France and place in the hands of the King? Thou should'st have had the task, could Scotland have afforded to part with so gallant a heart and so strong a blade, but she could not. He will, however, mention thy name to our good King, and should'st thou ever have need to fly this kingdom, and seek refuge at the court of St. Germain, the letter I have just penned will ensure you a warm reception."

Sir Andrew's heart was full; he could only lay his hand upon his breast and bow.

"And now, my friends, draw near and let me shake hands with one and all of you, in turn," said Dundee, with difficulty controlling the painful trembling of his limbs, and turning his bloodshot eyes from one to the other.

Silently and sadly, they complied with his request. Dumbarton was the last to approach his couch, and as he took his hand, Dundee said,—

"Old comrade and friend, I need not urge

* The existence of this last despatch is denied by some authorities, but the weight of evidence seems to be in its favour.

thee to remain true to our King, because I know that thou wilt do so, whatever may hap in the future to shake thy allegiance. May this day's glorious victory be an omen of future success, and of a second restoration. Think of me kindly, for though I have done fierce and stern things in my time, I have been driven to them by necessity and by a tide of circumstances incident to these our troubled times; yet for all this I feel, and a glorious conviction is it, that my friends will ever remember my name with honour, and my foes with fear. As a last request, I beseech thee to be merciful to our prisoners, for they are our countrymen; release and bid them return to their homes in peace, tell them that such was the last wish of Dundee. Now, go, continue in that path of glory which I must quit for ever, and should you live to behold our beloved King once more, do not fail to tell him that James Grahame of Claverhouse with his last breath blessed him and died. Yes, God bless King James and confound his enemies!"

The wild dark eyes of the dying man flashed for a moment with all their old energy, as he uttered the cavalier cry; he waved his hand above his head, as though he still grasped a battle brand, then he fell heavily back and expired, just at the first faint gleam of daylight brightened the distant east.

The kilted chieftains and the Lowland warriors started and bent over him, the surgeon placed his hand to his heart and shook his head sorrowfully, for it had ceased to beat; the fierce spirit of that remorseless cavalier had flown for ever, and his magnificent features, as the rigidity and pallor of death overspread them, assumed the aspect of a beautiful marble statue.

A groan that burst from the lips of his brother as he knelt down and closed his eyes, the heavy sobs of a few aged Highlanders, and the low wail of a lament, as the pipers of Glengarry poured it to the mountain wind and echoing woods of Urrard, were then the only sounds heard within that chamber, where the terror of the Presbyterians, the idol of the cavaliers, and last hope of King James, lay prostrate, to rise no more.

Though by one faction styled *the last and best of Scots*, by the other a murderer and an outlaw, yet by the cause for which he died, and the manner of his death, he closed in glory a life of singular ferocity and turbulence.

His remains were hurriedly interred in the rural kirk of Blair Athol, and his buff coat, bearing the mark of the fatal bullet, and stained with his blood, together with his helmet, sword, and other relics, not forgetting the fatal green scarf, are still preserved at the ducal castle of Blair.

Remembering the dying desire of their great leader, the Highland chiefs liberated, the next day, all the prisoners taken at Killycrankie, on their parole of honour not to serve against King James, Colonel Ferguson of Craigdarroch being excepted, says Captain Crichton, in his "Memoirs," on account of his more than ordinary zeal for the new Establishment.

But we must hasten on to the more exciting and thrilling scenes of our narrative.

## CHAPTER XLI.

### A DIABOLICAL PLOT.

We came o'er the downs, through village and towns,
In spite of the sneers, and the curses, and frowns.
Drowning their psalms and stilling their qualms,
With a clatter and rattle, of scabbards and arms,
Down the long street, with a trample of feet,
For the echo of hoofs to a cavalier's sweet.

It was a clear and starlight night in July, that a small band of Highlanders landed on the southern shore of one of those firths that indent the whole coast of Scotland, and struck into the interior of the country, marching in single file, and at a pace that, for silence and speed, could be equalled by few besides North American Indians.

It was neither a walk nor a run, but a swinging step between the two, capable of being long sustained, and which carried them over the ground at the rate of at least eight miles an hour.

Their guide was evidently a man perfectly acquainted with the country he was travelling; for he looked neither to the right nor the left, but pursued his course in nearly a straight line, now across meadows and ploughed fields, then through narrow lanes, and perhaps, for a short distance, along a high road, through copse and thicket, over hedge, ditch, and bank, on he went with the untiring vigour and activity of a true mountaineer.

He was a man in the prime of life, tall, rawboned, and muscular, and possessed of the broad shoulders, narrow hips, and sinewy limbs, that characterize the Scottish Highlander. His countenance, naturally harsh and stern in its expression, was rendered still less prepossessing by the scar of a sabre cut, extending from the left temple across the cheek bone to the corner of long upper lip, which latter feature was covered by a thick moustache, black as the raven's wing.

He was clad in the full Highland dress, the tartan being so dark that in the uncertain light its check was undistinguishable; but the only thing remarkable about him, was the extreme whiteness of his sturdy legs, which, had he long worn the Celtic garb, would after such a burning summer as had just passed, been of the colour of mahogany, as decidedly were those of his followers. His head was covered by an eagle-plumed bonnet, and in his broad belt was a long claymore, a dirk, and a formidable horse-pistol.

From the moment this mysterious band of fifty men set foot on shore, they were evidently in a neighbourhood which they had to travel with great care and circumspection, and near to a military camp of some sort, for an occasional pibroch could be heard in the distance.

The lateness of the hour, however, the darkness, and the unfrequented paths they were following, rendered it improbable that they should be encountered or even seen, but nevertheless every precaution had been taken in case they were.

The dress and equipments were the same in all respects as one of the Jacobite clans, attached to the fortunes of the House of Stuart. They were all, with the solitary exception of their conductor, Highlanders, talking Gaelic, and familiar with the habits of those they were so unhesitatingly venturing amongst.

During a march of three hours' duration, they made but three rencontres, the first was some peasant woman, who wished them a good night and walked on, unsuspecting, taking them for Camerons, the more so as two or three of them struck up the air of "*Lochiel's Lament*," which was a favourite and popular tune in that district.

The second meeting was not got over so easily. A peasant on a stout mule came trotting up beside the party, with whom he seemed inclined to keep company. He entered into conversation with them, asked them where they were going, and whence coming, and what was the cause of so late a march?

The men had had their lesson, however, and were ready with their answers, but his curiosity was not easily satisfied, and his questions at last became embarrassing.

## CHAPTER XLII.

### THE CAPTURE OF DUMBARTON AND DOUGLAS.

At midnight in his guarded tent,
The Turk lay dreaming of the hour
When Greece, her knee in suppliance bent,
Should tremble at his power.
In dreams through camp and court he bore
The trophies of a conqueror.

"GET rid of that chattering fool," said the leader of the expedition to one of his men. "Fifty lives must not be imperilled for one."

"True," was the muttered response, and the man addressed drew his claymore silently from its sheath, and slackened his pace.

As the unlucky peasant passed him, his bright blade gleamed for an instant; there was a low gurgling sound, and then a body fell crashing through bushes and branches into the ravine that bordered the rugged road.

It was an hour past midnight, when the adventurous little band halted, in a lane that wound between hills covered with forest trees, from amongst which large irregular corners and pinnacles of rock, here and there, protruded.

Everything was still; the breeze had died away, and save the occasional screech of an owl or croak of a frog, not a sound was to be heard.

"In ten minutes we are there," said the mysterious leader to his henchman, the same who had cut off the peasant's head; "it is time to give the final orders."

The men assented, and the next moment the band of adventurers was collected in a circle around their leader, whose second in command addressed them in broad Gaelic, thus,—

"Men of M'Alpine, we are within musket range of the outposts of the Scottish army. Yonder light burns within the head-quarters of their general, the Earl of Dumbarton, the successor of Dundee, and almost his equal in bravery and skill."

He pointed, as he spoke, to a tiny star of fire that gleamed in the distance.

There was a movement of surprise amongst the men, at finding themselves, as it were, almost within the very grasp of the lion.

"That exalted personage, but nevertheless double-dyed traitor," continued the henchman, "we are going to seize and convey a prisoner to the camp of General Mackay. There are but few troops to guard him, and English gold has tampered with their fidelity, but should there be any attempt at resistance or rescue, with an appearance of success, remember that dead or alive we must have him, and that his head alone will be worth its weight in gold to the man who shall present it, to-morrow, at the English camp. And now, forward! *Bothwell Brigg* the watchword, the rendezvous here, in case of dispersion."

The men then again fell into their places, and the march was resumed. They had not, however, advanced a hundred yards from the spot at which this short pause had been made, when the pass was lighted up with a bright glare, and the reports of five score muskets resounded from the neighbouring hills, awakening a hundred echoes.

At the same instant, from amongst brushwood and bushes, hundreds of dark forms started up, and the blue bonnets of the Camerons, that gallant and most dreaded of clans, became dimly visible through the darkness, as the Highlanders hurried down the hill-sides to the attack.

"Cursed luck, I have cast the dog-throw," exclaimed the leader of the expedition, as he fell heavily over a foot of a tree, "we have lost; but the game was well worth the risking, and perhaps the other expedition may succeed better."

He had been struck by two balls and died almost instantly. More than a third of his company had been killed or desperately wounded by the volley they had received, but notwithstanding this heavy loss and the desperate situation in which he found himself, the henchman, who was as yet unhurt, did not seem to despair, or at any rate he was resolved to sell his life dearly.

"Fight to the death, my men," cried he, as he snatched up the musket of one of the dead men, and taking a steady aim at a Scottish officer, who was leading on his men to the charge, shot him dead.

The Southerners gathering courage from the example of their new chief, poured in a volley upon the enemy, which for an instant checked their advance.

But the odds were too large for the issue of the contest to be long doubtful.

A gallant but vain attempt was made by the Southerners to retreat along the road by which they had come, fighting as they went, but after twice driving back the enemy, by the desperate impetuosity of their attacks, they found that they were completely surrounded, and might as well die where they stood.

A general discharge of the Highlanders' long Spanish muskets, who were enraged at the resistance of this handful of men, brought the matter to a conclusion; five Southerners, who still remained on foot, threw down their arms and begged for quarter, but were instantly bayonetted.

When the smoke of the final volley had cleared away, the Highlanders lighted torches, in order the better to despoil the bodies of their dead foes, a proceeding which was very deftly and speedily effected, after which the flambeaux were again extinguished, and the hardy mountaineers dashed off to the right and the left, back to the cantonments, from which they had been summoned by a peasant lad, who had become casually acquainted with the plot to seize upon the person of the Scottish General, and had hastened to divulge it to his chief, Cameron of Lochiel.

HE URGED HIS STEED AT A FURIOUS PACE ACROSS THE MOOR.

Change we the scene to the interior of the head-quarters of the Earl of Dumbarton, which two bodies of Southerners were striving to reach on that eventful night, trusting that the lax vigilance of the Highland outposts, and the influence of English gold, would enable them either to slay the great Scottish leader or bear him away captive—a plot which, if successful, they felt sure would demoralize the whole Scottish army, and perhaps, indeed, break it up altogether.

We have detailed the fate which attended one of these detachments, presently we will narrate whether the other succeeded any better in its fell scheme.

Dumbarton's head-quarters was a squalid looking little inn, which, judging from its isolated position, could scarcely have been resorted to, even in tranquil and peaceable times, by more than half-a-dozen people in the course of the week.

Built in an angle, formed by some large masses of dark-coloured rock, the house was invisible to persons approaching from the east or south, while to the north lay a thick forest of oak and chesnut trees, stretching up to the very door, and on the west the ground was rugged and broken, with a narrow sheep-track winding like a whitish line over the rocks, amongst which it finally lost itself.

The Earl of Dumbarton occupied a large smoky room, that composed the whole of the basement storey of the inn. He was attired in full Highland uniform, and strode impatiently up and down the damp and filthy floor.

He was evidently annoyed at something, for from time to time, an angry exclamation would escape him, and he would give a fierce stamp with the heel of his shoe, or a hasty clutch at the basket-hilt of his sword.

Once or twice he paused opposite to the large projecting chimney, and gazed for a moment into the log fire that was smouldering on the hearth, or pulled up the wick in an iron lamp that hung from the rudely-fashioned mantel-shelf, and then resumed his monotonous promenade.

The second occupant of the dingy chamber was a boy, apparently about twelve years of age, to judge, at least, from his diminutive stature and delicate features.

He was crouched down upon a low bench in the chimney corner, his elbows on his knees, his chin resting on his hands, and his large restless eyes, black as jet. glittering from amongst a profusion of tangled curls of the same colour, that hung over his neck, shoulders, and cheeks.

After some continuance of his restless walk, the Earl's patience seemed to be fairly exhausted. Stopping suddenly, he drew from his pocket a handsome gold watch, and looked at it by the light of the lamp.

"Eleven o'clock," he exclaimed, "and not yet come. Something must have happened."

But even as he spoke, the hoarse challenge of a sentinel was audible without, and the next instant a tall stalwart form stalked into the room, and casting aside his loose horseman's cloak of scarlet, revealed the form and features of Sir Andrew Douglas, who, with sorrowful brow, approached his friend and leader.

"Well, Douglas, what report do you bring me," asked the Earl.

"But an indifferent one, my lord; the Highland clans have begun, as of old, to quarrel among themselves, and the Irish Brigade are in open rebellion, and swear that they will follow no one but Colonel Cannon, whilst the whole army is unmistakably demoralized, and ready to split into fragments."

"And Sir Hugh Mackay, with ten thousand troops, is within a day's march," said Dumbarton, angrily. "We dare not offer him battle under such circumstances."

"We have scarcely any choice but to do so, my lord; if we retreat further north, we shall not be able to procure sufficient food for the army, and besides, at the first retrogade movement, I feel convinced that each separate chief will lead his clan home. We must fight, and if God wills it, fall; for to retreat a foot would be to break up the army," answered Sir Andrew.

"Oh! would that I had my old regiment of Scots Royals, fifteen hundred strong, and thou thy thousand Life Guardsmen, glittering in their scarlet and steel; then might Cromdale Haughs tell another tale than it is, alas! destined to tell ere to-morrow's sun has set," said the Earl of Dumbarton, sorrowfully.

"Do not despair, my lord; a stirring address might even now unite our quarrelsome chieftains in amity for a time. Summon a council, speak to them words of fire, such as you uttered at Ipswich, such as Dundee was wont to speak, and all may yet be well. Come, my lord, no time is to be lost."

"My friend, let us go together; my heart and brain seem on fire. We will not retreat; nay, in less than five hours we will advance as a river rushes towards a desert, knowing that its sands will absorb and consume it," said the Earl.

They were about to leave the half ruinous inn together, when a shot was heard, and then a heavy blow against the door, followed by a deep groan.

Then half-a-dozen shots followed in rapid succession, doors and windows were burst open, and in an instant the room was full of Southerners.

Swords flashed in the torchlight, and helmets, epaulettes, and accoutrements, glimmered and glinted in the uncertain rays, and amid the sound of trampling feet and the clattering of arms, voices might have been heard shouting "Seize them both. Shoot them down—alive or dead, what matters it—they are both outlaws, and each of their heads is well worth a thousand silver crowns."

But neither Dumbarton nor Sir Andrew Douglas cared to rate their lives so cheaply; their swords were long, their arms were strong, and they laid about them with such good-will, that half-a-dozen of the red-coated foes soon writhed on the floor. But what could two do against two-score, and ere long they were overpowered, borne to the ground, and bound hand and foot with strong cords, whilst gags were thrust into their mouth.

They were then dragged out of the inn, placed on two horses, and, surrounded by their captors, were forced, *nolens volens*, to gallop with them at the top of their speed, in the direction of the British camp.

---

## CHAPTER XLIII.

### A STORMY COUNCIL, AND HOW IT WAS TERMINATED.

March! march! why the deil do ye no' march,
Stand to your arms, my lads, fight in good order;
Front about, ye musketeers all,
When ye come to the English border.

With beat of drums, the following morning, there was dire confusion in the Scottish camp, for their general was missing, the brave, the chivalrous Earl, who had already attained almost as great a popularity with the stalwart Highland clansmen, though not in all cases with their chiefs, as had the ill-fated but brilliant Dundee.

Some unprincipled and malignant chieftains reported that he had deserted his men and abandoned King James' cause, but the unmistakable tokens of a struggle at his head-quarters, where the floor was covered with the bodies of dead Southerners, with pools of blood and torn fragments of the Earl's plaid and uniform, soon proved these malicious assertions to be false.

Then a stormy meeting was held in the tent of Sir John Macdonald, whereat were present the Chiefs of Lochiel, Glengarry, and Clanronald, the brave Sir Hugh Bellechin, Sir William Wallace, Andrew Grant of Glenmorriston, and other officers, who leaned on their swords and regarded each other, in many instances, with glances the reverse of friendly.

"Hereditary right will face the rock; as the senior chieftain and the leader who brings the greatest number of armed men beneath his banner into the field, I claim to be appointed commander-in-chief of the forces," exclaimed Sir Evan of Lochiel, in Gallic, as he grasped his dirk.

"Hoot, toot, mon, the blue bonnets of Glengarry will follow in the wake of no other clan in the Highlands," cried another, fiercely, "if you dare to assume the chief command, I will lead my men out of the field without their striking a single blow there. By heaven, I will."

"And, certes, the scarlet feathers of Clanronald shall not be far in the rear, for they will obey no commands but those of their own chief, who is determined not to lose another man in such a hopeless struggle as is now being maintained," echoed a third, with dogged resolution.

"I propose that Sir William Wallace assume the chief command; he bears a noble name, and one which is in itself an augury of success," said an Irish colonel, with some hesitation.

"Bah! a Lowlander! we will none of him," growled two or three of the Highland chiefs, as they handled their dirks with a half-threatening gesture.

"Let us cast lots, then, for him who is to command us; the matter can be decided in no other way, and whilst we wrangle for place and power the army without is getting demoralized, and the foe is moving down to crush us *en masse*," said Grant of Glenmorriston, with a reckless air.

"A good proposal; let us decide by the cast of the die, then no one can complain if the very fates declare against him," echoed Sir Hugh Bellechin; "Glengarry, Clanronald, Lochiel, are you with us?"

"Aye, aye, the dice-box—the dice-box," was the general cry, and a drum was quickly turned on end, the cups and cubes produced, and Sir Evan took up the dice to make the first throw.

He rattled them in the box for three or four seconds, and then cast them forth upon the drum-head. The throw was "deuce, ace."

"The dog-throw, by the gods! my chances are *nil*," he remarked grimly.

Clanronald grasped the dice-box in turn and threw sixes.

He uttered a cry of joy which caused several brows to knit with anger, and several hands to grasp their sword-hilts.

Then all the other chieftains and officers present in turn threw the dice, but not one amongst them could make a double-six.

Clanronald was, without doubt, the general chosen by the fates to rule the Scottish army, but yet the election did not appear to give satisfaction, and Lochiel, at length said angrily,—

"Rather than follow Clanronald, my clan shall march back to-morrow to their mountain fastnesses, 'tis a long cry to Lochan!"

"Ye need not be so proud, Lochiel, for we once humbled ourselves to follow behind your banner," sneered Clanronald.

"When was that?" demanded Lochiel with some surprise.

"When your whole clan—aye, every mother's son of them—ran away from us at the Race of Dunbar, and we followed them for three miles, till our green tartans were dyed of the same hue as their crimson ones, and our arms were weary with smiting them down," sneered the chief.

"Lying hound, have at thee!" cried Lochiel, fairly foaming at the mouth with rage, and he bestowed a hearty buffet on his rival's face.

Clanronald's sword was out in an instant, nor was Lochiel's slow to follow; cuts and thrusts were quickly exchanged, and the example being contagious, others followed it with avidity, and the *mecle* would have become a general one had not a tall swarthy man suddenly stalked into the te t, and said, in a stern commanding voice,—

"Sheath your swords, gentlemen, in the name of King James. Do the faithful sheep-dogs quarrel and fight among themselves when they know the wolf to be prowling around the fold? In heaven's name, my friends, are there not sufficient Southeners' throats to be cut that you must needs be flying at each other's?"

The combatants paused, and seemed half inclined to sheath their weapons, but the effect of the stranger's words was only transitory and quickly steel again clashed against steel in desperate and mortal combat, sparks of fire flashing freely from the clanging weapens.

"Hold, on your lives," shouted the tall dark stranger, this time in a voice of thunder. "He who does not put up his sword at my command shall die within the hour, riddled by the bullets of a file of my Irish brigade. Gentlemen, ye quarrel about that which concerns ye not, for a position which neither of ye can fill; for I am commander of the forces."

Had a cannon ball fallen in their midst the assembled Chieftains could not have been more astounded. Every sword flashed quickly back into its scabbard and a score of voices cried, "To the proof! to the proof!"

"Behold it, under the sign manual of the King himself," answered Colonel Cannon, for he it was who had so suddenly stilled the commotion, and as he spoke he flashed an embossed piece of vellum before their eyes covered with writing flourishes, and having a large seal appended. "Such is the will of the King, and you have but to bow to it as I should have done had one of you been elected in my place. God save King James!"

Few of the assembled Chieftains echoed the loyal cry; they loved their King and would have bled to the death in his cause, as they had amply proved by former acts of bravery and devotion; but stubborn Highland pride now stood in the way and prevented unity of thought and feeling, and brows were still bent in distrust and anger, though now more with indignation that an Irishman should be placed over them than in ill feeling towards each other.

"Colonel Cannon?" they muttered disdainfully as they drew themselves up, exchanged glances of hauteur, and twisted their wiry moustaches.

"Aye, Colonel Cannon," responded that officer, firmly, "whom ye will from this minute obey, loyally, zealously, implicity. Beware, for I will hang, draw, and quarter, the proudest chief amongst you at the first symptom of mutiny I observe in him; not from any personal animosity, but to prevent the contagion spreading, and for the sake of the good cause. Come, gentlemen, the tent is surrounded by my Irish brigade; will any of you force me to resort to extremities?"

For a minute there was a dead silence, then Cameron of Lochiel cried, "Until the approaching battle is over I will be leal and true, regarding you as our general; then I shall look upon you again as the man, and sword-point to sword-point, avenge upon your body the insult you have just offered to myself, and my brother chiefs. Aye, that will I, rest assured."

"Sufficent for the day is the evil thereof. I am content with thy answer," answered Cannon. "And now what say the rest of you?"

The replies of the other Chieftains were very similar to Lochiel's, but Colonel Cannon accepted them as sufficent, and answered,—

"That is well, and now let us hence, and form our little army in battle array, for I hear the drums of the advancing Southerners beating the point of war. Let us forget all personal animosities for a time, and thinking only of our King try to retain what Dundee so nobly won at Killycrankie, *victory*."

They then all quitted the tent and betook themselves to their different clans and companies.

## CHAPTER XLIV.

### THE HAUGHS OF CROMDALE.

Lochiel, Lochiel! beware of the day
When the Lowlands are gathered in battle array;
For a field of the dead rushes red on my sight.
And the clans of Culloden are scattered in fight.
They rally and bleed, for their kingdom and crown,
Woe, woe to the riders who trample them down;
Proud Cumberland prances insulting the slain,
And their hoof-beaten bosoms are trod in the plain.

The morning had broken dull and cold, the grey clouds swept hurriedly over the sky like charging squadrons, and the wind whistled over the bleak moor, on the high elevations, to the north of which was drawn up the Scottish army, only three thousand strong, in order of battle.

Away to the left drums were heard to beat, and anon came the frequent blast of the trumpet and the warble of the bugle. Then troops were descried forming slowly and quietly at the other end of the vast plain as if about to commence a safe and easy march. Horse and foot next took their places in long line, and here and there officers and camp followers were seen walking carelessly about, while at other spots some more rigid disciplinarians might be observed putting their men into better order and galloping hither and thither in all the bustle of command.

But as these Southern hosts approached nearer to the steep undulations whereon the kilted warriors of the north were already prepared to receive them, activity and temporary confusion succeeded the quiet regularity which had been before observable; reconnoitering horsemen were hurriedly recalled, musketeers were seen filing off to the left, the cavalry were collecting on the wings, the foot began to form line in the centre while a brilliant staff were discovered moving slowly from point to point, and from time to time a glittering horseman galloped away from it and seemed to convey orders to this or that regiment in different parts of the field.

Meanwhile the Scottish army remained quiet spectators of this martial scene, and standing in array on the summits of the hills patiently awaited the contest.

It was about twelve o'clock when the Southern trumpets sounded the advance, and as the first cannon shot boomed forth over the yellow gorse-clad plain, and through the grim gorges beyond, one long shout rent the air, breathing defiance to the mere handful of men who dared to bar their advancing course.

Onwards dashed the wave of Southern war, and General Cannon, afraid to order any of his Highland regiments to advance, lest the command might lead to a flat refusal on the part of some morose Chieftain, and thus set an ill example almost sure to be followed in other quarters, he merely permitted them to act on the defensive, a style of fighting to which Albion's warriors have ever had a strong aversion.

The battle lasted for three hours and was fought with dogged courage, but with little enthusiasm by the Scottish army. At the end of that period of time Lochiel had been driven in on the left by Leven and Mackay, and Clanronald on the right by Hastings' English regiment and Ramsay's lowlanders; while heavy bodies of cavalry were charging the centre, and every minute threatening to cut the little army in two.

Half an hour later both the right and the left wing were broken, and two or three clans were flying across the plain and falling by hundreds beneath the flashing swordblades of the English dragoons who gave them no quarter.

Presently the Royal Standard, of King James wavered and fell, and exposed to the fierce fire that rolled along the front of the English line, General Cannon himself wildly spurred to rescue it. As he galloped however to the spot where he had seen it disappear, lo! it rose again, only once more to sink as its last bearer was shot through the heart; and at the same instant a wild shout of victory rent the air, a shout which poor General Cannon was spared from hearing, for a round shot cut him in two just as it rang shrilly forth.

In sad confusion and disarray, the Scottish army then gave way at all points; discipline and order were completely lost among them, officers were without men, and men without officers; the slaughter was terrible, for it was wholesale.

Numbers of the Highland Chiefs and officers of note were taken prisoners or slain, and happy were the latter, for nearly every captive fell afterwards by the bullet or the headsmans' axe; mercy was rarely, indeed, shown in those days.

Such was the battle of Cromdale, which marked the utter prostration of King James's banner in the north, and it was followed only the following week by the battle of the Boyne in Ireland, which also terminated disastrously for the Stuart cause. Again King James had to seek refuge in France, where he was kindly received by King Louis, and allotted the Palace of St. Germain as a residence.

## CHAPTER XLV.

### CORGARF AND ITS GARRISON, THE WRECK, THE SAVED!

PASS we over the space of three weeks, and shift we the scene to the interior of the strong castle of Corgarf in the Western Highlands.

It was a dark and stormy evening, the sun had long dipped below the distant hills, and wildly drifting clouds of copper and leaden hue obscured the sky.

The copper tint soon disappeared, but the heavy leaden masses were momentarily increasing in extent and density, spreading over the heavens like a huge shadowy pall.

The wind was roaring fitfully amid all the towers and turrets of feudal Corgarf, and the usually sluggish and tranquil river that washed its base, roused from its accustomed quiet by the fierce tempest rolled in inky billows beneath the walls, dashed its feathery spray against the hoary cliffs upon which the fortress stood, while occasionally some mighty wave more powerful than the rest would cast its glittering saline particles even through the narrow windows above into the very rooms of the castle.

Beside one of these windows stood an old weather-beaten warrior of about sixty-five years of age, and by his side, with one white delicately-shaped hand resting on his shoulder, was a young girl of surpassing beauty.

She might have been between nineteen and twenty years of age, with a bright brunette complexion, and light brown hair, which was braided on her snowy brow, and glittered like threads of fine gold.

Her full and eloquent hazel eyes sparkled beneath long-fringed lashes, and delicately-pencilled brows, her teeth shone like two long strings of pearls between the red coral lips that were usually wreathed in a sweet but yet sad smile, while her attitude unstudied, and yet full of grace showed her exquisitely-proportioned and rounded figure to advantage, for its symmetry could not be concealed even by the stiff and unbecoming costume of the period in which it was arrayed.

Her companion, who was also her father, presented the very impersonation of ancient Roundhead chivalry.

The cast of his countenance was noble, but the features were stern, and harsh in expression.

The high forehead was open and unwrinkled, but the closely cropped hair, bushy eyebrows, and voluminous beard were white as the snows of winter.

The light grey eyes were restless and haughty, the lips compressed, and a slightly sarcastic curl, was their prevailing characteristic, while across the nose and right cheek was scored the dark purple seam of an old sword-cut, the glorious memento of some hard-fought battle field.

The old soldier was attired in a costume of buff-leather, he wore a dark steel cuirass and backplate, and his feet were encased in huge jack-boots, adorned with long steel spurs; attached to his belt was a heavy sword in a coarse leathern sheath which was balanced on the other side by a formidable brass-mounted holster pistol.

Both father and daughter were gazing from the iron barred window at the storm without, and after a silence of some minutes duration, the latter said.—

"Methinks, father, the tempest increaseth in fury, and the rising moon only serves to make the scene appear more fearful. Hark to the roar of the waves; they sound like the billows of the ocean. See how white the foam is, and the wind whistles amid the towers as though it were striving to overthrow them stone by stone."

"Fear not, my child, the towers of Corgarf stand too firmly on their foundations to be upset by a capful of wind; besides, the fortress has experienced a thousand gales such as this; yet nevertheless, the storm is very terrible, and I never before saw the meeting of the waters so rough. There seems to be a perfect whirlpool forming in mid-channel."

Flora Macclesfield, for she it was, trembled as she gazed towards the spot indicted by her father, for, in the middle of the stream, where the river first met the current of the ocean, the black billows had apparently centred all their fury, and the roar was deafening, as the waves threateningly raised their snowy crests, and whirled round in a boiling circle, like the mad waters of the Maelstrom.

"Oh, it is dreadful!" she exclaimed, with a shudder. "Alas for the poor sailors who are exposed to its violence, for, if the tempest is so terrible here, what must it be on the open sea?"

"Perchance scarcely worse than it is here, maiden; and, as for the sailors, a gracious Providence will protect them as it does the rest of us."

Both Flora and her father glanced hastily around at this unexpected reply, which was uttered in a man's voice, distinguishable by a strong nasal twang in the delivery, and their eyes simultaneously encountered the tall gaunt form and long-drawn countenance of the Reverend Ebenezer Makepeace, the chaplain of the castle.

In stature this remarkable addition to the party was considerably above the middle height.

He was also very thin, with high shoulders, legs, slightly bandy, and had long arms, terminated by bony hands of huge size.

He was attired in a suit of black of the true Covenanting cut, and his ill-shapen head, which, devoid of the usual appendage of throat, appeared as though stuck between his shoulders without the power of being moved, was long and dismal, being surrounded by lank black hair, smoothly brushed, and reeking with oil.

His forehead was high and narrow; his eyes small, black, and glittering like those of a basilisk; his nose long and aquiline; while the yellow saffron complexion, the high cheek bones, the wide mouth, with its thick red lips, and irregular projecting teeth, composed a *tout ensemble* of the somewhat equivocal charms of the intruder.

He drew back as he encountered the gaze of the Commandant and his daughter, and casting his eyes on the floor said,—

"Worthy Governor, pray pardon my interruption, but I came to announce that the evening meal awaited you."

"If so, we are ready for the evening meal, worthy Master Makepeace, as I daresay thou art, for I will warrant you preachers are ever recollecting the hours of feast, and forgetting those of fast. Art thou as hungry as usual, Ebenezer?"

"Yea, verily, I feel as though a little corporeal sustenence would do the inner man no hurt. The labourer is worthy of his hire; there is a time to eat and a time to fast, and now that the Lord hath delivered the bloody Philistines into our hands, it is the season to be joyful, and to drink the oil of gladness."

"It must be something stronger and more savoury than oil to make thee glad, or to give thee a cheerful countenance, Ebenezer," replied Sir Stephen Macclesfield, with a covert smile; "but lead the way to the supper room, and we will follow thee."

Then offering his arm to his lovely daughter, they quitted the window, and proceeded towards the northern tower.

Contrary to the custom of the period, Sir Stephen Macclesfield (now by the weak caprice of a monarch, restored to full favour at court, and intrusted with the command of this important Highland fortress) did not take his meals at the same table, or in the same room, as the officers and soldiers of his garrison.

This evening, the supper was spread in one of the private apartments of the castle, and there were present only two guests—the one being Ebenezer Makepeace, the other a young man attired in military costume, and apparently of about thirty years of age.

He had handsome, but somewhat sinister features, and pierceing black eyes, which ever appeared wandering and unquiet. He sat beside our heroine, and was, by turns, painfully polite or pointedly inattentive, while the lean chaplain, after having muttered grace, devoted himself entirely to the good things before him, and appeared unconscious of aught that was going on around.

A bright fire sparkled in the wide open grate, and three oil lamps lighted the apartment, and revealed the lofty oak-raftered ceiling, the faded tapestry that adorned the walls, and which waved to the cold breeze that swept in through the rickety and badly-constructed casements, and also disclosed to view the nature of the viands before which our quartette were seated. A huge round of beef, a jugged hare, and a portion of a roast peacock, being the principal dishes, whilst side plates of fruit and confectionery also graced the board, and the necks of half a dozen bottles of wine rose above them.

"Well, Albert," said the Commandant, after a pause, "what news hast thou brought us? how prosper our armies in the field, and what are the tidings of James Stuart, and his rebel army?"

"James has lost all on the banks of the Boyne Water. Ireland is ours from Sligo to Cork Harbour. Not a dozen men would muster around the Stuart banner, were it again unfurled in either of the three kingdoms; and the last of the race is again a fugitive in France."

"Is it, indeed, so? Now heaven be praised; but in truth this is all fresh news to me, for we are so shut up, and cut off from the rest of the world, in this old rat-haunted castle, that we learn but little of what is going on in the outer world."

"Nay; I should have fancied that the presence of cousin Flora would not have allowed gloom or care to become residents of the same atmosphere. I would that I had so charming a companion to beguile my tedious watch at Culcross."

And, as he spoke, the young soldier, whom the Commandant had called Albert, cast a loving glance at Flora, and then took her hand in his.

Our heroine, however, drew it quickly away, and a red flush mounted to her cheek, as she replied,—

"I pity the poor girl who has nothing better to do than amuse you. To many it would prove an irksome and a disagreeable task."

Albert bit his lip with vexation at the rejoinder, and quaffed a huge goblet of wine to conceal his mortification, but Sir Stephen said, angrily,—

"Methinks you might be more courteous in your speech, child; I fear that a border castle is but a poor school for politeness."

"Albert should reserve flattery and hollow compliment for those who like them," was the young lady's retort; "but hark! what was that?"

As she spoke, above the roar of the waters and the wild whistling of the wind, there echoed the boom of a distant gun.

Everybody sprang to their feet and listened.

But the next moment a flash of lightning darted through the room, a heavy peal of thunder reverbrated amongst the towers and turrets of the castle, like the crash of heavy cannon, and then a violent gust of wind blew in part of the casement of the window, and dashed the shattered particles of glass over the floor.

"Bless my soul, what a storm," exclaimed the old commandant, as he strove to prevent the extinguishment of the lamps by stuffing a chair-cushion into the aperture.

He was interrupted in the execution of this very feasible project by hearing heavy steps on the outer staircase, and the room door was unceremoniously thrown open by a burly trooper, who exclaimed, breathlessly—

"Commandant, there is a large sailing-craft drifting up the river towards the castle rocks; she is firing distress guns. What is to be done? we await your orders."

"Fix a beacon fire, then, on the walls to warn her to keep off. If she strikes the rocks on this side of the river she is lost."

"I don't think she obeys her helm, Sir Stephen, but your commands shall be attended to."

And he was about to leave the room when the commandant called him back.

"Prepare the boat, and get some strong ropes quickly. Place the latter on the windlass at the western portal, and be ready, with six men, to launch the boat at a moment's notice, for we may be able to save a few lives, even if the worst comes to pass. Now, children, let us proceed to the cliff-door in the room beneath the Wallace chamber, and see what we can see of this ill-fated vessel."

As they passed out of the room, the loud report of a third gun was audible close by.

It was answered by the harsher roar of the wild tide and howling wind.

Meanwhile, the tempest had increased in fury, and when our little party reached one of the embrasured windows of the Wallace tower, the scene presented was one of fearful magnificence.

The full moon shone out from amidst heavy rifts of leaden cloud upon the dark inky masses of tossing billows below, and in mid-stream, the spot where the waves of the firth met those of the river, the uproar was terrific, for the waves there whirled round in a mad circle, lifting their snowy crests far in the air, and hissing and roaring as they again sank, only the next instant to be tossed still higher and fiercer towards the sky.

---

## CHAPTER XLVI.

### MEETING OF FLORA AND SIR ANDREW DOUGLAS.

Directly towards the whirlpool, which was clearly defined by the surrounding darkness of cloud and water, one white sail was hurriedly flying, and although the wind had suddenly shifted dead ahead, and the snowy canvas fluttered heavily against the mast, this mysterious craft, dipping and plunging to every wave, was rushing madly on her doomed course.

In her bow three figures were dimly discernible.

Then a red flash broke from her deck, a wreath of smoke curled upward in the air, and the boom of another gun came over the seething waters.

Before its echo died away, the excited spectators saw her on the very margin of the swirl.

She rocked for an instant like a drunken man, then, lifting her bow quite out of the water, her mast toppled over the side, and, with the speed of a racehorse, she rushed into, and vanished amidst, the mist and spray.

Flora Macclesfield uttered a shriek as she beheld the vessel disappear. Albert Cunningham, with arms folded, looked on with an air of stoical indifference, and the chaplain, falling on his knees, uttered aloud in a nasal twang a few prayers, to which nobody appeared to listen.

Amid this din, the commandant's voice rang clear and hearty, as he issued different commands to his men, who were grouped together beside the portal that opened, or, in fact, overhung the sheer edge of the cliff, beneath which rushed the angry and foam-crested waters.

"Now off, my brave hearts, to the water-gate, launch the boat, and row out to see if any one can be picked up; but don't go too near the whirlpool, for I can't afford to lose you. Peter Giles, do thou keep watch on the tower, for the tide is setting in this way from the Firth, and it would not be improbable if some of the crew of yon sloop were to drift hitherward."

In prompt obedience to the mandate, several sturdy troopers of the garrison rushed down to the boat-house, which was cut out of a rock on a level with the river, and reached from the castle by a subterranean staircase and passage. A minute later, propelled by six flashing oar-blades, the heavy barge, mid clouds of seething spray and mist, was boldly racing out towards the scene of the catastrophe.

At this critical period, a cloud passed across the face of the moon, but the fiery radiance of the beacon light on the Wallace tower shed a lurid glow on the tossing waves immediately beneath, even so far as the shiny ridges of black rock which lay nearly a stone's throw from the cliff.

Suddenly Flora Macclesfield looked towards this rock, and uttered a startled cry upon perceiving a head and shoulders appear above the fierce tide, an upturned face, pale and ghastly, surrounded by long wet dangling hair, gazing up at the illuminated window, while the evidently drowning man seemed as though, with exhausted strength, he were vainly endeavouring to clutch on to the jagged edges of the rock to which the waves had borne him.

Flora called to her father and pointed out to him the drowning man.

"There!—there!" she said, "quick, or he is lost."

Cunningham moved not, and a sneer crossed his lips, as he exclaimed:—"Why so anxious, Cousin Flora? See you not by his long hair that the man is a Jacobite—a son of Belial—let him drown, 'tis a rascal the less."

"I only see that he is a fellow-being in mortal peril," was the reply. "O, father, what can we do?"

She turned to where Sir Stephen had stood; but he had rushed to the windlass, and a moment later his manly voice was heard shouting—

"Ho! there, my man, look out for a rope," and the old Commandant, who had secured the end of a long cord to a small ringed case ball, with a strong arm and skilful aim, threw it, with the rope attached, right over the rock to which the stranger was clinging, and luckily within reach of his hand.

"Now hold fast, and I will haul you up," he again halloed, in a voice that was audible even above the roar of the tempest, and hastily securing his end of the rope to the windlass roller, he prepared to wind it in.

With failing strength the drowning man laid hold of the strong cord, and, knowing that the waves would also help to bear him towards the castle cliff, some twenty yards distant, he wreathed a coil around his arm, and turning on his back, for he was too feeble to swim, he prepared to float across the narrow passage.

"Well done!" shouted Sir Stephen in tones of encouragement, as he beheld the rope swing nearly perpendicularly over the precipice, "cling on bravely with leg, arm, and hand, and in a twinkling you are landed."

As he spoke, the windlass, with a low creaking noise, began to revolve, the drowning man was hauled out of the water, and after dangling in the air for about a minute, during which time his brain seemed to whirl, and a million fiery stars appeared as though flitting before his eyes, he felt himself seized in a strong, powerful grip, and became aware that he was once more standing on firm ground, and safe from the deadly perils of the black rock and the whirlpool.

"Thanks, thanks!" he murmured, "you have saved my life," and then, his strength failing him, he fell on the floor insensible, beside the body of Flora Macclesfield, who had swooned away some minutes previously.

The Commandant raised him in his arms and halloed—"Cunningham, Ebenezer, come hither and help me to carry this poor half-drowned fellow to the hall-fire. It is the fatigue of swimming, and the excitement of being saved that have knocked him up. I don't think he has swallowed much water."

Five minutes later the rescued man was seated in the open settle of the hall, and slowly returning to consciousness. A dram of strong whisky poured down his throat by the Reverend Ebenezer Makepeace, and the intense heat of the blazing log-fire, contributed greatly to his restoration, and ere long he was able both to sit upright and to converse with those around him.

"Where are my gallant comrades?" was the first question; "am I the only one saved amongst them all?"

"I fear it has gone ill with your companions; we sent out a boat to their assistance, but, alas, it has returned without avail; no one has been picked up, and it is a miracle how you escaped; for there is a perfect whirlpool in mid-channel, and your vessel, if I mistake not, was drawn into its very vortex."

It was the old steward of the castle who spoke,

for Sir Stephen had, upon perceiving the first faint signs of approaching consciousness show themselves in the rescued man's face repaired to the bedchamber of his daughter, who had not yet recovered from her heavy swoon.

The young man shuddered as the steward spoke and then replied,—

"It is through God's mercy alone that I did escape, and next to him I have to thank you, my friends, for I could not have held on to the rock a minute longer, and had you not thrown me a rope I should have been lost."

In the countenance and form of the rescued man there was much to interest and admire. Tall and finely formed, his figure was both graceful and athletic; his features, clearly cut, were at the same time pleasing, and expressive of the utmost frankness and good nature; his hair was long and curling, his forehead being broad and high, and slightly scarred on the left temple as by the passage of a pistol bullet, while both his peaked beard and heavy moustache, pointed sharply upwards, were black and glossy as jet.

The costume of the stranger was unmistakably that of a Royalist cavalier, for his breeches were of white satin, slashed with blue; his doublet was cloth of gold, trimmed with costly fur; and his sword-belt glittered with jewels in the ruddy fire-light.

From his left shoulder depended a short cloak, also of white satin, edged with miniver, and his feet were encased in boots of untanned leather, the wide open tops being fringed with lace, while the heels were adorned with long gilded spurs.

The cavalier's plumed cap had been lost amidst the seething waters of the river, and the only weapon he bore was a small poignard in a velvet sheath.

For a few minutes the position was rather embarrassing to all parties; but presently the Commandant returned to inquire after the rescued man, and perceiving him recovered so far as to be able to sit up and converse, he shook hands with him, and congratulated him warmly on his escape.

The cavalier very gracefully returned thanks, and then added,—

"Sir Governor, by the uniform of your garrison, I perceive, as well as from your own costume and demeanour, that you hold this castle for King William, so I presume that I am to consider myself a prisoner."

"Not by any means, Sir Cavalier; had I captured you in battle or in siege, sword in hand under the banner of James Stuart, my lawful captive would I have held you, but you are here by the dispensation of Providence. You did not come against these walls in hostile guise, but were driven hither by wind and tempest. I will, therefore, not take advantage of the chance. You are a guest only within these walls, and to-morrow shall be at liberty to depart at will, in whatever direction it may please you to journey. Meanwhile as you are recovered from your immersion, we will conclude the evening with a bottle or two of choice wine, a bowl of punch, and the imbibing of the pleasant herb for which we have to thank the immortal Raleigh."

The stranger bowed his acknowledgments, at this speech.

"Here, Jeremiah," continued Sir Stephen to a tall trooper, who stood near, "bring hither wine and tobacco, and brew us a bowl of thy best punch, for the manufacture of which, in spite of that long name and longer face, thou art so worthily famed. We will listen to thy adventures over the social glass, Sir Cavalier."

"You overwhelm me with your kindness and hospitality. Your chivalrous courtesy renders me eternally your debtor. In return for life, liberty, and this hearty reception, I can but offer you the hand and the friendship of a Royalist and a soldier. I am Sir Andrew Douglas, late captain of King James's Scottish Life Guards."

"What! the most daring cavalry officer in the Scottish army, who turned the fortunes of the day at Killycrankie, by that headlong charge on the English guns? By heaven! you are he, too, who was my guest at Carlisle, and who afterwards saved my dear child's life in the Cathedral Close, when she was about to suffer martyrdom. Thy hand, thy hand, my boy; this is indeed a joyous meeting."

"What, Sir Stephen Macclesfield! is it indeed you? Faith to be candid, I had forgotten your countenance. And Flora, where is she?" stammered Sir Andrew.

"In her chamber just recovered from a heavy swoon, caused by over-excitement concerning the safety of the ship which has just foundered. Had she known that you were a passenger therein her distress would have been still greater."

"Oh, Sir Stephen, can I not at once see her?" asked our hero impatiently.

"Yes, boy, that you can, and delighted will Flora be to see your face again, for your name is ever on her lips, and your love, I warrant me, cherished in her heart. Come, follow me, I will take you to her presence."

But it was not needed, for, guided by some instinct which told her that one she loved was near, Flora at this moment entered the vast hall with timid and uncertain gait, but, catching sight of the young cavalier her demeanour suddenly changed, and with a light bounding step and a little cry of joy she crossed the tesselated floor and cast herself into his arms.

"Come away, come away, children, don't be making fools of yourselves before such an audience," exclaimed Sir Stephen, in a half-whisper, half growl, for he had a great horror of a scene, and he bustled the young people out of the hall and up the great staircase to one of the reception rooms in the Bruce tower forthwith.

Five minutes later, beside a wide fireplace, with its ruddy flames and crackling logs, our trio sat and conversed, while the firelight flashed upon their picturesque costumes, and on their happy faces, dimly discernible through the cloud of smoke that the still raging storm beat down the ill-constructed chimney, while the dark oak floor glittered beneath the rays of the oil-lamps that were lighted in many parts of the hall, as did the banners, armour, and warlike weapons that hung suspended from the tapestried walls.

## CHAPTER XLVII.

### FLORA AND SIR ANDREW RELATE THEIR ADVENTURES.

Froth it up, girl, till it splash every curl,
October's the liquor for trooper and carl;
Bubble it up, merry gold in the cup,
We never may taste of to-morrow night's sup.

(Those red ribbons glow on thy bosom below,
Like apple-tree bloom on a hillock of snow).

"Why, Flora, my own darling, how came you here, and how happens it that your father is again restored to favour at Court? Tell me your adventures, dear one, from the hour that I quitted you at Edinburgh Castle, now more than a year and three months ago, until the present time," said Sir Andrew, at length.

"Nay, dearest, first tell me thine," was the fond reply.

"No, that is scarcely fair; for another half hour I shall hardly feel equal to the task, but I have strength to listen, if I have not yet quite sufficient to talk; so, if you will first tell me yours, my adventures shall be duly narrated to you in turn," said the young royalist, pressing his lips to the young girl's forehead.

Thus urged, Flora Macclesfield commenced as follows—

"You must know," began Flora, "that I remained an honoured guest within the walls of Edinburgh Castle until Sir John Lanier, with a powerful siege train, and overwhelming forces, at last compelled the Duke of Gordon to yield at discretion.

"The women and children within the garrison were allowed to go wheresoever they listed; but every male defender was marched off into captivity, and the majority of them have since perished, either by the axe, the gibbet, or the bullet.

"The Duke of Gordon was alone missing, and at this Sir John Lanier and the Williamite officers were very wrath, for there was a heavy amount of blood money on his head, and the pockets of these worthies were as nearly dry of red money as the block on Tower-hill was dry of red blood, and both thirsted for a fresh supply.

"Fancying that the duke must have escaped dressed in female garb, the order that the women and children should be permitted to leave the castle and city unmolested was hastily rescinded, and I and another lady, who bore me company, first heard of this whilst partaking of an humble breakfast in a coffee-house in the Canongate.

"Dreading that we might yet be subjected to a long and tedious imprisonment, we gave out that we were the wives of two officers in General Mackay's army in the north, and were about to repair to the Highlands to rejoin our husbands, with some difficulty hired two horses, and mounting in hot haste, lost no time in leaving Edinburgh behind us.

"On we rode, sad enough at heart, until midday, by which time we were very wearied, and catching sight of a secluded farm-house at some distance from the high road, and nearly concealed by trees, we rode thither to seek rest, food, and shelter.

"This farm-house was an old, large place, with a comfortable kitchen, and a blazing fire on the hearth, and quite in the chimney-corner, though it was the 23rd of June, sat an old man wrapt in a frieze coat, and eating his porridge.

"There was an old woman, too, in a blue and white knit hood and red flannel petticoat, sitting in a chair by the dresser spinning, not with a spinning-wheel, but with a distaff, and there was a young woman also, skimming the pot that hung over the fire, and another middle-aged woman in a lawn cap, and bore lace pinners, the mistress, looking into a large metal pan of milk, which the dairymaid was stirring as though she had eyes for nothing else.

"It's all along of her," said the old woman, turning sharply round and breaking her thread, 'and this is her doings, too, said she; 'faith I will have her burnt one day.'

"'I wish I'd given her that piece of bread,' said the dairymaid, 'for the curd is plainly bewitched, and will never come.'

"As she spoke she raised her head, and perceived us, and then there was much bustling and the mistress, with many curtsies, asked pardon for her neglect, but the case was, she said, that she feared they were all bewitched.

"I had heard much of witches and witchcraft in my English home, and I cannot but say I believe that such things may sometimes be; but the stories these people told me were so silly, that, had not my heart been too heavy, I think I should have laughed outright.

"There was an old woman, they told me, who dwelt in a wood, some ten miles off, and she had caused their cart to stick fast in a lane, and had bewitched a whole pan of milk, which was to make cheese; moreover, she was attended by an imp, whose howling frightened the whole neighbourhood; and many other stories did they tell us, for their whole talk was of their farm, and of this witch of Balesboro' Wood, as they called her.

"The people, however, were kind, and heaped our wooden trenchers with chicken pasty, and brought us a great bowl of custard, and drew their oldest mead and barley wine, and then the mistress showed us into a pleasant chamber, with a half-tester bed, and blue check hangings; and the chimney was filled with a great bow pot, and being heartily tired, we slept soundly for some hours.

"When we awoke, it was still early in the afternoon. Oh, how slowly passed the time. We continued to sit up in the chamber that had been allotted to us, for although we had told the farmer's family the same story concerning ourselves as we had told at the coffee-house, yet I feared that in conversation we might unwittingly betray ourselves.

"My companion, fair mistress Annie Laurie,* feared so too, so we kept closely to our room, nor did we go down stairs until twilight had well set in.

"We had scarcely entered the common sitting-room, when the carter came in, who had just returned from selling the dairy produce in Edinburgh, and he told how great an excitement still prevailed in the city concerning the escape of the Duke of Gordon, and that nearly all the females who had quitted the castle in the morning had been re-captured, and that the rest were being diligently searched for and could not escape, for that the whole country round was being scoured by troopers, who were especially anxious to secure the person of one Flora Macclesfield, against whom a death warrant was still extant.

"Overcome by terror, and to conceal the emotion from those present, I turned towards the window, flung open the casement, and looked and

* Annie Laurie was a real character, and figured conspicuously in history about this time.

listned; but there was nothing either to be heard or seen.

"It was very kind of those worthy people to ask us to stay the whole night at the farm, and we accepted the invitation, but again early retired to our chamber.

"It was a bright evening, and when at length night came on, it could scarcely be called so; for the deep blue sky only shaded each object, and right opposite our window clear twilight lingered. How anxiously I looked out, fearing to see I knew not what; but nothing met my gaze save two or three fields, and a narrow road, the same we had pursued in the morning, and the desolate moor beyond.

"'Dear Flora, come to bed,' cried Annie Laurie, 'do try and sleep, and recover strength, for we know not what's before us, or how soon we shall need it.'

"'I cannot sleep, Annie,' said I.

"'Nay, lay down at least,' persisted she, 'for to-morrow night Heaven alone knows where we shall lay our heads.'

"'There is danger threatening us here, Annie; let us flee,' said I.

"'Not until midnight, and then we must march without beat of drum,' she said gaily.

"I sat down again at the open casement, and Annie got out of bed and sat by my side to comfort me, cheering me with words of hope.

"Ten struck, eleven, and then, oh, how long did it seem to twelve!

"'Hark!' said Annie, and she laid her hand on my arm. 'Footsteps! and the tramp of horses! Heavens! if it is us they seek!"

"I rose up and looked out. The low trampling sound came nearer, and presently I could just discern men and horses.

"'They are Swart Ruyters,' cried Annie, and she clasped her hands and wept aloud.

"Oh, how I strained my eyes as the troopers passed along almost within musket-range of the house, and I caught sight of one form that made my blood curdle in my veins! Surely there he was, the leader of the second troop, the rider of that horse that looked so much darker than the rest, even though all were black. Surely that was my terrible foe, Sir Edward Hamilton, but they passed at too great a distance to allow, by the starlight, of more than mere conjecture, and yet I felt that it was he.

"A little later we perceived a small body of foot sweeping onwards in the stillness of midnight in the same direction as that taken by the horse, and we could even hear the rustle of their tread on the grass.

"Another hour, oh how long, passed, and then Annie Laurie arose from the bed, whereon she had again flung herself, saying, quite calmly, 'We must prepare for the worst, we must quit this place, and that speedily.'

"She took off my gown, and unfastening the long hanging sleeves that were then worn, she took out the lead that was sewn at the bottom and slipt four gold pieces into each instead; she then unripped my hood, and between the velvet and the lining she put some letters of my father's, and money within them, and lastly, sewed my mother's miniature and my gold chain into my girdle, which, for greater security, she buckled under my gown.

"These preparations were but just finished when we heard a noise at the gate, and then a voice, a woman's voice, speaking in accents of pain.

"We rushed down and opened the front door, and beheld a lady seated on a jaded horse, the breast of her habit dyed with blood, she was wounded to death.

"The people of the house were now up, but too much affrighted to be able to render any assistance, so saying nought to them, Annie and I ran out, lifted the wounded lady from her saddle and led her in.

"No sooner had we laid her on the sofa than, recognising us, she exclaimed, 'Flora, Annie, thank God you have escaped! but there is no time to lose; the troopers are close upon my trail, and the bullet of one of them has proved swifter than his horse. It has sped my life away, but I die happy, oh, so happy!' and with these words she lay back and expired.

"The mistress of the house informed us that she knew who we were, and dared not harbour us, though she would not betray us. Alas! the poor dead girl had unwittingly betrayed us in her last moments.

"The good farm-wife behaved very kindly, however. She gave us food, and lent us each a large country cloak, and told us that if we would go about half a mile along the moor in the opposite direction to that in which the Stadtholder's troops were patrolling, we might find shelter under some elder bushes, and at nightfall she would come to us and show us where to go.

"I doubt not but the woman told us rightly, and I doubt not but that she meant to come to us, but we knew not a step of the way, and we most likely took a different path, so onward we went, looking out in vain for the elder bushes, and quite bewildered on the wide moor.

"How long we wandered I know not, but we were sorely tired; and as we saw some trees at a distance, we made towards them.

"Oh, how pleasant was their shade, and how soft the bank beneath them. It was well that we reached that place, for I think that I could not have walked a stone's throw farther.

"A little stream ran hard by, so I went and sat down beside it, and bathed my head in its water, and after a while was refreshed; but Annie Laurie was very anxious to find a shelter, and as she thought she could see smoke among the trees, she set forth towards it, bidding me wait her return.

"I had not sat long alone before I heard a low mournful noise—a kind of whine—and looking round I saw, under the farthest tree, a huge black dog, miserably thin, who held out his fore-paw to me, and looked as though asking help.

"I always loved dumb animals, and well do they know who love them, so I went to him, and found that his paw had been terribly torn, as though in a trap.

"Well, I pitied the poor creature, who looked so piteously up in my face, so I dipped my kerchief in the stream and carefully washed the wound, and bound it as well as I could with a strip of linen, which I tore from the covering of the bundle I carried.

"It was but a little time after, when I heard a trampling of horses. Oh, how I longed for Annie to return, that we might seek together some more secure place of refuge; but she did not come, and the sounds drew nearer, and I could now hear voices, and the clink of steel bits and sword-scabbards.

"It was a troop of Swart Ruyters making search after the duke, for I heard a voice, which I plainly distinguished as that of the ferocious Hamilton, say,—

"'A thousand pounds to whoever finds him;' and then—'Beat about here, for, if he is not caught. we may find the death-doomed traitor, Flora Macclesfield, for whom a reward of five hnudred pounds is offered, or some of the other lady rebels, who are worth just five pounds a head.'

"And he uttered a reckless laugh as he concluded.

"I started up; my peril was imminent.

"If they once commenced systematically to beat the bushes, the troopers could not fail to discover me.

"But which way should I go? that was the all-important question.

"The dog then looked earnestly up into my face. and limped off towards the right, and then stopped, as though bidding me follow him.

"I felt that he was the instrument ordained for my deliverance, and I did so, implicitly.

"It was a long, a narrow, and a tangled path that he pursued, and how far I know not; only I know how rejoiced I was to hear the voices and footsteps of the rough soldiers sounding fainter and fainter in the distance.

"At length we came to an open space, and on one side were two very large beech-trees, and under them, though you might scarcely see it, a low miserable hut, scarcely better than a cattle-shed, and in the dog went, and I followed.

"It was so dark inside that I could see nothing, but I sat down on the floor, little thinking that any one besides myself was within, when suddenly I heard a harsh, croaking voice say,—

"'Come, Rutterkin,' and as I looked again there seemed to be an old woman at the farther end crouching over a few lighted sticks, and patting the dog.

"'Good mother, said I, 'pardon me, bnt I've lost my way, and am sorely wearied.'

"The old woman rose up and hobbled towards me, and fixing on me the fiercest pair of blue eyes I ever saw, said,—

"'Who are you, and what do you come here for?'

"The poor dog now came up, and laid his wounded paw on my lap, for I was too faint to rise up from the floor, while the old woman stood staring at me as though she would look me through.

"'Who are you?' she said again, 'and with silver buckles in your shoes, too? Such do not often tread my floor.'

"'Indeed, good mother, I have lost my way,' said I again.

"'Dost thee know her, Rutterkin?' asked the old woman to her dog; but the poor half-starved animal was smelling and scratching at the bundle in which was the food the farmer's wife had given us, so I opened it, and took out a piece of bread, which he devoured greedily.

"At this the old woman set up a scream, exclaiming, with a laugh,—

"'*White* bread, white bread, white manchet bread! Ay, Rutterkin, 'tis long since you or I saw the like.'

"'Good mother, take some,' said I, again opening the bundle.

"She snatched a piece of bread and a piece of pasty from it, as though she had been starving (which indeed was the case), while the dog leaped up, and laid his maimed paw on my shoulder, and tried to lick my face.

"'He loves you,' said the old woman, 'poor Rutterkin, who hath been hunted and hounded from tything to tything, he loves you ay, the lady with silver buckles in her shoes hoth fed the witch's dog with white manchet.'

"Oh! what did I feel then! I had not much fear of witches as such, but I knew they were outcasts and abandoned creatures, and she was poor, even to starvation; how eagerly she had eyed my silver buckles; how certain she was that I was a lady; ay, and I had not in gold pieces enough to make her fortune? I dared not look towards her, but I glanced towards the door; could I not, though so faint, at least strive to escape?'

"Just then my eyes fell on a little bird that had flown in, and was busily picking up the crumbs at my feet.

"'God careth for the sparrows,' said I, 'surely He will care for me.'

"How swiftly this thought darted into my mind, a blessed thought! so I looked up to the old woman,—'Good mother,' said I, 'may I stay here and rest?'

"'Ay, that you shall,' said she, 'for I know well who you are—you are one of the ladies who quitted Edinburgh Castle this morning, and for whom the soldiers are even now searching. Nay, you are she for whose capture a reward of five hundred pounds is offered, and whose death warrant is even now in existence; but fear not, I will not betray you, and here you are safer than in a church, for who of all the country round will enter the witch's hut, the Witch of Balesboro' Wood?'

"Oh, how strange that I should have been led thither to the saving of my life.

"Well, the old woman gathered fresh fern, and spread my cloak on it, and made me lie down and then she bathed my feet, all the while the poor dog kept watch beside me, looking in my face with its half-human eyes.

"But I was much distressed about Annie Laurie, so the old woman promised to seek for her, and quite worn out I fell asleep, I know not for how long.

"When I awoke I looked up and there was dear Annie by my side. and there too was the faithful dog Rutterkin licking my hand.

"Oh, how odd it appeared that the daughter of Sir Stephen Macclesfield, late a Colonel Commandant of a city, should be lying in a miserable hut, the strictly-brought-up Puritan the guest of a reputed witch!

"What strange extremes, and yet at that very time the e extremes were linked together by the bond of a common danger, for the godless soldiers who burnt the Bibles at Peebles would as soon have hanged me as the old witch.

"More than a fortnight we stayed with the witch of Balesboro' Wood, for a hot pursuit was during all that time made through the country for the Duke of Gordon, who the wise heads at

Edinburgh seemed determined to think had made his escape in the character of one of the ladies who had been permitted to leave the castle on the morning of its capitulation.

"During that entire fortnight she fetched us food from the neighbouring farms, and made enquiries concerning the patrolling of the troops, so that at the earliest opportunity we might be enabled to continue our journey in safety, a time which at length, thank God, arrived.

"The old woman procured us a stout nag, with a saddle and pillion, a rough countryman's suit for Annie, and a female peasant's dress for myself. And so we mounted, Annie sitting cross-legged, as became the character she had assumed, with her beautiful hair all bundled up under her rough Glengarry bonnet, and her face dyed a dark brown so as to resemble sun-tan, whilst I occupied the pillion behind, with a market basket on one arm and the other thrown around Annie's waist.

"'Go due north to Dumfermline, Mistress Flora Macclesfield,' said the old woman, 'and there thou wilt meet thy father and a noble train of horse and foot. He is restored to royal favour, and is on his way to assume the governorship of the fortress of Corgaf, on the Firth of Dornoch. With him thou wilt be safe. Adieu.'

"'Mistress Annie Laurie,' she continued, turning to my companion, 'accompany thy friend to Dumfermline, and there thou shalt meet thy affianced husband, Sir Walter Fenton, of that Ilk, wing, I say unto you thou wilt be his wife within the month.'

"We parted from the old woman with hearty thanks, though putting little faith in her predictions, and pressed her to take four gold pieces, but she would not, for she said they might bring her into trouble, so we gave her what silver we had, and an address whereby in future she could communicate with us, should she ever be in want.

"She asked me for a keepsake, which I was right willing to give, so I made her take a solitary gold piece; it was one of the Commonwealth, and a hole had been bored in it, so the poor creature said that she would keep it for luck's sake, and we bade her farewell and rode quickly away.

"Without any further perils we arrived at Dumfermline, and the very first person we met was Annie's affianced husband, Sir Walter Fenton, and whilst we were at breakfast in his noble mansion that overlooked the high street, martial music was heard in the distance, and presently a procession of horse and foot soldiers passed beneath the window, and in the commanding officer I recognised my father. Thus did the witch's prophecies come true in every particular, for within a month Annie Laurie was married to her lover, and I accompanied my father hither, where we have remained ever since."

. . . . .

Sir Andrew pressed the lovely girl to his heart, and imprinted a kiss on her cheek, much to the consternation and scandal of the Reverend Ebenezer Makepeace, and then turning to Sir Stephen, said,—

"If it is not an impertinent question, sir, may I ask how you were fortunate enough to be restored to King William's favour so speedily?"

"Why, King William, God bless him! never knew of my iniquitous impeachment by the queen, prompted as she was by that arch-fiend, Sir Edward Hamilton. Directly the noble Dundee rescued me from my horrible dungeon at Carlisle, I rode on the spur to London, obtained an interview with the king, and told him the whole of the facts of the case. Of course, my restoration to favour was immediate; William of Orange was not going to deem a traitor one who had fought and bled under his banners for one-and-twenty years, and had thrice saved his life in French, Dutch, and Spanish campaigns, so he gave me the governorship of his old fortress, which you see I still retain."

"And now, Andrew, tell us your adventures since you left me under the protection of his grace of Gordon on that terrible night of riot and bloodshed in Edinburgh," pleaded Flora, letting her fair head sink on her lover's shoulder.

## CHAPTER XLVIII.

### SIR ANDREW'S NARRATIVE.

Thus urged, our hero began his narrative in turn, and told in detail every historical event of the campaign in the Highlands, and every personal adventure connected therewith, until he came to the evening whereon he and the Earl of Dumbarton had been made prisoners in the lone hut on the Houghs of Cromdale, at which point we will also take up the narrative for the benefit of our readers.

. . . . . .

"We were gagged and bound, so that we could not help ourselves in the least," he continued, "and in that state we were carried out of the hut and placed upon two horses, and surrounded by a troop of English cavalry, whose chargers' feet were shod with felt, so that they should make no noise while the steel sword scabbards of the troopers, the curb, chains, and every other jingling accoutrement were muffled for the same object, and we were borne away from the Scottish camp at a swift gallop.

"We travelled for at least sixteen hours without stopping, except to obtain relays of horses, and so the second night drew on, and at dusk we encamped in a grim and rocky defile, with piles of granite hills rising tier above tier on our right, and dusky woods stretching away for miles on our left, above which, at some little distance, rose the towers of a castle.

"The troopers, who were about twenty in number, lighted a fire, and proceeded to warm themselves, and to cook their rations, whilst Dumbarton and myself were left bound, propped up against a couple of stunted pollards, and at our back a dense little grove of hazel-bushes.

"Here we were left to ponder upon our approaching fate, which we knew would be either the halter or the block, most probably the former for myself and the latter for the Earl, and to hatch some plan of escape, which as yet seemed a matter of impossibility, so well were we watched and guarded.

"The face of nature was now beginning to get very indistinct, the light had nearly faded out of the west, and we began to calculate that in another hour the moon would be up, and then all chance of giving the English dragoons the slip would be impossible.

"At this moment we were startled by a voice whispering in our ears, 'Hist, I am a friend, and have followed you more than a hundred and fifty

THE HIGHLANDER SINGLE-HANDED DEFENDED THE PASS.

miles on horseback and on foot, to effect your deliverance. Sit still, and I will cut your bonds, then I will creep ahead and steal some of those rascals' weapons for you: faith we will trick the Southern loons yet.'

"As he spoke, still keeping under the shadow of the hazel bushes that grew right up to the stunted pollards, against which we leaned, the Highlander drew a skene-dhu from his belt and severed our bonds in a twinkling; oh, what a joy it was to feel ourselves free.

"He then crept snakewise forward in the long grass, and stole two sabres and four pistols, belonging to the revelling soldiery, together with a bag of powder and some bullets, and returning with them in the same stealthy manner, placed the weapons in our hands.

"We then perceived for the first time that he was a tall, stalwart, red-haired Athol man, with an eagle-plumed bonnet, a hairy sporan, richly chequered plaid, tartan trews, and silver buckled shoes, and that he was armed with cuirass and back plate, and bore his target of bull's hide, studded with brass bosses, on his back, whilst in his belt was a heavy broadsword, balanced on the other side by a brace of formidable pistols.

"'To the hills,' he said, impressively; 'clamber up those rocks, noble Earl, and thou too, brave Life Guardsman; they are easy for Highlanders to climb, and a hundred feet up, a silvery maple tree marks the entrance to a cave, wherein I'll be bound these Southerners will never find ye; I will stay to cover your retreat, and will rejoin you anon—away, I say.'

"We would have urged him to accompany us, but one glance at his face assured us that he was not to be dissuaded from a course he had resolved on. We therefore clambered up the cliff as well as we could, with our numbed limbs and ill-adapted attire.

"Before, however, we had ascended more than fifty yards, the moon suddenly shone out, and the troopers discovered us in an instant, and with loud cries started up from their camp fire.

"With arquebuss balls flying around our heads, we hastened on, while the Highlander threw himself on his knees on a projecting ledge of rock and gallantly defended the ascent, by hacking and hewing with his broadsword at the heads of the ascending troopers, many of whom he slew before he was himself despatched by a pistol bullet in turn.

"His bravery, however, secured our safety, for we gained the cave, and although the troops searched the cliffs for hours they totally failed to discover us.

"Since that fearful night myself and Dumbarton had been fugitives in the Highlands, and only yesterday succeeded in inducing the captain of a small coasting craft, at Invergordon, to carry us over to France. We set sail, but a storm arose and drove us north, and finally wrecked us in this Firth of Donoch. I am the sole survivor, and the gallant Earl of Dumbarton sleeps his last sleep beneath nine fathoms of blue water. Well, anyhow, that is a better death than one by the headsman's axe on Tower Hill."

When Sir Andrew had concluded his narrative, the little party broke up, for it was now one o'clock in the morning, and retired to their respective bed-chambers.

## CHAPTER XLIX.

### AN UNWELCOME ARRIVAL.—DOOMED TO DEATH.—A RESCUE.

Early the following morning Sir Andrew Douglas rose from his couch. He had dreamed of his beloved Flora, and he now arrayed himself with more than his usual care, ere he quitted his chamber to repair to the lower apartments of the castle.

Arrived at the hall of state, he found it empty, and upon questioning a trooper who, with sword and armour clanking, was pacing up and down the room, he learned that Sir Stephen Macclesfield was going the morning rounds and that his daughter had not yet risen.

To pass away the time, therefore, the cavalier strolled lazily up and down the polished oaken floor, ever and anon pausing to gaze from the arched and mullioned windows at the landscape without.

The morning sun shone brightly upon the little town of Corgaif, with its square towered church and white-washed cottages, upon the gently sloping hills at its back, carpeted with purple heather and yellow broom, and further away its rays rested on the dark woods of Costerphire, whose bare boughs were encrusted with a sparkling network of hoarfrost, until the view was bounded by the mighty cliffs of Ruart, whose hoary brows rose in shear precipices, eight hundred feet above the highest of the forest monarchs, that flourished their leafless branches at their base.

Immediately below the walls flowed the now tranquil waters of the Firth, for the tempest had ceased, and the silvery waves rippled on once more in the usual monotony, and the dark earthen colour of the water alone indicated the terrible storm which had so lately ruffled the treacherous tides. But the distant heath looked fresher and greener, for the wintry thunder speat, and the glassy slope outside the castle walls glittered with rain drops, as though they were sparkling jewels.

As he gazed with admiration at the scene and thought upon the fate of the noble Earl, his late companion in arms, who was sleeping his last long sleep beneath the waters of the Firth, the blast of a bugle echoed shrilly from without, and upon looking once more in the direction of the village, he beheld a troop of horsemen slowly approaching the castle walls.

They were attired in the yellow uniforms of the Dutch brigade and wore buff coats, with iron helmets, corselets and back plates, and were mounted on fine grey chargers.

At their head rode a stalwart warrior, attired in a vivid scarlet uniform, while his dark locks and swarthy visage were surmounted by a polished steel morion, adorned by a perfect cloud of crimson and white plumage. His further defensive armour consisted of a cuirass and back plate, and his feet were encased in huge jack-boots, which, together with his breeches, were of untanned leather. A long sword hung at his side, and on his breast glittered a silver medal, and while he sat his dark bay charger like a true horseman, his whole bearing was that of a thorough soldier.

On the left of the officer rode a trooper carrying the national banner, and on his right a trumpeter.

The other troopers rode a few yards in the rear, and Sir Andrew found that they were twelve in number.

Whilst he was looking at the approaching cortege, and trying to remember where he had last beheld the handsome but stern face of the commanding officer, the report of a calvern, from the tower above, rang harshly out upon the still morning air.

The clash of arms, the shrill clangour of a trumpet, and the rattling of heavy chains ensued, as the drawbridge was lowered on the approach of the little party of armed men, who the next instant crossed it, and disappeared from view around the angle of the tall flanking tower of the Norman portal.

With a sigh our hero turned from the window, and as he did so an opposite door opened, giving admission to Flora Macclesfield.

The fair puritan looked even more beautiful than she had done the night before, and Sir Andrew, full of love and enthusiasm, sprang forward and clasped her in his arms.

Flora blushed crimson and her eyes sought the ground, as she said,—

"Andrew, you must follow me. A company of Dutch dragoons has arrived at the castle, and my father bids me to tell you that for a few hours you must submit to be concealed in the blue chamber, for if once you are discovered, he can neither say nor do aught to protect you from a superior officer in King William's army."

"I like not hiding from a foe, dear Flora, yet if your father wishes it I will do so."

As he spoke he raised her hand to his lips and kissed it fervently, whereupon Flora blushed deeper than before, and said hurriedly,—

"Dear Andrew, hesitate not a moment, but

THE DEATH OF THE MARQUIS OF ANNANDALE.

follow me to where all the Dutchmen in England could not discover you," and turning round, she tripped lightly across the hall, followed by the Royalist Cavalier.

Threading several gloomy passages, they at last gained a large and handsome room.

"We are now near the place of thy concealment," said our heroine, and lifting the heavy tapestry she struck the wall, and Sir Andrew heard the click of a spring, as a secret door opened and disclosed a small apartment within.

"This is the blue chamber," said Flora, as she and the knight entered, "and here you must stay until you receive tidings that you may quit it with safety."

"And you will bear me those tidings, sweet Flora?" asked Sir Andrew.

"Perhaps I will myself," was the laughing retort, "but now be quiet, and to make all still more secure, I shall lock you in and not part with the key to a soul," and bounding out of the room, before the young Scot could detain her, she shut the door, and as the lock shot back into its securer, he heard a merry laugh without and then little light footsteps crossing the adjoining room and along the oak floor of the passage beyond.

Hours passed on, hours of long and weary solitude to the lonely captive, uncheered as they were by the presence of her he loved more than life.

Many strange sounds had during that time reached him in his confinement, such as the frequent sounding of trumpets, discharge of guns, and loud laughter of soldiery.

At length it seemed as if voices and footsteps echoed close by, and as he breathlessly listened, they drew nearer and nearer yet, and then ensued other sounds, namely, a heavy knocking and hammering against two sides of the room wherein he was hidden, and he could hear oaths and impatient exclamations frequently exchanged.

The truth suddenly burst upon him. A search was being made, a search for him, and the Dutch soldiery were sounding the panelling, in the hope of discovering a secret door, whose hollow reverberation to their blows would apprize them of its existence.

A cold perspiration stood upon the young cavalier's brow, less at dread of his own probable fate, if discovered, than at the thought that his being found concealed in the castle would again imperil the position and safety of those who had given him shelter and protection, even as they had done at Carlisle.

For several minutes the rapping continued, and then a loud shout of exultation announced that the secret door had been discovered.

The blows thereupon grew heavier than before, but the door stood firm, and presently a voice, which seemed very familiar to Sir Andrew, cried,—

"Avaunt thee! blow open the lock with your carbines; we cannot stay to batter the door down. Let us unearth the Jacobite fox with all speed."

The next instant three shots startled the stillness of the dark gloomy chamber, into which a ray of light suddenly darted as the door fell crashing inwards, revealing in the aperture the gleaming headpieces and weapons, dark scowling faces, and stalwart forms of the Dutch troopers, whilst a hoarse voice shouted,—

"In, in, ye ferrets, and drag the Jacobite rat forth, we will hang him from the highest battlement of the castle, and the false governor and his traitor daughter, one on each side."

"Thou wilt never live to see either execution, bloodthirsty miscreant," cried Sir Andrew, recognizing in the voice, and the tall form that for an instant darkened the doorway, his remorseless enemy Sir Edward Hamilton, whom upon three different occasions he had left for slain, and drawing his sword, he dashed forward, determining either to cut his way through the mass of Dutchmen, or at all events finally to settle his account with Sir Edward this time.

Hamilton did not perceive his foe rushing upon him out of the darkness, until the blade of the Life Guardsman clashed against his own, then his face grew almost livid with suppressed hatred and passion, and he hissed between his clenched teeth,—

"Ah, this time, malapert Scot, thou wilt not escape me, I have sworn to slay thee, and now thou forcest upon me an opportunity. Die, rascal, die!"

He attacked our hero with great vigour and pertinacity, and the Dutch soldiers, at a sign from Hamilton, held aloof, nor offered to take any part in the contest.

For more than five minutes, the vaulted chambers rang with the shrill clash of steel on steel, and sparks of fire flashed from the clanging weapons. Foot by foot, however, Sir Edward Hamilton had to give way before the superior address and more consummate skill of the young Royalist, and at length he who had begun the combat so arrogantly was fain to call upon his troopers to interfere.

"Coward!" yelled Sir Andrew, delivering a fierce lunge full at his opponent's chest.

His blade was, however, caught upon the sabre of a Dutch trooper, or assuredly its point would have drank the wily Hamilton's heart's blood. The next instant four troopers attacked him simultaneously, and after defending himself bravely for a few minutes, his sword was broken short off up to the hilt, by a blow from a partisan, and then he was pinioned from behind, borne to the ground, and overpowered.

"Ha! ha! lies my enemy then so low?" exclaimed Hamilton, with a mocking laugh.

"If so, 'tis not thy hand, dastard," retorted Sir Andrew, fiercely.

"Say on, say on, hard words break no heads, thou cans't not escape me this time, my slippery knave, in five minutes thou will be hung even higher than Haman."

"You hung me once before, but I escaped. See that you run not your own head into the noose that you have contrived for me. By heaven, something tells me that you will."

"Now may the foul fiend wither thy tongue," said Hamilton, turning pale, for he was fully embued with the superstition of the age, and the words of the young Royalist made the very blood run cold in his veins. He recovered himself in an instant, however, and cried,—

"Away with him, away with him, to the summit of the Donjon tower."

Thus adjoined, Sir Andrew was lifted to his feet, for he had been bound with cords, so that he could not move without assistance, and his guards closing around him, he was half-led, half-forced along passages, and through rooms, and up steep spiral staircases, until he found himself on the summit of the Castle's highest tower.

Here, to his dismay, grief, and consternation, he found Sir Stephen Macclesfield and his beloved Flora, also bound, and standing as prisoners amidst a troop of Dutch guards.

From the top of the tower had been run out three long poles, and a rope and slip noose had been attached to each, and they now dangled loosely and ominously therefrom.

Gladly would Sir Andrew have exchanged some words with his beloved, but it was not permitted him, nor was he allowed to approach within many yards of her.

She was very pale, and the young Scot could see that she trembled in every limb.

By her side stood her father, erect and dignified, his arms folded upon his broad breast, and the voluminous waves of his long grey beard floating majestically over them.

The Dutch guards looked stolid and motionless as statues of bronze; but around them, and trebling them in numbers, crowded the soldiers forming the garrison of the castle, excited, gesticulating, furious at the treatment to which their Commandant and his daughter were subjected, and only kept in restraint by their respect of and awe for the Royal Warrant, which, with the Queen's name attached thereto, authorizing the arrest and execution of Sir Stephen and Flora Macclesfield, wherever and whenever found, the dark-browed Hamilton kept flaunting before their faces.

And now a noose was adjusted around each of the passive victims' necks, and Mynheer Van Dunk only awaited his leader's order to give the signal for them to be launched into eternity.

He was about to do so, when, so suddenly as to appear almost magical, a small party of dragoons and Highlanders were observed immediately beneath the castle walls, and the next instant a trumpeter sounded a parley.

Sir Edward Hamilton immediately recognised in their commanding officer, who was equipped in a brilliant dragoon uniform, and rode a noble bay charger, the young Marquis of Annandale, one of King William's favourite and most promising officers.

The dragoons who accompanied him were men of his own regiment, who, in the devotion to their leader and chief, would obey his orders in everything; and the Highlanders, who clustered on the left, were clansmen of the Isles, firmly attached to the cause of the Stadtholder.

"The most noble the Marquis of Annandale to Sir Stephen Macclesfield, governor of his Britannic Majesty's castle of Corgarf, sends greeting," began the trumpeter, having ceased his warlike blast.

Sir Stephen could not reply, for a formidable gag had been thrust into his mouth, but Hamilton did so for him, saying,—

"Sir Stephen Macclesfield is no longer commandant of this castle. I hold it under a royal warrant, and, by royal command, am about to execute the last sentence of the law upon the person of the traitor thou inquirest after."

"The date of thy warrant, and by whom signed?" demanded the marquis.

"'Tis signed by the Queen in person—and as to the date, what matters that to thee?" retorted Hamilton, who had his own reasons for concealing the fact that the warrant was nearly two years old; but evidently the marquis had some suspicion of this, for he sneeringly replied,—

"Because, perhaps, it is dated at Carlisle, and if so is null and void. Any how, I would learn the name of him who is entrusted with so terrible and so important a duty, and I would also demand instant admission within the fortress."

"I am Sir Edward Hamilton, Colonel of his Majesty's third regiment of Swart Ruyters, and also a Lieutenant General in the Dutch service," was the reply.

"Then art thou art also a double-dyed traitor and perhaps worse, and I am the bearer of despatches to every fortress and commander of forces in Scotland, to have thee shot like a dog, without trial or condemnation, wherever thou should'st turn up."

"Villain, you lie; the charges against me, what are they?"

"Time enough to tell them when we stand face within the castle," answered Annandale.

"That will never be, Lord Marquis, for even at this moment thou diest," hissed Hamilton, between his clenched teeth, and snatching a petronel from the hand of one of his troopers, he raised it to his shoulder and hastily pulled the trigger.

The bullet sped true to its mark, the Marquis clapped his hand to his breast, a little jet of blood spouted from between his fingers, and deluged his white uniform. He reeled in his saddle, and would have fallen therefrom had not a young Highland chief rushed forward and caught him in his arms.

"Sir Donald, 'tis my death wound," muttered Annandale. "In my right breast pocket thou wilt find the warrant for this rascal's execution; see that it be carried into instant execution. The villain wrote to Louis of France, that for a sum equal to three thousand pounds in English money he would assassinate King William in Westminster Hall. Louis, like a noble-minded monarch and a true man, immediately forwarded the letter to William, and I have it now in my possession."

"Had the uncanny looking rascal a thousand lives they should all be forfeited for such a deed," retorted the Highland chieftain, in husky passion; "but, my lord, can we do aught for you before we force our way into this hornets' nest?"

"Yes, lay me on the grass, then lose no time, or he may yet wreck his threat on the old commandant and his other captives, for I see he has three gibbets rigged out," answered Annandale, feebly, and in a voice scarcely articulate.

He was lifted from the saddle according to his request, and laid upon the soft heather, with a horseman's rolled-up cloak for a pillow.

The dragoons then dismounted, and having piquetted their horses prepared, in company with the Highlanders, to force their way into the interior of the fortress.

They need not have been so anxious, however, concerning the fate of the three doomed captives, on the summit of the Donjon tower, for no sooner had the men-at-arms and retainers of Corgarf become convinced that Sir Edward Hamilton was acting on his own authority more than under valid royal warrant, than they determined to rescue their beloved commandant, with his daughter and guest, themselves.

With loud cries they threw themselves upon the stolid ranks of the Swart Ruyters, and a deadly conflict ensued, in the midst of which Sir Edward, thinking only of his own terrible doom if captured, turned round, gained the tower steps with a couple of strides, and fled precipitately down them, not quick enough, however, to elude the observation of some of the garrison, who turned promptly to pursue him.

Arrived at the foot of the staircase, he knew not which way to proceed, but in this dilemma a young officer sprang out of the doorway close at hand saying,—

"Follow me, I owe thee no love, but thou hatest this Cavalier Douglas, and that hate constitutes a bond of sympathy between us, and makes me wish to save thee from death. Quick, and we may yet evade the bloodhounds who are at thy heels."

It was Albert Cunningham who spoke, the young officer whom we have introduced in a previous chapter, as being the nephew of Sir Stephen and the cousin of Flora.

His face was now distorted by angry passions, for he loved his beautiful cousin, and the knowledge acquired on the previous evening, that all her affections had long ago being given to Sir Andrew Douglas, had changed his usually calm, equable temper to one better befitting a fiend; oh, what will not disappointed love sometimes make of the best of us?

He now felt that he would do anything to save the man who hated one whom he also hated, even at a personal risk to himself, so he again impatiently bade Sir Edward to follow him, and running on before, led the way through intricate passages, vestibules, and corridors, until they gained a spacious hall, at the other end of which a broad flight of stone stairs with massive carved oak balusters led to the banqueting hall, from whence an exit could be gained on to the terrace walk, and the verdant slopes leading down into the castle moat.

Could the banqueting hall be once reached, escape for Sir Edward was perhaps possible, and Albert Cunningham urged him forward by telling him that life hung upon his speed. Before, however, they could gain the staircase, a dozen pikemen belonging to the garrison burst through a side door just in time to bring Sir Edward to bay, ere he had planted his foot on the first step.

Albert Cunningham, who was in advance, not willing to compromise himself further, bounded up the steps, half-a-dozen at a time, leaving Sir Edward to his fate, who seeing at a glance that if he followed his example, he would assuredly be thrust through the back with a pike, faced round, drew his sword, and stood upon the defensive, exclaiming,—

"Come one, come all, but let him who values his life the least be in the front, for my sword is thirsty and will drink one or two hearts' blood ere I am overcome, I can promise you, so have at the rapscallions."

Then the clash of steel against iron awoke all the echoes of the old hall. Down went one sturdy pikeman weltering in his gore, away whirled the head of another, spinning like a cricket ball along the tesselated floor, while the body fell prone to earth in all its black iron and buff leather panoply, but against the halbert of a third Sir Edward's sword snapped off right up to the hilt, and then half-a-dozen springing upon him at once he was speedily dragged to the floor, overpowered, and bound helplessly with cords.

"Guards, drag the villain to the summit of the Donjon tower and hang him to one of the gibbets that he had destined for a better man," exclaimed the young Highland chief, who with his followers, had by this time obtained entrance to the fortress and reached the hall. "I will presently follow to see whether his master, the devil, will interpose to save him."

With their armour and partisans clanking as they strode, the men-at-arms, nothing loth, then hurried their prisoner towards the place of doom. In less than five minutes they had reached it, when a long pole was run out from the battlement, a still longer piece of rope being attached thereto, and all things being ready the noose was thrown over his neck and tightened.

"Now, fellow, for thou art a disgrace to knighthood, and so I will not address thee by thy title, make a short shrift, for thou hast but a minute to live. At the end of that time thou wilt leap from the battlement," said the Highland Chief, sternly.

"I have no shrift to make, I have already prayed that all the curses of the damned may rest on you all for ever," was the savage rejoinder.

"I do not fear thy curse, and I defy the power of the evil one," said the Highlander, who inherited some of the superstition of his race; "Now leap off into eternity."

The ill-fated knight stood upon the narrow battlement, he looked down and more than a hundred feet below he saw the sharp-pointed stakes that rose like a wall of crossed pikes from the dry ditch that encircled the tower. Then his eye rested on the weird pole and the loose dangling cord, that the next instant would be tightened with the weight of his own body, as he swung in mid air.

He turned ghastly pale at the sight, and a convulsive shiver ran through his frame, while he shut his eyes for a moment to recover his faculties.

"Prick him with your daggers, my merry men. Spur the hound to the leap," cried the Highland Chief, drawing his sword.

The men-at-arms were about to obey his commands, when Sir Edward Hamilton turned round, and darting at Sir Andrew Douglas a fiendish glance of deadly hatred, he exclaimed, "We shall meet again in this world yet," and sprang boldly into the air.

A simultaneous cry burst from the beholders, and Highlanders, dragoons, and men-at-arms ran to the parapet to look over.

They had seen the stout pole bend beneath the weight of its living burthen, and the rope tighten and give one fearful swing, but upon looking over into the abyss below, they beheld the long cord dangling in space. Sir Edward was gone!

"Saints of heaven, the devil has taken more interest in his chosen servant than I gave him credit for," exclaimed the Highland Chief, devoutly crossing himself. "He has been spirited away by no mortal agency—unless, indeed, the noose was defective and he has fallen into the ditch below."

"If so we should have heard his screams, as he was pierced by the sharp spikes, aye we should see him now as he lay writhing on their points," remarked a dragoon.

"And as for the noose, though perhaps I am told to say no better was never looped, it would not have given way under the weight of twenty such men. Besides, M'Alpine, behold, the noose as well as the man is gone, the rope is severed and scorched by fire immediately above the loop knot."

"Ah! then it must be the foul fiend who has aided him," retorted the chief; "doubtless the burn is the impress of his fiery talons as he released and flew away with him. It is no good bestowed further attention on the matter, so hasten to release these noble prisoners, whom the miscreant was about to hang."

The soldiers rapidly complied with this mandate, and in a few minutes Sir Stephen Macclesfield, Flora, and Sir Andrew Douglas, stood free and unfettered before their deliverers, to whom they returned the most ardent and grateful thanks.

"I suppose I am to consider myself your prisoner?" said Sir Andrew to the Highland chief, as he saw that the latter recognised in him a Royalist.

"I have not said so," responded the latter, with a smile, "I see only in you a guest of Sir Stephen Macclesfield's. Ill would it become me to arrest you in that capacity—ill, moreover, would it become a chief of the Isles to betray to Southern cruelty and wile a scion of the noble house of Douglas, the greatest, truest, best of Scottish names."

Sir Andrew grasped the young chief warmly by the hand, his heart was too full for words.

"The gallant Marquis, who was shot down by that rascal Hamilton, does he yet live?" asked Sir Stephen Macclesfield, at this juncture.

"No, Sir Stephen, he lies stiff and dead on the

SINGLE-HANDED HE CONFRONTED THE MEN-AT-ARMS.

green slopes without, his wound bled inwardly, but in his dying moments he begged that he might be permitted to bleed his last beneath the blue vault of heaven," answered the chieftain, with some emotion.

"God save him, he was a gallant soldier, and 'tis thus that most of his ancestors have breathed their last; their backs on Scottish heather, to which their life's blood had imparted a still richer dye, and a broken brand in their strong right hand, that they wielded well for Scotland's glory and for Scotland's honour," said Sir Andrew Douglas, fervently.

"I doubt it not, may God reward them, but let us now descend to the banquet hall, for doubtless, Sir Scot, thou and thy train are sorely in need of both food and wine," said the Commandant, and leading the way with his daughter, the whole party quitted the donjon tower and repaired to the lower apartment of the spacious fortress.

It was moonlight—the bright moonlight of an autumnal night, and, within a small room in the western wing of Corgaf, stood Flora, with her eyes fixed upon the blue vault of heaven and the glittering stars, which seemed as though they were the eyes of angels glancing down in pity and sympathy upon her through the open casement.

Motionless and cold as a marble statue she appeared, as, with her hands clasped over the back of an antique chair, she gazed upwards at the sparkling firmament, her eyes dimmed, and her long fringed lashes wet wlth tears.

At length a light cloud swept across the moon, and, with a sigh, Flora then turned away from the window, and, falling on her knees by her bedside, sought relief in prayer.

Suddenly she was roused by a dark shadow crossing the moonlit wall opposite, a light footstep sounded on the wooden floor, and then a voice whispered in her ear,—

"Fear not, dearest Flora; it is I."

What a thril of pleasure rose in the heart of our heroine as she recognised that voice and knew that Sir Andrew was beside her.

---

## CHAPTER L.

### ESCAPE FROM COGARF CASTLE.—PURSUIT.

FLORA was about to utter a cry of joy, but a hand was gently laid upon her mouth, and the young knight hurriedly whispered,—

"A single sound, Flora, might destroy us both. I have just seen your father. He bids me not put faith in the assurances of the English officer, for his second in command has over-persuaded him with his counsels, and he intends to forfeit his pledged word. To-morrow, if I abide here the night, I shall be sent a prisoner to London, where the block or the gibbet will yet be my doom, while your father fears that you also are in danger."

"What does my father wish us to do then?" asked Flora, breathlessly.

"To escape together, and to seek France with all haste," was the reply.

"Let us go then, I am ready," was the smiling retort.

Speedily a portion of her female attire was laid aside. a plumed cap donned, and slouched well over her face, her little form being concealed by a horseman's cloak. The next minute, with the assistance of her companion, she passed through the open window, descended the rope ladder, and stood in the pure night air beside her lover in the deserted bastion court.

"Courage, Flora, the worst danger is past," said Sir Andrew, as he felt the fair girl's arm tremble within his own. "The sentinels that should challenge our exit have been removed by your father's connivance, and concealed by a of trees on the hillside, beyond the walls, two good steeds stand picquetted. In a few seconds we shall be in the saddle, and then we may laugh at Annandale's dragoons and the Swart Ruyters to boot."

The happy girl made no reply. What could she fear under the protection of him she so fondly loved and trusted? And with as rapid steps as the unevenness of the ground and the darkness rendered practicable, they fled from the castle towards the grove of trees.

A few minutes' brisk walking brought Sir Andrew and his fair companion to the little cluster of elms and beeches indicated; which stood around and overshadowed the green turbid waters of the Whynn Pool.

Here, to his vexation and dismay, the young cavalier discovered that the horses the commandant had promised to send, were not awaiting them, and while the two fugitives stood irresolute and uncertain what course to adopt, they saw lights flashing in the windows of the castle, and heard the shrill clangour of the alarm bell burst wildly forth upon the cold night air.

"Andrew, we are lost," said Flora, clinging convulsively to her lover's arm; "our flight is discovered, and that bell will call both Swart Ruyters, and dragoons to the saddle—for heaven's sake, let us away."

"Keep up your courage a little longer, dear one," was the reply, "for yonder in the hollow scarcely a quarter of a mile distant is the village and its snug hostelry. Once let us reach that, and we will get a good horse I'll be bound."

So saying, he took Flora's hand, and at their best speed they ran down the slope and across the hollow beyond in the direction of the hostel.

As they approached its door, they saw that its inmates were already astir, for roused from their slumbers by the sound of the bell, some were hurrying forth to learn the cause of the uproar, while others with night-capped heads thrust out of upper windows, increased the confusion by loudly questioning each passer-by.

Aware that the less attention they attracted the better, Sir Andrew, bidding Flora follow him closely, led the way under the shadow of a high wall, directly towards the stables. The yard gate was luckily open, the doors all unlocked, and darting into stable after stable in quick succession the cavalier at last discovered a magnificent black charger, which he hastily harnessed and led forth into the paved yard.

Vaulting on to its back, and acknowledging the proud steed's impatient neigh by patting its arched neck, he held out his hand to assist Flora to mount, and placing her little foot lightly on his, she sprang up behind him, and then like a flash of light they dashed through the open gate and into the street beyond.

A large crowd was by this time collected in front of the inn, and riding down the street at a rapid trot, their armour and sword scabbards clanking, and the moonlight glistening upon their brass helmets and long lances, came about a score of Swart Ruyters.

Sir Andrew saw that no time was to be lost, and giving his horse the spur, he pressed him through the mob, knocking over those who stood in his way, and utterly regardless of the shouts and imprecations that greeted their passage.

"There they go—the Jacobite and his mistress—'tis they, 'tis they; after them, brave lancers, stop them, slay them!" and with such like cries, mingled with hisses and groans, the crowd fell back, to make way for the Swart Ruyters, who, now fairly on the track of the fugitives, swept after them at a hand gallop.

The last house of the scattered village is soon passed, but the lovers had scarcely reached the bottom of the steep hill beyond, when their pursuers turned the corner ot the top, and catching full view of their prey, with triumphant shouts urged their steeds still faster on the trail.

The race for life commenced.

Before them lay another steep ascent, and unwilling that the brave steed should be put to his full speed too soon, the cavalier held him well in hand, and contenting himself with keeping a clear hundred yards ahead of his pursuers, he strove to sustain the courage and confidence of his companion by words of encouragement and hope.

The brow of the second hill is gained, and Flora clasps her white arms still closer around Sir Andrew's waist, for the night air grows chill and cold.

One look back at the village, at the grey walls of its feudal castle, its dark circling woods, and the bright river that winds along, looking like a huge silver snake in the moonlight; a hasty and frightened glance at the galloping horseman, and the black charger dips lightly down the descent beyond, bounds over a flashing rivulet, and then, stretching away for miles beyond them, they behold fertile plains and patches of brown heather.

But this was no time to admire the beauty of the landscape, for faster and faster rush on the dusky Swart Ruyters, and swifter and swifter the fugitives fly before them, the black charger making but lightly of his double burden and throwing the white foam spumes like wintry snow flakes, as if in sport, over his glossy coat.

Along the level road, across a white common, where their hoof-strokes ring hollowly on the yielding turf, and their shadows flit like spectres over the green-sward, then once more into the road again, yet still the race continues.

Like lightning they sweep through the village of Arbroath, and so on and on until the towers of Drumcalth rise to view, and then the battlements of Coldeen on the summit of a wooded hill to the left.

Already five miles had been run, and their pursuers had not gained an inch of ground during the last three, while some of their horses were already knocked up, and others with heaving flanks, dilated nostrils, and laboured breathing, evinced unmistakable signs of giving in.

Pale, shivering, and rendered giddy by the headlong speed at which they were journeying, Flora Macclesfield still clung to her companion, who had contrived to throw his left arm around her waist, the better to enable her to keep her seat in the saddle.

To her it appeared as though hedges, trees, and cottages, all flew past, while the white road seemed to flow under the horse's feet like a ghostly river, and more vengeful and fierce every instant looked the bearded faces of the Swart Ruyters, and louder and louder sounded the hoof-strokes of their galloping horses, and the clatter of their arms and accoutrements, as with the untiring ferocity of the sleuth-hound they followed on the trail.

At that moment the black charger stumbled over a stone that unfortunately lay in the path, and both horse and riders came to the ground together.

The cavalier was instantly again on his feet, and bending forward, he lifted Flora from the ground, and remounting, they continued their mad flight.

They swept down another hill-side, and Sir Andrew uttered a cry of joy upon perceiving that a dense white fog filled the old vale below; in another five minutes they were in its midst, and so thick was it, that Sir Andrew could scarcely see the black charger's head before him.

. . . . . .

An hour later, two dark forms, mounted on a weary and lagging steed, slowly descended the steep lane which led to the town of Dulcoath, and having gained the first long straggling street, drew rein and looked anxiously around, as though uncertain which way to turn or what course to adopt.

In spite of the earliness of the season, a heavy snow-storm had set in; a strong east wind swept up the valley, and howled dismally among the distant woods, and the heavy flakes, mingled with pattering hail, blew against barred door and closed window, clothing road, field, and house-tops as with a silvery pall.

The town beadle, with his cocked hat and long grey cloak, his horn lantern and brazen staff of office, had just performed his sixth round, notifying to all who, amid wind and storm, could hear his words, that it was "past eleven o'clock, and a dreary night," which duty over, the good man had complacently adjourned to "St. Andrew's Cross," a small hostelry in the High-street, in order to get a warm by the inn fire, and console himself with a stiff glass of a liquid somewhat stronger than pure water.

The storm raged with great fury, but the two forms on the one horse seemed to heed it not. Towards their left the red fires of numerous iron foundries shed a crimson glow as of blood upon the surface of the pure snow, and the same lurid light gleamed upon the large meres of water that lay around, revealing the dark moving forms of the workmen, who still plied their busy calling, and tinting the dense clouds of black smoke, which eddied away in sulphurous wreaths before the wind, with streaks of coloured light.

On their right a different scene presented itself, for there, dark and gloomy, lay the high road to the port, far a-down which they beheld the flicker of advancing lights, as of some slow-moving vehicle struggling through the snow.

The stranger, who sat in front, shook his head sadly, and then turning towards the street that lead northward to the High Cross, exclaimed,—

"Onwards, brave steed, the death hounds are on our track, but we may distance them yet." And again he plied his long lance spurs.

The horse put forth all its strength to obey this last call, but in vain, its powers were spent. Each moment the snow grew deeper, so that before the horseman could gain the brow of the hill the noble charger with a faint neigh sank in the gathering drift, and no effort of rein or spur could induce it to rise more.

Then the riders, perceiving that longer delay would be dangerous, after looking anxiously around to see that no one was within sight, almost a needless precaution on so boisterous an evening, prepared to continue their journey on foot. This course they soon found that the deepness of the snow would render impracticable, tired and feeble as they already felt. Their only remaining hope, therefore, was that they might perchance be able to obtain shelter and food beneath the roof of some favourer to the Jacobite cause.

. . . . . .

Notwithstanding the wintry night without, there is comfort and content in the little parlour of old Hob Helshender's pretty ivy-mantled cottage, for a bright wood fire sparkles in the open grate, before which, stretched at full length on the matted hearth-rug, reposes a sleek tabby cat.

Upon the round oaken table lies the frugal evening meal, a good Dutch cheese and a loaf of home-made bread. The parish sexton, aided by an oil lamp and a pair of horn-rimmed spectacles, is reading aloud a chapter from the Bible, and his worthy spouse, who is his junior by some years, sits in her accustomed chair on the opposite side of the fire-place, busily engaged with her spinning wheel, while their only daughter, the pretty Phœbe, occupies a seat beside her mother, and with her blue eyes fixed upon the glowing embers, listens alternately to the reading and to tht roaring wind and to the pattering hail without.

At length the good sexton's dissertation was interrupted by a knocking at the outer door, and upon Phœbe withdrawing the bolts, the latch was hastily raised, and two strangers, tired and way-worn, their plumed caps and dark grey cloaks covered with snow, strode into the apartment.

The eldest of these unlooked-for visitors was apparently young and handsome, but his face was thin and careworn, his hair and beard long and unshaven, while his uniform, tarnished and faded, was unmistakably that of a royalist cavalier. His companion was more plainly dressed, but kept his hat slouched over his eyes, so that his face could not be seen.

"My good friends," exclaimed the eldest, as

he entered the room, "pardon our disturbing you at so unseasonable an hour, but we are outcasts and fugitives, and as such beg of you one night's shelter and protection. We are, moreover, in danger, our foes are on our track, and the gallant charger that has borne us from Cogarf since moonrise lies dead on the road. Our only hope is that this heavy snow storm has induced our foes to relinquish the pursuit. Can you, then, bestow on us food and shelter? We will pay you well for both;" and so saying, the stranger drew a purse from his pocket.

---

## CHAPTER LI.

### THE PLACE OF HIDING BENEATH THE CHURCH.—ESCAPE TO FRANCE!

"WE seek not reward for the hospitality which both duty and inclination prompt us to offer," replied Hob Helshender; "so replace thy purse unopened, sir cavalier. Our frugal supper lies as yet untouched; sit down, both of ye, and partake of it with us, and if thy foes come we can offer thee concealment as well as shelter."

Thus received, both Sir Andrew's and Flora's fears and anxieties were considerably relieved, and they presently found themselves seated at table, and doing justice to the humble fare, for they had tasted nothing for twenty-four hours, and Sir Andrew related to their worthy host, who turned out to be a staunch Jacobite, the full details of the close of the campaign, of their escape the previous night from Cogarf, and of their pursuit thither.

Just, however, as he had concluded his narrative the tramp of advancing hoofs was heard in the snow without, then came the shrill neigh of a horse, and while a heavy knock thundered against the outer door, a hoarse voice without shouted,—

"Open, in the name of the King! We are in search of two traitors; open quickly, or we will batter down the door."

The old sexton sprang to his feet, exclaiming,—

"Sir cavalier, we have not a moment to lose; my daughter will conduct you both to a place of concealment; follow her."

"Phœbe," he continued, turning to his fair child, "you know the spot, *the left eye of the death's head.* Go, while I stay to parley with those who knock so loudly."

The soft cheek of the lovely peasant girl was flushed with many and varied emotions as her eyes met those of the eldest of their guests, whom she now motioned to follow her.

The next moment they had passed through a door at the back of the cottage, and found themselves in the churchyard.

Both Sir Andrew and Flora heard the crash of wood, and the echo of angry voices as their guide closed and locked the door through which they had passed behind them, and they knew that their pursuers had forced an entrance into the house, but a soft voice murmured, reassuringly,—

"Fear not, cavalier; there is no danger, but follow quickly!"

The storm had by this time ceased, and the pale moon shining through the drifting clouds shed a ghostly radiance upon the old churchyard, with its quaintly cut tombstones and snow-covered graves.

The dark massive walls of the church, with its tall tapering spire, and traceried windows, stood before them.

Before a small oak door, on the northern side of the building, Phœbe Helshender paused. The cavalier and his fair companion were quickly by her side.

Drawing a key from her pocket, she inserted it in the huge old-fashioned lock.

The creaking hinges then slowly turned, and the next moment the fugitives and their guide stood within the sacred edifice.

All here was as still as death.

They had entered close to the communion-table, the spot where two years ago had stood the high-altar, with its massive golden crucifix and tall wax candles; and Sir Andrew bent low, and made the sign of the cross, for he felt that he stood upon holy ground.

The moonlight, streaming in through the great southern window, flickered upon the pedestals of the early Norman pillars and Gothic arches, and on the delicate carving of the dark oak roof; but the eyes of the fugitives dwelt not long on these; they scarcely, indeed, thought of their own danger, for their gaze was rivetted upon the features of their deliverer, who, by the pale radiance of the moon, they could almost fancy to be some guardian angel or holy saint, sent specially to deliver them from danger and from death, for her face and form bore an air of almost more than earthly beauty as, lighting a waxen taper, which she held in her hand, she glided noiselessly towards the southern aisle, and stopped before a richly-sculptured tablet, which was affixed to the thick wall.

The monument presented on its face a marble statue of Time, life-size, holding in one hand an hour-glass, and in the other a human skull.

"Now," exclaimed the pretty Phœbe, in a half-whisper, "we are come to the place of thy concealment, for no living soul knows the mystery of this old tombstone, save my father and myself," and so saying, she placed her finger within the eye-socket of the effigy—Death's-head; and yielding to the pressure, the skull hastily revolved, and the whole frame of the tablet falling back, as though on concealed hinges, disclosed behind it a dark archway and secret staircase, cut out of the thickness of the wall.

Down this staircase, which was very narrow, the cavalier and his companion wonderingly followed the light steps of their guide.

It was terminated by a trap door, but upon touching a spring, this also opened, and after descending another long flight of steps, they entered what to all appearance was either a naturally-formed cave, or else an artificially-constructed dungeon, for it was apparently formed out of the solid rock, and was small but dry, and apparently contained tolerably pure air.

"Here," exclaimed Phœbe, as she once more turned towards Sir Andrew and his companion, "is the place of thy concealment. It is not a very warm or comfortable spot, but it is one of security, as more than one royalist fugitive could testify; therefore, fear not, for you shall be regularly supplied, both with food and light, and soon I trust that I shall be able to come and tell you that you may once more go forth into the world with safety."

"I trust so, indeed, fair maiden," answered Sir Andrew, sadly.

"That hole which you see to your right," continued Phœbe, "leads, through devious paths, to a wood a mile distant from the town, but part of the way is, I believe, blocked up by masses of fallen rock and earth, and thus rendered impassable. The spot whereon we now stand is twenty-five feet immediately beneath the flooring of the church. Now, farewell; I have told you your surroundings, in a few hours we shall meet again."

So saying, Phœbe, who, during her conversation, had been securing a lighted candle in an iron bracket, which was nailed to the side of the cave, turned round, and, with a smile of angelic sweetness, bounded through the dark archway by which they had entered, and, before the astonished cavalier could find words wherewith to express his own and Flora's thanks and gratitude, she had ascended the long flight of stone steps, and securing the trap-door behind her, was out of hearing.

Several days passed away, yet every night after the town clock had struck the eleventh hour, a fair female form, bearing in one hand a lighted taper, and in the other a basket, flitted down the dim southern aisle of St. Michael's Church, bearing food and consolation to the lonely captives.

At length, however, these visits were to cease.

Some time had elapsed since the soldiery of the Stadholder had left the town, the danger of capture appeared over, and the road was once more open for our hero and heroine to pursue their journey unmolested.

Phœbe Helshender, true to her promise, bore them the welcome news that it was practicable for them to leave the damp vault in which they had for so long a time lain concealed; and her own brother, and eight other hardy Highlanders, escorted them in safety to a little cove in the Firth of Dornach, where a lugger lay waiting to convey them to the friendly shores of France, which, after a five days' voyage, they reached in safety.

The parting of Sir Andrew with Phœbe's brother and his eight gallant friends we represent in a spirited engraving.

## CHAPTER LII.

### A CHANGE OF SCENE.—A BALL AT THE PALACE.

It was not often, in the gloomy eighteenth century, that the old palace of St. Germains, then the residence of a dethroned English King, threw off its stately air of accustomed gloom, and assumed the aspect of gaiety and mirth. This particular evening was a exception to the rule.

Towards eight o'clock the large saloons of the palace were well-nigh full; for the last hour the paved streets, as well as the square courtyard of the mansion, had resounded to the rumble of carriage wheels, the sharp click of horses' hoofs, and the hum of many voices, as guest after guest made their appearance, and quickly vanishing from the gaze of the outer world, within the dim shadow of the old Gothic portico, ascended the broad oak staircase towards the reception-rooms.

To one of these noble apartments, now fitted up for the ball, we will conduct our readers, and acting as master of the ceremonies, proceed to introduce them to some of the company who are there assembled.

Upwards of three hundred wax candles adorn the huge candelabra that hangs suspended from the carved ceiling, and shed a mild and silvery radiance over the polished oak floor, heavy drapery, and tapestried walls of the noble apartment, flashing back, as it were, in showers of light, from the rich jewels and glittering appointments of the assembled multitude.

The apartment, though large, was nevertheless as full as comfort and harmony of motion would allow, for already three hundred guests were present, and the rustle of silks and satins, the flashing of jewels and cloth of gold, the heavily-laden perfumed air, and the perpetual murmur of subdued conversation, made up the chief features of the scene.

The musicians, however, had not yet arrived, so the guests, to pass away the intervening time, lounged on the sofas and fauteuils, promenaded the reception-rooms, or else gathered in knots and groups, and conversed on the various and all-absorbing topics of the day.

Every variety of dress might there have been seen. The costly and elegant costume of the cavalier, with his long floating hair, peaked beard, and carefully curled moustache, his slashed doublet, in many cases, covered with gold and precious stones, Vandyke collar of foreign lace, and long straight rapier, forming a strong contrast to the tightly-fitting scarlet or blue coatee, the twisted gold epaulettes, long jack-boots, powdered wig, and white cravat, which distinguished many of the French officers who were present.

Among the latter sons of the sword was a tall, strongly-made military-looking man, about forty years of age, whose handsome, though sinister, countenance would anywhere have commanded some attention.

His face was dark and sunburnt, with a keen black eye, and a closely-clipped moustache, the latter indicative of foreign service. His green velvet coatee was trimmed with gold lace, edged with sable, while the dark curls of his Ramillies wig flowed profusely over his shoulders; his waist was compressed by a broad leather belt, secured by a gold buckle, from which depended a long straight rapier, and his nether person was accoutred in polished leather jack-boots with gilded spurs.

This personage was Captain Louis Pelissier, of the 5th French Light Dragoons, but ere long our readers will be introduced to him in another character, one in which they have met him ofttimes before.

Another half-hour has passed away, and then a slight murmur of interest and surprise runs through the room, for the musicians have taken their places in the gallery, and just as the opening notes of the brass instruments ring musically forth, the folding-doors at the lower end of the vast apartment are thrown open, and a fair young girl, leaning lightly on the arm of a cavalier who is splendidly attired in a costume of rose colour and silver, enters the room.

Then followed a great flutter and movement as the beautiful unknown, with her handsome chaperone, advanced up the room, and many an earnest conversation was suddenly hushed, many a deep flirtation abruptly brought to a close, the half-uttered words of love changing into subdued exclamations of surprise and admiration as she swept along, and whispered observation of "How lovely!" "Beautiful as an angel!" passed from mouth to mouth.

After the ceremony of introduction was gone through, several sets of "La Viennese," a fashionable dance of the time, somewhat similar to the modern quadrille, were formed, Flora Macclesfield, for she was the beautiful stranger, dancing with our hero, Sir Andrew Douglas, for it was he who had led her into the room, and having for a *vis-à-vis* Louis Pelissier, the Captain of French Dragoons, who had secured for a partner a young French lady known to Flora, and who was at the time a visitor at the palace.

Several other dances succeeded the Viennese, and Flora Macclesfield, being the belle of the room, did not lack partners, but at length, somewhat fatigued with the exertion, and oppressed by the heat, she once more accepted the arm of Sir Andrew, and suffered him to conduct her to a deep recess formed by one of the large bay windows of the saloon, and here, seated on a superb ottoman, they watched for many minutes through the interstices of the massive velvet hangings which screened them as it were from the gaze of everybody the gay scene around, and the sparkling throng who still mingled in the dance, where

> Soft eyes looked love to eyes that spake again,
> And all went merry as a marriage bell,

forgetful of the troubles that had darkened the past, and unmindful, in the gaiety and mirth which marked the present hour, of what fate might reserve for the mystic future.

Flora's lovely and love-beaming eyes were now turned upwards to those of her companion, who, gracefully leaning against the back of the velvet ottoman on which she was seated, and bending forward so that his long perfumed hair almost mingled with her silken tresses, was pouring into no unwilling ear, in that low silvery tone of voice, which is either the token of real feeling or else its imitation, those impassioned words of love, which although she had listened to it a thousand times before, seemed, when issuing from his lips, to be ever new and ever welcome.

Sir Andrew Douglas was now an accepted lover, and their danger and perils over, only one short month was to elapse before he hoped to lead the fair and gentle girl who was now hanging so fondly on his every word to the altar, there to claim her as his bride before all the world.

The ninth of the following month had been fixed upon for the wedding, and it is needless to add that all parties looked forward with anxiety and pleasure to the happy day that should unite two such young, trusting, and fond hearts in the holy and mysterious bonds of wedded life.

But to return to the course of our story. A full hour had passed away, yet still the lovers talked on. They saw not the mazy whirl of the dance nor heeded the spirit-stirring strains of the band; the velvet curtains hid them effectually from view, as there, reclining against the downy cushions of the ottoman, her head gently drooping on his shoulder and his right hand abstractedly playing with the waving ringlets of her glossy hair, they spoke in whispers of the future and pictured the happiness of their approaching bridal day.

So engrossed, indeed, were they in their thought and conversation, that they heard not the sound of approaching stealthy footsteps, and great was the surprise of both when the velvet curtains were momentarily drawn aside, and the tall commanding form of Captain Louis Pelissier stood before them.

At sight of the abrupt intruder, Flora sprang to her feet, and the brow of the young cavrlier momentarily darkened, as his right hand wandered, as if by instinct, to the hilt of his bejewelled rapier.

The French captain, who, like many other of the guests, now wore a velvet half mask, observed not the nature of his reception; but without deigning to bestow a single glance upon Sir Andrew Douglas, turned to the lady, and, with a low bow, remarked,—

They are forming "La Volta," may I have the honour of dancing with you, mademoiselle?" and without waiting for a reply, he took her hand in his.

The fair girl drew it hastily back, annoyed at his presumption, and at the amatory glance with which he had thought fit to accompany his words, and Sir Andrew Douglas curtly remarked, "This lady is already engaged, sir."

"So it would seem, in more ways than one, and I do not greatly admire her taste either," replied the captain, with a mocking, sarcastic laugh, and anger gleaming in his fierce, dark eyes, as with a threatening glance at Sir Andrew, and a half-muttered curse in English, he turned and strode haughtily away.

The hot blood mounted to the young Scot's cheek, and springing to his feet, he was about to follow the Frenchman, but Flora caught him by the cloak, and, with many prayers and entreaties, begged him to remain by her side; so, perceiving that that was neither the time nor the place to resent the insult which he had just received, he suffered himself to be calmed down, and smiling to reassure Flora, who looked now pale and frightened, he offered her his arm, and led her towards the dancers, while Captain Louis Pelissier, as he called himself, fired with jealousy and anger, and annoyed at the *exposé* he had just made of his feelings, without a word to anyone, secretly left the palace, and proceeding to the stables, mounted his black Smolenski charger and galloped away.

## CHAPTER LIII.

### THE ROAD TO PARIS.—A STRANGE RENCONTRE.

FLORA MACCLESFIELD soon forgot, amid the exciting whirl of "La Volta," a dance very nearly resembling the modern valse, the fears and anxieties which the angry *rencontre* of her lover with the French captain had for awhile occasioned, and as dance followed dance in quick succession, and the flying hours chased each other merrily along, for time ever passes quickly when we most wish it to linger; the bright rose tint once more gleamed warmly in her fair cheek, and her bright eyes again shone with all their wonted brilliancy.

At length one deep musical stroke from the

PHŒBE'S BROTHER AND HIS EIGHT FRIENDS BID ADIEU TO SIR ANDREW.

palace clock proclaimed the first hour of the morning, and the folding doors at the end of the saloon being thrown open, disclosed, in the adjoining apartment the tables spread for the banquet.

At the same moment the brass band in the gallery breathed forth the martial and spirit-stirring strains of a military march, and the cavaliers and gentlemen choosing their partners, began to move towards the supper tables.

Flora Macclesfield took the arm of a handsome young cavalier, who was attired in a brilliant uniform of rose colour and silver.

It was Henry de Vandelem, lately a cornet in King James's Scots Royals, but who, on William's accession to the throne, a year previously, had resigned his commission.

This young officer was a friend and companion of Sir Andrew Douglas, and it was of that cavalier that they were speaking, as amid the blaze of light, the clangour of music, the buzz of conversation, and rustle of the rich and gorgeous dresses, they swept into the inner saloon, wherein a collation was spread for a thousand persons, the long tables being covered with every delicacy, both in and out of season, while the scene presented was one of great magnificence.

But we have neither space nor object to enter into the details of the banquet, or of what took place afterwards. Suffice it, therefore, to remark that the gaiety and merriment were kept up until a late or rather an early hour, for four o'clock had struck before the guests began to disperse.

Then the rumble of wheels once more resounded in the narrow streets of St. Germains, as in carriages, Sedan-chairs, on horseback and on foot, the company quitted the palace; the fiery radiance of the torch links casting into momentary obscurity the faint lights of the oil-lamps, which glemmered like stars above, and when the deep-toned bell of St. Mary's convent struck five, the dark outline of the old palace, now the abode of an English king, was illumined only by the newly-risen moon, and no noise broke the stillness of the morning save the soft murmur of the river, the rustle of the leaves, or the dull heavy rumble of some early waggon journeying on the high road towards Paris.

It was sbout half an hour after the last of the guests had taken their departure, that two figures might have been seen standing alone upon the broad stone terrace of the palace.

These forms were male and female, and the bright moon shed as it were a flood of silvery light upon the gorgeous attire, the laced cloak, and the plumed cap of the cavalier, and revealed also to view the exquisitely lovely features and long waving tresses of his fair companion, who, still wearing her ball dress, and glittering with jewels, now stood beside him.

It was Sir Andrew Douglas, and his companion was the beautiful Flora.

And the light of the same autumn moon shone on the dark, and already in many places, the crumbling walls of the old palace, and played fitfully among the carved pedestals and quaint statues that adorned the terrace walk.

Immediately below them, and gleaming in its onward course like a stream of molten silver, flowed the clear waters of the Saye, and about half a mile down its side, on the opposite shore, the towers and battlements of the Château of Concressault rose to view, thrown forward in clear relief by its dark wooded background of oak and elm.

Altogether the scene presented was one of surpassing beauty, and so doubtless thought our hero and heroine, as they gazed silently and thoughtfully at the moonlit view before them.

Sir Andrew was the first to break silence, as, pressing the slender form of his fair companion closer to his heart, he said,—

"Flora, my beloved, I must now bid you adieu; 'tis hard to tear myself from your side, even for a day; but it must be done. In a few hours we meet again, and soon—very soon now—you will be my bride, and then we shall seldom know what parting means: Come, good-bye, darling."

"Good-bye, Andrew, if it must be so," replied Flora, softly; "but remember to come back soon, for in your absence I feel very sad, and sometimes I have but ill forebodings of the future."

"Nay, nay, trust not to signs or omens, my Flora; half the unhappiness of mankind is caused more by shadows than by realities. Good-bye, till we meet again;" and so saying, he imprinted one burning kiss upon her marble forehead, and pressing her little hand, which was adorned by more than one costly ring, within both of his, he once more bid her adieu; and descending the broad flight of stone steps towards the garden, disappeared from her sight in the deep shadow of one of the buttresses of the palace.

Five minutes later he was in the saddle and outside the gates.

The dull grey light of early dawn was slowly usurping the dominion of the radiant queen of night, when Sir Andrew Douglas rode up the long steep hill which led out of the village in the direction of Paris. In the streets all was still gloom, for the tall old houses on either side cast a dark shadow over the paved road which was scarcely dissipated by the sickly glare of the oil lamps, which, suspended by ropes from window to window immediately across the street in a manner still seen in a few quaint old towns in Lower Hungary, swayed backwards and forwards with every gust of wind, and shed a vague uncertain light upon the course of the passers by.

Upon reaching the top of the Rue de La Villette, the young Scot turned to the left, and passing the market-place, soon found himself cantering along the high road in the direction of Paris, now only a few miles distant.

Few people were yet astir, for it was still very early, and all nature appeared wrapped in repose; but the cool fresh air of morning played gratefully upon the fevered brow of the young cavalier after the prolonged revelry and excitement of the night, and reining in his magnificent grey horse to a walk, a proceeding which the noble animal appeared by no means to relish, he sank into a profound fit of musing.

So deep, indeed, was our hero soon involved in his own reflections, that for many minutes he heard not the sharp ring of horse's hoofs on the hard road behind him, but when at last they did strike upon his ear, he turned in his saddle, and, to his surprise, behold a strange horseman, mounted upon a powerful black charger, spurring furiously in his rear.

As his pursuer drew nearer, Sir Andrew Douglas saw by the heavy blue cloak which draped his person, as well as by the plumed shako and jack-boots, that he was an officer in the French army and not a highwayman, as he had at first conjectured, and then the impression that the stranger was no other than Captain Louis Pelissier flashed to his mind.

Our hero, however, was not permitted long to guess who the stranger might be, for when he again looked round a voice hoarse with rage, cried,—

"Halt, sir cavalier, halt, or by every fiend in hell you are a dead man," and before the Scot resolved whether or not to comply with a request so insolently uttered, his pursuer was alongside, and reining in his panting and foam-flecked steed so suddenly as to throw him right aback on his haunches, he turned towards our hero and disclosed the sinister and now furious countenance, not of Louis Pelissier, but, now when unmasked, unmistakably that of his old foe, Sir Edward Hamilton, the *ci-devant* Colonel of Swart Ruyters.

"What pressing business is it that you have with me that necessitates your riding at so headlong a pace, Captain Edward Hamilton," said Sir Andrew, with a sarcastic sneer, as he now fully recognized his foe, and laid his hand on the hilt of his rapier in readiness for action.

Hamilton held a long steel-barrelled horse-pistol in his right hand, but he now returned it to its holster, saying,—

"'Tis well, sir cavalier of the blue and silver, that you thought not of flight, for if you had increased your speed but to a trot, an ounce bullet should have scattered your brains to the four winds of heaven. My mission concerns us both."

"State it then, and that speedily, sirrah, for I have but little time and less patience wherewith to listen to idle boasting," replied the Scot, with a sneer.

"Then it is this," retorted the bravo, with an oath—"I require from you an apology, and, what is more, an immediate one, for your insolence at the ball last night. Come, be speedy with it."

And, as he spoke, his countenance gleamed with the fury of a demon.

"I am sorry that Captain Louis Pellissier, alias Sir Edward Hamilton, demands what he will never obtain," replied Sir Andrew; "but a Scot never craves pardon, save when in the wrong, and seldom indeed, then."

"Then if you will not render an apology, we must fight it out—unless, indeed, you choose to brand yourself with the name of coward, you can-

THE DEPARTURE.

not evade rendering me satisfaction by way of arms," retorted Hamilton.

"I shall not seek to," retorted Sir Andrew with a laugh. "On the contrary, I accept your challenge, and only regret that it is you who offer it; for, let me tell you that, had you not overtaken me now, you would have been favoured with a written cartel immediately upon my arrival home. Name, then, your time and place, choose your weapons, and I will not shrink the contest," said Sir Andrew.

"Then let it be under the lightning-blasted oak that grows in the moat of the ruined Château de Concressault at the ensuing midnight, for there there will be no one to disturb us, and for weapons I propose rapiers," replied Sir Edward.

"Be it as you will," responded the Scot.

"Find, then, a second—I can easily obtain one—and see that your hand trembles not, my young carpet knight, for you have to do with one who seldom omits to pink his man."

"Fear not for me, Edward Hamilton, for perchance I may effect what the hangman, when last we met, failed to accomplish."

And with these words they parted, Sir Andrew Douglas turning into a bridle path on the right, which led to his residence in the little village of Luneville, and Sir Edward Hamilton, fuming with a terrible rage at his rival's parting words, and breathing muttered curses, once more retraced his way to St. Germains, secretly overjoyed that the cavalier had consented to rapiers for weapons, because at them he was an adept, and proceeding at a hard gallop so as to be in time for morning parade.

---

## CHAPTER LIV.

### THE MOAT OF THE CHÂTEAU DE CONCRESSAULT.

The green leaves of summer had already begun to dry and crisp beneath the scorching sun.

The ripened corn undulated in golden waves before the gently passing breeze, and many a reaper was whetting his sickle in the broad valley of the Saye.

It was the day succeeding the ball, a lovely morning in September, and Flora Macclesfield sat alone in her boudoir within the eastern wing of the palace.

Reclining in an elbow chair which was drawn up to the window, our heroine gazed long and abstractedly through the open casement.

Her eyes rested upon the bright and glittering landscape without, yet, strange to say, she saw it not. The white flaky clouds which swept through the blue ether high overhead flew on unnoticed, and she listened not to the clear notes of the skylark as he trilled forth his daily song of praise. Her window opened on to the terrace walk, and overlooked the gardens of the palace, where, amid the buzz of bees and summer butterflies, choice flowers of a thousand different tints and varieties expanded their little leaves and petals to the welcome sunshine, while the fragrance of the creeping plants that clung around the carved pedestals and quaint old statues was wafted refreshingly into the apartment.

The same glorious orb of day that shone so cheeringly over hill and plain among the bright flowers of the parterre, and on the glittering waters of the distant Saye shot a stray beam through the deeply mullioned window of the boudoir which played among the waving tresses and dwelt like a halo of glory above the snowy brow of our fair heroine.

On that fair young brow a cloud of care appeared now to rest, the dark spirituelle eyes glistened with unshed tears, and the general expression of the countenance was one of pensive grief, Her head rested on her hand, and her gaze, as we before noticed, was fixed unconsciously on the broad terrace walk.

On the sunny pavement without a momentary shadow was now cast. It was that of a man, and the next instant the graceful figure of Sir Andrew Douglas stood beside the window.

With a cry of mingled joy and sorrow, our heroine awoke from her reverie, and bursting into tears, threw herself into her lover's arms.

The young cavalier embraced her tenderly, and then putting back the long waving tresses from her forehead, said in a voice full of emotion,—

"Flora, dearest Flora, why do you weep? you are not wont to be so sad. Tell me the reason, and I will endeavour to assuage your grief, you are pale and distressed."

"Andrew, I am both," replied the fair girl, with a deep sigh, "my heart is heavy with an unknown sorrow, and every passing breeze seems to warn me of a coming evil. Last night, too, I dreamed a dream, and that also was ominous of ill."

"But you should not put credence in these gloomy forshadowings, which have no meaning save those in which your fancy chooses to drape them," replied the young cavalier with a laugh, as he lead her to the sofa, and seated himself by her side.

Then taking her little hand in his, he continued,—

"Tell me your dream, my Flora, and I will read you its signification, for such visions as these must always be interpreted by their contraries."

"Methought, then, that I saw you lying in the clear moonlight beneath the widely spreading branches of a large tree. A stream of blood flowed from a wound in your side, and formed a pool among the tall grass on which you lay. As I gazed in mute horror at the sight, a dark form hovered before me, and pointing towards you said, 'Behold the corpse of him you love—go, join him, for you are the bride of death.' So saying, the dark shadowy form again vanished, and with a cry I awoke."

A cold shudder ran though the frame of the Scot as Flora related her dream, for the mention of the bleeding body, and the large tree, caused his thoughts to revert to the old oak in the moat of the Chateau Concressault, the spot where his duel with Sir Edward Hamilton was that very night to come off. But in a moment he recovered his composure, and laughing at her superstition, as he termed it, he strove to reason her out of her sorrow, and restore her to her usual spirits.

In this, however, he did not succeed. Flora listened trustingly and lovingly as ever to his words; but, for once, they failed to bring the bright rose-tint to the cheek, or the sunshine to the eye. In vain did Sir Andrew put on an appearance of a gaiety and mirth which he was far from feeling—all was of no avail; and when the shades of evening fell over hill and valley, and he rose to take his leave, Flora gave one low moan of agony, and fell fainting in his arms.

Her lover laid her on a couch, summoned her attendants into the room, and then, as if fearing that if he stayed longer his resolution and his composure would alike vanish, he imprinted one long passionate kiss upon her cold brow, and stepping through the open casement, mounted his horse and rode quickly away.

Ere his departure, however, he had given a small sealed packet into the hands of the chief waiting maid, with the request that it might be delivered into her mistress's own hands if he did not return by an early hour on the morrow.

. . . . . . . . . . .

It is night, once again the queen of darkness has usurped the place of the glowing sun, and bathes both hill and vale with its mild effulgence.

In glittering beams it falls upon the towers and turrets of the Château de Concressault (scarcely then a ruin), and shines brigtly upon the still waters of the Saye, that sweeps by close to its outer walls.

It reveals also to view, about a mile distant, the town of St. Germains, with its stately palace, its squared-towered church, and raised terraces, and glistens flickeringly upon the waving foliage of the oak and beech trees, which immediately surround the dilapidated edifice.

One of these, a mighty oak, stood within the very moat close under the northern tourelle of the Château, and its dense heavy foliage kept the bright moonlight at bay, throwing a deep and sombre shadow far around its gnarled trunk and widely-spreading branches.

Beneath that dark shadow, still and motionless as a statue of bronze, Sir Edward Hamilton awaited his rival. It wanted half an hour to the appointed time of meeting, yet he had already been long on the field, and with eager expectancy did he now listen for any sound that might warn him of the near approach of his hated foe.

Of the result of the combat, strange to say, the *ci-devant* Swart Ruyter had not the least apprehension; an adroit swordsman, he had already fought many a duel with the rapier (a weapon the use of which he knew few Scots were acquainted with), and had never yet missed pinking his man, so his mind being at rest on that score, his thoughts now wandered upon his second scheme, namely, the best means to be employed for securing the person of peerless Flora, and of bending her to his will after he had brushed for ever from his path the person of her lover.

The Captain's reverie was, however, at length disturbed by the crackling of the surrounding brushwood, mingled with the unmistakable sound of horses' hoof-strokes.

At the same moment the powerful black Smolensko charger, which he bestrode, threw up its head and uttered a shrill neigh, and then emerging from amongst the shadow of the surrounding trees into the open space of green sward which lay close to the northern tower, appeared a solitary horseman, mounted on a beautiful bay steed, and attired in the rich and gorgeous uniform of a royalist cavalier.

At this critical juncture of affairs, the moon set behind a cloud, and the whole scene was immediately enveloped in darkness.

Then the cavalier reined in his horse, and drawing his rapier, looked cautiously around as if he were uncertain, in the sudden gloom, whether his adversary had arrived or not.

His doubts on that point were, however, soon solved, for Sir Edward Hamilton, irritated by delay and impatience for action, after a hasty glance at the fleeting clouds, and a deep imprecation at the sudden darkness, spurred his horse from under the shadow of the oak tree, and appeared before him.

Without a word passing between them, the rivals then neared each other, and with a sharp crash the ringing blades met.

Sir Edward Hamilton had previously determined that, in the beginning of the fray, he would act merely on the defensive, trusting to his skill in swordcraft to save him from hurt, until his adversary, exhausted and unfeebled by his attack, should becom an easy prey; but now his plans were entirely altered, for, aware that in the present dim light his swordsmanship would prove of little or no avail, he resolved to assume the offensive at once, and by pressing his antagonist with blow on blow, thus affording no time for counter attack to throw upon him the difficult task of maintaining guard, a proceeding, on account of the present darkness, almost impossible long to perform.

It was Sir Edward, therefore, who struck the first blow; but great was his astonishment when he beheld his rival's weapon fly from his grasp, and the young royalist left utterly defenceless before him.

With a yell of ferocious joy, Hamilton recovered his guard; for a moment the combatants regarded each other in silence; but the cavalier blenched not, and then the Swart Ruyter spurred forward, and with one fierce lunge passed his rapier through his rival's body.

Uttering one long piercing scream of agony, the cavalier fell headlong from his horse, to all appearance lifeless.

Sir Edward then quickly sprang from his charger, and placing his foot on the body of his prostrate foe, exclaimed, with a reckless laugh—

"Ah! ah! my gay Jacobite, my rapier point has let daylight in through that laced doublet of thine, and, I hope, taught thee better manners."

He paused for a reply, but none came, only a deep groan of pain, and he was about to spurn the body with his heel, when the heavy cloud which had hitherto obscured the moon passed away, and with an exclamation of surprise and horror, the villanous Swart Ruyter started back as he discovered in his bleeding victim the form of a lovely woman, and recognised the lovely features of Flora Macclesfield.

The distant clock of St. Mary's Convent struck the hour of midnight, and as the vibration of the last stroke, mellowed by distance, died musically away, a sound, as of crackling branches, aroused Sir Edward from the agonised hell of his own thoughts, and at the same moment a solitary horseman leapt his gallant steed over the low brushwood and rode towards him.

"I fear that I have kept you waiting, Captain Louis Pelissier, but yet I am hardly behind my time," exclaimed the new-comer, who was no other than Sir Andrew Douglas.

"The object of our duel is over, Sir Cavalier. She whom we both loved lies cold in death. Look yonder!"

As he spoke, Sir Edward pointed to the body of the hapless Flora, and then, with a fiendish laugh, he flung himself into the saddle, and giving his horse the spur, was out of sight before Sir Andrew could comprehend the full meaning of his words.

The young Scot looked anxiously to the spot pointed out, and there, lying among the tall rank grass, he perceived the form of Flora, while the beautiful bay palfrey on which she had ridden to the field, with drooped head and trailing rein, stood beside his mistress, and gazed mournfully upon her pale face and blood-bedappled dress.

Despite the male attire, the Scot immediately recognised the bleeding form before him as that of his betrothed bride, and with a cry of despair he sprang from his horse, and sinking on his knee beside her, he exclaimed, in accents of horror and alarm—

"Flora! my Flora! what means this? How do I find you thus? Oh, speak to me if you yet live."

On hearing that voice, every tone and accent of which she knew and loved so well, a faint flush again rose to the marble cheek, and opening her dark lustrous eyes, the dying girl gazed upon her lover with a look of deep affection and delight, but which told him, by its terrible calmness and unearthly brilliancy, that there was no hope.

Then, with an effort, she said softly,—

"Andrew, dearest Andrew, grieve not for me, I have but fulfilled my destiny, for only last night it was in a dream revealed to me, that by the sacrificing of my life I might save yours. At first I understood not the meaning, but your letter, which came into my possession before you intended it to, made all clear to me, and dictated the course ordained for me to follow. I have not shrunk from the ordeal, and so the prophecy is fulfilled, for you are saved and I am the victim. —the chosen bride of death."

"Oh, Flora, what is this you tell me?" exclaimed Sir Andrew, as the whole horrible truth burst upon him. "In your noble devotion to me, you have imperilled your own life, for one who little deserves such a sacrifice, for one who, if you die, will have no wish to survive you. Oh, Flora! I would rather have suffered death and the torture a hundred times than one hair of your glossy tresses should suffer pain; you cannot, shall not die."

So saying, the cavalier tore his silk sash from his shoulder, and unclasping the velvet doublet that covered the snowy breast of that beautiful noble-hearted martyr, strove with trembling hands, to staunch the blood which slowly trickled from the deep sword-gash in her side; but he strove in vain, for, in spite of all his efforts, the crimson stream of life flowed on, and each moment the fragile sufferer became weaker and weaker.

"All your efforts are useless, Andrew," she whispered, at length. "I have but a few minutes more to live. Only raise my head, that I may look upon you once again before I die; upon the face that I have loved so long, that I used to dream of in the night time long ago. Oh, Andrew, may I soon look upon you again in a brighter and better world."

Her voice grew husky and thick, and with an effort she strove to pray.

Her lover gently raised her head from the damp sod, and now it rested on his arm, while his own cheek just touched her pale forehead, as he bent over her in silent sorrow and unspeakable grief.

For several minutes, she lay still and motionless, her lips moving as if in prayer, then she strove once more to speak, and in a voice so faint and low as to be scarcely audible, she said,—

"Andrew, my beloved, the moment of dissolution is nearly come, for a coldness at the heart tells me that death is nigh; but now I fear not its approach, for you are with me. I would that my dear father were also here, but that wish is vain. I will not ask you to remember me with the same feelings that you ever professed, besause I have faith in your love, and know that it will be lasting; but I have a request to make, namely, that I may be buried in the west corner of the old Protestant cemetery at St. Germains, for there the bright sun ever shines, and the summer flowers blossom the thickest."

With a faltering voice did Sir Andrew promise compliance with her wish, and then she again exclaimed,—

"Andrew, my spirit is departing. Give me one more kiss, 'twill be the last and the dearest of all, and may God look down and bless you for evermore."

With a deep feeling of intense love and agony, the young Scot complied with this artless request.

He fondly pressed his lips to those of the dying girl, and even as he did so a cold shiver passed through her frame, the fringed lashes drooped for ever over those spiritual eyes, and gently and silently as a snow flake on the water, the soul of the beautiful Flora flew from its earthly tenement to the presence of its maker.

For upwards of an hour did Sir Andrew Douglas sit beside the corpse of his beloved Flora.

His countenance remained calm, though there was in it an expression of settled and unaltered despair, and his tearless but bloodshot eyes were fixed upon her face as though he were endeavouring to impress every lineament of those beloved features on his mind, before the dark grave hid them from his sight for ever.

Never in life had Flora Macclesfield looked more lovely than now, although her beauty was that of another world.

Her head rested on the soft turf, pillowed as it were by wild flowers; and the long black hair, wet with the night dew, fell in all its glossy luxuriance around it, forming a strange contrast to the pure and beautiful throat and deathly pallor of the soft cheek, on which the long fringed lashes drooped calmly, as if in sleep.

Her lips, too, were parted in a half smile, and there was an unearthly radiancy of expression on the placid countenance, so often observable in those who die happily and in peace.

Her slender form was now wrapped in Sir Andrew's richly laced-velvet mantle, but the two small delicate hands lay crossed upon her bosom, for so her lover after death had placed them.

At length the expression of the cavalier's face changed, and after twice passing his hand across his clammy brow, as if to collect his thoughts, he rose to his feet, but, after a moment's consideration, again stooped down, and carefully severed with his dagger two long tresses of hair from the flowing curls of the unconscious dead.

One of these he placed within the folds of his doublet, and then he entwined the other around the bare blade of his dagger, and made a terrible vow, that from henceforth his whole life should be devoted to revenge, and that he would never rest until that glossy ringlet of his betrothed bride was dyed crimson in the blood of the assassin.

This done he cast one more sorrowful glance at the corpse, and then silently mounted his charger and galloped off in the direction of the village of Luneville, in order to procure aid to bear the remains of her he had so fondly loved back to the palace.

. . . . . . . .

It was a clear autumnal morning, and all nature looked calm and beautiful, as the funeral procession of the unfortunate heroine of our tale passed through the narrow streets of St. Germains on its way to the Protestant Cemetery.

Slowly and solemnly the deep-toned minute-bell boomed forth its cadence of woe, startling the busy rooks from their nests, and breathing its hoarse notes of warning to all who chose to understand their meaning on the uncertainty of human life, as amid the tramp of feet and whisper of many voices, the dark coffin, with its heavy velvet pall, surmounted by a silver cross, was borne through the winding paths of the graveyard towards its final resting place.

Arrived at the western extremity of the cemetery, the procession halted; then the coffin was placed gently on the ground, and amid the most profound silence, broken only by the boom of the passing bell, the murmur of the gentle breeze, and the occasional sob of some sorrowing mourner, there arose the solemn tones of the old clergyman in the last and most impressive ceremony of the church.

At its conclusion, there was a hush still more profound, then the coffin was once more lifted from the ground and carefully lowered into the deep grave.

But when this was effected, when the first

spadeful of loose earth fell with a hollow ring upon the lid, a loud cry burst from amidst the surrounding mourners, and Sir Andrew Douglas, unable longer to restrain an unconquerable impulse, sprang forward and threw himself headlong into the yawning grave.

The unhappy cavalier was, however, soon again extricated therefrom by his friends, and raving with a wild delirium was driven home to his own residence.

---

## CHAPTER LV.

### THE CHURCHYARD AND THE BATTLE-FIELD. CONCLUSION.

THE grave was then hastily filled up, the green turf replaced, and the sorrowing procession slowly retraced its way towards the palace.

No heavy stone monument with its pompous inscription marked the spot where rested the mortal remains of the fair and hapless heroine of our tale—the beautiful Flora Macclesfield—but her last wishes were fulfilled, for her grave was covered by the verdant turf on which the first wild flowers of spring blossomed and the setting sun shed its parting rays of glory.

Towards that quiet grave every day for five long years one solitary figure bent his feeble steps. It was the old puritan soldier, Sir Stephen Macclesfield, who had quitted military service and gone to reside at St. Germains in order to be near the last resting-place of his only and beloved child.

Thus did he pay his last tribute to her memory, but at length he, too, was taken away, and then that quiet mound knew no mourners.

. . . . . .

Great was Sir Edward Hamilton's delight when, upon his return to St. Germains, he found awaiting him a sealed dispatch, which had just been brought from Paris by a government courier. It was to the effect that Captain Louis Pelissier (by which name the reader must recollect that the *ci-devant* Swart Ruyter was known in the French service) should immediately break up his quarters at St. Germains, and march with his regiment to Phalsbourg, there to join the new military expedition destined for service against the Dutch in the Lowlands of Holland.

With the utmost alacrity, did Hamilton obey his instructions, and half an hour after their receipt, the 5th Light Dragoon, with colours waving in the pure morning breeze, defiled at a trot through the deserted streets, and took their way eastward.

It was with a feeling of intense satisfaction, though mingled, perhaps, with a shade of sorrow, that he saw the palace, square-towered church, and gabled roofs of St. Germains, each moment left further in his rear, for he knew full well that after the fearful occurrence just transpired, it was no safe place for him longer to remain in.

Now that he had no object left to reward the risk run, he feared the vengeance of Sir Andrew Douglas, who, he knew, would soon be on his track ; he dreaded, also, the resentment of the old knight, Sir Stephen Macclesfield, who, he concluded, would be sure to come over to his daughter's funeral, and he also knew well that the sword of many an exiled cavalier would be drawn to avenge the beautiful Flora, the avowed belle of the exiled court, and that most probably he would be forced to fight duel after duel until he at last met the fate he so richly deserved, unless he speedily left so dangerous a neighbourhood.

These reflections made him pursue the line of march as speedily as possible, and not a man or officer in the regiment knew of its destination, until the closed gates of Phalsbourg rose proudly and darkly before them.

When, therefore, Sir Andrew Douglas, after seeing the body of the ill-fated Flora safely borne to the palace, proceeded towards the cavalry barracks, intent upon revenge and retribution, he found the huge iron gates barred, and learnt, upon inquiry, that two hours previously the regiment had quitted the town, but could not discover for whither.

Then followed the funeral, which we have already described, but after the young Scot recovered from the delirium and fever which followed that event, he entered the army of the King of France, hoping, thereby, some day to meet with his enemy, and also that amid foreign scenes of adventure and excitement he might, in some degree, erase the morbid melancholy that preyed upon his soul.

Meanwhile, Sir Edward Hamilton, alias Louis Pelissier, dreading more and more every day a rencontre with his rival, deserted from the French army, and joined that of William III., in Holland, under the baton of Lord Churchill, who once more gave him the command of a regiment of Swart Ruyters.

We must now pass over an interval of nine months, and hurry onwards to the closing scene of our narrative.

It is a bright morning in the June of 1692, and on the south bank of the Sarbelles, the army of Louis XIV. makes a gallant stand against the overwhelming forces of Lord Churchhill.

The French forces are drawn up in two lines, immediately opposed to the deep and dangerous fords of the river, with the extreme left of their position defended by a morass, and their rear resting on the village of Maestrecht.

On the opposite side of the stream, and almost within musket-range, lay the overwhelming forces of the Elector William, a motley collection of Belgians, Hanoverians, and English, all confident of victory, and well supplied with every necessary for rendering success certain.

Amongst the numerous forces, both horse and foot, that composed the centre of the French line of battle was a picked regiment of cavalry, the Horse Chasseurs of the Guard, and the gorgeous uniforms, matchless chargers, and imposing bearing of this fine body of cavalry were prominently conspicuous among the raw levies that immediately supported them.

Their commanding officer was no other than our old friend, Sir Andrew Douglas, who had by this time been promoted to the rank of colonel in the French army.

He had walked his horse to some paces in advance of his men, and was intently watching the movements of the enemy, for he was aware that in the army of Lord Churchill there was one whom he thirsted to meet, and that one was Sir Edward Hamilton.

For many months had our hero sought his old foe with the untiring ferocity of the sleuth-hound; but without success. Now, however, the Fates appeared to smile upon his hopes, for already, amid the dark masses of troops that line the opposite shore, he had discovered the tall commanding form of his hated foe, and a whisper at the heart tells him that the crisis of both their destinies is nigh.

Meanwhile, the battle has commenced, for General Dundas, under cover of a fierce cannonade, led on his three regiments of infantry to the charge.

They cross the morass without opposition, and fell fiercely upon the French right flank.

Before that headlong British charge, the raw French levies waver and gave way, and ere they can re-form, a charge of Dutch cavalry renders their confusion irretrievable, and with the utmost precipitation they throw down their arms, and fly towards Maestrecht, while the victorious cavalry thunder in the rear, sabring the fugitives by scores, and riding them down like a field of ripe corn.

While this brief but terrible conflict was proceeding on the French right wing, the centre of the British army, under the command of Lord Churchill in person, also passed the force without interruption, and forming on the opposite bank advanced to the attack.

Then the order was given to three regiments of infantry to charge them at the bayonet's point; and notwithstanding the overwhelming majority of the enemy, the French with loud cries *Vive le Roi* rushed forward to the combat.

The allied infantry, upon seeing the movement, came to a halt, and with their front ranks remained with their long muskets and bayonets at the charge, the rear kept up a hot and destructive fire upon the advancing French columns.

Before that terrible fusillade, the French troops perished by hundreds; rank after rank fell to rise no more, yet still the survivors pressed on.

Another moment, and they are up to the very muzzles of the English guns; the front line of Hanoverians gives way, victory seems certain, but suddenly a heavy squadron of Dutch cavalry arrived to the supportof their wavering comrades, and the scale of battle is turned.

The brave French, taken in flank, give way, and become a mass of scattered fugitives.

The French general witnessed this repulse of his picked battalions with a gloomy feeling of despair; but no time was to be lost, for, in another minute, unless checked, the dark squadrons of the enemy's horse would have gained the brow of the hill, the key of his position, so, urging his charger to a gallop, he dashed up to the Chasseurs of the Guard, and, pointing to the enemy, exclaimed,—

"Sir Andrew Douglas, you must lead your men to the attack; another moment, and the heights are lost, for all the troops in your front are giving way; on you and your gallant regiment depends, perhaps, the fate of the battle."

"Then, general, it rests with men who will welcome death rather than defeat," exclaimed our hero."

And, drawing his sword, he turned to his troops exclaiming,—

"*Vive le Roi; chargez en queu la troupe!*"

He urged his noble charger to a gallop, and the next moment those fiery horsemen were sweeping with headlong speed down upon the dark squadrons of advancing cavalry, the steady gallop of their black horses shaking the earth as, like an ocean wave, crested with glittering steel, they rolled swiftly onwards.

Then there was the crash of steel as the band of dauntless heroes plunged right into the overwhelming masses of the foe, and, before the irresistible shock, horse and horseman rolled together on the plain.

A brief play of sword-blades in the air, and the white plumes of the Horse Chasseurs swept like a vision through the overthrown ranks, and hurling the enemy down the slope they fairly drove them by scores into the rushing waters of the river.

It was then that Sir Andrew Douglas discovered, amongst the retreating masses of the enemy, the tall commanding figure of Sir Edward Hamilton, and with a wild yell of joy, he dashed forward in pursuit.

The Swart Ruyter was vainly endeavouring to rally his crest-fallen followers, who, plunging into the river in one irregular line, were striving to gain the opposite shore.

At this moment it was that Sir Andrew Douglas reached the bank. He saw his hated foe below him, and at once dashed into the water.

One or two powerful strokes, from his swimming charger, brought him alongside with his rival, and before Hamilton was aware of his proximity, he had gripped him by the shoulder belt, and with a fierce cry of, "Murdering villain, you have escaped me thrice, but now we have again met, and your last minute in life has arrived," he dragged him from his horse.

Sir Edward recognized his opponent, and endeavoured to draw his sword, but in this he could not succeed, and then grappling together with the desperate impatience of mortal hate, the rivals disappeared beneath the rushing waters of the river.

Twice did a hand, grasping a long dagger, appear above the stream, the bare blade of which was entwined with human hair; at its second appearance, the bright steel and raven tress were dyed red with blood; then both hand and dagger disappeared for ever, and not a ripple remained upon the surface of the silvery stream to mark the spot where those two fierce revengeful hearts had sunk to their last rest.

But the avenger's vow was fulfilled, the blood of the peerless Flora avenged.

We need not enter into minute details of the rest of the battle. In spite of the chivalrous bravery of the French horse, they were at length driven back, and almost destroyed to a man, by the reserve forces of Lord Churchill, who bore everything before them, and the French general, seeing at length that the battle was clearly lost, ordered his forces to fall back upon their entrenched position at Dulecken.

Thus ended the last episode in the life of the last cavalier of Scotland, and with it our story is concluded.

THE END.

www.ingramcontent.com/pod-product-compliance
Lightning Source LLC
Chambersburg PA
CBHW081156170626
46813CB00009B/3214
* 9 7 8 1 5 3 5 8 0 1 2 4 9 *